The Heart of a Hussar

A tale of chivalry, love, and conflicted loyalty set in 17th century Poland

(Book 1 of 2)
by Griffin Brady

Copyright © 2020 by Griffin Brady.

All rights reserved

This book is a work of fiction. Names, characters, places, and incidents are the product of the author's imagination or are used fictitiously. Any resemblance to actual events, locales, or persons, living or dead, is coincidental.

No part of this book may be reproduced, or stored in a retrieval system, or transmitted in any form or by any means, electronic, mechanical, photocopying, recording, or otherwise, without express written permission of the publisher.

ISBN 978-1-7354558-1-5
ISBN 978-1-7332763-3-7
ISBN 978-1-7354558-0-8

Cover design by Jenny Quinlan, Historical Editorial
Map by Cathy Helms, Avalon Graphics LLC
Edited by Jenny Quinlan, Historical Editorial
Proofread by HippoCampus Publishing
Printed in the United States of America
Trefoil Publishing

Dedication

For my late father-in-law, Russ. If we have past lives, you were surely a valiant winged hussar. Thank you for your courage and kindness, for your steadfast support, and for raising your amazing sons. You were the living, breathing embodiment of everything we love in our heroes, and you will be in our hearts forever.

Table of Contents

CHAPTER 1 ~ Under Fire 1
CHAPTER 2 ~ Spoils of War 9
CHAPTER 3 ~ Oliwia 17
CHAPTER 4 ~ Dancing on Jagged Stones 23
CHAPTER 5 ~ Foreigner 30
CHAPTER 6 ~ Commonwealth 37
CHAPTER 7 ~ One Summer Afternoon 43
CHAPTER 8 ~ Savage 49
CHAPTER 9 ~ Loose Ends 56
CHAPTER 10 ~ The Biaska Chorągiew Husarski 62
CHAPTER 11 ~ Biaska Castle 73
CHAPTER 12 ~ Destinies Built on Sand 81
CHAPTER 13 ~ Heretic 91
CHAPTER 14 ~ Szlachta 102
CHAPTER 15 ~ Wąskadroga Castle 109
CHAPTER 16 ~ Tournament 120
CHAPTER 17 ~ And Now We Feast 132
CHAPTER 18 ~ Cultivating a Warrior 148
CHAPTER 19 ~ Campaign 164
CHAPTER 20 ~ Border 175

CHAPTER 21 ~ Emergence 185
CHAPTER 22 ~ The Tatars 194
CHAPTER 23 ~ Winged Warriors 213
CHAPTER 24 ~ Rich Nobleman, Poor Nobleman 232
CHAPTER 25 ~ Homecoming 243
CHAPTER 26 ~ Jacek's Command 258
CHAPTER 27 ~ Jacek's Folly 272
CHAPTER 28 ~ The Porucznik 281
CHAPTER 29 ~ Gifts 293
CHAPTER 30 ~ Katarzyna's Plan 313
CHAPTER 31 ~ Walking in Shadows 322
CHAPTER 32 ~ A Promise to Keep 334
CHAPTER 33 ~ Choices 343
CHAPTER 34 ~ Anyone Will Do 359
CHAPTER 35 ~ She was in a Wreath and Comes in a Cap 376
Glossary 391
Historical Figures 394
Author's Notes 398
Timeline 403
A Hussar's Promise ~ Excerpt 405
Acknowledgments 415
Connect 415
Also by this author 418
About the author 419

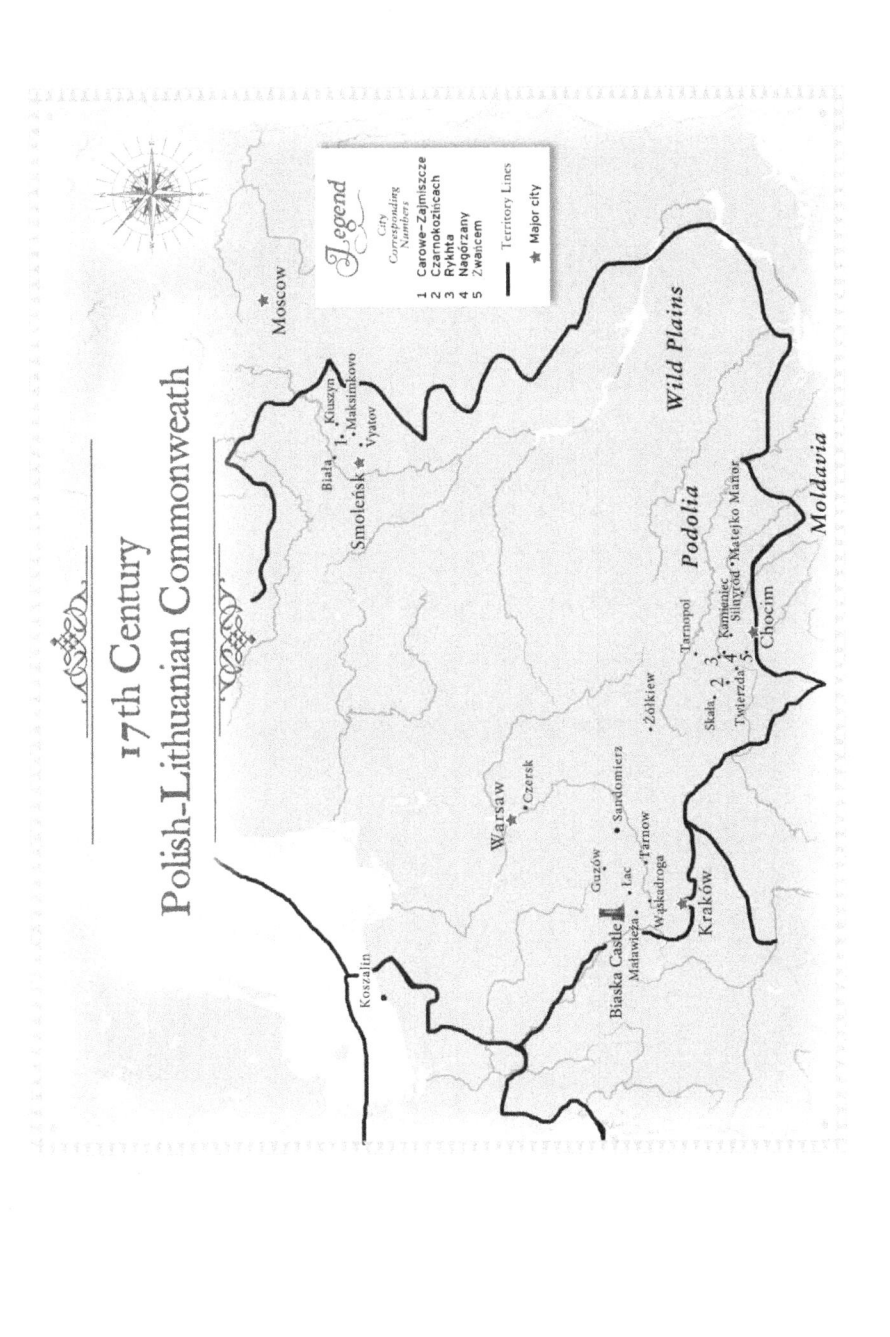

CHAPTER 1

Under Fire

Battlefield near Kłuszyn, Muscovy
July 4, 1610

Jacek yanked on the reins, curbing his warhorse beyond the reach of enemy guns. Heaving breaths burning in his chest, he glanced at the bloody sabre in his grip, still attached to his wrist with a lanyard. When he'd ridden into the enemy, he'd thrust eighteen feet of *kopia* squarely into a soldier whose face he never saw. He'd only felt the gratifying bite of the lance's steel tip and the impact juddering along the length of the shaft and up his arm right before it shattered and the man cried out.

The fierce fighting that followed had been a jumble of cold, slashing steel; gritted teeth set in grim, bloodied faces; the tang of coppery blood mixed with horse sweat and acrid smoke from gunpowder and burning villages. He'd pursued the enemy as they fled and now stood quite alone on the outer fringes of the eerily silent forest. As if waking from a dream, he looked about; it was still morning. The air was thick and ripe, adding to the sheen of sweat covering his exposed skin. He bit down on his leather glove and tore it off before running his hand over his armor and padded thighs. He felt his way around his body, his spirit lifting with each undisturbed inch he discovered.

Movement between the trees jolted him back to the present.

"Jacek!"

Narrowing his eyes, he scanned the battle haze that hung from the evergreens and birches like gossamer veils draped over a hundred brides. A horse and rider cantered toward him, and he recognized his best friend, Henryk, looming out of the murk.

Henryk drew alongside, scrutinizing Jacek through the leaf-shaped nose guard of his helmet. "What the devil were you trying to do back there?"

Jacek gave his friend a hard stare, masking his unease at his own reckless bravado. Why in God's name had he done it? "Kill the enemy. What else?"

Henryk's horse turned in a circle. "By leading the charge through one small gap in the fence under fire? Since when have you had a death wish?"

His breathing leveling once more, Jacek crammed the glove in his belt and glanced at his friend.

"I have no death wish. I volunteered, and the captain sent me in." *And God and all the saints saw fit to safeguard me.*

As Henryk stared at him, Jacek continued. "I saw Lieutenant Górnicki go down." His own words jarred him, sending a fresh stab of dread through him.

Henryk let out a snort and shook his head. "No doubt the captain would have picked you to lead the charge whether you volunteered or not. I want to see the look on his face when he realizes your blood does not soak the battlefield."

Jacek felt a rising urgency and dismissed the remark. "Does Górnicki live?" His voice sounded choked.

Henryk looked away.

"Henryk! What of Górnicki?"

Henryk exhaled. "I don't know. I was rows behind you. By the time I went through, the gap had widened and the melee was well underway."

Jacek tugged on his reins and pulled away. Henryk positioned his horse across Jacek's path.

"Out of my way, Henryk. I need to go back," Jacek ground out.

"No. You don't. We have other places to go."

"Get the hell out of my way," Jacek nearly yelled, as much to cover his alarm as to convince Henryk to move. He backed his horse, but Henryk shifted and blocked him again.

"You may outrank me by one year, but I have my orders. The infantry has arrived, and they ready the guns. You are headed the wrong way, my

THE HEART OF A HUSSAR

friend. If you insist on continuing, you'll likely get yourself and Jarosława"—Henryk nodded at Jacek's horse—"blown up, and Lord Eryk will have my head on a pike. Unlike our beloved captain, I venture he wishes to see you alive."

Jacek stopped and stroked his mare's neck. Shouts rose in the distance, but the small patch of ground where he and Henryk stood was steeped in preternatural quiet. No birds trilled; no insects hummed; no leaves rustled. The pawing of a hoof and his charger's soft snort were the only sounds.

Henryk smirked. "Don't look so dumbfounded. We are to continue pursuing the enemy. You get to live a few more minutes and, with any luck, kill another dozen before they kill you."

The big animal tossed her mane, jingling her turquoise-encrusted bridle. The clank brought Jacek back to the reality of the battle that had started before dawn only hours before.

Jacek looked up at his friend. "Lead on."

Just then, the guns boomed, their reports roaring through the woods, followed by the dull popping of firearms. Wordlessly, he and Henryk turned and rode toward the terrible noise.

With a satisfied eye, Lord Eryk Krezowski surveyed the battlefield from his vantage point atop his warhorse. Pride swelled inside him. Despite a sleepless night plodding through rain and mud, his men had fought valiantly, battering the enemy's defenses in charge after ferocious charge. Why would he have expected any different outcome? Every one of his winged hussars had performed as he knew they would.

He glanced skyward, and his elation turned to disquiet; not all his warriors were accounted for. He crossed himself, then sagged with a deep breath, praying neither his lieutenant nor his best warrior, Jacek Dąbrowski, were among the battle's casualties.

The day was growing hot, the clamminess curling itself upward in a creeping vapor that carried the fetid smell of blood and death along its tendrils. Eryk looked toward a cluster of men. Among them was the general, Crown Field Hetman Stanisław Żółkiewski, negotiating terms with the defeated Muscovite army's mercenaries. As Eryk pondered their exchange, a horse and rider caught his eye, and he raised his commander's mace.

"Captain," he called.

"My Lord Eryk." Mateusz reined his horse beside Eryk and pulled off his helmet, ruffling his short chestnut hair with a gloved hand. Only twenty-eight, the fissures of Mateusz's craggy face made him appear far older than Eryk's thirty-two.

"What news of the men have you?" Eryk asked.

"We lost Górnicki. Two missing, presumed dead. Five wounded; the barber-surgeon assures me they will survive. Overall, it appears the casualties on our side were a fraction of the enemy's. Quite remarkable, really."

"Who is missing?"

"Jacek Dąbrowski led a charge between the fences and came under fire. Neither he nor Henryk Kalinowski has been seen since."

Bile rose in the back of Eryk's throat. "You know this for certain?"

Mateusz removed the glove and swiped his hand over his forehead. "I have seen Górnicki's body. No one has seen Dąbrowski or Kalinowski since the charge—they didn't fall back. But it's a mess over there." Mateusz jerked his chin toward the battlefield. "I can only assume they're dead and have yet to be uncovered."

"Perhaps they were part of the pursuit," Eryk posed.

"Those soldiers have all returned," countered Mateusz.

"Losing Górnicki is a blow. If Dąbrowski and Kalinowski are lost, it is a bitter disappointment. They are fine officers," Eryk said quietly, recalling Jacek's eager yet earnest face when he'd first come to train with Eryk six years ago.

Mateusz shrugged and turned a piercing blue-green stare on Eryk. "Despite unbelievable odds, we triumphed, and you should take comfort in that. Better to lose a few of the inexperienced younger men who have no wives or children to grieve them."

Eryk glared at the man beside him. "You forget yourself, Mateusz. Those inexperienced young warriors, as you call them, were as battle-hardened and courageous as any I have had the privilege of fielding. They may not have wives to grieve them, but they have mothers."

THE HEART OF A HUSSAR

Mateusz sighed, glancing upward as he shifted in his saddle. "Of course, Eryk, I did not mean—"

"You will either address me as 'Lord Krezowski,' 'Rotmistrz,' or 'my lord.'"

"Yes, my lord." Mateusz settled the helmet back on his head, wiggling it in place. "I will check on the rest of our company." He turned his horse and pulled up short.

"Sweet Jesus, I cannot believe it," he muttered.

Eryk glanced over his shoulder. Two winged hussars rode toward them, a string of horses in tow.

"Dąbrowski!" Mateusz barked. "Where the devil have you been?" Out of the side of his mouth, Mateusz grumbled, "With the Muscovite camp whores, no doubt."

Eryk ignored him as Jacek and Henryk slowed to a walk, stopping in front of Mateusz.

"Sir," Jacek rumbled and looked past Mateusz to Eryk.

"Jacek. Henryk. It's good to have you back. What happened?" Eryk asked.

Glancing at Mateusz, Jacek nudged his charger's flanks and pulled up before Eryk.

"Begging your pardon, sir, but the infantry had begun their pursuit of the Germans, and Colonel Dunikowski ordered us to support them. As we returned from that effort, more of ours started after Shuisky's retreating troops but many … ah … stopped to gather treasure the Muscovites tossed aside, so we turned and chased that lot nearly four leagues."

Eryk's eyes flicked over Jacek's and Henryk's saddles. "I gather by your empty saddles you did not join the plundering." His gaze rested on the tethered horses.

"No, sir. But we found these foraging on our way back and rounded them up. We will deliver them to your camp."

"Keep your prizes. You earned them." Eryk's eyes wandered to Mateusz, who seemed to fume. "Mateusz, take Kalinowski and check on the others."

Weariness weighed heavy in Eryk's bones, but he kept his shoulders erect as the two retreated. He glanced at Jacek sitting straight and tall in his saddle. Though bloodied and bedraggled, his garb was unmistakably that of the winged hussar. A padded red coat skimmed the knees of dark breeches tucked into yellow leather boots. Over this, he wore gleaming steel armor that covered chest, back, and shoulders. A thick black leather shoulder strap held his depleted powder horn and cartridge box. Clasped at his neck was a snow leopard hide, and atop his head a plumed helm.

Eryk's costume was like Jacek's in all ways but one. Eryk wore a mail skirt that fell just above the knee. At the back of each man's saddle, mounted to the cantle, rose a slender wooden shaft that held a row of eagle feathers. While Eryk's stood defiant and unscathed, Jacek's was missing feathers and listed precariously.

"A little worse for wear, eh, Jacek?"

"Nothing a hot meal and a sound sleep cannot cure, my lord."

The two men stood side by side, surveying the scene in reverent silence. The battlefield, only recently a simple swath of farmland, was thick with churned, wet earth and troughs of milky brown sludge mixed with blood. Black smoke curled upward. Upon the enormous field sprawled broken and bloody bodies—those of men and horses—together with the smashed remains of lances, wagons, and fences.

Small movements on that field became silhouettes of men lifting and carrying their friends and fellow soldiers away; or homeless villagers—men, women, children—tearing through clothing and saddles; or servants delivering death blows to wounded enemy soldiers who thrashed in misery, or to the stray horse who struggled to stand on shattered legs.

"A great victory for Hetman Żółkiewski." Eryk's eyes remained fixed in front of him. "Perhaps he can convince more to surrender when we return to Carowa-Zajmiszcze."

"When do we return, my lord?"

"Today, after Żółkiewski has finished here. However, once *our* company reaches camp, we pack up. We begin our journey home tomorrow."

In the periphery of his vision, Eryk caught Jacek's head swiveling toward him. He faced his surprised officer. "Our work is done. With the time we have already spent at Smoleńsk and Biała, we have overstayed our obligation, and Żółkiewski has no money to pay us." With a pinprick of guilt, he went on. "Other companies have lately joined the campaign, and with harvest approaching, the king has agreed to release those who have been here longest."

THE HEART OF A HUSSAR

Not one to shirk a fight, Eryk was tired, and though he kept it to himself, he was grateful to be headed home.

The company trudged the eighteen miles back to Carowa-Zajmiszcze that night, some nodding off in their saddles as they went. Morning brought an unremarkably gray, overcast sky that mirrored the men's faces. Eryk looked on as servants disassembled and stored each hussar's camp in that man's wagons, alongside his weaponry, clothing, blankets, and dwindling provisions.

The company's field clerk sidled up to Eryk with a shuffling gait.

"My lord?"

Eryk turned and looked down at the slim, spectacled Jew with moustache and wild black hair peppered with white. The fastidious bookkeeper was surely devoid of any ability to smile.

"What is it, Aron?"

"I have taken inventory of our foodstuffs, sire, and we are perilously low. We must consider resupplying for the journey home."

Eryk's brows knotted. "And you are just now telling me this?"

Aron's own brows knitted together. "Begging your pardon, Commander, I thought to get what victuals we needed from the camp followers, but Hetman Żółkiewski has claimed nearly all of it."

Eryk followed the clerk to the supply wagons and blew out a breath as he looked over their paltry stores. His mind whirred.

"Send the captain to me," he instructed.

The clerk scurried away.

When Mateusz appeared, Eryk was beside a wagon, deep in thought as he palmed the wagon's rail.

"Mateusz. We need to replenish, and we will have to forage until we reach Poland. You will take the main bulk of the company while I take a detachment with me to get what we need."

Mateusz frowned. "Where do you intend going, my lord? Any settlements close by are already looted, and game is scarce."

Eryk nodded, fiddling with the hilt of his sabre. "There are villages farther distant—beyond the better-traveled paths—that might do. Vyatov, for instance, which is not too far from Maksimkovo. It's on Muscovite soil, so I do not expect a welcoming population, but the villagers might accept payment or barter in exchange for our direst necessities. If the folk are friendly, they might be sympathetic—or at the very least, not hostile."

"Should you not appoint someone else to lead this foraging mission? A senior retainer or Dąbrowski, for instance." Mateusz's frown held fast as he unstoppered a waterskin.

"I want be to be sure ample food remains for the villagers, even if Vyatov is an enemy hamlet. With harvest near, we have an even chance of provisioning without taking everything. As for letting someone else lead the detachment, Jacek is more than capable. But if we run into looters, they will be our own countrymen in a plundering mood and more likely to heed *me*."

Mateusz leaned his head back and drank water from the skin. He dragged his sleeve across his mouth. "No pillaging under your watch, my lord, even if they are filthy Muscovites who kill us?"

Eryk crossed his arms. "They are not the ones who kill us. Their *soldiers* do the killing, and plundering that treasure is vastly different from taking everything the settlers have. They are simple people trying to scratch enough from the earth to feed themselves and their children. I will not tolerate harming them unless we are provoked. The men have always understood and abided by my edict, and you know this."

Mateusz capped his waterskin. "Just as I know those children grow into men who would murder us all."

Usually a man in control of his temper, Eryk let his fatigue and irritation get the better of him. As Mateusz wheeled to leave, Eryk cleared his throat.

"Mateusz. Send Dąbrowski to me. I'm promoting him to lieutenant and will be bringing him with me."

When Mateusz looked back at him, Eryk noted the flash in his eyes. "Careful, Mateusz. I can also promote him to captain."

Mateusz's mouth opened and snapped shut.

CHAPTER 2

Spoils of War

The new lieutenant took the news with his usual solemnity and went straight to work organizing the detachment. No smile, no extravagant words. Within the half hour, Jacek had enlisted a score of hussars, together with servants and *pacholiks*—the hussars' retainers—and two score were ready to ride to Vyatov.

As Eryk observed his freshly anointed lieutenant, it occurred to him that, at twenty-two, Jacek was the youngest lieutenant in the company's history. But despite his youth, Eryk was confident the choice had been judicious. Time and again Jacek had earned the men's trust through unbending self-discipline—as he'd done by forgoing rich plunder to hunt the enemy. A professional soldier, he was committed, almost to a fault, to the company's success and had been since Eryk had known him. He would doubtless perform his duties admirably.

Both men stood beside one another, checking their horses' trappings. Eryk glanced at Jacek. "Tell me, Jacek. Why does Mateusz dislike you?"

Jacek was inspecting a stirrup. "I was not aware Captain Zalewski dislikes me, my lord."

Eryk chuckled while he straightened a buckle. "Then you must be the only one to think so. What did you do? Sleep with his wife?"

Eryk had meant it as a joke. But when he registered the slight jerk in Jacek's ordinarily smooth movements, he gathered he had inadvertently struck upon something.

Jacek led the detachment as they rode away from the main squadron and veered toward the village three hours distant. Over flat terrain covered in scattered patches of dense forest upon fields, he pondered his unexpected promotion. While he'd expected the advancement since he'd set his sights on leading the company years ago, it had come far earlier than he'd planned. He only wished they'd followed Żółkiewski's army. He hadn't quite tired of testing himself against the enemy, but more important was his desire to distinguish himself in the hetman's presence.

The hetman had King Zygmunt's ear, and if Żółkiewski should mention individual feats of valor on the battlefield, well, Jacek's deeds might be among those. He owed Lord Eryk four more years of service, and he meant for the king to hear his name at least once in the time that remained. The prestige of such an utterance carried with it the promised path to what he most coveted.

Mateusz doubtless suspected Jacek's ambition, which fueled his superior's growing disdain—that and Mateusz's belief that Jacek vied for Eryk's favorable treatment. *Let him believe what he wants. The devil with him.*

Keeping his focus forward, Jacek studied the dirt track below him and the blur of trees beside him and blew out a sigh. The odds of Żółkiewski noticing him were as long as the interminable path they followed—even with the promotion. No matter. He would continue making and taking opportunities as they came—like riding in the front line or stepping into his dead lieutenant's place. He crossed himself as he recalled the man he replaced, a man he'd admired.

As they emerged from the pines and rounded a bend, Jacek drew in his reins sharply, Lord Eryk and Henryk pulling up beside him. His nose was assaulted by pungent black smoke and his eyes by red-orange flames licking thatched roofs, spiraling ash skyward. They had arrived too late.

THE HEART OF A HUSSAR

"Jacek, take them with you," Eryk ordered as he pointed to a group of hussars behind them. "Henryk and I will take the rest. Head to the north. We'll swing south."

Jacek drew his sabre and barked out commands. The weary cavalrymen urged their horses and raced toward the village.

Everywhere was chaos. Polish soldiers—thugs, really—rode horses through screaming villagers, trampling some as they lofted lit torches atop the cottages. Women covered children in their arms as foot soldiers attacked with all manner of weapons in a bloody, disorderly rage. Some village folk resisted the ravagers, but most became their victims instead.

Jacek raised his sabre, and the winged hussars sprang into action, transforming the aggressors into the hunted as they bore down on them. Their armor glinted dully in the flat light as they scattered the marauders before their poised blades. Fatigued as they were, the hussars were still a terrifying sight to behold, armed and armored in their battle regalia. Jacek's aim wasn't to murder their compatriots, though he wasn't keen to acknowledge them as such. Rather, he meant to drive them from the village and the people they brutalized.

He wound his way through the mayhem, confident the hussars would soon have the instigators on the run. Little could be done for the devastated settlement.

Seeking a broader perspective, he was walking his horse out of the fray when a desperate struggle came into view and seized his attention. Through the thick smudge of smoke billowing from a burning cottage, he made out a man's body crumpled across the front threshold. A woman lay just beyond, inside the doorway, as still and as dead as the man.

Another man, very much alive, wrestled with a feminine form in the yard between Jacek and the cottage while a small boy tugged on his leg, keening pitifully.

"Leave her alone!" the child cried.

The woman, doubtless the boy's mother, thrashed and kicked with an unbound desperation, making her a more difficult victim to subdue than her slight body insinuated. The man grunted his displeasure as he tried to overpower his quarry. Seeming to lose patience, he raised a wicked dagger, intent on crashing the hilt into the base of her skull.

"Stop!" Jacek bellowed. "Release her!"

The man's head jerked up, fury twisting his face.

"Why should I?" he snarled, wrenching his captive across his body. He lodged the honed point of the knife against her exposed slender white neck. It was then Jacek realized she was a mere girl.

Sitting erect, unmoving and taut as a drawn bowstring, Jacek appraised the man. He was doubtless a soldier but surely could not be among the higher ranks—a peasant foot soldier or a pitiful pacholik, perhaps, but no more. His garments and arms bespoke a lowly station, and his wretched mount was nothing like the warhorses favored by Polish cavalry. He had no telltale pennons or adornments, and though he wore a traditional cap, it was devoid of the common decorations: showy feathers, medallions, brooches. At this moment, countryman or not, he was a foe.

"Are you part of a Polish company?" Jacek demanded.

"Why does it matter?" the man growled, holding his weapon to the struggling girl. He yanked her dark plait hard, exposing a silver chain that encircled her neck and plunged in a long, narrow V under her bodice.

Eryk pulled alongside Jacek, and in a tight voice said, "Because he's deciding whether to kill you where you stand or spare your life this once because of your ignorance. Not that ignorance excuses your despicable behavior."

The man laughed malevolently. "And you two will stop me?"

"I only need him." Eryk pointed at Jacek. "And should I need more, then we two and the rest of my army, you pathetic bastard."

"I am an officer in Aleksander Lisowski's regiment, and I'm entitled to my spoils. This girl is my reward," the soldier raged. "You can keep the brat and sell him to the Tatars." He kicked at the youngster, now folded over his knees, crying inconsolably in the dirt at the girl's scrabbling feet.

One of Lisowski's lost men? Perhaps the Crown tolerated them, but Jacek did not. They were brigands, the lot of them, good for naught but carrion. Dispatching this one would trouble his conscience not a whit.

From the corner of his eye, Jacek saw Eryk lean forward and relax his reins as he rested his hands on his saddlebow. His shoulders eased, and he continued in a drawl. Jacek transferred his sabre to his left hand and slid his broadsword from its sheath beneath his left thigh.

"I am Lord Commander Eryk Krezowski of Biaska. Be you truly an officer, legitimate or not, I am your superior. Therefore, *I* choose my spoils first. If any remain, you pick from what is left. That girl is part of *my* booty."

THE HEART OF A HUSSAR

Unruffled, Eryk delivered this news juxtaposed with the strange tableau of seething soldier, struggling girl, and forlorn boy. Jacek's gaze remained fixed on the assailant, and he detected a flash of recognition in the man's eyes upon hearing Eryk's name.

One second, then two more ticked by. Eryk stood in his stirrups with a roar.

"Do you understand?"

Jacek and Eryk positioned their blades with deadly speed, leveling them at the soldier. Materializing from the smoke, the hussars sifted in and ringed them in a half circle. Eryk continued in a cold, calm voice as Jacek stepped his horse closer and aligned the tip of his broadsword with the man's neck.

Try it, filth. Go on! Jacek checked the wicked grin quirking a corner of his mouth.

"If you choose to die this day," Eryk began, "say whatever prayers you wish to say now before you meet the devil, and we'll be done with it. But if you choose to live, you will drop your weapon and free her. I don't give a damn either way. If she dies along with you, I'll be disappointed, but it will matter little. She'll be one more dead Muscovite." He shrugged.

Eryk's demeanor, paired with the blood and gore still streaking his cuirass, bespoke his lethal meaning. For several heartbeats, he scrutinized the soldier, who had grown still save his darting rat's eyes. Flames licked their way through the thatch and wood of the cottage, crackling and popping as they cast off fiery showers of embers. The man lowered his dagger and released the girl, shoving her to the dirt.

She grasped her throat and coughed in raspy breaths while the boy smothered her back with his small body, racked in sobs.

"I will have your name, soldier," Eryk growled.

The man's chest heaved, his nostrils flaring. "I am Romek Mazur," he spat.

"From where do you hail?"

"I hail from nowhere. I only serve Lisowski."

"Truly a lost man, then." Eryk straightened in his saddle. "Romek Mazur, hear me. As one of Lisowski's band, you are a marked man in Poland. I could kill you now and be lauded by the Crown for saving them the trouble. Be grateful I am feeling generous and design to spare your life today. If I hear of you preying on innocents again, be assured I will finish what I began here today."

Romek's eyes blazed with hatred. "No Muscovite is an innocent."

"She is a girl undeserving of what you had in store for her. Now go before I change my mind."

The riders moved aside as if they were one long palisade gapped in even widths. Romek scurried away and jumped atop his steed, spurring a quick path out of the village.

Eryk jerked his head at him. "Let's go."

As Jacek reseated his blades, he glanced at the boy and girl. Whether it was the light or some other trick of the eye, he couldn't say, but for a moment he saw his sister in the bend of the girl's head and the delicate curve of her shoulder. But that couldn't be so, if for no other reason than his beloved sister had died years ago. A familiar, unwelcome pang of guilt stabbed him, and he immediately buried it.

"What of them, Commander?" He tilted his chin at the children.

"We cannot bring them with us," countered Eryk.

Jacek looked around the leveled settlement. "There is nothing left here." He had no idea why it mattered; they were the enemy, after all.

"You understand I did not actually intend taking her as plunder." Eryk darted his gaze to the girl on her knees in the dirt.

"I do, yes," Jacek replied evenly. He waited.

Eryk sighed and walked his horse toward them. The girl, who had grown silent when her strangling breaths abated, wrapped her arms around the boy.

"Please!" she implored in Polish. "I will go with you, but please do not hurt him!"

Eryk leaned over his horse's neck and murmured, "Where is your family, girl?"

She glanced over her shoulder at the two bodies in the doorway.

"All dead, then?"

She nodded as she looked back up at him, meeting him squarely with dry eyes.

He straightened, backed up, and nodded at Jacek. "Get the girl." He swung toward Henryk. "Bring the boy."

THE HEART OF A HUSSAR

Henryk deftly dismounted, seized the youngster, tucking him under his arm, remounted, and secured the child before him. The snuffling boy twisted, but his efforts were for naught.

The girl lifted her face as Jacek approached. He was struck by fear-filled light eyes in featureless, dirt-smeared skin; flashes of porcelain peeked from the stripes of filth. He was also struck by the fact that she pulled herself up, clenched her fists at her sides, firmed her trembling chin, and glared at him. Her fright now masked by audacity, he realized she was not a girl, after all—not yet a fully bloomed woman, but she soon would be. If she lived that long.

Her bravado crumbled as the boy renewed his weak struggles.

"We will not harm either of you, but you cannot stay here." Jacek extended his hand. "Vyatov is in ruins, and your people have either fled or been killed. Come."

Oliwia held her ground and peered up at the hulking, metal-clad warrior defiantly, belying the fear rippling through her body. She could have been looking into the face of an angel of death, but she willed her spine and legs to keep her upright. Then she noticed something out of place when taken with his fierce appearance. Though his feathered helm encased most of his face and obscured his features, sympathetic deep blue eyes fixed on her from either side of his broad nose guard. With his hand held out, palm up, he beckoned her to accept his offer.

"There is nothing for you here but death. Or worse. Come," he urged.

She glanced back at her brother, who had calmed in the other soldier's saddle. Shuffling her feet, she reached out a hesitant hand to the man on the combat horse. He leaned down and wrapped his arm around her waist, the metal of his arm guard digging into her hip as he hoisted her in front of him. Something hard rested against each of her knees, and her eyes fell on pistol butts protruding from red leather pouches on either side of the saddle. Behind her, the cold, unforgiving metal of his breastplate pushed against her shoulder blades. The odor of a man hard at work—but strange and different from anything she knew—wafted over her. Though she tried, she could not suppress a shudder. She scanned the group of grimy, grim-faced warriors, then darted her eyes to her brother once more.

You must stay strong for Filip, Oliwia. Stay strong.

Yes, Mother, I promise I will.

The lord—their commander—signaled with his raised forearm, and the riders fell in behind him in an orderly column. The pillagers had long scattered, and the village was empty and wholly ablaze. The heat of the flames brushed her cheek as they engulfed the scattered buildings one by one, like a great slithering beast devouring one carcass after another. As the riotous conflagration claimed structures, so did it claim bodies in its path, and she covered her nose.

The lord led them away with a shout. "Let's put this stench and madness behind us before it catches us up in it!" Soon little would remain of her home but char and ash. She swiped at a wayward tear.

In the blink of an eye, her life, everything she knew, had been erased.

Again.

CHAPTER 3

Oliwia

They rode hard, putting space between them and the wreckage of Vyatov, stopping at intervals to rest and water the horses. During one such break, the lord announced they'd crossed the Muscovite border and were on their home soil once again. A cheer tore through the warriors, but the news sent a cold tremor through Oliwia.

Entering a thick wall of cool woods, they threaded their way single-file among the tree trunks supporting high canopies above them. As the sun moved across the summer sky, its rays peeked through the dense veil of vegetation, sending shafts of light to the forest floor below. The cavalrymen guided their mounts to a grassy clearing beside a stream flanked by clumps of thick bushes and lush, shady trees.

Men dismounted and scattered like purposeful ants, unbundling supplies from saddles, freeing horses and each other from armor, gathering wood, and setting up tents. The commander headed to a seemingly abandoned wagon and cursed aloud about paltry provisions, then ordered a small hunting party armed with bows and arrows into the trees.

The soldiers carrying Oliwia and her brother lifted them onto trampled, damp grass and peeled away. Oliwia swayed where she stood, pins and needles stabbing her legs and feet. The lord grasped her arm and walked her to a tree, where he steadied her against the solid bark, keeping her upright.

"Are you well?" he asked.

She nodded, snatching breaths, and splayed a hand across her belly. "Yes, my lord, thank you. My legs are a bit numb. I am unaccustomed to riding a horse."

He removed his feathered helm and ruffled his matted dark hair. She stole a glance as her breathing calmed. "May I have some privacy to take care of my needs? And those of my brother?"

He gave her a curt nod and barked at a soldier. "Lesław! Take them downstream to the pool. Stay close, but give them privacy."

The soldier snapped to the command. "Yes, my lord."

Pressing herself against the tree, she kept her eyes riveted on the lord, whose attention was drawn to the bustling camp. She studied him; this was the first time she had seen any of the soldiers' faces unobscured by helmets. Under the dirt was a handsome, tanned face with strong cheekbones and a sculpted jaw darkly dotted with stubble. Above a full mouth was a straight nose, slightly flattened at the tip, that broadened and knobbed between the eyes. Those eyes were rich amber brown, clear and deep set. They turned down at the outer corners, giving him a thoughtful but sorrowful look. His thick black eyebrows were bunched in a frown, and she thought she recognized a ferociousness tempered by kindness. Perhaps she was safe with him.

"My lady?" The soldier's words startled her; soon she stepped away from the tree and joined her brother.

She kept a tight hold of Filip's hand and followed Lesław down a narrow, rutted path between slender branches he held back for them. Though he was not as big as the commander, he was still a sizeable man, and he blocked her view as she tailed him. She looked around furtively. Which way could she run if she had to? Could Filip keep up?

Soon the path gave way to a wide, flat, sandy patch beside a still pool carved from the stream, and the soldier stepped aside.

"I will wait up the trail until you call out." He pointed to a copse they had just passed.

"Thank you," she mumbled, watching him retreat as she held her breath.

THE HEART OF A HUSSAR

"Lieutenant Dąbrowski, I have not yet congratulated you. You reached your new rank far sooner than planned." Henryk smirked as they handed their mounts' leads to their retainers.

"Only because we lost Lieutenant Górnicki. I would have preferred to earn the position later, with Górnicki still alive and in charge," said Jacek somberly.

Henryk nodded. "He was a good man. It does, however, bring you within a step of replacing the captain. May your rise to his position be just as swift. The man's insufferable."

Though he didn't disagree, Jacek held his tongue.

Henryk pulled off his gloves. "Strange that Lord Eryk brought the children along, especially as one is female."

Jacek shrugged. "She's just a child. She won't pose a problem, unlike the women Lord Eryk forbids. Besides, we will doubtless deliver them elsewhere within a day."

Henryk didn't ask what had possessed Jacek to plead for them, nor did Jacek volunteer the reason. He still didn't know himself.

Making his way across camp, Jacek detected an air of restrained joviality. The servants' luck in hunting had been prodigious, and there would be an abundant rabbit stew tonight. Aromatic smoke from the cooking fire swirled lazily into the sky while the men went about their tasks.

His stomach grumbled as he stood amid a small group gathered at the edge of the clearing. He had been the last to inspect the camp and therefore the last to shuck his armor. Several soldiers talked and laughed as his retainer, Marcin, loosened Jacek's pauldrons and arm iron.

Marcin looked up from the vambrace he held and stared across the clearing; he stopped in mid-movement. The jabbering and good-natured teasing among the men ceased. Jacek followed Marcin's gaze to where it fixed on the girl emerging into the sun-filled clearing from a screen of shrubs.

Thick and dark, her damp, unbound waves cascaded over her shoulders and down her back to her small waist. The face hidden by grime in the village now glowed like ivory, highlighted by rosy cheeks and lips. Slender, she held herself erect, and Jacek judged the top of her head barely reached his shoulder.

The camp had stilled, and as he looked around, most of the men's eyes were directed to the exact object Marcin's were fixed upon.

"She has the most beautiful eyes I've ever seen," Marcin rasped.

"Close your mouth. She's a child, for Christ's sake." Jacek thumped his retainer's chest. "Save it for the whores. Tell any of them they've the most beautiful eyes you've ever seen, and you're likely to get twice what you pay for."

Behind him, she chided the brother she tugged along, her words echoing through the now-quiet camp. "But you just washed, Filip! How can you be filthy already? Now we must return to the stream!"

Eryk strode toward the children. "Perhaps you would both care to eat first, my lady. I am sure you're hungry, and I venture he will need washing after the meal as well."

The girl jerked like a panicky rabbit about to wind up in the evening's stew. Jacek felt an odd pull to cross the clearing to her, to soothe her, to let her know she had nothing to fear. Instead, he remained rooted where he was and watched as she drew in a breath and regained her composure. She trembled slightly, though her voice did not betray it.

"Thank you, my lord. I will do as you suggest." A heartbeat later, she added, "I thank you, my lord, for providing for us."

Eryk smiled and gave her one quick nod. Their brief exchange broke the spell that had mesmerized the men, and now the buzzing resumed. Marcin darted Jacek a sheepish look and finished removing his armor. Jacek shook his head.

Across the clearing, Eryk bid the two to sit on a log, and he took a seat on a nearby boulder. "What's your name, girl?"

"I am Oliwia," she replied in a small voice. "And this is my brother, Filip." She glanced at the boy beside her.

"I am honored to know you, Oliwia, Filip. You already know I am Lord Eryk Aleksander Krezowski of Biaska, and I am the *rotmistrz*—the commander. I am in charge of these men," Eryk said, waving his hand around the camp.

The boy sprang from his seat and squawked, "Thank you for bringing us here, Eryk!"

THE HEART OF A HUSSAR

Oliwia pinched her brother, making him yelp. "Filip! You are to address this man as 'my lord' or 'Lord Krezowski,' but never by his Christian name!"

The lord's mouth curved up on one side in a small, indulgent smile, and he inclined his head to Jacek approaching them from across the clearing.

"Allow me to introduce my lieutenant, Pan Jacek Dąbrowski. The proper way, Filip, to speak to members of Polish nobility is to address them as 'Pan.' All the hussars you see here, those dressed in red—and most of their retainers—are from the noble class; therefore, you will call them all 'Pan.' When you meet a noblewoman, you will address her as 'Pani.' Pan Dąbrowski is second in command here; you may also address him as Lieutenant Dąbrowski."

Jacek's long strides brought him to Eryk's side quickly. He dipped his head to Oliwia and Filip and brought himself up to his full posture, feet hip-width apart and hands clasped behind him.

Oliwia glanced at her brother, mortified she had been unable to rein him in. Yet she was relieved he seemed to have forgotten, for the moment, the slaughter in Vyatov. Filip's gray-blue eyes sparkled, and he grinned from ear to ear as he eyed the lieutenant. She had to tilt her head to look up at the man, and when she did, her breath caught. Even devoid of the steel that had covered his upper body, he was intimidating.

Lieutenant Dąbrowski stood a half-head taller than his commander, with squared-off shoulders and a lean, powerful physique. Doubtless he was the biggest man among the squad. He was the biggest man she'd ever seen. Though young, he held no vestiges of youth—there was no softness. His face was strong and chiseled, accented by a straight nose and full-lipped mouth. A well-defined jawline came to a squared-off point and was scattered with stubble much darker than his brown hair, which was shot with gold. Wide eyes of sapphire blue reflected a deep intensity and were fringed in long, dark lashes. His sable brows were gathered in a scowl, a deep shadow between them. But as he looked down at Oliwia and Filip, his fierce visage transformed with a smile, displaying straight white teeth.

Despite the smile, Oliwia shuddered inside. She'd shared a saddle with this man, this looming beast who could crush her with a single blow of his meaty, scarred hand. She flicked her eyes away lest he glimpse her growing alarm.

CHAPTER 4

Dancing on Jagged Stones

After a meal of fresh rabbit mixed with groats and mushrooms, an air of fatigue and solemnity hung over the camp with the descending darkness. It blanketed them with a peculiar hush, save some susurrations amid the clustered men.

Filip pointed at a cup Eryk pressed to his lips. "Is that *wodka*?"

A generous gulp later, Eryk examined the cup. "Yes, it is. Would you like some?"

Filip shot Oliwia a glance, and she shook her head vigorously. "Thank you, my lord, no. The ale quenched his thirst."

Eryk chuckled. "It was a jest, Filip. You need more seasoning before drinking among these men," he said with a sweep of his hand. "Besides, I always prefer wine to wodka, but alas, I must wait until we're hosted at a decent estate before I'm offered such a luxury."

"Everyone in our village drinks wodka," Filip blurted.

Everyone in our village is gone. Oliwia held her breath. Though she couldn't see her brother's face, his small body leaned against hers, pliant and warm. If he understood their loss, he wouldn't feel so at ease, she reassured herself.

"How old are you and Filip?" Eryk asked her.

From her perch on a log, Oliwia answered, "My brother is six, and I am fifteen years."

"Have you kin anywhere besides Vyatov?" Lord Eryk leaned back on his hands, his ankles crossed.

"No, my lord." She was careful to mask the clench in her gut.

He looked somewhere distant and scratched the back of his head. Oliwia's eyes bounced between Lord Eryk and the rod-straight lieutenant. Though Pan Dąbrowski hadn't paid her much mind, his face a study in boredom most of the time, when he did look her way, his dark blue eyes drilled into her. So when Eryk announced she and Filip would sleep in the shelter of a tent between the two of them tonight, panic bloomed in her belly.

She opened her mouth to speak, only to snap it shut.

"I assure you, you'll both be safe. What is it you fear?" Eryk urged.

How could she tell him her fear resided wholly with his menacing lieutenant? "It is … it is …" she faltered.

He waited, watching her. Jacek stood and excused himself, inviting Filip to follow. Her brother jumped up. In a bid to regain her composure, Oliwia tugged the necklace from her bodice. At the end of the chain was a silver cross with a high luster and no adornment. Calmed by its comforting familiarity, she raced forward.

"It's just you told that … that man, you would as soon he kill me. That it would make no difference …" She trailed off, eyes downcast.

Eryk erupted in a laugh, slapping his hands against his thighs, startling her. "Is that what has you worried?" When she nodded, he continued. "I'm sorry if what I said frightened you. I didn't mean it. Well, I meant what I said to *that* vermin, but not to you. I do not harm children. I do not kidnap women, enemy or otherwise. I do not trade in human slavery. Nor do *any* of my men. To do so would make us no better than the mongrel Tatars." He turned his head and spat. "I did not want him to harm you. If he thought I cared, he'd have just as soon slit your throat. Do you understand?" He lowered his head and peered at her.

She lifted her chin. "You called him a lost man. What did you mean?"

The lord drew in a great breath and settled his arms across his chest. "To understand that, you must first hear of an adventurer named Aleksander Lisowski. He is a nobleman who once rode for the Crown. He is cunning and ruthless, an excellent cavalryman and skilled fighter. Some call him bloodthirsty. During a time when the Crown was remiss in paying soldiers their wages, Lisowski mutinied and formed his own regiment of irregulars. They fight for the Crown, then switch sides and fight for our enemies, the Swedes. They are opportunists who receive no formal wages. They take their pay in plunder." Here he stuttered.

Oliwia remained still, appalled yet fascinated, eager to hear more.

"They are not particular about whom they victimize, and they commit atrocities in their own homeland—similar to what they did to your village. The Crown attempts to keep them occupied off home soil and looks the other way when they fight Muscovites—begging your pardon. They are known as the *chorągiew elearska*—the lost men." He paused a beat. "Does that answer your question?"

Oliwia nodded, pondering the fate from which she and Filip had been saved, though she had little idea what fate faced them now.

"Good. Let's get some sleep."

A short while later, lying atop thin layers of blankets between the commander and lieutenant, Oliwia held her brother close and stared at the lieutenant's broad back mere feet away. If she scooted any farther from him, she risked backing into the lord. From the stillness of the second's form and his rhythmic breathing, punctuated by an occasional snort, she judged him to be asleep and no threat—for the moment.

Vigilance kept her adrift in a restless twilight, and cruel images flashed through her head. Animals bawling as they burned in a barn; Jans and Magda, the people the lord had mistaken for her parents, so easily overcome by a Polish brute; the smithy's daughter fleeing, only to be overpowered and dragged off. Her screams echoed in Oliwia's head; she sent a silent prayer heavenward.

Squeezing her eyes tight, she conjured an angel. Her mother's crystal-blue eyes—so like her own, she'd been told—danced and sparkled as she smiled at Oliwia. Oliwia watched her ghostly white child's hand reach up to touch her mother's dark brown hair. Its softness brushed her fingers.

I promise I will be a strong girl, Mother.

Jacek opened his eyes amid an awakening chorus of woodland birds. He was more tired after his fitful sleep than when he'd first stretched out. In the weak light of the predawn sky, he made out the petite form sleeping an arm's length from him, her brother's smaller body tucked in her arms. Eryk's blanket was empty, and Jacek set off to find him before the men roused.

He located his commander at the edge of the pool, pulling his fingers through his damp hair, seemingly lost in thought. Jacek scanned everything in his purview but saw only the small, clear pool, deep enough to submerge a grown man to his shoulders. A stack of boulders blocked the stream's current, allowing only gentle flows through a jumble of rocky gaps. Willow shrubs crowded the edges of the sandy ground, dense and green. The water reflected the graceful elm and willow branches arcing above while damselflies and midges skimmed soft ripples across its shimmering surface.

Jacek stripped and plunged into the brisk water, bringing his mind and body to full alertness. He emerged and shook water from his hair and limbs. After he dressed, he dropped beside Eryk on the sandy strip limning the pool. Eryk stared ahead, and Jacek followed his gaze. Pulling in three deep breaths, he focused on a gnarled, knotted birch trunk on the far side of the stream.

Eryk broke the silence. "She says they've no family left, and I have no desire to return to enemy territory and search. I see nothing to be done other than to bring them to Biaska."

Jacek held still while Eryk continued. A hard edge crept into his commander's voice. "You know what this means, yes? If we bring them back with us? We have at least four weeks of travel before we reach home, and this girl, this young woman will be a distraction."

His eyes fixed on the warty burl, Jacek shrugged. "Possibly."

"These are good men, honorable men. But they've been away from home a long time, and they have battled hard," Eryk said. "I do not wish to place too great a temptation in their paths."

"Then permit them more frequent visits to the brothels," Jacek offered.

Nodding, Eryk untangled a stray twig in his hair. "As we travel, the only men I entrust her with besides myself are you and Henryk."

Jacek's head pivoted, and he arched an eyebrow at his lord.

"Well, now that I think on it a little harder," Eryk corrected with a small grin, "perhaps not Henryk, after all. I think the boy will be safe with him though."

THE HEART OF A HUSSAR

Both men chuckled. Henryk had the reputation of being a courageous, tough warrior and a fearsome foe. Henryk also had the reputation of being an irresistible charmer of all women, and this earned him a different sort of admiration among the men. He indulged as fully as he fought.

"Henryk can be trusted with the life of anyone under your protection. Besides, he would not molest a child," Jacek said.

"Apparently, you haven't noticed, but she's not such a child. Turning her over to him might prove too great a lure; he's not invincible. The wisest course is to have her ride with just the two of us."

"Understood, my lord."

Eryk smirked. "On further thought, as *you* are the one who advocated rescue, you will take her for the journey."

Jacek bit back a protest.

An hour later, amid servants stowing away the camp, Jacek readied Jarosława. He murmured in his mare's ear as he cinched her girth.

"It wasn't my choice. I'd prefer not to be crowded, but she's not big and cannot weigh much. You and I will manage the inconvenience."

Like the others, he didn't don his armor, for they did not expect any battles this day, and they wanted to move quickly in the summer heat. Unlike the others, he relinquished his pistols, his *pałasz*—the broadsword—and war hammer to better arrange himself and his passenger. Though he still carried his prized sabre, dagger, and bow and quiver, the missing arms unnerved him.

Horses stood ready in the clearing, and men began clambering into their saddles. He mounted as the girl approached, her eyes darting over Jarosława. Extending his arm, he jerked his head, signaling it was time to go. When he leaned down to her, she stumbled backward.

He suppressed his annoyance. "Come closer so I can help you up."

She shuffled toward him, and he encircled her middle. She bucked as he hauled her up.

"Stop," he scolded. A pang of guilt softened his tone. "Ease yourself. I have you. I won't let you fall."

Oliwia's insides flipped, then flopped, and her limbs were nearly frozen with fear. But she did as the lieutenant commanded and found herself propped face-forward in the saddle. His muscular thighs straddled her bottom while her legs bestrode the saddlebow and dangled on either side of the big stippled gray horse. It took some shifting, but they finally fit together like puzzle pieces.

As they walked the trails curving through the wood, the lieutenant's warm breath fell on her hair and she smelled his musky scent—more pleasant than yesterday's version. The heat from his unarmored body seeped through her gown, and she sat forward to evade every sensation emanating from him. The action garnered a grunt from him. A forearm corded with hardened muscle snaked around her waist, pulling her back up in a straight position snugged against his chest. She squeaked.

"My lady," he hissed. "I think it would be most comfortable for us both if you were to stay as upright as possible."

She bobbed her head like a sprinting pigeon. At least her back was to him, and she was spared his stormy eyes scrutinizing her.

And so they trudged in and around the thick trees. When the woods gave way to rolling meadow, the horses cantered. The summer sun had climbed high, and the heat shimmered through the grasses. A few leaden clouds lumbered overhead, threatening a rainstorm later that afternoon, but all else was still.

Midday, they took refuge in a shade-dappled grove beside a stream and ate a simple meal of bread and cheese. Oliwia and Filip sat among several hussars, her brother's head wagging back and forth between the bantering men. He seemed dazzled and distracted, and she sent a grateful prayer skyward.

The rest of the afternoon passed without threat from nature or man. Heat rose and enveloped the group in torpor as they rode through field and wood, and Oliwia's body rocked to the rhythm of the horse's steps. Soon her head flopped to one side, and the lieutenant raised both arms and braced her, then tipped her back against him. She startled fully awake, pulling herself away from him.

"Was I asleep?" she said in a fluster.

"Yes, my lady. Or you were about to be. I feared you might fall over, so I pulled you back."

"Oh, I see," she muttered in a voice thick with sleep. "Thank you."

THE HEART OF A HUSSAR

She ran her fingers through her hair in a nervous gesture, horrified when an errant curl caught in his mouth. He freed it with a sputter. Her back now rigid, she searched for something to say.

Unfortunately, she blurted the thought consuming her.

"Are we your prisoners?"

CHAPTER 5

Foreigner

Momentarily stunned, Jacek did what all good soldiers do. He bought time while deflecting an attack. "I beg your pardon?"

The girl twisted in the saddle and regarded him over her shoulder. Her face was flushed; he doubted it was from the heat.

"During the midday meal," she said in a steady tone, "I heard your men say we are on Polish soil. Judging by the sun, we are traveling southwest, away from Muscovy. Have you taken my brother and me prisoner?"

"Of course not."

"Then where are you taking us?" she posed—quite rationally, he grudgingly admitted.

"When my commander learned you have no family, he decided to safeguard you and bring you with us to his estate. First we will catch up our company, then we all travel to Biaska, in the southwestern part of the Kingdom of Poland. It's a fortified castle among a line of fortresses guarding the western border. Do you know Kraków?"

She nodded. "Whenever I go with my ... When I would visit the fair in Maksimkovo, merchants would tell stories of Kraków, its grand cloth hall, and the king's beautiful palace on the hill."

His eyebrows inched up his forehead. "Wawel Castle. Soon it will no longer be the site of the king's court. His Majesty ordered the

THE HEART OF A HUSSAR

reconstruction of the Royal Castle in Warszawa and relocates there." He couldn't fathom why he was bothering to tell her this.

"But why?"

"The king is a goldsmith and employs an alchemist. Part of Wawel burned years ago from an experiment gone awry. Warszawa is also closer to the Muscovite border, and Sweden, where he hails from."

"Did you witness the fire?"

He suppressed a chuckle. "No. But when I was six, I went to Wawel with my grandfather. His father served Zygmunt the Old, which is how he gained his estate, my family home."

She had been swiveling her head back and forth and now turned and looked at him again with a deep frown. "Why?"

He flicked the reins impatiently. Her questions tossed him off balance, as though he fought for footing atop a rolling log in a swift river.

"He saved his commander at the Battle of Łopuszno in 1512," he replied hotly. "And killed many Tatars."

Shaking her head, she said, "No, I meant why did you go there with your grandfather? It must have been quite an adventure for a young boy."

Her guileless expression sucked all the wind from his bluster.

"It was, yes." His voice was colored with sheepishness. "He took me and my brothers to see a portrait of the battle showing my great-grandfather among the warriors."

"You come from a long line of soldiers, then. How many brothers?"

"Three older, one younger." He smirked. "And before you ask, two older sisters and one younger."

Her eyes widened. "Such a big family! Do your parents live?"

"Yes." With melancholy, he added, "Our family was larger once. My mother lost several children … and I had another sister." The words escaped before he could swallow them. He never spoke of Ruta.

You remind me of her.

"How long has she been gone?" she asked gently.

"Seven years. She was my twin. She died of ague." Ague he'd been sick with and passed on to her. The ache returned, and he flicked the reins again, clearing his throat.

Oliwia nodded and faced forward. A few minutes later, she glanced back. "So we are not prisoners? We are free to go?"

"Go where?" he asked with bemusement. She replied with a shrug.

"Muscovy will soon be part of the Commonwealth," he boasted, "So you're as good as a Pole now—or Lithuanian, if you prefer. If your family ... If you're Orthodox, you might choose to be Lithuanian as they too are Orthodox. Most Poles are Catholic, but you are free to choose your religion." He cocked his head to the side to look at her.

She drew in a sharp breath, and her face darkened with a fierce glare. "What makes you so certain Muscovy is about to become part of your precious Commonwealth?"

"Because your boyars signed a treaty, and our Prince Władysaw is now their tsar," he retorted with equal fervor. "I was fighting nearby, at Smoleńsk, when it happened. That city will soon surrender to us. I just returned from Biała, where the Muscovite commander withdrew when he heard we were marching to liberate our garrison. And only two days ago, we marched to Kłuszyn, where we routed a Muscovite force many times greater than ours! And they ran! With an army like that, it's only a matter of time before your country falls." His heart hammered against his ribs.

Her eyes became two glittering moons. "So it's true!" she whispered right before she twisted away and showed him her back. Her shoulders seemed to sag.

Why the hell am I arguing with a fifteen-year-old girl who's just lost everything, for Christ's sake?

For the rest of that long afternoon, she didn't speak to him. When they stopped to encamp, she scrambled out of the saddle, tumbling to the ground before he could reach out to soften her landing.

Oliwia scanned the soldiers' faces from a safe distance as they sat around the fire. Her predicament hit her with full force. She was one girl, and a small, unarmed one at that, among scores of hardened warriors. Hardened *enemy* warriors. On their way to join hundreds more. On foreign soil. With sharpened steel. But where could she go? To survive, to keep Filip alive, she must stay with them. She had no choice.

The people of Vyatov had tolerated the Poles, learning their language to trade with them. But elsewhere in Muscovy, Poles were despised. She had listened to the stories, and she'd heard the lament of the "three plagues." Typhus, the Tatars, and the Poles.

The Polish soldiers who had destroyed her village had been evil. But outside of the lieutenant, *these* men didn't seem like evildoers. Hadn't her father—her real father—fought on the side of the Poles? Surely he had seen something noble. And Lord Eryk had taken her and Filip—to safeguard them, the lieutenant had said—when he could have left them behind to starve or worse.

But then there was the enigma that was the prickly lieutenant. She shuddered. He had glanced her way a few times tonight, but she'd ignored him. Or tried to. She struggled to envision him laughing among his siblings but could only conjure his forbidding face with a bloody weapon to hand.

Bone-weary, she stood and stretched in the firelight. Several sets of eyes turned to her, and the faces they belonged to smiled before turning back to their dice, their pipes, and their songs. She stepped to the tent set up for just her and Filip and rolled herself in a nest of blankets with her slumbering brother.

They are not bad men. We are safe in their care. We have to be.
Stay strong, Oliwia.
Yes, Mother.

Sometime in the night, she was wakened by thrashing and cries. Before she gained full consciousness, a large figure loomed in the tent, and her heart leapt to her throat.

"Are you all right?" The lieutenant's voice, soft and low, came from his hulking outline. He knelt beside Filip.

Her brother keened, and the lieutenant sat him up and shoved his limp, sweaty person into her arms before retrieving a lantern. Hovering over the flame, he peered at her while Filip sobbed against her.

"I was on guard outside your tent when I heard cries," the lieutenant whispered. "He'll be better now." He nodded toward the snuffling heap in her lap with the scrawny arm clamped about her neck. The lantern light might have deceived her, but she thought the lieutenant's eyes shone with sympathy, not the disdain she would have expected. Before she could thank him, he had melted into the night, leaving behind the lamp.

By morning, Filip had recovered, babbling cheerfully as if naught had happened during the black hours. Oliwia resolved herself to riding with the lieutenant again, and though he still scared her, her fear had receded a shade. He was not so frightening as he had been at the outset.

The landscape seemed to stretch for miles, green and flat, with the occasional hump in the land or dark green grove on the horizon. As they traversed an endless sea of grasses, Oliwia sought to make peace.

"Lieutenant, what do you like to do?" she ventured with a backward glance.

His lip curled up at one corner, and he looked to the side as if calculating. "I like to eat, and I like to dance."

He must have seen astonishment on her face, because he chuckled.

"From the time I was a boy, I was taught, like other sons of noblemen, all the knightly arts, including how to dance."

She tried in vain to imagine him spinning joyfully in a reel. "What else were you taught?"

"Warfare," he replied easily. "You look surprised. It's no different for any of these hussars." He waved his hand.

Then he told her about the soldiers traveling with them. They were heavy cavalry, he said, sent into battle for one purpose—to smash enemy lines. But not all in their number were hussars. Jacek explained she was looking at a spectrum of circumstances: the middling nobility, the poor nobility, and the yeoman class.

The nobility, the *szlachta*—who fancied themselves descended from the Sarmatians—ranged from the wealthiest landed magnates to those rich in name only. Though they considered themselves as equals, their differences in wealth shaped their station in military service, he explained. The cavaliers dressed like him—armored, in red or saffron boots and a cardinal coat called a *żupan*—were heavy winged hussars. The elite cavalry.

"When a rotmistrz, like Lord Eryk, receives a letter of recruitment from the king, he calls forth trusted hussars. They report, ready to swear an oath to his standard, with their *poczets*—their retinues—consisting of servants and pacholiks, whom they outfit and feed. Hussars also bring their own horses and provisions."

He pointed to men dressed in gray żupans. "They are servants—tenant farmers or their sons—who sometimes fight in Lord Eryk's company. In darker cloth or faded red are pacholiks. Some of them are poor noblemen—like Marcin. Their families are long on dedication and short on the funds needed to equip them to be husaria."

She frowned. "If Marcin is a nobleman, then …"

"He is like other pacholiks, fighting and laboring for the hussars they serve."

"Will he someday be like you and have attendants serving *him*?"

"Possibly. Marcin strives to prove his prowess and acquire enough wealth to finance a retinue of his own, thus rising from pacholik to hussar. A pacholik's fortune depends upon his master and chance."

"Have you other servants?"

He shook his head. "My poczet is Marcin and me. He does the work of four men."

As he described his Polish domain, Oliwia grew enraptured by the narrative delivered by the deep voice rumbling through his chest, vibrating her back when she sat against him. She nearly forgot to be afraid.

The troop had been traversing a boggy brown field, with Jacek's warhorse lumbering behind the outriders. A loud rapping sounded; horses were reined to a stop. Jacek tensed, swiveling his head until a pacholik pointed at a copse.

"Look," Jacek laughed, stabbing his finger toward the top of a dead tree. What resembled an immense cap rested precariously in the crook of a sturdy branch. Rising from it were two white heads affixed with long orange beaks. One beak clattered, the noise bouncing between the trees.

"Have you seen a stork nest before?" he asked. She shook her head, mouth open, staring at the large birds.

When the horses resumed, Oliwia glanced around and found Marcin. The dark-haired, dark-eyed young man lagged behind with other retainers. He looked to be eighteen, and his features and easy manner reminded her of the cartwright's son in Vyatov. A sudden jolt tore through her. In her mind, an image bloomed of the young man bellowing, running, flailing his fists desperately as he threw himself at the soldiers abducting the smithy's daughter—the maiden who was to be his wife. But he proved no match for hardened soldiers. Oliwia's vision shifted to his glassy brown eyes, staring blankly as he lay in a pool of his own blood. *He is dead.*

Mid-afternoon, they stopped by a rivulet barely contained within its shallow banks, cattails growing thick like a palisade alongside it. After watering horses, shaking out stiff limbs, and letting blood flow into numb backsides, the caravan resumed.

"How did you become a hussar?" she asked once they were underway.

"From an early age, I was taught riding and combat. My father employed a mean old bast—hussar who trained my brothers and me in exchange for quarters and meals. When I was sixteen, my sire sent me to Lord Eryk for more instruction."

"Why?"

"I had outgrown my teacher, and like most wealthy lords, Lord Eryk had his own army of highly trained soldiers. I was honored when he asked me to remain at his garrison. It was there I joined his husaria. We are called *towarzysze*—companions or comrades."

"Companions to whom?"

He shrugged. "Companions to one another and to the rotmistrz, since we campaign together. And now I serve Lord Eryk year-long."

"Are your brothers hussars?"

"The two oldest ones fulfilled their military obligations in other capacities and now help my father manage the estate. The next oldest is a hussar who fights on behalf of his wife's clan, and at the end of his turn, he will parlay a favorable royal post. My younger brother trains at home."

"Are your brothers married?"

"The oldest three are."

"And you?" It hadn't occurred that this gruff soldier might have a wife. She glanced at him, trying to imagine such a creature. Would she be pliant and kind? Or as steely as he?

"No," he said with a tight smile. "I have much to accomplish before I take a wife."

"Such as?"

He looked away quickly, and she fretted his silence was a signal she'd pushed too far.

CHAPTER 6

Commonwealth

On a long exhale, Jacek leveled his eyes at hers. "I want land of my own. I will never inherit my father's estate, and despite my parents' wishes, I will not gain holdings through marriage. So I must acquit myself on the battlefield and gain the king's recognition. If I prove myself worthy, as my great-grandfather did, the king may reward me with a Crown estate. As long as there is land enough to hunt and cultivate timber and wheat, I will need nothing more."

Except the satisfaction of seeing the looks on his sire's and brothers' faces when they first stepped onto his estate. That vision—with the stinging memories of their heedless ridicule—made him more determined than ever.

The squad reached a meadow of high grasses, riding side by side in one long line. The sun pulsed in a cloudless deep blue sky, showering them with hot rays.

The girl swatted at a swarm of gnats. "Why does Lord Eryk have a private army?"

He took a swipe at them too. "He has vast holdings. As lord, he's duty-bound to protect them and his people. In times of war, which seem to be *all* the time, his force is available to the Crown. As rotmistrz, he can raise more troops in addition to his private army if the king or the Sejm—that's Parliament—calls for it."

"And did Parliament call for your recent ... forays?"

He chuckled mildly. "No, but the king did, and Hetman Żółkiewski serves the king. Lord Eryk, in turn, supports Żółkiewski. So when Żółkiewski sent a plea for more troops, Lord Eryk led us to Smoleńsk and eventually to Kłuszyn. Since I've been at Biaska, we've gone on campaign every year—sometimes for the king, at other times for magnates such as Żółkiewski. It's an exciting life."

She quirked an eyebrow at him. "Have you ever met the king?"

"Almost, at Smoleńsk. One day I shall."

A fierce frown drew her dark brows together. "Who does Poland fight? Besides Muscovy, I mean?"

"It's not only Poland, but Lithuania too—the entire Commonwealth. Since the treaty of Lublin united the two countries some forty years ago, the borders stretch forever and are always in need of defending. To the east, well, you already know that one," he said uneasily. "To the north, we fight the Swedes. To the south, the Turks always threaten, and they send their damned, er, that is, their dogs, the Tatars, to fight us and raid our country for slaves. And nobles fight among themselves. All are reasons for a permanent force."

She grimaced. "Those same dogs raid Muscovy too."

More questions led to more answers. Unlike the strained quiet of their ride the afternoon before, today's journey passed swiftly, and Jacek found himself grateful for Oliwia's company.

They broke camp before dawn the next day under the threat of gathering clouds and were riding before the sun lit the gray murk on the horizon.

"Everyone seems hurried this morning," she remarked.

"Lord Eryk is anxious to cover ground and reach the company. Judging by the clouds, we are in for a downpour, which means we will in all likelihood set up camp early."

They rode on in silence for a stretch until Jacek spoke up. "I expect you are weary of my ramblings after listening to me all the day yesterday. You have said little of yourself. Might I not hear from you?"

She shrugged. "You already know all there is to know. Filip and I come from a peasant village. We have—uh, had—no knights there, no towarzysze. No nobility at all."

"It is not tales of knights or nobility I care to hear."

THE HEART OF A HUSSAR

"You would hear silly stories of peasant children?"

"What is wrong with peasant children? They are like all other children, yes? They eat, they sleep, they terrorize one another. Boys chase girls with frogs and pull their braids, and girls exact their vengeance in devious ways when no one is watching. No different from noble children."

She glanced back at him with a smirk. "They are quite different, my lord. Besides, I still have questions."

"What questions did you not ask? I believe I have answered them all."

"Why is it everyone among you is dressed differently?"

Was she distracting him to avoid talking of herself? Darting his eyes to the lowering ceiling of steely clouds, he decided to indulge her. At least her endless questions kept his mind off the drudgery of the flat march and the damp wind whistling around them.

"Lord Eryk does not provide livery, so these hussars outfit themselves and their poczets. However, he does provide leopard pelts to his senior officers. They come from Asia and Muscovy, I'm told." He smiled inwardly. "The pelts, not the officers."

Oliwia glanced over her shoulder, and he tilted his head to meet her gaze.

He anticipated her question. "Mine is stowed in my wagon presently."

A beat passed before she asked, "Does your horse not get tired from carrying you all the time?"

"I bring more than one horse on campaign, as you will see when we catch up the company. Most times I have five."

Her eyes and mouth grew round.

"A hussar needs more than one so he can keep them fresh for battle. And if one is injured or killed, he has replacements," he explained.

She stiffened. Had he upset her with talk of the horses?

"Have you a rock?" she hissed, her eyes fixed on a squat shrub ahead.

Bewildered, he shook his head. "Why?" He glanced around, alert for wolves.

"I should like to knock that fat, silly pheasant senseless for our supper," she whispered as she pointed. As if hearing her plan, said fat, silly pheasant made a great beating of its wings and lifted laboriously into the sky.

Jacek did not mask his skepticism. "You could have hit that thing?"

She shrugged. "Maybe, though I am much better with a sling."

He laughed, and she twisted in the saddle and peered at him, her brows knotted together.

"Have you never thrown rocks at a bird?" she demanded.

The challenge in her question thumped him with surprise—and amusement.

"Of course. All boys do. And some girls, apparently," he chuckled. "You're a cheeky young miss."

"I am *not* a child," she huffed. "I'll have you know I was to wed in a month."

His eyebrows flew to his hairline. "So soon?" he blurted. And he hadn't meant a month was soon, but rather fifteen summers was soon. Though the practice was common enough, Jacek had been raised in a clan that did not encourage marriage at an early age. *"A bride should not be a child who has yet to reach womanhood!"* his grandmother would have exclaimed were she alive.

He scratched the back of his neck. "A boy in your village?" he ventured.

"No." Her voice was so soft he barely heard her. "A widowed merchant of forty-nine."

"Surely this wasn't a union *you* desired?"

She shook her head, and he thought her slight shoulders shuddered. "I had no choice. The man had offered my mast—" She paused and drew in a breath. "He had some wealth, and so, you understand, the marriage was of great benefit."

Ha! Of great benefit to the randy old merchant, no doubt. Jacek squelched his disgust.

She swiveled her head to him, her luminescent eyes on his. "Do Poles believe in forced marriage?"

He shrugged. "There are arranged marriages across all classes, and royalty especially, of course. But no, Poles are free to choose their spouses; even peasants and nobles sometimes intermarry. In the case of my older sisters, they did not wed before reaching eighteen years, and they chose for themselves. Their husbands enhanced my family's standing, of course, but they were love matches nonetheless." It was his family's way, and he found nothing lacking in it. "Women in Poland are considered as equals. Partners."

She gave him a shy smile. "Perhaps there is benefit to becoming a Pole, or a Lithuanian, after all."

THE HEART OF A HUSSAR

He didn't add that some, notably the clergy, not only viewed women as inferiors but also opposed educating them. On this point, his family also differed, for his sisters had all been schooled.

After a long interlude, when he thought she'd fallen asleep, the girl surprised him by prodding him about battles and enemy armies, Muscovites included. He reveled in military strategy, and soon any fatigue that had threatened to overtake him evaporated. His enthusiasm for the telling grew as he explained tabors, caracoles, and one formation after another in precise detail to his solo audience.

"What purpose do the wings serve?" she asked.

Jarosława pulled to the right, intent on an inviting lush patch of grass, and he tugged the reins to bring her back on course. "The wings distinguish us from other cavalry. *And* their fluttering frightens enemy horses as we charge in, as do the pelts. One frightened horse will spread that fear among the others, leaving enemy riders in disarray."

And so the conversation continued.

Jacek couldn't remember encountering a female who had shown curiosity in subjects most thought exceedingly masculine and dull. When in the company of ladies, he had noted most of the prattle centered on fashion and who said what about whom. Many starry-eyed girls would ask a soldier about his acts of valor but never cared to hear about the battle itself or the strategy behind it.

There was, of course, a less genteel world that brought him into conversations with the fairer sex. Women with whom he shared the occasional intimate encounter were likewise uninterested; talk was superficial and brief. Their fascination in him matched his in them and had everything to do with the immediate and the physical, not the intellectual. While whores were happy to let a man blather about anything he wanted, their feigned interest held only as long as his coin or the next customer's patience. So it was with no little wonder that he spoke so freely to a mere girl of fifteen in a way he'd never spoken to a woman of any age or social standing.

Eventually, even he wearied of military tales. One afternoon he began recounting some of the antics he and his brothers would get up to and the trouble they suffered at the hands of their harangued servants and overbearing sisters.

"See this scar?" He pushed up his *kolpak*—his cap—and pointed to a divot just above his eyebrow.

She turned her head and glanced at him. "How did you come by it?"

"My oldest brother shot me with an arrow." When she fired him a skeptical frown, he said, "No, really. He did. He told my mother he had been aiming at a squirrel on a branch above my head."

"And what did your mother do?"

"After she had him whipped, she took away his quiver and arrows and gave them to me. From then on, I goaded him endlessly, certain I would end up with his entire arsenal."

"And did you?"

"No. Instead I suffered his pummelings until he turned twelve and was sent off to study at a magnate's court. My other brothers took over the beatings in his stead. But I showed them all when I grew to be the biggest of our lot." He grinned.

Oliwia laughed throughout the telling of his misdeeds, and he found himself moved to divulge more. Maybe it was because she asked questions he wanted to answer. Maybe it was because she didn't titter or squeal. Maybe it was because he was forced to be so close for so long. Whatever the reason, the words seemed to flow from him, giving way to an animated mien quite out of character for him.

The rain pushed everyone into their tents early that night. Jacek lay on his back with fingers laced across his belly, listening to the rhythmic chorus of plops against the canvas. Before slipping into a dreamless sleep, he imagined what awaited him in the morning: soggy countryside, a grimy girl, and the myriad stories he would regale her with. For the first time in months, his nighttime musings held no unpleasantness. No thought of an enemy, no thought of danger. No thought he would soon face both.

CHAPTER 7

One Summer Afternoon

The following midafternoon, the detachment trudged single-file into dense wood through humidity so heavy it seemed to steam from the ground beneath wheel and hoof. On one side, the trees rose up a hillock ten feet above the track, while the other side was forested flatland. Long shadows fell over their path, creating pockets of stifling darkness.

An outrider abruptly motioned a halt and unsheathed his sabre. The signal rippled through the troop, and a fire sparked inside Jacek. Any illusion of languidness vanished as men and horses snapped into a practiced mass of motion.

Urging Jarosława toward the back of the line, Jacek barked orders to servants encircling the wagon. He came alongside it, hauling Oliwia from his saddle and depositing her atop the heap of equipment in its bed.

"Stay here! Get low, and stay here! Do not let them see you!"

Marcin appeared beside him. Jarosława danced in a circle, Jacek holding her reins loosely as he pivoted with her.

"They will protect you!" Eyes fixed on Oliwia's, he gestured toward the servants swarming the cart, his hand reaching up to snatch an oncoming projectile flying through the air, seemingly of its own volition. Without looking, he grabbed the sheathed pałasz Marcin had plucked from the wagon and tossed at him. Jacek unwound it and seated it swiftly, belying his racing pulse.

"*Oliwia!* Do you understand?" Jacek boomed as Marcin handed him his *nadziak*—the war hammer.

Dazed and wide-eyed, she dropped into the bed and nodded. Jacek turned Jarosława and galloped toward his brothers-in-arms, kicking up clods of earth as he went. They tensed on their horses, bristling with armaments as they faced the sloping woods. From the corner of his eye, he saw Henryk riding for the wagon as if he ran from the devil.

What in blazes?

Ah, Christ! Filip!

Henryk tossed the lad to his sister, turned, and spurred back, falling in beside Jacek. The group drew together in formation. Jacek gripped his nadziak and drew in a steadying breath.

Horsemen erupted from the wall of woods, sweeping down the rise. More men followed on foot, tattered men, scrabbling down the slope like agitated, overgrown beetles. They bore down, swords glinting. Hussars fired wheel-locks into them, the thud of gunfire reverberating off the walls of trees. Heavy puffs of white-blue smoke spread an opaque haze over the scene.

Jacek surged into the onslaught, swinging his nadziak as men came together. The hammer head landed on the snout of an adversary's horse with a reporting crack, reverberating the impact up Jacek's arm. The force from the strike carried into the next beast. Its inertia spent, the weakened blow still caused the animal to turn its head, exposing its rider.

Now!

Jacek arced the nadziak and buried its claw in the man's cheek. Bone split, and the man screamed as flesh tore away. Muscled meat flashed, dark red, blood pouring from the gaping wound as Jacek wheeled away. Rooted in his saddle, he swung the war hammer into an enemy shoulder, connected with taught gristle, then backhanded it across another's midsection, slowing them both.

He pulled away, readying for the next assault.

Come on! Come get me!

Three rushed at him. He kicked at one, connecting his metal-heeled boot with the man's chest. The man reeled sideways. His saddle seemed to give, and it slipped. Jacek followed with a powerful blow to the man's mount, toppling him when his horse jerked. The animal bolted into its rider's erstwhile companions' path, stamping, blocking adversaries as it crushed its former rider, now prone below its hooves.

While the beast flailed, the two other horses backed up, panicking, tangling themselves and their riders. Jacek seized one man's reins, swiping the nadziak's claw at his chest. The man twisted, and the point skittered down his side and punched into his thigh. Bellowing, he jerked his reins, but Jacek held them fast and heaved his elbow into the man's nose with a resounding *crunch*. Blood gushed over the man's unkempt moustache, dribbling into his mouth and off his chin. He grabbed at his nose, and Jacek yanked the nadziak free, turning with a shout to strike the man's companion.

But he wasn't fast enough.

The man's sabre flashed as it carved across Jacek's body, the curve slicing his middle. Fabric tore. *Mother of God!* He didn't look down. Instead, he locked on his attacker's fiery eyes and thrust the nadziak at the man's chin. The man's orbs rolled backward. Surging Jarosława into him, Jacek kicked out and sent him to the ground.

Jacek barricaded himself with the now riderless horses and paused, gasping. There was no pain, no burn of the blade. Sucking in air, he looked down. No blood. He brought his head up, his eyes sweeping the scene, taking in flashes. Mounted men smashed and hacked at each other with unbridled ferocity. Some battled on the ground, sidestepping stamping hooves. Behind him, Henryk dueled two from his charger. Farther off, Eryk swept his sabre like a scythe, slashing at the enemy.

Horses neighed, metal crashed and rang; shouts filled the hollow between the woods.

Jacek tightened his grip on his nadziak, ready for the next onslaught, and stole a glance at the wagon. Enemy riders peeled off, heading for it.

No, no, no!

Blood had been pumping furiously through his veins since the fight began, but now an extraordinary burst exploded. It mixed with a killing rage and coursed through him. Roaring, he swung the nadziak with a two-handed grip. Crushing and clawing, he drove into the men before him with both ends of the war hammer.

Oliwia knew nothing of warfare, yet it was apparent Lord Eryk's men were the better trained. But they were outnumbered by the combatants engulfing them. She soon lost sight of them as the chaos became one boiling mass of men and horses shrouded in dust and smoke.

A band of foes broke from the main group, riding toward her, seizing her attention. With swords held high, they came at the men guarding the wagon.

Oliwia tugged on Filip's tunic. "Get down!"

Filip dropped to his belly and became part of the camp supplies. She threw herself over him, covering his slight body. Squeezing her eyes shut, she hunched her shoulders, abjectly aware her linen gown was no shield.

Please, God! Protect Filip. I swear I'll do whatever you ask of me.

As she lay atop her brother, steel clanged and men yelled. The sounds grew closer, louder. She raised her head. A leathery, lank-haired man battled Marcin beside the wagon, so close she could see him gritting yellowed teeth. They grunted and growled like two snarling wolves. Marcin's horse rocked the wagon when its rump pushed against it.

Pulling herself up, she fumbled in the equipment, hauling her brother out. She set him at the farthest corner of the cart, motioning for him to stay low, and turned back to the struggling duo.

Men clashed all around her, but she stayed fixed on Marcin and his foe. As they grappled in their saddles, they began a slow tumble over the side of the wagon, and she stumbled to the corner where Filip had squatted a moment before.

He was gone.

Her stomach heaved into her chest, and her racing heart accelerated. She fought down the terror gripping her and scattered whatnot as she burrowed. She searched in vain. A brown blur darted on the ground, snagging her eye. With visceral dread, she turned toward the motion; her brother's small form ran toward the screening woods.

She screamed, but Filip vanished into the greenery. Crouching in the cart, she searched the main fracas for Jacek, Henryk, Lesław—anyone she could call to her brother's rescue—but could not distinguish hussar from enemy within the obscured turmoil.

Closer at hand, Marcin's assailant clobbered him with a heavy hilt, doubling the pacholik over. The enemy locked his eyes on hers. In a fleet decision, she did the only thing she could.

She lit from the wagon.

Blood pounding through her, Oliwia sprinted toward the opening where her brother had disappeared moments before. Something thundered behind her, gaining on her. She flew upward, momentum flailing her feet, hoisted through the air, landing hard on a saddle. An odious cloud engulfed her. Was this one of Eryk's men?

An iron hand squeezed her left breast, and a nasty, raspy voice clucked in her ear.

"You're a pretty one!"

Not Eryk's man!

She pummeled and clawed at his sinewy arm, to no avail. He rode hard and fast, wrenching her tight until she could scarcely breathe, driving the fight from her as she struggled to keep her wits. She tried to cage her fright, tried to keep her bearings. Landmarks flew by, obliterated in a blur of foliage.

They slowed, snaking their way over a thick carpet of rotting vegetation, deadening the sound of the mount's steps. The echoes of battle receded, replaced by the stillness of a forest asleep on a hot, lazy afternoon. Her captor stopped his horse within thick trees ringing a clearing.

No more sound. All was quiet.

They were alone.

The man slithered over the side of his saddle, dragging her with him as he sank into the layer of leaves. He smelled of ale and decay, and Oliwia stifled a wave swelling in her gut.

His arm cinched about her waist, he hauled her to a tree trunk with a substantial girth. Barely taller than she, he was stocky and strong. Very strong. He tossed her at the trunk, knocking the back of her head. She righted herself awkwardly, fighting to recover her voice. That voice came out as little more than a squeak when she faced him. He was more hideous than his reek.

Hard, thin lips under an unkempt bush of a brown moustache revealed brown stumps where front teeth should have been. Bloodshot obsidian eyes beneath a ridged brow were set in a pitted face, and they gleamed as they looked her over. Oily brown hair hung in a hank to one side. The other side was shaved, exposing a scabby ear with a missing lobe. Fear spread through her like countless pinpricks.

Pinning her to the tree, he yanked at her bodice, covering her mouth with his, preventing her from crying out. This time she didn't manage to withhold the retching rippling through her, and she gasped, inhaling his putrefied breath. She brought her knee up with force, but he moved just in time and avoided the strike.

"A feisty one! I like that. I'll have me a taste now," he snickered as his tongue laved a slobbery trail down her neck and chest.

Oliwia wriggled and flailed, fighting to escape his grip. She drew in air to scream, and he clamped a greasy, grubby hand over her mouth, muffling her.

"Not yet, princess. Wait till I'm inside you—then you can scream with pleasure," he cackled. He thrust his pelvis against her, gyrating and grinding, his breathing growing more piglike. Grinning hideously, he shoved her to the ground and fumbled with his breeches.

Oliwia heaved herself up, but he was on top of her, forcing her back down, trapping her arms under her as he wrenched the hem of her skirt. The gown ripped, and he pushed it up to her knees. She twisted her legs together, desperate to lock them. He slammed his knee into the apex of her thighs, and she groaned as pain radiated from her core. Dragging in another breath, she rallied, bucking under him. For naught. Her thrashing would not hold him off much longer. Without any binding, he had fixed her arms and hips. Panic washed over her; her limbs were of no use, and she couldn't reach any part of him to bite.

Bare skin, something hard and revolting, grazed her flesh as he rucked up her skirts, exposing her thighs. She redoubled her effort to wrest herself away from him, but he only pressed his weight more forcefully on top of her, driving her body into the forest floor. She squeezed her eyes shut.

He let out a loud grunt, and his weight was gone. Uncomprehending, Oliwia blinked and rolled away, panting as she drew herself up to her knees, readying to burst into a run. Then she heard a growl that brought her to a halt. When she turned toward the sound, the sight greeting her flushed relief through the whole of her body.

Never had she been so elated to see anyone.

CHAPTER 8
Savage

Jacek stood beside the spot where she'd just lain, his large hand wrapped around the brute's neck. Oliwia's attacker was on his knees, his hands clutching at Jacek's wrist as he emitted truncated gasps and wheezes. Jacek sent him sprawling with one powerful shove. The man coughed and sputtered.

Suddenly, swiftly, he sprang to his feet and drew a dagger. A well-placed strike of Jacek's nadziak sent the knife sailing from his grasp. The man howled. Staggering and choking, he grabbed his arm and teetered backward. Jacek stepped into him and hurled him into the moldering leaves.

The man's breeches gapped open, exposing his anatomy, and he scrabbled to secure them. Gone was the menacing visage; he looked ludicrous with the hulking lieutenant looming over him. Jacek thrust his boot on the man's chest before he could rise. A bloody nadziak was poised in Jacek's right hand as if taunting the man beneath his foot, daring him to make a move.

He glanced over his shoulder at Oliwia. "Are you all right?"

Despite the throbbing between her legs, she picked herself up and nodded, scattering leaves. "Yes."

Jacek turned back to the wretch on the ground. Oliwia wrapped her arms around herself and watched as Jacek bent down and hauled the man up, slamming his back against the trunk where he had pinned Oliwia only moments ago. The man lost his breath in a *whoosh*, sliding the length of the trunk, crumpling on the ground. Jacek seized him and pulled him up again. Groaning, the man glared at him. With a murderous glower of his own, Jacek leaned into him until he was mere inches from his face.

"So you force yourself on defenseless girls? You cast-off spawn of a devil's whore!" Jacek spat. "You couldn't gain a woman's favor any other way."

Between heaving breaths, the man replied, "She's yours? I had no idea, your honor. You can't blame a man for trying. She does taste very sweet."

Oliwia flinched, expecting what didn't come. Instead of running the man through, Jacek pulled back, fixing his forearm across the brute's barrel chest.

"Who are you?" he asked calmly. The man appeared startled.

The question was not what Oliwia had expected. She'd anticipated a different outcome—a deadlier one. She watched, transfixed.

The man didn't answer. Jacek asked him again, dropping his voice, drawing out the words.

"Who ... are ... you?"

The man seemed to tremble. "I am Dariusz of Koszalin."

"You are a long way from home, Dariusz of Koszalin, are you not?"

"That I am, your honor."

"Who do you serve?" The lieutenant's voice was even, almost melodic, and his posture seemed relaxed.

Twitching, the man replied, "I ... I cannot say, my lord. My companions and I was ... We was hired by a man named Leszek—he gave no other name—who said he was the magistrate for a great lord."

"Hired for what purpose?"

A sheen of sweat slicked Dariusz's waxy face. "To deliver justice for a terrible crime committed against the lord's family."

The lieutenant appeared indifferent. "What crime?"

"Leszek did not say."

"Who is accused of this crime? Who were you hired to kill?"

Dariusz appeared confused. "Why, Lord Krezowski and his men. *You*, lord."

Jacek's eyes flickered. "What did this Leszek look like?"

THE HEART OF A HUSSAR

Dariusz swallowed and licked his lips. "I ... I don't know, your honor. Me and the men ... we'd had a bit to drink, and it was dark. He ... All I remember is he had a strange-looking eye. Clouded like. White."

"How did Leszek come to hire you?"

"We ... At least I ..." Dariusz sputtered.

"Come, Dariusz, spit it out. The truth now," Jacek said blandly.

"He found me in a tavern west of Smoleńsk. I forget which village."

"And the others, they were mercenaries like you?"

To Oliwia's amazement, Dariusz scoffed. "Not mercenaries! Swords of justice for a Polish lord!"

Jacek stepped on Dariusz's foot while he forced the spiked end of his nadziak into his crotch, then leaned on his forearm a little harder. His actions elicited a choked cry.

Oliwia hugged herself tighter and drew in a sharp breath.

"I would choose my words judiciously if I were in your boots, Dariusz. You might lose something you value."

Is the lieutenant smiling?

"Begging your forgiveness, your honor."

"So Leszek led you to us—"

"No, lord," Dariusz interrupted. "Leszek gave instructions to one from among us, a big man named Witek. He's the one what brought us here. He's dead now, killed by your men."

Puzzlement flashed on the lieutenant's otherwise inscrutable face. "Where was Leszek during the skirmish?"

"I don't know. I never saw him after he hired us. Only Witek spoke with him." Dariusz's voice took on a groveling note. "Have mercy, lord. I'm a simple townsman who only sought a bit of treasure."

"What were you promised?"

"Leszek said we could choose any reward when the job was done. Coin would follow."

"Ah. And you chose to pluck your prize before the job was finished, yes?"

Oliwia studied Jacek. He maintained a placid look, as if bored. She imagined him yawning at any moment. A tic in his jaw and the look in his eyes, however, told a different story. It seemed as though a storming ocean tossed in those eyes, wild and dark.

Dariusz squirmed, his face slimy with sweat. Jacek let up for an instant only to slam his forearm back into the man's chest with the full force of his weight. The claw of the nadziak dug a little deeper. Dariusz let out a groan and cursed.

Jacek continued in the mild voice. "You see, Dariusz of Koszalin, you were entitled to nothing because you killed no one. The soldiers—the *hussars*—you attacked all survived. Your friends, however, did not fare so well."

The man's eyes darted from side to side as though he watched a bee flying to and fro. He sucked in a breath and, in a wavering tone, asked, "Are you the lord we served?"

So swift as to be unreal, Jacek brought the spike of his nadziak up, twisting it as he buried it in the man's torso. Oliwia's blood ran cold. A terrible cracking sound, and the man's body lifted with the powerful thrust. His mouth fell slack, and he stared, wide-eyed.

"No, you son of a bitch, but I *am* the lord who's sending you to hell," Jacek snarled. "You deserve the same mercy you were about to show a helpless girl."

He stepped back, and Dariusz slithered in a twitching heap to the foot of the tree. A wave of nausea rose, and Oliwia covered her mouth, but she couldn't tear her eyes away. Jacek planted his boot firmly against the now lifeless body and yanked out the nadziak, wiping it on the man's filthy breeches. He turned to her and held out his hand.

Frozen in place, she stood as if her feet were staked to the ground. She blinked rapidly and began trembling, her arms wrapped around herself. The scene had unfolded from mere feet away, and her mind still reeled, trying to reconcile it all. Numbness that had cocooned her in a fuzzy haze fell away, and emotions crashed through her. Overcome with gratitude and admiration for the man who'd saved her, she was also swamped with fear and horror.

He appeared so calm as he stood, hand extended, looking at her. If she hadn't known him, hadn't glimpsed gentleness in his soul, she would have whirled and run. He hulked over her and the dead man at his feet, but it was so much more.

The blood of his enemies had sprayed and crusted over his skin and clothes. His deep blue eyes were narrowed and reflected an onyx glint, yet his breathing was even. He hadn't broken a sweat. Though he had just ended a man's life—violently—he seemed at ease, as if he'd taken a leisurely stroll through a summer garden. As if there wasn't a bloodied corpse at his feet. His composure terrified her. His appearance, the weapon he held, and the ruthlessness he'd just demonstrated made Oliwia hesitate. *Is this the same man?*

"Come, Oliwia. Filip awaits. We must leave now. Those who did this may return." He canted his head, and his eyes transformed back to their normal sapphire, topped with the usual scowl.

The voice rumbling from the warrior was kind—the same one she'd been listening to as he'd woven his lighthearted boyhood tales. But it did little to warm her. Chills raced through her body, and as she shambled toward him, her feet felt as if they dragged boulders.

"Oliwia?"

Jacek stuffed the war hammer in his belt and stepped to her. A voice echoed in her head, telling her to run, to get away. But she couldn't move, couldn't talk. Couldn't breathe.

He swept her from her feet into his arms.

"I have you," she heard him say softly. "None will harm you, I swear it."

Vaguely aware he carried her across the clearing, a thought drifted through her clouded mind: How could two such different men occupy the same body at the same time?

Though she couldn't be sure—and she didn't care to ask—Oliwia reckoned screaming from the woods signaled the men of Biaska gave the ambushers no quarter.

As eager crows began gathering on tree branches, Eryk's warriors prepared to leave. Among the few who had suffered wounds was Marcin, bloodied but mercifully whole.

Another pacholik, a tailor by trade, handed Oliwia needle and thread to repair her torn gown, and she numbly accepted the gift right before Jacek helped her into his saddle and mounted behind her.

They rode hard and long, leaving the carnage far behind. When at last they set up a hasty camp, darkness had snuffed out every streak of light on the horizon. A swirling wind bore a boggy, sour stench. The hussars huddled at the fringes of the lone fire, talking in low voices amongst themselves.

Oliwia couldn't make out their words from where she sat with Filip. Disheveled, weary, with damp decaying leaves tangled in her hair, she meticulously pulled strand from strand, picking out bits of vegetation. Concentrating on her grooming distracted her from the events of mere hours before.

While putting distance between herself and the terrible place in the woods had helped dissipate her fog, it was riding with Jacek, his solid warmth at her back, that had pulled her from the brink of a void. The savage warrior she'd witnessed had given way to the milder version of himself, and it was the latter she chose to see despite his menacing glower. She now understood the scowl wasn't meant for her.

Beside her, Filip hunched close as if his arm had been stitched to hers. At times, he burrowed into her side. Though his clinging slowed her grooming, she didn't mind. She'd been his mother practically since he'd been born, and soothing him came naturally, though today she was as likely to scold him for running off.

In hitching words, Filip had told her how the lieutenant had already berated him. Her consternation at this statement was overridden a breathless minute later when he told her the lieutenant had likewise praised him.

"I was hiding, and I saw you captured. I followed as far as I could. I knew you needed help, so I ran. The lieutenant was riding through the forest, searching for us. I helped him find you. I stayed hidden and guarded his horse until he brought you back."

Stunned, she asked if he'd seen or heard anything and held her breath.

He shook his head, bobbing his brown curls. "No. Perhaps a yell, but nothing else."

"Well done," she said softly.

He looked up at her and, with a tentative smile, said, "That's what the lieutenant said."

She kissed the top of his head and pulled him close. He'd get no scolding from her this day. Like she, he was resilient, but she suspected the sorrow and horror of these last days had finally wrapped their tentacles around his child's spirit and thrashed it soundly. He wouldn't be a normal boy if they hadn't.

She held him for a long while, and he let her, the closeness as much for her as for him.

CHAPTER 9

Loose Ends

Jacek stared at the fire, aggravated. His instincts had been overthrown by an internal voice yapping that he was not only soldier, but protector, compelling him to leave the fight early to succor Oliwia and Filip. In doing so, he'd placed his squad at risk.

Eryk's voice pierced his thoughts, and Jacek raised his head abruptly to find all eyes on him. "She says she wasn't violated," he replied, "which confirms what I saw. Not that the bastard wasn't trying his damnedest. Had I been a moment later, he would've succeeded."

His shoulders easing, Jacek glanced through the swaying flames. Had he let Oliwia be taken, he wouldn't be looking at her across the fire right now because she'd be dead—after being horribly used. This girl brought to mind too many memories of Ruta; he couldn't have left her to such a fate.

Inwardly, he admitted Oliwia had shown courage, and something akin to admiration rose in him as he watched her struggling with her hair. That a girl so small could fight so hard and recover her wits as quickly as she had was praiseworthy.

He felt the men's questioning gazes still fixed on him. "She gave him everything she had. She was losing the battle when I arrived, but she'd fought him just enough to slow him down. After witnessing what I did, I saw no reason he should continue drawing breath."

THE HEART OF A HUSSAR

Eryk nodded. "We knew the girl was a fighter. He told you he was from Koszalin? Why a Koszalin man? Why this attack at all? It makes no sense."

Jacek shrugged. "He resembled a steppe Cossack more than a Koszalin townsman. He claimed a man he'd never met, named Leszek, hired him and the others to kill us all for an unknown lord, to exact revenge for an unknown crime; that they were led by yet another man, Witek, whom he didn't know. A string of disconnected details."

"Yet he used *my* name. Might they have been Lisowski's band?"

Jacek shook his head. "Too undisciplined. Besides, Lisowski's men are far too shrewd to engage hussars."

Eryk turned to Henryk. "And you, Henryk, what did the man you questioned have to say?"

"Just before he died," Henryk paused to cross himself, "he pointed out this Witek's corpse. When I looked the body over, I recognized he'd been the one shouting orders. There was nothing in his pockets, no identifying marks, no way to know who he was. But the manner of his death was puzzling."

"Yes?" Eryk prompted.

Jacek's brows furrowed.

"He was killed by an arrow through the heart—a perfect shot. But it wasn't any of ours. The fletching was unlike any I have seen," Henryk said.

Eryk looked at Lesław. "Tell the men what you told me."

Lesław cleared his throat. "I saw a man crouched just behind the hillock in the woods, holding an empty bow. He was watching the melee as if he didn't belong, like he'd been hunting and stumbled across it. I thought it odd because he was reloading, but then he stopped."

"Then what?" Jacek's puzzlement grew as his brain sorted the information, sifting for a forgotten nugget.

"I looked away for a second, and when I looked back, he'd vanished. I checked, but he left no trace."

Jacek exchanged glances with Eryk before addressing the group. "Did any of you find personal belongings on any of the bodies or horses?"

Murmuring "no," they shook their heads.

Jacek looked at Eryk and raised an eyebrow. "Whoever ordered this attack took pains not to be discovered. Have you made an enemy of a 'great lord'?"

Eryk let out a mirthless laugh. "The only lord I suspect of being an enemy is my cousin Antonin, and he is 'great' only in his delusional mind. He does not have the means to pull this off. And *were* he capable, he would not attack so far from home. Besides, he may be a repulsive son of a bitch, but neither of his eyes is milky."

Jacek shrugged. "We will search for clues among the belongings the servants recovered."

The group disbanded, and Jacek remained beside the fire, fidgeting with the twisted silk of his sash—or what was left of it.

Henryk jerked his chin toward him. "Good thing you had that on."

"It's beyond repair, but it did what it was supposed to do." Jacek inspected the ruined fabric. "Better a ruined sash than a ruined belly. I will buy a new one in Kraków."

"*If* we reach Kraków."

A starless night hovered beyond a filthy window in a grubby tavern. Two men sat in a dim corner, heads bent together in quiet conversation over a small oak table. One had been wearing a hood he reluctantly pulled off when the bartender, apparently a man concerned with decorum, ordered him to do so.

The hooded man was not one to take orders from a peasant or a merchant, but he withheld the urge to snarl at the man behind the bar, the likely owner of the squalid establishment. *Best not draw attention.* Instead, he had nodded and turned before shucking the hood and threading his way to the dingy corner.

"Stop grumbling about your hood, Romek. No one here notices—they're not even looking at you. All they care about is what's left in their cups and if they have enough coin for another," Romek's drinking partner admonished.

Romek unhooked his metal tankard from his belt and set it on the table, then emptied the remainder of an earthen bottle into it. "Still, some of these men might recognize me, *Leszek*."

THE HEART OF A HUSSAR

"If you kept your cowl up at all times, I doubt anyone got a good look. If I were you, I'd be more concerned with what Krezowski will do if he finds out who was behind the attack."

Romek stared at the insolent man across from him. Though the light was dim, Romek could easily make out his milky eye. "You're scared of a mongrel like Krezowski?" he scoffed.

Dymitr, the man's real name, was a new hire—not one of his troop—but he asserted himself as an equal. "Of course I am! And so should you be, if you have any sense."

Romek was exercising a great deal of control to ignore the insult. He swallowed another sip of bad wodka with a grimace. It burned his throat on its way to his stomach. "Where the devil did you find those flea-ridden curs anyway?"

Dimytr growled, "They were idle soldiers looking for a job."

"Bah! Maybe they fancied themselves soldiers, but they were not engaged elsewhere for a very good reason: no one else wanted them. Half the bastards were drunk. Some could barely stay astride." Romek let disdain color his voice.

"Why don't you try it next time? See how well you do putting a force together with such short notice and so little pay," Dymitr retorted.

There will not be a next time.

Dymitr held up the jug and called to a tavern maid, who sashayed to their table, swiveling her wide hips. Dymitr ordered with a wink and a squeeze. She then turned her attention to Romek. He looked away, but she kept at him, prodding him in the shoulder.

"You're a big, strong one." She leaned forward, revealing ample cleavage, and ruffled his hair. He nearly gagged from the discordant touch.

A familiar spark ignited inside him, one that flared white-hot. Keeping his head turned, he reached his hand up her skirt and grabbed her thigh, digging his fingers into the soft flesh of a woman who indulged too much and worked too little. She yelped and tried to pull away. He knew he should let go, but her cry fed the spark. He dug a little deeper, relishing the feel of his nails cutting into her skin, then released her. It happened so fast that neither Dymitr nor anyone else knew. Only her, and she left the table as soon as she could escape. Romek indulged himself with a smirk. She wouldn't be back. She was just like the others. *Stupid bitch.*

He slowed his breathing while Dymitr droned on.

"The competent mercenaries are all fighting right now, and even if they weren't, this paltry booty wouldn't have convinced them to go against a score of husaria. Those curs, as you call them, were the only ones willing to strike, and even *they* took convincing."

One more gulp, and Romek recovered. He tossed back the contents of his cup. A different barmaid arrived at their table, setting down a jug of *piwo* with a thud and a slop. Her demeanor all business, she quickly wriggled her way back through the patrons. Dymitr topped off their tankards.

"From what I witnessed," Romek groused, "most of them took one swipe with a blade, then ran like frightened women. They completely failed at the mission! This is not the outcome I paid for."

"Then why didn't you join the fight and show them how it's done? Lead them, for Christ's sake?" Dymitr snorted. "We can complain all night long, but it solves nothing."

Control it, just like with the tavern whore.

Romek slugged his drink. "You're sure no one can identify us?" Though he acted as though he were skeptical, Romek wasn't worried. The hussars had finished off everyone involved without learning a thing. Life was short in this part of the world.

"God's teeth, yes. Like I told you before, Witek was the only one who could tie us to the attack, and I took care of him myself. Perfect shot too." Dymitr toasted himself and swigged a mouthful of piwo. "Will you try again?"

"Another attack is out of the question." Romek bristled at the thought of strategizing with this filth. Dymitr wasn't szlachta; he was beneath Romek.

Dymitr sneered. "So what's the next brilliant plan?"

Romek glared at him. "The next plan is you stay here while I return. We keep our mouths shut."

Raising his tankard in another toast, Dymitr chuckled. "Lucky for you. You'll leave this godforsaken part of the world."

Romek ignored Dymitr's remark and threw back the rest of his drink.

"Where do I find you when I need you?" Dymitr downed the contents of his tankard as well and wiped a grimy sleeve across a hard mouth.

"I'll find you."

With that, the two men stood and blended into the crowd like smoke, passing out of the door before anyone knew they were gone.

THE HEART OF A HUSSAR

Hours later, Romek waited in the shadows. A man stepped through a dimly lit doorway, and Romek followed him, melting in and out of trees as he went. The man stopped and undid his trousers, whistling softly. When Romek heard the telltale splatter in the dirt, he moved swiftly from behind, yanking up the man's chin. Before he could cry out, his throat was sliced and he fell forward, landing in his own urine.

"Told you I'd find you." Romek let out a soft chuckle. "So damned predictable." Romek glanced back at the hovel laughingly called a brothel, but no one stirred.

He kneeled beside the man and waited. Waited for the twitching to stop, waited for the final sputter. Then he grabbed the man's hair, pulling his head up. He stared into two lidded, vacant eyes; one of them glistened like a pearl.

The last detail had been dispatched. Romek congratulated himself.

CHAPTER 10

The Biaska Chorągiew Husarski

Another day of travel, and the detachment at last beheld their company moving ponderously, like a massive turtle with feet of slow-rolling wagons. They were heading through an open meadow toward a dark green palisade of woods standing like a fortress wall in the distance.

As she had throughout their journey, Oliwia sat before Jacek in his saddle. Filip rode with Lesław, and his wide eyes tracked the guards as they threaded their way toward the mass undulating over the field. The towarzysze's vivid żupans were dwarfed by the sea of gray uniforms surrounding them.

Some towarzysze wore an array of animal pelts, causing Filip to exclaim with each new discovery. He reminded Jacek of himself when his hussar master had first appeared at his father's estate, bedecked in his illustrious finery; his father had told him not to gawk.

"Liwi, look at the wolf's head!" Filip pointed. A head dangled from a bushy gray wolf hide behind its host, bouncing as he rode.

A smile teased a corner of Jacek's mouth, and he walked Jarosława toward Filip, one hand resting on his thigh. The mare fell into an easy gait beside Lesław's and Henryk's mounts.

Henryk looked over at the lad and chuckled. "Like that one, do you?"

THE HEART OF A HUSSAR

Filip nodded vigorously from his perch in front of Lesław, then whipped his head around, looking Lesław over with grave curiosity.

"He's wondering what that smelly pelt of yours is, Lesław," Henryk offered.

"It's a bear. I wrestled him myself. Enormous black beast with tremendous claws and razor-sharp teeth." Lesław bared his teeth and raised his arms in a savage pose. "Foul-smelling creature, he was. Had a wicked look in his eyes, and he was intent on having me for his supper."

Filip fairly fizzed. "What happened?"

"I showed him which of us was the more powerful and had *him* for *my* supper."

Filip was carp-mouthed. "You wrestled him?" Lesław seemed to transform into a hussar of special distinction in the child's eyes.

Lesław grinned. "I did."

"You killed him?"

"I did."

A huge smile split Filip's face. "How did you do it, Pan Lesław?"

"With one hand around his neck. I held the other behind my back, having no need of it." He waggled his bushy eyebrows and his even bushier moustache; his dark eyes shone with amusement.

Henryk chortled. "It was a baby bear, Filip. Only so high," Henryk indicated an eighteen-inch span with his gloved hands. "And its mama had left it behind, so it was mostly dead when Lesław found it."

"This pelt is too big to be from a cub," Lesław scoffed. "And the hat came from the same animal." He pointed at his kolpak, adorned with a jeweled pewter medallion nearly swallowed up in the thick brown-black fur cuff.

"Where you did find it?" Filip asked.

"Find it? Bah! It found *me* when I was hunting red deer."

"Speaking of hunting, look what just got dragged in," a voice rattled behind them, sending dread through Jacek's bloodstream.

Mateusz drew even with Jacek but didn't look at him. Rather, his gaze fell on Oliwia, and a greedy smile broke out over his leathered face. "And what have we here?"

Oliwia had been intent on the large group swallowing them up—the full husaria company, the *chorągiew husarski*—and she'd been overwhelmed. The sight of so many warriors was beyond disquieting. Not a woman among them.

Upon hearing the unfamiliar voice, she felt Jacek tense at her back. When she looked up, a man with chestnut-colored hair and blue-green eyes stared at her, smiling from within a reddish beard. His expression reminded her of a wolf baring its teeth. Broad-shouldered and fit, he sat shorter than the lieutenant but was every bit as intimidating.

He scrutinized Jacek, drawing his dark red brows together. They resembled bushy slashes above his penetrating eyes. A shiver sped up Oliwia's spine.

"Where are your manners, Dąbrowski? Introduce me to your enchanting companion."

The men quieted. Henryk's features had fixed in a frown while Lesław looked straight ahead. When Oliwia glanced back, the man's smile broadened. It did nothing to increase his appeal.

He kept his eyes riveted on her. "So, Dąbrowski, did you get her from the camp followers? A little dirty, perhaps, but she's one of the better looking ones you've had."

Jacek reined in Jarosława, bringing the horse to an abrupt stop. Henryk pulled in a sharp breath and huffed out a curse. He guided his horse across their path toward the stranger and gave him a hard look.

"Mateusz!" Lord Eryk called. "A word."

Mateusz chuckled, slithering his eyes over her before peeling away. "Another time perhaps." Her innards felt greasy.

Henryk and Lesław relaxed their postures as they watched the man ride off, but Jacek remained a wall of taut muscle behind her. She thought he grumbled under his breath.

"Who is that?" she asked.

Henryk's answer was surprisingly subdued. "Mateusz Zalewski, the captain of this company."

THE HEART OF A HUSSAR

Behind her, Jacek rumbled, "Stay away from him, my lady."
She twisted her head and stared at him; his warm breath ruffled her hair.
"Captain Zalewski. Stay away from him," he repeated.
"Oh."

Discomfited, she let her attention drift back to the soldiers riding through the forest. Shafts of light illuminated otherwise dark pockets of shade, and the color of the men's attire shifted as they moved in and out of shadow. Light caught and glinted off metal.

She squinted, imagining a mix of collaborative predators—wolves, bears, leopards, lynx—moving through the woods in place of the men who wore their hides. The exercise occupied her mind, helping her forget her aching legs and the captain's unmistakable leer.

Days after they'd joined the company, Oliwia found one among them whose company she should have feared but welcomed instead. Father Augustyn had twinkling gray eyes and a cheery smile. A round man, he was nearly as wide as he was tall. His dumpling body was topped by a ball of a bald head. As he performed his priestly duties, he waddled, ducking his head in and out of a liturgical book while he mopped his sweaty brow. Had the priest not been so earnest, she would have found him comical.

His very manner put her at ease as she watched him performing unintelligible rituals—unintelligible because they were Catholic and conducted in Latin, a language mysterious to her, for it resembled no other language she knew. Observing from afar, she absentmindedly slid her cross along its length of chain as she tried to pick out words. She'd heard them since leaving Vyatov, for Latin was also the language spoken by the noblemen around her.

In Vyatov, worship had been done in her country's tongue. Similarities in the rituals, however, allowed her to follow along in varying degrees. As she stood between two trees, listening to the masculine mumbles emanating from the men assembled for Mass, a thought niggled at her. Catholics and Orthodox had their differences, but did they hate one another as they hated Protestants?

Protestant! The word reverberated in her head, sending chills through her limbs.

Father Augustyn chose just that moment to look up, directly into her eyes, as though she'd shouted out the word. The look jolted her, making her feel as though her belly hosted a bag of snakes. He bent his head back to the open book, but her stomach would not calm. She immediately tucked the cross inside her bodice, burying it as far as it would go.

The next day, she rode in companionable quiet before Jacek. Without thinking, she tugged the cross from her bodice and skittered it along the chain.

"I've been meaning to ask." His deep timbre startled her. She glanced over her shoulder, and he pointed. "About your cross."

Panicky, she turned away and stuffed it back. It hung up along the way, and she fumbled about in her attempt to conceal it.

He humphed in apparent annoyance. "Is a bee stuck in your bodice?"

Squaring her shoulders, she twisted toward him.

"I am fine, thank you." She sought a distraction. "I do have a question."

His eyebrows shot up. "What, another one? I do believe you've wrung every single answer from me."

She stared at him as she racked her brain in search of what was, in this moment, a very elusive question.

"What does *amor patriae nostra lex* mean?" she blurted.

He leaned his head to the left and looked at her curiously. "It means 'Love of country is our law.'"

She hurried on. "So a hussar goes to war out of duty, for love of country?"

"It certainly isn't for the pay," he quipped. "We receive a wage when we serve, but it's not enough to cover the cost of joining a campaign. Just look around you—at the horses, for instance. The cost of one warhorse equals many years' pay.

"Beyond the horses, there are saddles, tack, armor, weapons, feed, and on and on. Only the kopia is provided to us. *We* pay for everything else. It doesn't take much for a hussar's equipment to outstrip a decade's wages. If not for love of country, there would be little reason to leave one's comfortable home and place oneself at death's door."

She shot him a conspiratorial smile. "Little reason other than a land grant, yes?"

THE HEART OF A HUSSAR

He smirked. "And that is a very good reason."

Oliwia let out a small sigh of relief when he made no further mention of the cross.

They encamped close to the Vistula, in the imposing shadows of Czersk Castle's three towers, a sennight's march to Biaska. Throughout the journey, the scouts had diligently sought—and found—towns, villages, and estates where they could set up camp. Though the men might have preferred the delights of Warszawa, it was a day's ride north from their current path. Czersk proved a desirable alternative, for it was a flourishing town bursting with all manner of goods and entertainments. Once a beloved destination of Zygmunt I's wife, Queen Bona, it was she who had spurred its return to a thriving center during her reign.

The Biaska chorągiew, however, was more impressed by the welcome they received from the town's animated citizens who greeted them as though they were King Zygmunt III's personal entourage, owing in no small part to their victory at Kłuszyn. When their squadron rode in, folk lined up and showered them with delicacies such as they had not enjoyed in a long while. Jacek and his brethren eagerly stowed their stale rations, scarfing up fresh cheeses, bowls of *bigos*, juicy fruit tarts, and cherry-infused piwo.

Here, as they had in other towns along the way, the men mingled, taking full advantage of drink, food, and female companionship—it would have been impolite not to. Though he had relaxed his rules, Eryk still demanded restraint, and the men mostly abided by his wishes.

As an officer, Jacek could have been billeted and enjoyed the comforts of a clean bed for the two days they stayed. Instead, he chose to remain in camp. It was here where he was startled awake from a rare nap by a boisterous Henryk bursting into his tent.

"What the devil are you doing? Aren't you ready?" Henryk stepped over to his cot and kicked Jacek's boot. "Get up, man! You're wasting time."

Jacek grunted and sat up, extending his arms overhead in a luxurious stretch. "Ready for what?"

"Women! The brewery! Women! They will not wait forever, even for you." Henryk cajoled with a little shove, and Jacek glowered at him. The glower wasn't hard to come by; he'd been enjoying his slumber immensely.

"Well, come on, then, now that you're well rested for tonight's diversions." Henryk waggled his eyebrows. "Make yourself pretty, and I will wait for you—if you're quick about it."

Jacek pulled a hand through his hair and yawned. "I'm not going."

Henryk threw up his arms. "What? Again? Why the hell not?" Then a huge grin crept up his face. "I've got the perfect girl picked out for you. She's got curly blond hair, big brown eyes, and tits out to here." He held his hands a foot from his chest. "You might smother to death, but I wager you'll die happy."

Jacek arched a skeptical eyebrow.

"What? Come on!" Henryk entreated. "So maybe I exaggerated, but she's got many admirable attributes, and she's waiting to meet you."

Jacek shook his head. "Not this time, Henryk. Find her someone else, or keep her yourself."

Henryk looked at him, dumbfounded, then suddenly brightened. "Ah! You've taken a liking to a camp follower, haven't you? Which one? The pretty redhead I saw you talking to?"

"Get going, Henryk. You don't want to be late." Jacek flapped his hand dismissively.

"You dog!" Henryk gave him a smug smile and a finger wag.

When Henryk left, Jacek lay back on his cot and stared at the planes of the canvas ceiling; his mind wandered to the redhead. She *was* pretty. But she was also a virtuous young woman, the daughter of the leatherworker, and he wasn't interested in virtuous young women. They all expected to become wives. The sort he was interested in—if one could call it that—were those he could leave without a backward glance. Forgettable. Uncomplicated. Undemanding.

His fingers tapped out a tattoo on his chest. The thought of wheedling a girl like the pretty redhead had been appealing not so long ago. But she would want him to hold her all night, maybe make love to her a few more times, then awaken dreamy-eyed beside her in the bright morning. While he wouldn't have objected to coupling more than once, he wanted none of the rest of it—not the sleeping beside her, nor the waking up beside her either.

THE HEART OF A HUSSAR

And it wasn't just maids like her. It was also lonely widows and frustrated wives. Of course there were always whores, and he had no compunction about leaving them behind as soon as he was done, but they'd never held great appeal for him to begin with, so he seldom frequented the brothels.

He laughed out loud. Without conscious effort, he'd slipped into a state of curmudgeonly semi-celibacy. Surely he was too young for such a condition. But overall, it seemed *easier,* at least for now, to forgo female companionship altogether, for it forestalled entanglements—and unwanted consequences from said entanglements. It also made confession go more smoothly.

Jacek wasn't clever with banter, nor did he care to be. His words, like his manner, were spare. Unlike the dashing Henryk, he wasn't easy with charming the fairer sex; he chafed with the effort. Flirting was as foreign to him as an unbroken night's sleep had been on this campaign.

Besides, if his itches became too great for him to scratch on his own, he usually needn't look far for aid. His stature, both physically and within the company, drew opportunity to him more than he desired it. There always seemed to be at least one woman who considered him a worthy challenge and set about overwhelming his reluctance. In turn, he sometimes succumbed and welcomed the distraction, but mostly he found would-be lovers insipid impediments to his paramount objective—his ambition, which had seduced him wholly and become the mistress he slavishly adored.

Jacek stood and wet his face and neck, giving them a good buffing. Pulling on his kolpak, he set out for the barber's tent. He hadn't gone far when he received a servant's message ordering him to report to Mateusz.

Heaving a breath in and out, he braced himself before announcing his arrival at his superior's tent. After being invited to enter, he found Mateusz seated, digging dirt from under his fingernails with his eating knife. Mateusz did not offer him a seat, so Jacek stood, his gaze straight ahead. Mateusz had to twist his neck to look up.

"So, Dąbrowski, you're the lieutenant now. Did you kill Górnicki to get the post?"

So that was it. No subtlety, no niceties.

Mateusz chuckled. "No need to look so offended. It was a jest." He pointed his knife at Jacek. "Look at me when I speak to you." Jacek complied, and Mateusz continued. "I'm not sure what you did or said to the rotmistrz to compel him to promote you. Maybe he only did it because you've been there so long—"

"Yes, sir. I arrived three years before you." Jacek couldn't help himself. He pressed his lips together, endeavoring to hold back more imprudent utterances.

Mateusz scoffed. "As I was saying, I want it known I do not agree with his selection. There are men far more qualified for the position than an incompetent, arrogant whelp like you."

"I'm sorry you feel that way, sir." Jacek kept his tone even.

"Mark my words, you *will* be sorry. I will do everything in my power to show Lord Eryk what a poor choice he made. And what in blazes are you doing with that Muscovite peasant in your saddle? Ha! I can *imagine* what you're doing with her." He let out a chortle and leaned forward, his ruddy brows pulled together.

Jacek clasped his hands behind him in stony silence, if for no other reason than to hold his fists in check.

Mateusz looked him up and down. "In case you've forgotten, *I'm* your immediate superior." He jabbed a thumb at his chest. "If you want to get in my good graces, Dąbrowski, you'd be smart to offer me your plunder. The horses you captured *and* the girl—for at least a quarter of an hour now and again." A wicked smile stretched across his face, highlighting the weathered cracks.

Jacek gritted back his words and willed his boots to stay planted to the ground, imagining them fastened by roots deep below the earth's surface. He searched his thoughts for a retort—an *acceptable* retort.

"Actually, Captain, Lord Eryk claimed her and assigned me to safeguard her. As for the horses, I lost my share to Henryk in a game of dice." Jacek silently congratulated himself.

Mateusz stood abruptly and leaned in to Jacek, fixing his blazing eyes on him. Jacek girded himself. The captain's face hovered so close Jacek could make out enlarged, black pores and spidery lines spreading like red starbursts over his nose and creviced cheeks.

"Don't cross me, Dąbrowski," he snarled, emitting a whiff of stale garlic, "or you'll find out just how dangerous I can be. And you had better not let that girl out of your sight if you hope to safeguard her. Now get out."

THE HEART OF A HUSSAR

Jacek left, striding purposefully through camp, his increasing pace matching the growing alarm bells in his head; his visit to the barber was all but abandoned. He'd told himself the reason he hadn't accompanied Henryk on his hedonistic forays was because it would have been unfitting to abandon duty for pleasure, but he admitted to himself in that moment that Oliwia was another reason he remained behind. He'd been loath to turn the girl over to another and risk subjecting her to the captain. But what if his momentary lapse, his self-indulgent nap, had left her at his mercy?

At last, he glimpsed her on the fringes of camp, hunched over her lap as she sat in a familiar folding chair. He veered toward her. She held very still, and his alarm bells clanged louder. Was she hurt? When his shadow fell over her, she jumped, then broke into a wide smile.

"Lieutenant! You startled me. I hope you don't mind. Marcin lent me one of your chairs. He said you approved."

The cacophony in Jacek's head died down as he registered she was seemingly in good health, with no lacerations or lumps, although the fingers on her right hand were smudged in black. "No, of course I don't mind. What are you doing?" His voice was harsh, and he thought she flinched—not what he'd intended.

"The field clerk gave me a spare piece of paper—he said it would be all right—and I've been making some drawings with a bit of charcoal to pass the time." Her eyes darted from his face to the paper in her lap.

"You draw?"

She let out a nervous laugh. "Well, that is a matter for debate."

"Show me." He held out his hand. She obeyed, and his eyes lit on a partially sketched wagon being drawn by oxen. Below it were letters, of which he only understood one, and the year. He pointed to the writing. "What is this?"

"It says 'provisions wagon, Poland, summer, the year of our Lord 1610.' And below that—"

He cut her off. "Below that is *été*." *French for summer.* "Did you write this?"

She seemed to grow nervous. "I practice my letters so I do not forget, and so I can teach Filip."

The girl could write? In French? Jacek schooled his astonishment. "What is this other language?"

"English, Lieutenant."

Awkwardly handing it back to her, he opened his mouth and quickly closed it again.

Men began shouting gleefully, pulling his attention to several towarzysze wrestling on the ground. Other hussars surrounded them, laughing and jeering, their fists jabbing the air. Within the circle of spectators ran Filip, round and round, his eyes dancing.

Oliwia turned toward the commotion. "Filip enjoys the company of your men. They've been very kind to him. I think it helps him to … to forget."

Jacek put aside the puzzle of her writing, fixing his eyes on the contest. "Has anyone bothered him? Or you?"

From the corner of his eye, he detected her mouth forming a perfect little O. "No, no one at all, although I would not have been surprised."

He met her gaze. "Why?"

Her hands fidgeted in her lap, smearing the charcoal. "We are of Muscovy," she replied in a tiny voice.

"Not anymore," he countered glibly. "Hetman Żółkiewski marches on Moscow." Her crestfallen expression shot a pang of guilt through him. He cleared his throat. "What I meant to say was that you are part of Biaska now. We will be there in seven days, if the weather holds."

CHAPTER 11
Biaska Castle

The weather held. After traversing an endless landscape of wide river valleys, they at last climbed rolling hillocks thickly covered in pines and brilliant green-leafed birches. Streams that fed the big rivers grew smaller and rockier, and the company weaved between massive boulders as they made their way across the terrain. Mountains and cliffs of stone rose abruptly, as if erupting from the ground.

It was late August, and they had missed the harvest festival—the *dożynki*—but home was only two days away. They pushed their mounts, eager for reunions.

Eryk guided his warhorse to the outer fringe, distancing himself as he spiraled into contemplations of Katarzyna, his wife of ten years. Would he find, by some miracle, they had finally conceived before his departure, and she awaited him with a swaddled baby son in her arms? An heir at last? He dismissed the rattling thought she might not be there to greet him at all.

When Eryk first met Katarzyna, a month before their wedding day, he was the reluctant half of an arranged marriage between two landed families. He'd been twenty-two, and though not as surly as Jacek nor as self-indulgent as Henryk, Eryk had nevertheless been a self-centered young man determined to maintain his liaisons.

With light green eyes and hair that seemed to be spun from gold, Lady Katarzyna of Reczyn had captured his attention, and thereafter his heart.

He'd never expected to fall in love with her, nor had he imagined loving anyone as wholly as he did his Kasia. He'd broken off his other relationships, never to be tempted again. Over the years, the depth of his devotion had grown and exposed a vulnerability he had never known.

As he thought of his wife now, a shiver of panic moved through him. Losing her would be far more devastating than any wound inflicted by an enemy. He crossed himself, a small prayer on his lips before rejoining the main group.

"Let's get on home!" he exclaimed. A cheer broke out and rippled through the men.

Standing among the foreriders, Jacek surveyed Biaska Castle in the distance as it rose from an expansive sea of grasses surrounded by pine forests. They were gathered on a ridge with a sweeping view of the fortress, its bucolic green fields, and the village sprawled to the north of it, its thatch-roofed cottages resembling clustered brown rushes.

Jacek exhaled a breath, and his shoulders eased as he did so. He never grew tired of the sight before him.

Situated upon the high point of a knob, the castle appeared to grow out of the rock beneath it. The entire structure was made of smooth, creamy limestone that fairly glowed. Behind toothed battlements, a distinctive multistoried round tower jutted from a massive wall of stone, and atop it sat a dark onion bulb resembling a Turkish minaret. The turret anchored a blocky keep and stood like a sentinel beside the castle's stone gateway. Across a vast yard stood three more towers, shorter and squatter, with sloping, peaked roofs. The entry to the castle yawned to an expansive drawbridge spanning a dry moat, with a second gate beyond.

"Almost there, eh, Lieutenant?" The soldier's voice held a smile.

"Soon they'll be celebrating our return, Stefan."

Suddenly, Jacek felt the fatigue that had crept over him like a weighty mantle. Though the sight of Biaska warmed him, the return was bittersweet. Górnicki's wife would soon know she was a widow.

THE HEART OF A HUSSAR

Firearms discharged and trumpets blared, signaling the men had been sighted. They now cantered, the vanguard with kopia in hand. Spear tips glinted, and the long bright banners waved and snapped boisterously to herald their arrival in showy fashion. Eryk was in the lead beside Mateusz. He could practically smell the stables and hear the horses' hooves clattering over the drawbridge.

Their numbers had dwindled as warriors had peeled off to their own manors. Those who remained descended the ridge, converging on a wide emerald plain that swept up to the castle's entrance. Around him, riders whooped, urging their mounts onward. Something forceful, a swell of energy, passed between them as they closed the distance to the castle.

Climbing the grassy hillock to the gateway, Eryk's heart raced with the excitement of returning to his wife's arms. He longed to hear her voice, to run his fingers through her silky hair, to kiss her and bask in her brilliant smile.

Human shapes congregated on the battlements, crowding one another. While enemies cowered in advance of such a spectacle, the same sight was cause for rejoicing among his people. He smiled inwardly as he watched figures jump and wave from above.

Eryk and his company rode into the immense courtyard, where they were waylaid in a joyful, chaotic jumble. He scanned the keep, and there she was. His heart leapt. Katarzyna stood at the top of the forestairs, framed by wooden doors leading to the great hall beyond. His eyes steady on her, he quickly dismounted, carelessly tossing his reins in the general direction of a servant, and ran up the steps two at a time.

"Eryk!" she squealed when he reached her, her smile broad and her arms wide. Tears spilled down her pallid cheeks.

As he lifted her off her feet, her blood-red velvet skirt swirling about her, he restrained himself for fear he might crush her. Slight since he'd known her, she seemed to have grown more diminutive during his absence.

Keeping her pressed to him, Eryk kissed her face, her lips, her soft hair. The cacophony around him fell away, and for long moments he hugged her as she murmured against his chest, as if there were only the two of them.

"I've missed you so, my love," he heard her say. "I was overjoyed when the outriders told us of your arrival."

He pulled back and smoothed her cheeks and the fine flaxen wisps escaping her headdress. "How fare you, my sweetest heart?" He looked into her teary eyes.

"I am well now you are home." Her voice grew anxious. "Are you ill? Are you hurt?" She began running her hands over him.

He laughed. "No, Kasia! Just tired, hungry, and in sore need of my fairest wife's company."

She grinned at him. "I am delighted I can help with all three."

He scanned her face as she ran a frail hand along his stubbled cheek. Her translucent, smooth skin was sparsely sprinkled with faint freckles. On either side of an upturned nose were light celadon eyes that shone with curiosity and calculation. Creases bracketed a thin-lipped pale pink mouth, making her appear far older than her twenty-seven years.

As he took her in, he tried to dispel his alarm. Eryk benefited from a robust constitution, seemingly immune from injury or illness. But in the last few years, Katarzyna had weakened and waned before his eyes. No one could tell him what ailed his lady or how to halt the advance of whatever ravaged her body, turning her peach-colored skin sallow and inflaming her joints with pain. Katarzyna had lost so much weight that her skin at times seemed to cover her bones like an ill-fitting garment.

Giving himself a mental shake, Eryk kissed her nose and lifted her above him while she laughed and begged him to put her down.

"I have gifts for you." He lowered her and surveyed the wild tangle in the courtyard below. "But first ..." He spotted a guard hoisting Filip from a saddle. Jacek, with Oliwia seated in front of him, lumbered across the drawbridge through the gates into the yard. "I'd like to introduce you to two new citizens of Biaska. At least one, I believe, will be of great service to you."

THE HEART OF A HUSSAR

As they had descended the ridge, Oliwia had been enthralled by the rolling fields with their neat rows, the swaths of pine forests, and the glowing castle in the distance. But after riding through the gates, she grew overwhelmed with all her eyes beheld—the massive oak doors with enormous trident-shaped iron hasps, the menacing points of the suspended portcullis, the towering block castle walls, and the throngs of raucous people. Now as she stood beside the lieutenant in a cavernous stone hall before a blazing hearth, she stared at an ethereal, elegant lady.

Catching herself when Jacek bowed, Oliwia darted her eyes down and gathered her gown in both hands. She curtsied deeply, praying her pins-and-needles legs would hold her up. Lady Katarzyna's tinkling voice implored them to rise. When Jacek raised himself to his full height, he towered over the lady, and she laughed—a delightful, infectious trill that spread laughter through everyone around her.

"Pan Jacek, it is wonderful to see you, but I fear I should have let you remain in a prone position so I could better look on you. If I have to maintain my head thusly for very long, I believe it will fall off."

Eryk and Jacek joined in her merriment while Oliwia stood tongue-tied, frozen in place, mesmerized by how the lady's soft green eyes sparkled and her cheeks pinked like two small, shiny apples when she laughed. Feeling grubby and disgraceful, Oliwia kept her downcast eyes glued to the stone floor at her feet.

"Sir," the lady said, "my lord has already told me a little of your journey, and I long to hear more. I understand you fought bravely. Now please make me acquainted with this lovely young woman at your side."

Intricate tapestries and limestone pillars blurred as Oliwia ascended stone stairs that seemed to go on forever. She trailed the linen-clad backs of two women who led her and Filip down a dimly lit passageway, their slippers shushing over wood planking. Torches glowed in the gloom at intervals, filling the air with an oily scent. Her head pivoting to and fro, Oliwia tried hopelessly to absorb it all.

Soon she and Filip were separated through private doorways. Oliwia was shepherded into a white-plastered bedchamber behind a sturdy, dark door that creaked on its hinges. A narrow shaft of light struck a red-and-blue carpet covering the board floor. The light streamed in from a small window set in a deep alcove beside a soot-smudged stone hearth with a cheery fire.

To her mortification, Oliwia was disencumbered of all her ragged clothing, and efficient hands scrubbed her from head to toe as she stood in a shallow tub of water. She twisted her legs together self-consciously and pulled her arms in, only to have them pried off, exposing her to the cold air. She withheld a squeal but could not restrain her squirming.

For as long as she could remember, she'd been taught to dress herself and perform her own ablutions. These she'd done capably for years without an audience of women clucking and fussing around her. She wondered if the same torture was being visited upon poor Filip.

When Lady Katarzyna appeared in the chamber, Oliwia had been outfitted with a whisper-soft white linen chemise, and her attention moved from her own discomfort to a fabric of duck-egg blue draped over the lady's arms. Lady Katarzyna laid the bundle across the bed's rose-colored coverlet as though it were a sleeping child, revealing a simple silk gown embroidered at the scooped neckline and hem in a scrollwork of bellflower thread. Oliwia bit her lip and stared wide-eyed at the lovely gown. It was the most beautiful garment she'd seen in a long while.

The lady gave her a kind smile. "Tonight's feast is for all here at the castle in honor of our lord's return. You and your brother are welcome, of course, and you may use this chamber tonight. We will sort a different arrangement tomorrow."

"Thank you, my lady." Oliwia swallowed her doubts and surrendered herself to Lady Katarzyna's maids. One was a small, silent girl named Nadia, whose dark eyes continually darted from Oliwia to her mistress.

The lady perched in a chair and extracted a small book from a sash wound about her waist. "I understand you read, Oliwia."

Oliwia turned startled eyes to her while the maids continued their attack, lacing and tying Oliwia into a semblance of order. The lady held up the cover. "What does this say?"

"I understand 'poetry' in the title, my lady, but little else. I … I am not well versed in French," she stammered. "I am better versed in English."

THE HEART OF A HUSSAR

The lady regarded her with sharp eyes. "Any other languages?"

"Reading and writing? Only the two. And poorly at that."

"I am curious to discover how it is you are familiar with two languages from countries far flung from Muscovy." Lady Katarzyna slid the book back into her sash and pressed her palms on her thighs. "But alas, we are late, and my curiosity must wait for now." The lady's demeanor was calm, curious, and Oliwia eased her shoulders a bit as the maids finished attiring her.

She was guided to a chair beside the fire, where Nadia tugged a brush through Oliwia's tangled hair. Oliwia gripped the chair's arms in a white-knuckled clutch. The sun had melted into the horizon, and the room was dark save the firelight and lit tapers. Her stomach growled but then fluttered each time the fine linen and silk caressed her skin or her thoughts danced to what awaited. Lady Katarzyna frowned and fussed over the taming of Oliwia's unruly waves, giving Nadia one set of directions and then another, at last flinging her hands toward the ceiling.

In the end, Nadia loosely piled Oliwia's damp, still-tangled locks atop her head, a few tendrils framing her face and spiraling down her neck, and secured them with a simple length of cloth. The cross remained where it always was, diving under her bodice and nestling between her breasts. When Oliwia at last stood and turned to Lady Katarzyna, the lady's eyes danced, and she clapped her hands.

"You look lovely, my dear. The gown is the perfect match for your eyes. Now we must hurry, or they will begin without us!"

Lady Katarzyna interlinked arms with Oliwia and tugged her out of the chamber beside her. The motion did nothing to assuage Oliwia's tattered nerves. Were they preparing to offer her up? Make her the main attraction—the virgin sacrifice—of unspeakable debauchery? She was among Poles, after all.

They floated down two flights of stairs to the great hall—rather, Katarzyna floated and Oliwia imitated her while her heart launched itself against her rib cage. Eyes cast down, she focused on her steps, missing the view of the great hall below until her feet alit on its stone floor. As she shuffled along, clean rushes rustled under her feet.

They neared a large platform supporting several sturdy tables of dark wood. Lord Eryk sat in the center and stood as they approached, extending his hand to his wife. She laid her own in his, and he pulled her to him, kissing her cheek.

He dipped his head. "Oliwia, welcome to Biaska."

Oliwia was ushered to a different table, where she plopped onto a wooden bench. Her head swiveled as she took in everything around her. There were no sacrificial altars, no wickedness lurking in shadow. Only people—well-dressed, merry people—talking, drinking, and laughing, many of them the men she'd come to know on the journey from Vyatov. The column of her spine relaxed ever so slightly.

Her eyes continued scanning the hall thronged with people. It was enormous! Like a row of straight trees, pillars rose from the stone floor. Lush tapestries in pale reds, greens, and golds covered soaring limestone walls. Evenly spaced along each wall were tall, deep-set windows draped with burgundy velvet curtains. In the middle of one wall, a lively fire blazed in a hearth taller than any man standing before it and wide enough to accommodate four comfortably. On the wall above the fireplace, crossed lances, brightly colored shields, and a coats of arms were displayed.

The tables were covered in white linen and all manner of gleaming platters heaped with roast venison haunches, sausages and capons, meat tarts, steaming bowls of aromatic chicken broth, plates of forest mushrooms in butter, and pewter cups filled with wine and mead. Oliwia's mouth watered as the fragrances intermingled and engulfed her.

At last, she found Filip standing before the fire, gawking at the ceiling above him. Oliwia looked up and nearly gawked herself. The stone columns fanned out in ribs spanning deep vaults of painted plaster. Exotic red swirls and gold starbursts against ultramarine graced the inner arches, looking altogether like an otherworldly night sky.

Throughout the room, candles flickered from sconces and candelabras, giving the space a cozy feel despite its cavernous size. Oliwia had heard of crumbling castles that were bleak and cold, but Biaska was none of these; it was richly decorated and well-tended. The atmosphere wrapped her up in a warm glow.

Suddenly, her apprehension, which she'd wrestled to the periphery of her consciousness, roared back. Peasants didn't belong amidst such luxury. Protestants didn't belong among Catholics. She was not meant to be here.

CHAPTER 12

Destinies Built on Sand

The rejoicing grew raucous, lasting into the morning with free-flowing mead, piwo, and wine. Consequently, when the sun rose, many a castle dweller was still abed. Jacek had exercised his usual restraint and thus did not suffer the celebration.

Besides making his head hurt, he'd found too much drink unfailingly eroded his judgment and inhibitions. Unlike many in his profession, he generally didn't become more enamored of a fight. Rather, he became more enamored of the fairer sex. On more than one occasion, he'd awoken in a bed he wished he'd never climbed into in the first place. What had seemed a splendid idea on a dark velvet night under alcohol's hazy cloud invariably proved a poor decision when the harsh cock's crow announced dawn's arrival, for he would find himself in the unseemly act of vaulting from said bed and its occupant.

Jacek smiled to himself as he made his way through the yard from the garrison, remembering how quickly Henryk had found himself among a bevy of women to entertain. They'd tittered and chirped like a flock of songbirds. Jacek hadn't lacked for female attention, not all of it welcome. Lady Barbara, a raven-haired beauty with dark, molten eyes, had sought him out with her feral smile—despite being Mateusz's wife. It had not been the first time. Had Jacek been tempted, bedding the wife of one's superior carried a weighty cost he was unwilling to pay. He'd worked too hard to risk losing it all for the fleeting pleasure.

So rather than her heady company, he had allowed himself to be enveloped by a chorus of feminine giggling, which in the end helped him put aside his own shortcomings as he lost himself dancing with the ladies.

This morning, he woke in his own bed, alone, and now quickly strode to the great hall to fill his rumbling stomach. As he entered, he looked toward the empty dais, but no drunken bodies sprawled across a table or the floor. The room was spotless, as though no celebration had concluded mere hours before.

An image of Oliwia's fixed expression flashed through his mind. She had watched the merrymaking with the eyes of a child on the verge of opening a beribboned gift. Lady Katarzyna and her maids had performed miracles on the girl. Had he not known better, he would have thought her older. Some of the lads *had* thought her older—or didn't care—and he'd dissuaded them from their amorous intentions. His actions had come naturally. He reckoned he'd safeguarded her throughout the journey and would just keep at it until she left, protecting her from any young men bent on doing what young men do.

"Good morning, Jacek. I trust you slept well." Eryk surprised him from his ponderings with a strident greeting.

Jacek's metal boot heels clicked on the stone floor as he headed toward him.

"Good morning, my lord. Thank you, I did." Jacek inclined his head.

"Join Lady Katarzyna and me in the solar." Eryk then called to a serving maid for food and wine for five.

"Of course, my lord." Puzzled, Jacek began following in his lord's wake.

The solar adjoined the great hall by a short flight of steps. Lady Katarzyna stood by a blazing hearth, and though it was a warm morning, the lady seemed to hug the heat radiating from the flames.

"Jacek. Thank you for coming," she greeted him quietly.

He bowed. "My lady, I hope you rested well."

Wordlessly, she sank into a carved armchair beside the fire, seeming to disappear into it. Eryk sat behind his desk and signaled Jacek to take the chair across from him. The lord's somber eyes appeared sunken, dark half circles smudged beneath them. Jacek smiled to himself. Had his chieftain celebrated overmuch?

THE HEART OF A HUSSAR

Two serving maids entered and laid out pewter plates with a wheel of cheese, meat tarts, a loaf of warm bread, and a large bowl brimming with plums and raspberries. They arranged five goblets and poured wine from a pewter flagon. After the maids quit the chamber, Eryk and Jacek heaped their plates, the lady declining refreshment.

"Mateusz has received a reply to the last of the inquiries we sent from the road. There is nothing illuminating about the ambush."

Jacek did not mask his disappointment. "What of the horses or the lettering we found?"

Eryk shrugged. "A crudely scratched *JM* on a hilt means naught, and the few marked saddles led back to stables from which the horses had been stolen."

Jacek's frustration simmered. "So what can be done?"

"For now, nothing. We continue probing, and we remain vigilant. But these are not the reasons I called you in here."

Jacek had just picked up a meat pie, which he quickly lowered to his plate.

"I've been thinking about our mysterious young Muscovites." Eryk bit into cheese layered on a hunk of bread.

How does this involve me?

Jacek popped a few grapes into his mouth and waited as Eryk filled his cup. "Lady Katarzyna and I spent a great deal of time last night discussing their future. I have come to a decision."

A smart rap sounded at the door. Oliwia opened it a crack and peered at dark blue cloth. Her eyes traveled upward and landed on the lieutenant's serious face, and she immediately opened the door. Her breath caught. He was so big, and so … well, so close. His form filled the doorway, and she fumbled before inviting him to enter all the way. For weeks, she had ridden with her back to him, and this perspective—him ducking his head and wide shoulders through the doorway—was an altogether foreign one.

Last night, standing tall in the high-ceilinged hall, he'd been surrounded by admirers making no effort to conceal the fact they found his stature, and most everything else about him, appealing—despite the facial fixture that was his scowl. She had been out of place and a little envious of their closeness to him. But now that *she* was close to him, his nearness caused her to step back.

This morning, he was dressed in a deep blue żupan of light, loosely woven wool, lined in canary-yellow silk. The hem fell below the knee, skimming saffron boots. In his leather belt loops, a dagger and his hussar's sabre were sheathed in their scabbards. Simple yet elegant in design, rows of silver strands wound around the weapons' gray-white sharkskin-encased hilts. Wood scabbards covered with black leather were wrapped in two double bands of silver. The sabre's scabbard featured a silver-and-gold-embossed diamond-shaped medallion and ended in a plain silver tip. Any other embellishment on his clothing would have been superfluous.

Jacek smiled at her without the scowl, and she recognized warmth in his intense sapphire-blue eyes. She fidgeted. After several heartbeats, he cleared his throat.

"Lord Eryk and Lady Katarzyna request you and Filip present yourselves. They wish to speak with you both and have tasked me with bringing you to them."

Her stomach turned a few flips, and her hand fluttered to her silver chain, but she squelched the urge to pull the cross out. "Do you know why?"

"I do, yes."

"Will we be returned to Vyatov?" she blurted. The question sounded absurd as soon as it tumbled from her lips. The lord wouldn't return to a demolished village in enemy territory—*their* enemies, not hers.

Jacek must have agreed, for a bemused frown creased his brow, as if he were an impatient elder dealing with a child. "It's best you hear it from the lord himself." His voice, though calm, held steel.

Confused emotions collided as she pondered whatever pronouncement she and Filip would face about their future. She was anxious to hear they were staying—the castle and the lady were beautiful beyond imagination, embodying a world Oliwia longed to be part of. But she was also anxious to hear they were not— this new world was elegant, and they didn't belong.

"Ahem." The lieutenant arched an eyebrow, and she realized she was staring at him. He said nothing to calm her unease. In fact, he said nothing at all. She blinked a few times.

THE HEART OF A HUSSAR

"Um, yes, of course. I will get Filip."

Squaring her shoulders, she smoothed her skirts. With a deep breath, she prepared herself to meet the lord and lady who held their fates.

Jacek raised his hand, palm up, toward the open door. "After you, my lady. Have you eaten yet?"

The flips had twisted into a knot in her belly, and she didn't think herself capable of ingesting anything. She shook her head.

"Well, if you are so inclined, a small feast has been laid out in the solar. I've no doubt your brother will be delighted to avail himself." Jacek nodded at said brother, who stood in the passageway, looking splendid in a smaller version of Jacek's attire.

Filip ran to Jacek's side, not seeming to notice Oliwia's outstretched hand. Instead, he craned his neck to look up at the lieutenant. As Jacek marched toward the solar, Filip mimicked his steps, looking like an awkward, stalking stork. Oliwia laughed to herself, and the knot loosened itself ever so slightly.

Jacek stopped at a hefty oak door that stood ajar, knocked, and pushed it open. Oliwia ground to a halt at the sight of the majestic lord behind an enormous, ornate table of rich, lustrous walnut, a neat stack of papers and books at one corner and a quill and inkpot at another. He was bedecked in a gold żupan and vivid red *ferezeya* accented in fur. A rolled sash of golden silk and a gem-encrusted belt encircled his waist.

The equally regal lady stood beside him in a gown of green-and-gold taffeta with poofed sleeves that swallowed her arms; white lace brushed her thin wrists. Oliwia was painfully aware of the grand surroundings and how poorly she fit them. She flinched when Jacek closed the door behind him and placed his fingertips in the small of her back, nudging her forward.

"Sit," Eryk instructed, not unkindly.

Katarzyna sank into a seat to her husband's right. "Yes, do sit and be comfortable."

Jacek placed his imposing self on Eryk's left, facing her and Filip.

Eryk leaned back in his chair. "Are you both rested? Have you had enough to eat?"

From the corner of her eye, Oliwia spied Filip nodding vigorously. "Yes, thank you, my lord, my lady," she replied for them both. "We want for nothing and are immensely grateful for your kindness and hospitality." She sat stiff-backed at the very edge of her seat, pins and needles tingling her scalp, her fingers, her toes.

Eryk rocked forward, resting his elbows squarely in front of him as he steepled his hands.

"You've only just arrived, but tell me if you would, do you like it here?"

Oliwia opened her mouth and looked from Eryk to Katarzyna and back again. Filip showed no such restraint. His six-year-old body seemed barely able to contain his exuberance. He nodded animatedly, his brown curls bobbing in time.

"Yes, my lord," Oliwia said. "Very much."

Eryk placed his still-steepled index fingers against his lips for an instant, then reached for his cup. "My lady and I are well pleased to hear it. I have come to a decision concerning you both. Lady Katarzyna joins me in this."

He took a deep swallow and set the cup down. "There being nowhere else for you to go, you shall remain here. Biaska is now your home."

Filip bounced in his seat; Jacek darted him a stern look.

Eryk's lips curved in a smile. "I can see this pleases Filip, but what of you, Oliwia?"

After the jolt of "Biaska will be your new home," she'd gone utterly numb.

"You are very kind, my lord, my lady," she managed.

Eryk thumped his hands on the desk. "It is settled, then! You are likely wondering about your stations here."

And so much more! Are we Poles now? Must we become Catholics? What does our future look like?

"Oliwia, you will be my lady's maid. You will serve her in any way she requires, and in turn, you will take direction on how a lady conducts herself."

"Yes, sire." Oliwia glanced at Katarzyna, who gave Oliwia a measured dip of her head.

"Now, Filip. We've a plan for you as well. You are to become a page, possibly a soldier in my company, and you will immediately move into the barracks with the men."

Oliwia gasped, and all eyes were on her—including her brother's.

"But, my lord, if I may, he is so young. Should he not remain with me for now?"

THE HEART OF A HUSSAR

Filip narrowed his blue-gray eyes at her. "But I *want* to live with the men, Liwi. How else will I learn to be a great soldier?"

Oliwia squirmed in her seat and interlaced her fingers so hard she might have twisted them off. Her knuckles whitened. This was not what she'd expected, but she felt helpless to stop it. Any of it. Her heart beat like a hummingbird's wings, and her eyes flitted between Eryk and Katarzyna.

"Do not fear, my dear," Eryk soothed. "Filip is the right age to live among the men and learn their code of conduct. He will serve Pan Jacek personally, and there could be no better mentor."

Filip whooped and raised his fists in the air. Jacek's eyes flicked to her bouncing brother, his dark brows knotting together. His high cheekbones seemed to blaze red. Oliwia swallowed a protest.

Jacek turned his head to Eryk. After acknowledging the compliment, he glanced back at Oliwia with arched eyebrows, as if to say, "You see? I said you would become a Pole." Her breathing came quick and shallow, and she opened her mouth to speak, but only a small, strangled "but" escaped her lips.

"I will see him safe. I will bring him to you whenever you or he wish it. He will be close, and he will be well cared for," Jacek assured her.

Oliwia slumped in her chair.

Just inside Muscovy's western border, Romek Mazur pulled up on his reins and walked cautiously toward camp, the late-summer night air heavy and humid. His horse limped, and he grumbled. He couldn't afford to lose yet another. They'd been unable to take any during the last raid. The beasts had been too emaciated anyway, like his mount.

As he threaded his way between thick, oppressive trees in the gloomy forest, his chest felt as though iron pressed on it. His breathing grew labored. Raucous voices sounded as he drew near.

For God's sake, what do they celebrate? We got nothing of value from those flea-infested peasants!

The inkiness around him lightened, and sweat that had been forming along his hairline evaporated. He looked up. The reflection of a roaring fire lit up the trees surrounding the clearing like massive torches, bouncing off the high canopies.

Fools!

When Romek emerged into the clearing, he erupted in curses. Soldiers—*his* soldiers—danced around a bonfire, hooting and laughing as they passed jugs and guzzled. Others were having a go with one of the women they'd taken, while those with their own women fornicated like beasts for all to see. Elsewhere, men wrestled with one another, throwing errant punches that hit dirt more than each other.

"Jesus Christ!" Romek stormed. A few heads turned his way, and men nudged one another. Untying a bundle from his saddle, he muttered to himself in disgust.

The tussling diminished, and the men began dispersing. A soldier by the fire took a pull from an earthen bottle. "What crawled up your ass, Lieutenant?" He shook the bottle at Romek. "Maybe you need some of this." A man's groan sounded nearby, and the soldier chortled and pointed at two figures in the shadows. "Or maybe some of that?"

Romek spat, keeping his repugnance to himself. He was likely the only man in camp who had no interest in the perversions the others fancied. But battering a woman's face purple and pulpy? There was an exciting thought to spark him.

"Where in hell's blazes is Fabian?" he shouted.

A dark, curly haired man broke away from a retreating group and loped over. He stared at Romek through wide black eyes set in a gaunt young face. "Sir?"

Romek stuffed his reins in the boy's hands. "Take care of my horse and get the hell out of my way."

He stalked off, raging as he went. He made his way to the back of the camp and ducked into a tent set apart from the others. It was dark inside, and he pulled in a breath as his eyes adjusted to the gloom. A wet cough drew him farther inside.

"Bella? Bella, love. I've brought you a potion," he called in a singsong voice.

Between coughs, a woman wheezed. "Over here, Brother."

She lay in the dark on her side, and he knelt beside her, running his hand over her hot forehead. Fear raced along his spine. "Why are you lying in the dark, Bella?"

THE HEART OF A HUSSAR

In gasps, she said, "The men grew loud. I was afraid, so I didn't light the lantern."

"Don't let them frighten you. They're only having a bit of sport." He spoke softly as he stroked her damp hair.

More wheezing. "Was it a good raid, then?"

"Not this time, I'm afraid. The only prizes are bottles of bad wodka and the few whores from that accursed village, and neither is worth more than a few hours' amusement. So the men will have their fun tonight, and they'll ride on tomorrow. You and I, Bella, we return to Poland. I have just come from Lisowski and told him I am through."

"I—I don't know if I'll be strong enough, Romek." She hacked a long series of wet coughs. "It's bad this time."

"It will pass. Let's get this medicine inside you. By morning, the coughing will be gone. You'll see."

He pulled her withered frame gently against his shoulder after she'd consumed the elixir. "Lean against me, Bella. Rest a while."

As he often did, he began to speak to her of a brighter day, a day when she was well and they both luxuriated in an estate of their own again.

"You will have so many servants waiting on you, you will need a list to remember all their names."

A small laugh led to another series of coughs. He paused, then went on soothingly. "And while you are ordering them all about, I will hunt on my fine stallion—one of many from our rich stables. It will be better than it was before the Krezowskis stole our lands from our grandsire. Do you remember Papa's stories?"

"Yes, he made it all sound so grand when we were children—especially when he was in his cups. I'm surprised you remember them so well. You were a boy when Papa died."

"I've never forgotten. I promised Papa I would set it right, and now I have another chance. The time has come to make the Krezowskis pay for what they did."

She sighed. "Romek, it happened long ago."

"It doesn't make it just, Bella. That family of thieves is responsible for taking what was rightfully ours and putting Papa in his grave."

"Papa drank himself to death. No one forced him," she said softly.

The conversation had wandered in its usual uncomfortable direction, so Romek arranged her makeshift pillow and laid her down.

"Sleep now, Bella. No more talk tonight."

CHAPTER 13

Heretic

Oliwia woke at daybreak, quietly stowed her pallet, and dressed. After a meal in the great hall, she slipped back into Lady Katarzyna's bedchamber. Though she'd performed the routine for the last fortnight—if so few mornings could distinguish it as a routine—the act still unnerved her. Her, here, amid lavish tapestries and oil paintings overflowing with maidens in countryside scenes.

Glancing toward a sumptuous white marble fireplace, the smell and pop of a lively fire reassured her it had been stoked. Her eyes skirted an oak mantel, ornately carved in patterns of leaves and thistles, and lingered on a gilded clock placed between two delicate porcelain ladies. A small voice startled her when it lilted from one of two armchairs set before the hearth.

"Oliwia?" said the lady.

Oliwia dropped into a deep curtsy. "My lady."

The lady held a book in one hand, and with the other, she patted the chair beside her. "Sit," she urged.

Clutching her skirts, Oliwia approached cautiously, awed by being invited to sit upon the plush cushion of red velvet. The carved chairs sat on either side of a table holding cups, a jug, and a bowl of fresh flowers.

You don't belong here.

Gingerly, she scooted into the seat, perching herself at the very edge. She sprang up quickly as though she'd sat on a bag of thistles, for in her awe, she'd forgotten herself.

"Have you eaten yet, my lady?"

"No, I have not. I have no appetite yet. Until I do, you may answer a question I posed when you first arrived." She leaned her head against the chair's cushioned back, appearing drawn. "'Tis rare for a noblewoman to read in her own language, and rarer still for a girl who's not of noble breeding. And yet you read two, and neither of them of this part of the world."

Oliwia cleared her throat.

Katarzyna gave her a sidelong glance. "Sit, Oliwia, and tell me what you appear so hesitant to divulge. Best spit it out."

If Oliwia could have squeezed her eyes shut and willed this moment away, she would have. Instead, she braced herself. "I ... well, ... that is, I *am* of noble blood, my lady. Both Filip and I." She drew in a breath and held it.

"What did you say?" Katarzyna stared at her with round celadon eyes.

Oliwia swallowed hard, but it did little to moisten her dry throat. She twisted her hands in her lap.

"You'd best pour us both some wine, Oliwia."

Oliwia stood, grateful for a moment to compose herself, and measured tawny liquid into twin goblets. Once the lady had taken a sip, Oliwia quaffed a quick mouthful and sat.

"Well, then?" prodded Katarzyna.

Oliwia swallowed a bit more. "The people we lived with at Vyatov were not our parents. Our real mother brought us there five years ago before she died. Only Filip and I remain."

Amid the soft crackles of the blaze came the soft silk-and-velvet rustle of Katarzyna's gown. Her eyebrows furrowed. "What happened?"

Oliwia let her gaze wander to the flames, though she didn't see them.

"The day she left, my mother gave me a letter and told me to read it after she had gone. Though 'twas only one page, her script was small and she filled every space on that paper. I kept it all those years, wearing the edges ragged from handling it. It was lost in the fire the day Lord Eryk and Pan Jacek came." Her breath hitched, and she paused before rallying on.

"But I can recite it backward and forward. If you wish to hear it, I will tell you what was passed on to me."

With a nod, Katarzyna took her hand and squeezed it.

Oliwia filled her lungs with air and blew it back out. "My mother was Lady Margaret Sewell, the only child of Lord Alistair Sewell. His wife died days after giving birth. He never remarried, and as he had no other children, my mother became everything he held dear."

Sewell Castle was close to Carlisle and the border between England and Scotland. Living close to the border invariably brought English and Scots together. One day the Lady Margaret, then seventeen, was escorted to the nearby village, where she spied a tall, handsome knight. The young man was accompanying his sister, and by chance they met. He stole her breath and her heart. Margaret learned this dashing knight was Alexander of the Armstrong Clan, the third son of a noble Scottish family.

Alexander was as taken with Margaret, but the bad blood between English and Scots did not favor a future together. Neither family sanctioned a union, but Margaret was determined. She would not give up her braw warrior. The two sweethearts eloped. Upon their return, both were cast out by their families.

The newlyweds found themselves struggling to forge their own path together. Alex ardently strove to provide for his young wife by doing what he did best—soldiering. Consequently, he was often away fighting on behalf of any Christian country willing to hire him. The young couple soon learned love alone did not feed or clothe them, nor did it keep a marriage whole.

"I was born while my father was away, and my mother named me Oliwia—for the olive branch. She prayed for peace so he would come home. My grandfather took us in, but my mother missed my father terribly, so she set out to recover him, leaving me behind. When she did at last find him, they returned to Sewell. But he did not stay long, for he argued bitterly with my grandfather, and neither man could abide the other."

Nadia swept in, and Oliwia swiped self-consciously at her cheek. Katarzyna ordered the little maid to refill their cups and leave.

"Go on," the lady urged softly. Oliwia drew in another halting breath.

The pattern—Alex leaving, returning, and leaving again—repeated itself throughout the years until at last he found a permanent post fighting in

Poland's army and sent for them. Margaret gathered Oliwia, bid Lord Sewell good-bye, and left England behind. Filip was born within the year.

Margaret and the children lived among the camp followers until tragedy struck. Close to the Muscovite border, Alex was felled by an enemy pike. Before he died, he entreated Margaret to have him buried in Scotland, but they had not saved enough coin. The only item of value was a Sewell family heirloom, a silver cross—not enough to barter with, and too precious to sell. So when a merchant named Jans offered to provide a home for Oliwia and Filip, Margaret had little choice.

The letter ended with Margaret passing the cross to Oliwia, explaining it had been handed down from her mother and her mother before her. She also promised to return one day.

Oliwia's eyes were riveted on the fire, and she fought vainly to check her tears. As they coursed down her cheeks, she brushed at them between snuffles.

"I watched for her every day, but she never came."

Oliwia did not get on well with Jans or his wife, Magda. Accusing her of laziness and willfulness, they whipped her, and Magda resented Filip's preference for Oliwia's affection over hers. She began whipping him too. Only twelve, Oliwia pitched herself at Magda one day, which sent the woman into a tirade. Enraged, Magda told Oliwia the rest of the story—what Margaret had been unable to write herself.

Margaret had been gravely ill, and she struck a bargain with Jans. In exchange for the children, he paid for both Alex's and Margaret's bodies to be returned to Scotland and buried beside one another. Margaret soon succumbed, and Jans upheld his end of the bargain.

"Magda unfailingly reminded me Jans was true to his promise, and we belonged to them, you see. Bought and paid for."

Oliwia felt the old stab of Magda's other words like slivers of glass lancing her heart. The woman had called her and Filip heretics. Oliwia lived under the constant threat they would be delivered to those who would torture and burn them. Madga had also told her they were lucky to get the paltry sum the creaky old merchant had offered to pay for her, for she was worth no more. Magda never revealed what the paltry sum was.

By far the worst pronouncement, however, was that Margaret—whom Magda also accused of heresy—hadn't loved them. "What loving mother would sell her children?" she'd repeated. And yet Oliwia could still see her mother leaning down to her, her wavy hair dark and loose. Oliwia stubbornly clung to the belief that Magda had it wrong. Her memories still nurtured the sound of her mother's lyrical laugh and the smell of summer blossoms that had enveloped her whenever her mother had held her against the soft, warm folds of her clothes.

Those same memories also hauntingly echoed her mother's last tearful words.

You must stay strong for Filip, Oliwia. Stay strong. There's a good girl.

Oliwia sat for long minutes until Katarzyna's voice stirred her.

"May I see the cross, Oliwia?"

Oliwia's veins turned icy as she dipped a shaky hand into her bodice and freed the necklace. Katarzyna peered at it, turning it this way and that, then drilled her with her light green eyes.

"Your mother, Oliwia, she was Protestant?"

Oliwia nodded slowly, dread spreading through her like pine tar, sticky and thick.

"And your father?"

"Catholic, my lady."

"But you spent a great deal of time with your mother, yes? And your grandfather?"

Oliwia swallowed hard. "Yes."

Katarzyna dropped the cross into Oliwia's palm, and Oliwia quickly tucked it back in its hiding place.

"Oliwia," she said coolly, "I would like you to find the head cook, Beata, and give her my list for the next days' meals. I am not well enough to deliver it myself."

"Of course, my lady."

As Oliwia departed the chamber, Katarzyna's eyes were fixed on something outside the window, her finger absently tapping her chin. Oliwia wanted to run through the passageways, but she slowed her steps and walked with a smooth, deliberate gait, soaking up everything around her— the smoky torches, the scarred wooden doors, the squeak of the wood boards under her feet. The lady knew Oliwia's secret now. She and Filip would soon be sent away, never to see these wonderful walls again.

The errand finished, she returned to Lady Katarzyna's bedchamber, but the lady was not there. Instead, Oliwia found Nadia pulling apart her pallet. The few items she'd been given were neatly arranged: a comb of bone, a dark blue ribbon, two snowy chemises, and stockings. Her heart plummeted, ready to tear itself apart.

"Nadia, what are you doing?"

The little maid wheeled, a startled look in her eyes.

"Begging your pardon, m'lady. Lady Katarzyna instructed me to remove your things."

Oliwia grabbed the possessions and clasped them tightly to herself as she looked on.

"Why?" Her hope was shattered, gone.

"Has Lady Katarzyna not told you? You are no longer to remain …" Oliwia did not hear the rest. Gradually, shreds of sentences pierced her thick veil of misery, "… a small trunk with two of m'lady's old gowns—she hopes they will be satisfactory until you get your own—and it is ready for your things …"

Oliwia shook her head. "Pardon?"

Patiently, Nadia started anew. "You will serve m'lady as her handmaid. As a noblewoman, you are to have your own chamber close to m'lady's. I have cleared a small trunk—"

Oliwia grabbed the maid's wrist, and Nadia's small brown eyes fairly bulged.

"Do you mean I am to stay?" Oliwia fought to restrain her exuberance, which threatened to overflow.

Nadia straightened, flummoxed. "Of course. I am sorry, truly I am, for thinking we were of an equal station. I hope I did nothing to offend you, Lady Oliwia."

Lady Oliwia!

Oliwia stared at her, unsure what to say. Nadia must have wondered at her ludicrous expression, for her brows scrunched together.

Within minutes, Oliwia had moved into her snug, private sanctuary. Alone, she twirled about, arms flung wide, before sailing onto the bed. She giggled and hugged herself as she scanned the room. It was beautiful. Wood beams spanned the ceiling, each one painted a unique, cheery pattern. Evenly spaced corbels adorned plastered walls while an eastern-facing mullioned window scattered prismed light across an ornate Turkish rug. She sat up, pulled off her slippers and stockings, and curled her toes into the carpet.

THE HEART OF A HUSSAR

Now her gaze landed on the four-posted bed and the fringed tester above. From the top of the tester hung sumptuous gold curtains banded in blue-embroidered silk and tied to the posts with matching tassels of gold.

She skimmed her fingers over an ivory counterpane embellished with indigo flowers and gold scrollwork, relishing the feel of it against her skin. Matching bolsters lined the wooden headboard, and she buried her face in them with a squeak. Then came a knock.

Jumping up, she straightened her gown and hair before opening the door. Nadia peeked at her.

"M'lady?" The little maid shoved herself through the opening.

"Yes?"

"Lady Katarzyna has arranged for Father Augustyn to join you and m'lady at the midday meal, and she said not to be late."

"Father Augustyn?"

"Yes, m'lady. And she wishes you to bring this." Nadia opened her hand, sliding a length of smooth beads into Oliwia's open palm.

After Nadia left, Oliwia ran her fingers over the rosary and looked around the chamber once more. Awkward though this new world was, she would fumble her way through somehow. And Filip would be safe. Oliwia was on her way to becoming what Jacek had told her she'd become all along—a Pole. A *Catholic* Pole.

"Oliwia, Father Augustyn is quite pleased with your progress. Filip's as well," Katarzyna said one day as Oliwia pulled a silver-handled brush through the lady's fine hair.

"Thank you, my lady. I enjoy the stories and the lessons in catechism, but the Latin ..."

"Yes, well, your smattering of French should help with that. Master Latin, and you shall have mastered the mysteries of Polish noblemen as well. And heaven knows we need all the help we can get to understand *them*!"

Oliwia laughed in concert with her lady.

"I'm pleased you've kept our little secret, my dear. We Poles are very tolerant when it comes to matters of religion, but still, to be wholly accepted as szlachta—at least in this part of Poland—will go easier if you are Catholic."

Oliwia ducked her head in agreement.

"And speaking of szlachta, we will have a gathering of many noble families in just over a month. Lord Eryk has announced a tournament to celebrate the Feast of Our Lady of the Rosary."

"What is that, my lady?"

"Why, it's the celebration of the day the Ottomans were defeated at the Battle of Lepanto in … 1572, I think it was. Or was it 1571? Nevertheless, we will celebrate here on October seventh. It will be nothing so grand as to draw hundreds of towarszyse, but it will lure several score of noblemen from nearby estates for a bit of sport followed by feasting and dancing. Truly, it's just an excuse for men to get together, drink to excess, and outdo one another. Oliwia, would you brush more on that side? Where was I?"

"Men outdoing each other, my lady?" Oliwia offered as she dragged the bristles through Katarzyna's hair. In spite of the bubbles popping in her stomach, Oliwia held back the smile threatening to spread across her face. The event would fall on the day she turned sixteen.

"Ah yes. Puffed-up peacocks bashing each other." Katarzyna picked up a silver comb from the dressing table and began turning it over in her hands. "In spite of all the men's boasting and *ridiculous* behavior," she laughed, "tournaments are enjoyable occasions for the ladies as well. It is like a festival with one grand feast at the end—a splendid occasion to show off a fine new gown and one's jewelry."

Katarzyna looked at Oliwia in the mirror. "Which reminds me, my dear. I have asked the dressmaker to bring up some bolts of fabric. She has a lovely pink silk I am anxious to see. It sounds as if it will suit you nicely."

Oliwia stopped brushing and glanced back at her mistress's reflection.

"Why have you stopped?"

"I did not expect to be attending, my lady, nor did I expect a gown of my own."

"But of course you're attending! You must learn how to conduct yourself at such affairs, and for that you need a proper gown, not my castoffs. How are your dance steps coming? You will show me, and I will see for myself. We must be sure you know them all by then."

THE HEART OF A HUSSAR

Lady Katarzyna set the comb down, then crossed her arms and leaned back.

"Thank you, my lady." Oliwia hovered the brush over the lady's head, unsure what to do next.

"Keep brushing, Oliwia. Now let me see. We have much to do in preparation—making more piwo, ordering barrels of wine from Kraków if we haven't enough," she looked up at the ceiling as she counted off on her fingers, "getting more girls from the village to cook and clean, readying the guest quarters ... Oh! And the men will want to hunt, of course, so the stable master and hunt master must be consulted ..." She trailed off. "You will help me with all of it. Then someday, when you are a lord's wife, you will know how to conduct such events."

A lord's wife?

Biaska Castle and its inhabitants buzzed like a hive of purposeful bees. Filip leapt down the bottom few forestairs and burst into a run across the courtyard, colliding with a basketmaker balancing a full load in his arms. Baskets scattered throughout the yard in a calamitous display. The man threw up his arms and cursed loudly. Filip spun in the dirt, sending up a cloud of dust. Then he bolted—and came to an abrupt stop when Jacek caught him by his shoulder.

Filip looked up. Jacek kept his hand clamped in place and arched an eyebrow.

Filip bobbed his head. "Uh, good morning, my lord."

Jacek said nothing. Instead, he turned the boy and pushed him toward the basketmaker, who muttered as he stamped about, gathering his goods.

"Good morning, Konrad." The man looked up at Jacek and stood as tall as his stout frame allowed, bringing his height even with Jacek's shoulders. When he pulled off his kolpak and bowed, his wavy black hair stuck to his head with sweat.

"My lord lieutenant, how may I be of service?" He looked from Jacek to Filip and back again.

Jacek glanced down at Filip. "It is not how you may be of service to me, but how my apprentice can serve you. Filip?"

Just then, Jacek's eye caught on a familiar form as she scampered down the forestairs.

Oh, Christ. Here comes mother hen, ready to peck my eyes out.

Filip shifted his weight from foot to foot, Jacek's hand still holding him in a viselike grip. He didn't ease up when Oliwia appeared beside Konrad. To the contrary, he tightened his grip when Filip remained silent.

"Ah, um, uh, I ..." Filip stammered. Oliwia, mercifully, held her tongue.

"What the lad seems unable to say, Konrad, is he will gather your wares and take them where you tell him."

Filip's mouth dropped open, and he stared up at Jacek.

"And for his insolence, he will give you a day's labor. Perhaps some hard work will loosen his tongue and allow him to apologize properly and remind him of his manners in the future." Jacek gave Filip a shove toward the spilled baskets. Though Oliwia flinched, her expression betrayed nothing.

"But, sir," Filip protested, darting his eyes to his sister, "Master Feliks expects me in the stables to work for *him*."

"You should have considered that *before* you ran over Konrad. I will tell Feliks you are occupied and will be late to your chores, but that you will appear ready to perform them all when you are done working for the basketmaker." Jacek nodded at the surprised Konrad. He glanced at Oliwia, expecting her to at least fix him with a fierce face, but she merely crossed her arms and scowled at her brother. Konrad had been clutching his kolpak and now crushed it on his head with a wide smile. Filip followed him, glowering.

"I thought you might want to take my head off," Jacek remarked when he and Oliwia stood alone.

"He must learn." Her tone was surprisingly airy.

He regarded her with mock astonishment. "The she-bear not defending her cub? Surely the world is on its head, and the sun may not rise tomorrow."

She gave him a wry smile and shook her head. "Not this time, Lieutenant. He was wrong. Now if you'll excuse me, I am on an errand for Lady Katarzyna." She pivoted from him.

THE HEART OF A HUSSAR

Her coolness threw him. The imp was actually walking away from him! He caught her up. "May I escort you somewhere?" He fell in beside her, giving her no choice.

"I ... Well, perhaps you can help me." Her calm expression seemed to slip into something akin to panic. "I am to see the stable master on behalf of Lady Katarzyna and ask if we've enough caparisons for the hunt, but I ..."

"I'm headed there myself."

When she didn't respond, he said, "You've never spoken to Feliks before, yes?"

"I have never spoken to Pan Feliks, nor have I addressed a stable master. I am not sure what to say."

"First of all, he is not Pan Feliks to you. You are Pani Oliwia to him, but not the other way round."

"What, then, do I call him?" she croaked.

"Call him Feliks. If you prefer, call him 'stable master.' Second of all, you *do* know what to say. 'Feliks, I require a count of caparisons for the upcoming hunt.' And he will answer, 'Of course, my lady.' If he says anything short of that, he will be reprimanded."

Jacek walked beside her, his hands behind his back. She clutched her skirts, dodging troughs of soupy mud as they went. Behind them, two dogs took turns barking at a cat. She stopped and looked up at him with a plea in her eyes. "Would *you* ask him? I'm not sure he'll take direction from me."

"Of course he will. You're gentry, and he knows his station. He *will* take orders from you."

"But I ..."

He turned her toward the stables. "Come now. I've seen that set to your chin. All you need do is stick it out as you're wont to do, and he will have no choice but to heed you. If you're to become a great lady someday, you must learn to order people about."

She smirked. "Would *you* heed me if I ordered you about?"

"Absolutely not. Not even my mother can order me about, so do not think to try, missy."

CHAPTER 14
Szlachta

Oliwia sat beside Lady Katarzyna in her sitting room, fumbling with a bit of embroidery. The work was tedious, the design more intricate than anything Oliwia had stitched before. Her sewing until now had been of a practical nature—mending a chemise, darning a hole in a stocking, repairing a torn sack. She hadn't needed to negotiate tiny bluebells with delicate leaves, and for what? A bit of frippery. And what was it she worked on? Part of a lady's cap? An apron? A bit of adornment for a table? Convinced she would never master this lady's pastime, she stabbed at the fabric square with a muted roar at the back of her throat, poking herself soundly on a finger pad.

"Ow!" She dropped everything and sucked on the finger before darting her eyes to the lady beside her. Lady Katarzyna seemed to be sleeping; Oliwia let out a relieved breath. After taming her wound, Oliwia reached over to slip a book from her mistress, but the lady clutched it as if her hand were a claw. She startled awake.

"Oliwia?"

"I'm sorry, my lady."

Katarzyna straightened and had Oliwia pour her a glass of wine. She sank back in her chair and, after a deep gulp, let out a long sigh.

"I want to stay awake for a time, so I will tell you a story, Oliwia. Biaska Castle has a rich history. You live here now, and you will know it."

THE HEART OF A HUSSAR

The castle and the estate belonged to the Krezowski family. Eryk Aleksander Krezowski was the youngest of three and the only male heir. His mother died when Eryk was four, and his sisters married and moved across the kingdom. At twenty-two, when he became lord upon his father's death, he was the sole Krezowski in southwestern Poland. Along with Silnyród, a lesser estate in Podolia near Hetman Żółkiewski's holdings, what came to him was a forty-five-hundred-acre estate of seventy-odd *łan*, or fiefs, eleven villages, and a fourteenth-century fortress in the Jura Highlands: Biaska.

"Hundreds of years ago, King Kazimierz the Great ordered castles built throughout Poland," Katarzyna said in a dreamy voice. "The fortifications by Kraków, of which Biaska is one, were vital, you see, to safeguard us from Bohemia. They also protected Kraków's trade routes and the royal court at Wawel.

"Eventually, the defenses were no longer needed, and castles fell into disrepair. Some passed to aristocratic Polish families like the Krezowskis, with their lands, the peasants, and all accompanying rights. The endowments were made in exchange for kinship, military service, heroism, to buy favor, or any other purpose that served the Crown."

The very reward Jacek aspires to!

Katarzyna handed her cup to Oliwia for a refill. After a few more sips, she continued, her posture seeming to ease.

"The nobleman was expected to continue the castle's upkeep and to defend the Crown when a *Postpolite ruszenie*—a feudal levy—was issued. Thus did generations of Krezowski descendants manage its holdings and military and governed its people. Eryk has enhanced Biaska's wealth. But now there is no heir to continue the proud tradition."

After another long sigh, Katarzyna continued. "The lord supplies trained knights for war. His garrison has other soldiers, of course. Infantrymen, dragoons, and artillerymen he's hired from other countries—Scotland, Spain, Wallachia, for instance. Your father might have been employed by such a lord. But Lord Eryk's hussar cavalry is made up of Poles he not only pays but has trained. At present, he retains nearly fifty.

"When Eryk ascended to the lordship, he assumed power within the szlachta *zamoża*—the propertied nobility—without fuss or bloodshed. It was a civilized transition, and now he is the law here. But his cousin wishes it different, I fear. Antonin is cunning, and he is covetous."

Oliwia was surprised by this, for she had heard nothing of a cousin. "His cousin, my lady?"

Another few sips. "Eryk's aunt married into the Wąskaski clan. Antonin is her son. The estate, Wąskadroga, was once a large, prosperous land holding. But Antonin's father was a poor manager who drank and gambled away the family's fortune. As Antonin came of age, his father died suddenly, and he inherited his family's lands along with his father's debts. The owner of those debts was a powerful magnate who had long coveted Wąskadroga, so Antonin struck a bargain."

Oliwia glanced at her mistress's empty cup and offered her more wine.

"Yes, please, and pour yourself some as well. It makes a good story better, and I can barely feel my hand at this moment, praise heaven. Now where was I?"

Oliwia filled the lady's goblet as full as she dared and handed it back. "Pan Wąskaski struck a bargain." Oliwia sipped at her drink, transfixed.

"Yes, of course. So the estate passed to the magnate with a portion carved out for the Wąskaski clan. Young Antonin went from being of the szlachta zamoża to the szlachta *cząstkowa*—the petty nobility, with little or no land. Wąskadroga is a mere fragment of its former size. What once belonged to the family exclusively—land and everything it yielded—is shared among Wąskadroga's overlord and neighbors. Antonin kept the fortress, and though it sounds grand, it is a burden with crumbling walls and decaying timbers. So while Antonin is part of a landed family, it is not a wealthy one. That, however, appears to be changing …"

Oliwia raised her eyebrows. Katarzyna's eyes twinkled above her cup.

"Back to Eryk now. As the only male heir, he was groomed for his inheritance from the time he toddled. When I met him, he was very much ready to become his lordship. And, Mary, Mother of God, was he handsome!" A distant look of melancholy transformed her features. "But then, he still is so very handsome. I am so privileged to be his consort.

"He is a generous, masterful lord. Like his father before him, Eryk rules Biaska with a firm but just hand, like a state of and to itself. Our riches do not rival those of the magnates, but we enjoy the ease of a noble family of means." She shrugged. "Eryk especially enjoys his independence from the royal court."

The lady glanced up at the ceiling and rotated her head around the room, looking altogether as if seeing it for the first time. Her coloring had pinked. Finally, she downed the contents of her cup demurely, shaking her head when Oliwia stood and reached for it. Oliwia sat back on the edge of her chair, her hands laced together in her lap.

"No more wine just yet. I have more to tell you about Eryk and politics. He does not care for it; he thinks it tedious. His involvement is limited to the issues he most cares about, the ones that most affect him and the estate."

She began counting on her fingers. "Electing a king—the king answers to the szlachta, not the other way round. Answering a military recruitment—he finds those rather exciting. And supporting resolutions that protect the szchlata. Am I boring you, Oliwia?" Katarzyna looked at her with glazed green eyes.

"Oh no, my lady. Please go on." Oliwia was fascinated with the world she knew nothing of and astonished at the ease with which the lady discussed it. The wine no doubt played a role; Katarzyna slurred her words slightly.

"I'm glad to hear it because no matter what the men tell you, a noblewoman must learn all of these nuances and intrigues, even if she would not discuss them openly."

Katarzyna closed her eyes and drew in a deep breath. When she opened them, she stared at the fire. "Eryk doesn't care to attend the Sejm, even though they only meet regularly every two years. He sends a deputy in his stead. Like most of his peers, he's part of the Chamber of Deputies—the lower house—and attending would help him build alliances with his lord-brothers, which I believe he must do. Many do not trust him, you see, because he would not join them during the Zebrzydowski Rokosz when they rose up against the king."

Oliwia's mouth gaped. "They rebelled, my lady?"

Katarzyna put her hand to her temple. "The king is Swedish and once ruled that country. His uncle deposed him and took the throne. Many believe Zygmunt still seeks to reclaim the Swedish throne—at Poland's expense. He also angered the nobles when he arranged his own marriage to Constance, the Archduchess of Austria, in 1605. He did so illegally, without the consent of the Sejm. In addition, he proposed abolishing the Chamber of Deputies, imposing a permanent tax on the nobility for a standing army, and I don't recall what else. The rebelling lords believed Zygmunt should vacate the throne.

"Matters grew worse, and Pan Zebrzydowski, the leader of the rebellion, called on Eryk to join them when they met the king's army in Guzów in July 1607. Eryk sided instead with Żółkiewski, and therefore the king. The Crown crushed the rebels in that battle. Eryk spoke to you of Aleksander Lisowski, yes?"

Oliwia could not suppress a shudder. "Yes, my lady. He believes Lisowski's men were responsible for the destruction of my village."

Katarzyna nodded gravely. "Well, Lisowski was one of those rebels."

"What became of the other noblemen who rebelled? Were they executed?"

"Last year, the Sejm granted them full amnesty, but resentments are still there. As one would expect." Katarzyna shrugged. "Eryk has scant tolerance for gamesmanship and little ambition for high-ranking posts, so he chooses to distance himself. He prefers the simple country life, surrounded by an idyllic landscape and easy rhythm. But sometimes I think it an unwise stance, for there are ambitious, ruthless men—like his cousin.

"I fear Antonin may strike Biaska one day. He is recently married, you see, to his third wife, a wealthy widow. His first wife died in a strange accident—fell down the stairs and broke her neck. He married his second wife straightaway, also a wealthy widow. When she drowned in the Vistula, he was enriched by her death, and he is no longer such a poor nobleman. I understand he is even buying back some of his family's estate. Even so, I am convinced he aspires to have more. I believe he covets Eryk's lands, for the soil is better here than at Wąskadroga."

The declaration startled Oliwia and filled her with questions, but Katarzyna handed her the empty cup and sagged in her chair, her eyes clouding. "Oliwia, I shall rest a while. Be a dear girl and help me to bed."

Jacek stood just outside Eryk's solar and announced himself. Low voices interspersed with pacing bootsteps drifted through the partly open door.

"Come," Eryk ordered. Jacek stepped beside Mateusz and stood at attention.

THE HEART OF A HUSSAR

Eryk swatted a sheaf of papers against the edge of his desk. "Jacek, Mateusz has been advising me of rumors my cousin Antonin is building up his forces."

Jacek tracked Eryk as he resumed pacing.

"I still do not believe he could have had anything to do with the ambush, but in spite of our inquiries, we've learned absolutely nothing. I thought perhaps to pay him a visit at his fortress and satisfy myself."

"Of course, my lord. When do we leave?" Mateusz asked.

"Two weeks, but you are not going, Mateusz. As captain of the guard, you will remain here. Jacek will be my second on this foray."

In Jacek's peripheral vision, Mateusz eyed him with a frown. Jacek kept his eyes straight ahead, trained on the lord.

Eryk's shoulders drooped. "I would have left sooner but for my wife's health. She is recovering from a bout of illness, and I expect her to be fully restored when we leave for my cousin's stronghold. I need to make it seem like a friendly visit, a family visit." Eryk chuckled mirthlessly. "I shall call on a man I neither like nor trust."

When the meeting ended, Jacek left the solar briskly, putting distance between himself and Mateusz. His effort did not get him far.

"Dąbrowski!" Mateusz barked.

Jacek bit back his irritation and turned to face his superior.

"Captain?"

They stood outside the great hall, poised at the top of the forestairs in a chill wind.

Mateusz's face was mere inches from Jacek's. "I know what you're doing, Dąbrowski."

Jacek looked down at him. "Sir?"

"You've set that brat of yours to spy on me while you ingratiate yourself with Lord Eryk. You're trying to steal my position." Mateusz pulled his gloves on.

Heat rose in Jacek's cheeks. "Begging your pardon, Captain, but I have given Filip no orders to 'spy' on you. If the boy is being a nuisance, I will deal with him."

Mateusz's mouth twisted in a snarl. "See that you do, Dąbrowski. See that you keep him away from me. And another thing. Stay away from my wife!" Mateusz was so close he sprayed Jacek's chin and mouth.

Calmy, Jacek removed a linen square and scrubbed it over his face. The captain's bloodshot eyes smoldered, and a vision of a deformed, split nose bleeding between them flashed through Jacek's mind.

In a low voice, Jacek replied, "I think, Captain, it would serve you better if you told your wife to leave *me* alone."

Jacek turned on his heel, but before he took a step, a hand clamped on his shoulder. He let the captain spin him around, calculating all the while. *One well-placed jab. One well-placed jab and a knee to the groin. Grab the back of his head and ram his face into the knee, hear the gratifying crunch. Watch the blood pour.*

Jacek clenched his fists. Mateusz stared at him for several heartbeats. Two of Mateusz's underlings called to him from the bottom of the forestairs, and Mateusz started to laugh. He smacked Jacek's cheek and pointed a blocky finger at him.

"Don't flatter yourself, Dąbrowski." He gave Jacek a rough shove, turned, and leapt down the stairs, still laughing.

Just then, Filip careened into the courtyard, his head down as he trod the rutted path to the forestairs. Mateusz took four steps out of his way and barreled over Filip, sending him sprawling on his backside in the dirt. Mateusz roared with laughter, spurring his two men-at-arms to join in.

"Why don't you watch where you're going, you little rat? Now stand up and apologize."

A hand gripped Jacek's arm as he readied to descend the stairs, and Henryk's even voice sounded in his ear. "Don't give him the satisfaction."

Feliks paced into the courtyard and pulled Filip up by the scruff, talking to him in a low voice Jacek couldn't make out. Filip looked up at Mateusz with blazing eyes and mumbled something. Mateusz wheeled toward Jacek and erupted in another round of laughter before turning his attention back to Filip.

"Apology accepted," he hollered. Mateusz started to walk away but stopped and pivoted. "And tell that sister of yours I'll pay her a visit soon."

Jacek jerked his arm from Henryk's grasp. Feliks caught his eye and shook his head, then grasped Filip's shoulders and spun him toward the stables.

"Jacek. Time for the midday meal. Come, before the food is gone," Henryk said. Jacek blew out a breath and trailed his friend, his hands still fisted.

CHAPTER 15

Wąskadroga Castle

A squadron of Biaska husaria rode toward Antonin Wąskaski's stronghold twenty-eight miles southeast. Eryk and Jacek led the column behind Izaak, the *chorąży*—the standard bearer—a young nobleman chosen by Eryk as the most promising leader from among the younger towarzysze.

The group traversed dark pine forests flanking Biaska, then rode through open, rolling meadows of harvested barley and rye. After a steady plod, the detachment arrived at the castle's outer walls as the sun hovered on the horizon.

While they waited to enter the gates, Jacek surveyed the crumbling structure. This was not his first visit to Wąskadroga, but the extent of the fortress's deterioration surprised him. By all accounts, Lord Antonin had acquired some wealth. What, then, did he spend that wealth on?

By the time they had entered the gates and dismounted, said lord awaited them in the yard, flanked by several guardsmen. He approached Eryk with a broad smile and arms flung wide.

"Cousin! You're looking well. I was delighted when I received your letter, though I'm disappointed you can only spend one night. I will do my utmost to tempt you to stay with the aid of my best Hungarian wine!"

The men embraced stiffly, followed by an exchange of reticent arm-grasps. Broad and robust, Lord Antonin stood eye to eye with his cousin.

A fairer, older counterpart, his additional eight years showed. His shoulder-length blond hair was lanky and streaked with gray. He shared Eryk's brown eyes, but his face was longer, looking as though his chin had caught when he exited the womb. A shaggy gray moustache and beard disguised a tight-lipped mouth and pocked skin. Less easily hidden by the whiskers, a livid scar—earned during a quarrel with another nobleman—stitched his jaw line.

After setting aside their weapons in the disarming room, the contingent ambled into the great hall, where people and dogs milled about the dingy space, the soot-streaked walls devoid of decoration. In spite of the aroma of fresh pierogis, the pungent smell of filthy rushes and animal waste assaulted Jacek's senses. He carefully picked a path across the floor.

Feigning casual interest, Jacek scanned faces, walls, and alcoves. Beside the blazing hearth were several large tables. Servants carrying all manner of cups, jugs, and platters bustled about, laying the evening meal atop bare wood. No linens graced these scarred tabletops, and the dinnerware appeared as battered as the surfaces they sat upon.

Antonin's men-at-arms, some already slurping soup, were a ragtag assemblage of mismatched soldiers. From their dress and arms, they appeared to be infantrymen—poorly trained and poorly mannered.

Jacek and the rest of Eryk's men were shown to a trio of tables arranged in a haphazard cluster. They nudged their way between motley dogs keenly awaiting sloppy eaters. Jacek strategically seated himself with a direct line of sight to Antonin, who sat beside Eryk at the main table. No women occupied the head table, which struck Jacek oddly. In fact, the only women present were the servants hurrying between tables and demanding diners.

The meal in full sway, a serving girl who had been attending Antonin's table suddenly appeared at Jacek's side and began exchanging dirty platters for fresh ones. She leaned in to Jacek repeatedly, brushing her breasts against his arms and shoulders as she chatted merrily at him. The excessive attention vexed him—her plump figure interfered with his view of the main table. She was so persistent that he elbowed her over to Henryk and resumed his scrutiny.

The girl reddened and flounced away, only to return several minutes later, her laces noticeably loosened and her breasts cresting the top of her bodice as if they were about to overflow their trappings. Thusly arranged, she plopped her ample bottom onto Jacek's lap and looped her hands around his neck. Startled—and irritated—he stood abruptly from the bench and spilled the girl onto the filthy stone floor, dousing her with a brimming cup of piwo.

"*Vacca stulta!*" he hissed at her in Latin. *Stupid cow!*

She yelped and swore at him, then abruptly glanced over her shoulder toward the head table. Jacek followed her gaze just in time to see Lord Antonin lower his eyelids and subtly shake his head. When the lord opened his eyes, he met Jacek's stare and immediately turned toward Eryk, laughing as if he had been engaged in a very amusing joke.

The serving girl squawked at him. "The least you can do is help me up, you big oaf!"

He reached down and pulled her upright, releasing her as soon as her feet were under her.

"You shouldn't sit on a lap when you're not invited," he growled.

She turned and stormed away. When Jacek sat back down, Henryk handed him a fresh cup of piwo, a smirk plastered on his face.

"Your charm is as smooth as ever. You do have a way with the ladies, Jacek."

"That one wasn't interested in me. She was following her lord's orders." Jacek jerked his chin toward Antonin.

"Probably. Otherwise, she never would have picked you over me."

The evening wore on, and the Biaska men laughed heartily, toasting one another before downing their full cups and calling for more. Their merriment drew attention, and before long Jacek led them in singing "Bogurodzica," the centuries-old Polish knight's hymn before battle.

To his relief, the girl never reappeared. Once the food was cleared away, he and his fellows joined Eryk, Antonin, and Antonin's officers in front of the maw of the stone hearth. Little care by the servants was given to cleaning, but the dogs made short work of any scraps on the floor, benches, and tabletops.

After seemingly endless toasts to one another's health, Antonin called for wodka to replace the wine, and the men threw it back.

"Your health!" someone cried for what seemed the twentieth time.

Jacek placed himself beside Eryk.

"So, Antonin, tell me. How go your estate's affairs?" Eryk asked.

Antonin eyed his cousin for a moment. "As you know, Cousin, my estate is not rich like yours. My family and I do not enjoy the same comforts as you and your lovely lady, but we manage."

"And where is your charming wife, Antonin? Where is Lady Helena? I hoped she would join us so I could pass along Katarzyna's best wishes. It has been too long since I've laid eyes on her."

Antonin paused and looked into the wavering flames before turning his gaze back to Eryk. "I'm afraid my Helena is quite ill. She has been abed for weeks now, and the physician doesn't know what ails her. It is why she did not join us this evening, although I am sure she would have preferred to be among us."

Jacek looked from Antonin to Eryk. Both men held a wooden posture.

"I am truly saddened to hear it. And what of your son and daughters? Are they well?"

"Yes, praise be to God. At Helena's request, I sent Maurycy to the Jesuit Academy at Wilno, and the girls to stay with other family. Helena fretted her illness would spread to them. So now I am deprived of my wife's company and my children, and I live like a lonely bachelor." He hung his shaggy head.

"I pray they return to you soon," Eryk said.

An awkward pause followed, then Antonin raised his cup to the Biaska group. "I hear much of your famous hussars, Cousin, and not just of their lusty drinking. I understand you enjoyed a tremendous success at Kłuszyn in spite of tremendous odds."

"Hetman Żółkiewski's strategy was brilliant. He sent in charge after charge, fooling the enemy into believing we were many. I witnessed much bravery that day from all our sons of Poland." Eryk flicked his eyes to Jacek. "Tell me, Antonin, how is your arms supply?"

Antonin and his officers froze. They might have been a cluster of men turned to stone by Medusa's stare.

Antonin cleared his throat. "Why is it you ask, Cousin?"

"I ask because there have been rumors of … disquiet … in the countryside, and naturally I wish to be sure you have enough to defend Wąskadroga." Eryk gave him a benign smile.

Antonin barked out a laugh. "Can one ever have enough arms?"

THE HEART OF A HUSSAR

Bland smile still in place, Eryk seemed to appraise his cousin's every tic and twitch. "I would be happy to inspect your armory and determine how best Biaska can help."

Antonin coughed, reddening as he attempted to catch his breath. "I beg your pardon," he gasped, "the wodka!" Recovering himself, he continued. "While yours is a very generous offer, I am in the process of acquiring more and have no need of aid." His eyes slid to his second, a wiry redheaded soldier. "Wouldn't you agree, Radek?"

Radek blinked rapidly. Antonin's eyes narrowed, large shadows painting darkness beneath them in the firelight.

"The armory is somewhat depleted but will not be for long," Radek at last rasped.

Jacek furrowed his brows while the comment hung among the small gathering. The fire popped, spilling embers to the stones. A serving maid circulated among them, topping off their cups until Antonin seized the bottle from her and sent her away.

"Well, the hour is late," he declared. "One last drink and I shall have you shown to your quarters."

Jacek trod the courtyard as two guards watched him from the battlements. Relieving himself against a dilapidated wall, he sang several stanzas of his favorite carol, "When Christ is Born," loudly and badly to no one in particular, then launched into a love ballad to his horse before weaving off in the direction of the stables. The guards laughed at him, telling each other what a stupid, drunk hussar bastard he was, then turned their backs on him. He smiled to himself. *Not such a stupid hussar bastard, after all.*

He reached the stables and briskly moved up and down the aisle, padding like a sleek cat. The smells of horse dung and old hay engulfed him. Despite the poor light, his eyes adjusted to the gloom. He picked out box stalls, where the horses rested, from the stalls where the stable hands slept. A horse snuffled, and he froze. Then came a man's huff and the sound of a body moving in straw, followed by a drawn-out sigh. Jacek counted ten beats, then ten more. All was quiet. He counted to ten yet again before stealing to the tack room.

An opaque pane let in diffused shafts of moonlight, illuminating the murk, and he inspected bridles, bits, reins, saddles, and any armor or weapon lying about. Discovering little of interest, he careened back through the ward toward the keep. His meandering path drew scant notice from the guards, and he headed for his target, tucked in a garrison tower rising several stories high. The armory.

Satisfied no one watched him, Jacek wound his way up the structure, creeping between torches from one pooled shadow to the next. Not all the torches were lit, making it easier to slither along the wall undetected. A cool, damp breeze soughed through the leaves and ruffled his kolpak. Two guards strolled along the ramparts, comparing their experiences with a certain tavern wench, their minds obviously not on their duties. *Just like the rest of Antonin's forces.*

He advanced toward a set of timbered doors glowing dully in torchlight, sliding on the balls of his feet to keep his metal heels from striking the stone walkway. When he reached the closure, he ran his hands over it and set to releasing a substantial iron latch. He twisted slowly, cautiously. As he maneuvered the rusty handle, he felt a sharp prod in his lower back.

Christ and all the saints!

"What are you looking for there?"

Feeling naked without his sabre, Jacek slowly turned toward two foul-faced guards. One pointed an arquebus while the other brandished a pałasz, now leveled at Jacek's abdomen.

Jacek glanced around himself, teetering in his boots.

"I'm looking for … looking for … For Christ's sake! Where the hell is this place? And why are you pointing that at me?" he hollered belligerently.

"You drunk fool. You're in the guard tower. Where the devil did you think you were?"

Jacek turned to the heavy doors once again and began rattling the iron latch.

"She told me to meet her here! She said she'd be waiting on the other side of this damned door, but she's locked me out! Faithless wench!"

"*Who* told you she would meet you here?" The guard gripping the blade—Jacek dubbed him Pałasz—frowned at him while the other—Arquebus—looked him up and down.

THE HEART OF A HUSSAR

Jacek turned partway to the guards, one hand still working the stubborn latch.

"I don't know. One of the serving maids. The busty one," he said in an irritated slur.

"What was her name?" Pałasz asked.

Jacek broke out in a grin and tried to elbow the guard, nearly stumbling. "I didn't catch it. My attention was elsewhere. She sat in my lap and said she'd show me her tits. So here I am!" He threw his idle hand in the air with a flourish.

The guards exchanged glances. Jacek turned back to the door, continuing his manipulations. *Just one look is all I need.* At last, the latch clicked and released. Just as the door gave, Arquebus grabbed Jacek's shoulder and spun him face-forward, burying a wicked uppercut squarely in his gut. Jacek folded over, coughing in amplified breaths, bumping the door ajar. His retching and spitting caused both guards to back away. Pałasz let loose a string of expletives and advanced once more. Drawing his booted foot back, he caught Jacek in the side and sent him sprawling beyond the doorway into a torch-lit room.

Jacek grabbed his middle, cursing and groaning loudly, then rolled onto his side. He lay still on a rough, planked floor. Arquebus aimed the butt-end of his gun at Jacek's head. Jacek struck quick as an eyelid's beat and grabbed his ankles, yanking the man down hard, before he could land a blow. Arquebus howled when his elbow struck the wood, and his firearm skittered out of reach.

"You stupid son of a bitch!" The man kicked his legs to disentangle himself from Jacek's hold.

Pałasz moved in, drawing the broadsword back.

"*Stop!*" A sharp voice rose from the ramparts beside the keep, and Pałasz stayed his hand, cursing as he turned toward the command.

Jacek released his grasp on Arquebus and lay immobile, one eye closed, the other a narrow slit. Arquebus lurched upright. The sinewy Radek advanced on Pałasz. As the superior officer approached his man, he shouted at him.

"What the devil do you think you're doing? This man is the Lord of Biaska's lieutenant! You were just about to run him through, you feeble-minded fool!"

Though Pałasz was taller than his lieutenant, he seemed to shrink to match his height. Arquebus had recovered his firearm and stood nearby, holding his elbow against his body.

Jacek moaned and turned his head, hiding his features from view.

"This man?" The guard pointed at Jacek and protested, "But he's too young to be a lieutenant. Besides, he doesn't look like a hussar."

"Did you bother to ask?" Radek's voice was low, seething.

"No. He was trying to get into the armory, and I thought he should be stopped," Pałasz answered defensively.

"Did you wait long enough to find out why he was trying to get into the armory?"

"Says he was here to meet someone—sounded like Krystiana. I think he made it up."

Groaning, Jacek pulled himself up gingerly on all fours, swayed, then crawled away and heaved. With a stolen glimpse, he noted Radek's fists balled on his hips and his face contorted in a grimace.

"You're not paid to think!" Radek snarled as he pointed at Jacek. "He's drunk! Any clodpole can see that! Had you bothered to find out why he was here before knocking him unconscious, you might have noticed he's dressed like a nobleman."

The guard shuffled his feet. Arquebus opened his mouth to speak, but Radek snapped at him and continued his rant.

"And why would he breach the armory in plain sight, you imbecile? Or at all, for that matter? I'm sure Krystiana *did* arrange to meet him. He's so sotted he couldn't find his way out of a privy right now. If you had half a brain, you'd've figured it out. Instead, you've assaulted him!" Radek's voice had risen to a squealing pitch, and Pałasz flinched.

"Now pick him up before I knock you on your ass next to him!"

Pałasz took a few steps, bent, and hoisted Jacek under his arms—or tried to. The guard grunted as he yanked on him. Radek snapped at Arquebus.

"Help get him up! Now!"

Jacek's chest hovered above the floor as the guards tried dragging him out. He cracked an eye and looked around in feigned confusion. He glimpsed another form, a familiar one, walking crisply toward them. *About time!* Jacek squeezed the eye shut.

THE HEART OF A HUSSAR

"Sir, I believe your man has gravely injured my lieutenant," Izaak piped up.

Jacek began to flail. "What the devil do you think you're doing? Release me, you halfwit! At once!" he slurred.

Izaak quickly stepped to his side, replacing the guard, who now relinquished his load. Jacek peered at his subordinate.

"Lieutenant. It is Izaak, come to help you to your quarters, sir."

"Where is the girl I was to meet?" Jacek demanded.

"She is, ah, she left, sir." Izaak seemed to fight a smile.

"Damn!" Jacek slumped and nodded his head. Izaak helped him in his awkward climb to a standing position and threw Jacek's arm over his shoulder.

"Thank you, Lieutenant," Izaak called to Radek. "I take responsibility for him now. I will say nothing of your men's assault on our lieutenant, and you will say nothing of our lieutenant's, ah, error. Agreed?"

Radek immediately agreed.

"Now get him out of here!" he yapped at Izaak before turning on his guards. "You two! You're relieved! Find replacements more competent than you—that shouldn't be difficult—then meet me in the guardroom."

Safely away from the battlements, Jacek stood, sliding his arm from Izaak's shoulders.

"Are you all right, sir?" Izaak panted.

Jacek stood rod-straight, brushing his żupan and breeches nonchalantly. "Was that not a little longer than was wise, Izaak? The man was about to run me through, and his friend nearly bashed my head in."

"Yes, sir. I am sorry. But you see, I could not roust their superior right away. As it was, I had to persuade him. I found him in a ... ah ... compromising situation. I don't think he's very happy with me either, but for entirely different reasons."

Jacek grinned and grasped his shoulder.

"I'm glad you're all right, sir." Izaak added with his ever-ready smile.

"As am I, Izaak."

The two men strode to Eryk's chamber. Lesław glanced up and down the hall after ushering them in.

Eryk smirked. "You're a bit disheveled, Jacek. No permanent injuries, I trust?"

"No, sire. Just a little sore. I'm grateful Izaak shadowed me. He arrived just in time. Much longer and I would not be standing here right now." He gingerly prodded his ribs.

Eryk was seated by the fireplace. The single slit of a window was uncovered, and the brisk night air seeped in, unmolested, sinking heavy into the stones already cold as chunks of ice. Beside him was a worn oak table with a small array of mismatched bottles and cups. He motioned Jacek to sit and nodded at the collection.

Jacek reached for a cup and a jug of piwo. He'd had enough wodka to last him months, even though he'd deliberately emptied most of it in spilled toasts. Still, his retching hadn't been entirely an act.

"Tell me what you discovered in your wanderings." Eryk leaned forward.

Jacek wiped out the cup, filled it, and took a gulp before beginning.

"I found nothing suspicious in the stables. The overall care was disappointing. There's improvement needed in that regard, just as there is in the great hall." He glanced around the chamber. "And in the guest quarters as well."

Jacek held up the jug, and Eryk shook his head, so Jacek poured himself another and returned the bottle to the tabletop. Lesław filled his own cup and sat as Jacek summarized his escapade in the guard tower, filling in details as Eryk asked for them.

"While the guards were enduring their lieutenant's wrath, I glimpsed his weapons store. Pan Wąskaski may have understated his supply. I would not call it depleted. He's well stocked, with an abundance of guns for a fortress this size."

Jacek then told Eryk of the servant girl's bid to distract him and her suspicious exchange with Antonin.

Eryk rubbed a finger over his pursed lips.

"Maybe it was nothing. Maybe she wanted to take a tumble with you, and Antonin had other ideas. It's certainly not the first time a woman's thrown herself at you. Nor the first time a husband or lover was unhappy about it."

Jacek shifted in his seat. "I wanted nothing to do with the woman, but she proved useful—without being present. I hope Henryk uncovers something helpful in the garrison."

THE HEART OF A HUSSAR

The four men huddled around the waning fire, adding what little fuel was available as they talked. Dawn readied to creep over the horizon when Henryk returned at last.

"Did you have any difficulty?" Eryk asked.

Henryk slumped into a chair and grinned. "Not when they saw the bottles I brought with me. And when I let them see the size of my purse, it wasn't long before I was gambling and drinking with them."

"What did you learn?"

Henryk accepted a full cup from Lesław. "All these soldiers have been hired recently." He took a deep drink and wiped his mouth. "They said a commanding officer, possibly even a hussar, will soon arrive and begin training them."

Jacek deepened his scowl. "Train them for what?"

Henryk shrugged. "Castle defense. They say Lord Antonin has been adding to his holdings and therefore needs to increase his army."

Eryk rested his chin in his palm. Save the breeze squeezing through the slit, the room was still. "It makes sense. It's what I would do. What I don't understand is why he didn't come right out with it? And why the deceit regarding his arms store? My cousin's always been a shifty bastard, and this bears watching." He paused a beat. "What of the ambush? Did you learn anything on that score?"

Henryk shook his head. "I recounted the event, and all seemed surprised. The tale had not reached them here. I believe they know nothing of it."

Jacek rose and began pacing. "What if Romek Mazur organized the ambush?"

Eryk seemed to consider. "What would his motive be?"

Jacek gave a shrug. "Vengeance for Vyatov, plunder."

"It's possible. But the men who ambushed us were in disarray, drunk. If Mazur is truly one of Lisowski's men, they would have been more disciplined, and he would have led them himself." Eryk rubbed his eyes. "The men we captured said they were recruited to kill us. But by whom and why? I seem to have acquired a mysterious enemy in that part of the world."

CHAPTER 16
Tournament

The castle's ordinarily quick pulse became frenetic in the week prior to the tournament. Noble families and their retinues arrived, filling chambers, hallways, grounds, and the great hall. Biaska Castle fairly bulged. Lords and ladies dressed in their finery paraded with their families and expansive entourages. Crisp canvas tents flying brilliant flags sprawled over the grounds. But for the boisterous fanfare and lack of cannon or catapult, the castle could have been under siege from the sheer number of encampments surrounding it.

An arena was created on a large practice field, and staggered benches were erected on three sides for the spectators. The lord's section, elevated on a platform in the middle of the stands, was crowned by dazzling striped awnings. Red-and-yellow Biaska banners flew from masts at each of its four corners.

The air was charged, the growing excitement palpable. As people thronged the castle, the din grew louder. With tournament day drawing near, the wagers and challenges built upon one another, rising to absurd heights.

As Jacek strode the castle grounds, taking in the bustle of carpenters, stable hands, and servants, eagerness percolated through his bloodstream. He surveyed the preparations with covert delight, smiling in spite of himself.

THE HEART OF A HUSSAR

While others would vie for the fat purse, his motivation lay in the opportunity to pitch himself against other warriors in the arena. Whether it was the finesse of spearing a piece of paper on the kopia's steel point or a full-out race, he would hold nothing back. And the more competitors, the better. The contest, the prospect of testing his skills—these got his blood up. Just as pitting himself against his older brothers, and triumphing, *still* did. Every single time. After a childhood of torment at their hands, he thanked God for the large body he'd grown into, flaunting his physical superiority against them at every opportunity.

"My lords!" Henryk heralded as he stepped in Jacek's path. He flung out his arms with flamboyance. "I give you last year's winner." Then he pointed both thumbs at his own chest. "It is also my pleasure to give you *this* year's winner. Jacek, why not forfeit now and avoid embarrassing yourself?"

A grin widening over his face, Jacek clamped Henryk's nape and shook him. "You may try to unseat me, but you will fail, just as you did last year ... and the year before ... and the year before that. When *was* the last time you bested me? I'm having difficulty remembering, it's been so long ago. Ah! I recall. Never!"

Henryk batted Jacek's arm away while his companions laughed. He lowered his eyebrows at Lesław. "I would not laugh so hard if I were you, my lord-brother. You have not beaten him either."

"No, no one has. But I clearly recall beating *you!*" Lesław guffawed.

"Bah!" Henryk waved his hand dismissively. "Jacek just likes to show off. It brings out his theatrical side. He wants to impress the ladies and make them swoon at his feet. Eh, Jacek? And speaking of ladies, did you notice who arrived with her father today?"

Jacek's eyebrows rose. "Izabela?"

"The very lady. And she searches for *you*, you dog. Shall I find her for you? I wager I can convince her to give you up for me." Henryk waggled his eyebrows.

"You won't be able to convince her to give up her *betrothed* for either of us," Jacek said. Then to himself, he added, "I did not expect her."

Though she scurried hither and thither delivering Katarzyna's orders, Oliwia paused at intervals to marvel at the preparations whirling about her. The merchants' fairs near Vyatov paled in comparison to this dazzling production, dubbed a "minor affair" by her mistress.

A day before the tournament, Oliwia stopped in a gallery along the inner perimeter of the great hall and peered out a narrow window. She could barely contain the excitement bubbling within her at the sights and sounds below. Music drifted on the air as minstrels milled about, practicing their songs amid chattering, laughing folk. The melodies almost masked the horses' pounding hooves and the hussars' good-natured shouts as they practiced in the arena beyond. She caught the muffled boom of firearms, signaling the gentry hunted in the woods.

And then there were the incessant smells. From the yard below, aromas from slow-roasting mutton, hot laundry swimming in enormous vats, smoking fires from the blacksmith's shop, and heaps of horse dung intertwined and spiraled upward, mixing with the smell of fresh bread and bigos wafting from the kitchens. Oliwia crinkled her nose and swiped the back of her hand under her nostrils, tempted to keep it there.

As she watched, spellbound, Nadia sidled up to her and peeked out of the same aperture. "We must not dawdle, Lady Oliwia," the little maid said softly.

With Oliwia's soaring rank, Nadia's behavior had shifted to the reverence reserved for nobility. Oliwia was kind to the girl, but she was not above using the difference in their stations. At this moment, she chose to invoke that gap and ignore Nadia.

"Look at them all, Nadia! So many people. And the colorful flags! Is it not exhilarating?"

Nadia shrugged her small shoulders. "It is no different than any other tournament. This one is smaller, perhaps."

"How many have you attended?"

"I do not attend them, m'lady. I merely serve our lord's family and his guests. But I have witnessed them all."

THE HEART OF A HUSSAR

Oliwia chided herself, for she would attend the contests and the grand fête afterward. Nadia would not. She realized she had no idea of the girl's age and sought to recover from her insensitive lapse. "How old are you, Nadia?"

"Thirteen summers, m'lady."

"So you must have seen at least that number. Tomorrow, I am sixteen, and this is only my first."

And it will be the most exciting birthday of my life!

Jacek woke in the early dark and blinked at the solid, dark-timbered ceiling suspended above him. He could just make out the individual rough-hewn beams overhead, and he picked a seam he could fix his gaze upon. As he exhaled, his breath billowed into a cloud with disappearing edges, escaping into the darkness above.

It was cold. Opposite his cot, ice had formed crystal spiderwebs along the bottom of the meager singular windowpane, filling its corners in soft arcs. He glanced at the fire's remaining embers, then shifted his eyes back to his focal point.

The air knifed into his lungs like slivers of ice. He pulled in three huge breaths and slowly expelled them, willing himself not to cough in the process. And not to think about winning today. Not yet.

By the end of the third breath, it had become easier, and as he released the warm mist, he unwound muscles that had bunched against the chill. He stared at the ceiling, at that seam, and thought of naught but breathing evenly. In and out. And again. Last night's dream nudged him from the back corner of his mind. It wanted—demanded—his attention, but he ignored it and continued to breathe while he stayed locked on the unwavering seam.

After what could have been either hours or no time at all, he broke his gaze and sat upright, cloaking his naked shoulders with a dense, dark hide. When he grasped its outer edges to fold them over himself, his fingers sank into the coarse fur. He absentmindedly wiggled them through the packed hairs before gathering both corners in one hand under his chin. The pelt's musky tang enveloped him, but his frosted nose hairs blunted its pungency.

With his free hand, he dragged a splayed-legged wooden chair to the hearth and re-enlivened the fire, coaxing the embers with a poke of an iron rod. He waited for them to catch in the thick gray ash. When they did, he carefully laid a log in the nest of dust and heat. Sparks popped and burst as the fire licked its way hungrily round the fresh fuel.

Propping bare elbows on bare knees, he leaned toward the fire, palms spread open to the flame. The hairs along his forearms glowed golden. At last, he let the remnants of his dream emerge. He glanced over his shoulder to the rumpled cot and the misshapen pillow where his head had lain, but she wasn't there. No one was there, and no one had been there. And yet the dream had been so *real* he'd had to check for himself.

A soft shape, blurred around the edges as though shrouded in mist, began to materialize in his mind. The deity of his dream. Though she seemed familiar, her identity was an utter mystery. Her back was to him, and long, dark hair spilled like waves down her bare back. She turned and looked over her shoulder, and he tried to make out the contours of her face. Just as he sensed the curve of a cheekbone or the upturned corner of her lips, she rotated away from him, eluding him like a fistful of fog.

He shut his eyes, his mind conjuring the feel of her beneath him, bringing the image to life. His body reacted to the vision, a stirring flushing through him, charged and hot. He drew in a deep breath, and with it he tasted the strawberry and honey of her mouth as he had in his reverie. Sweet, soft. So soft. His fingers, thickened from years of handling horses with bit and rein, moved on their own, retracing the silky skin along her jaw, down her smooth throat, over a chain to the hollow between delicate collar bones. In the dream, his fingers had lingered there, skimming the U-shaped curvature. When he had pressed his lips in that hollow, she had shivered and sighed against him, and she had whispered his name, over and over. But still he did not recognize her.

Unbidden, reality intruded. He relinquished his vision of her hair fanned across the mattress as she lay naked in his arms, enticing him to stay where he was. He shook his head again, like a shaggy, wet dog. He needed a clear head if he was to triumph today, which meant he needed to expel his enigmatic lover from his thoughts. Her presence in his brain dominated and muddled him. She had to go.

THE HEART OF A HUSSAR

He sighed and stood up.

Her excitement popping and fizzing along with the buzz of the crowd, Oliwia took in the field from her seat beside Lady Katarzyna. She spotted her brother stationed on the sidelines opposite the spectators' seats. Conscripted by Jacek for the day's event—not that he'd needed any inducement—he now stood in bug-eyed wonder among the pages as a vivid array of competitors trotted onto the tournament grounds, lances pointed at the sky. Oliwia held her breath. They were outfitted in their most brilliant reds, greens, and blues, and their armor was so highly polished it could have been used as a looking glass. Their mounts were no less resplendent.

Bouncing on her backside, she clapped excitedly at the startling sight of hussars parading past in perfectly spaced rows, their magnificent wings rising above their backs for all to look upon. The wings were crafted of wood shafts, some painted, others encased in rich red velvet. Into each, feathers were inserted in evenly spaced holes along the frames: eagle, crane, goose, swan, and vulture, among others. The entire assembly was then mounted to brackets on the soldier's backplate or on his saddle, producing the rather dramatic effect of winged knights riding in formation. Nothing compared.

The spectacular exhibit nearly cheered the gray skies out of their somber mood. And though she was told the display offered only a taste of a true winged hussar charge, she was nonetheless awed by the grandeur before her.

The trumpeters and kettle drummers led the showy parade. Behind them rode the standard bearer, holding an enormous Biaska flag, followed by the lord, the captain, and the lieutenant. The latter was hard to ignore. Clearly the largest among those vying for today's championship, his presence drew all eyes—not just hers. Jarosława carried her master, and it occurred to Oliwia the mare held herself as proudly as he. With each cheer that rose, the lieutenant seemed to grow taller, as if feeding on the noise.

Eryk dismounted and joined his lady while the competitors trotted to and fro with their gilded lances. They rode before audience members of the fairer sex, then leveled the tips of their kopie. Lady Katarzyna had prepared Oliwia for this ritual with a bundle of colorful emerald ribbons. Smiling, the lady stood with her own fistful of brilliant blue ones and was greeted by cheers among the competitors. As a line of cavaliers led by the captain came before the Lady of Biaska, she attached a length of satin to the kopia of every man who asked it of her. Oliwia followed her lead when the captain approached.

Now Jacek drew even with the Lady of Biaska and bowed to her from atop Jarosława. When she'd favored him with a ribbon around his unadorned lance, he turned his kopia to Oliwia, sending an unexpected thrill through her. She was surprised he entreated her for a favor, and her hands trembled as she fastened a length of brilliant green satin to his lance, feeling her smile lift high and her blush creep up her neck to her hairline.

Now what's he doing? Jacek headed purposefully to another young woman in the stands, a beautiful redhead who fluttered her eyes and giggled as she added her own adornment—an embroidered glove—which he retrieved and tucked into his belt. Oliwia's heart, which had been soaring mere moments before, stuttered a bit in descent. She glanced about herself uneasily, hoping none noticed. Relief inched through her when the lieutenant headed to the center of the arena, whooping as he went, ignoring untold other ladies who called and waved tokens from the stands.

With her eyes fixed on Jacek, Oliwia swallowed hard. Since when had looking at him caused her to feel like a dozen lanterns had just lit up inside her at once? *It must be because he's bedecked in his finest attire.*

Giving herself a mental shake, Oliwia bestowed ribbons—with very steady hands—on Henryk, Lesław, Izaak, and towarzysze she didn't know as they lined up. At last, the parade before her stopped.

With a wave of his gem-encrusted *budzygan*, his lord's mace, Eryk signaled the start of the games. Now they would get to the important part of the event. Across the field from her, Filip appeared delighted.

THE HEART OF A HUSSAR

The men participated in myriad races testing their abilities on horseback. One of these was a trial of riding skills where horse and rider galloped down a pair of tracks, pivoted, and bolted back, all while the horse's hooves stayed within an impossibly tight boundary. It was a drill they practiced constantly, and Jacek was confident he would take this race as he'd taken the first two. He mounted his mare, and Filip, standing beside him, hefted his sheathed sabre to him when he was seated.

"I have no need yet. Hold it until the next race," Jacek instructed.

Filip then did the unthinkable. He let Jacek's prized szabla slip, dropping it to the ground. Jacek let out a flurry of exasperated curses. The boy reddened and quickly bent, picked up the blade, and began brushing it off. Suddenly, his head bobbed up then went back down again, where it remained by the horse's belly.

"Filip!" Jacek snapped. "What the devil are you doing?"

Filip ducked his head out and drew himself upright. "I believe a buckle on the girth is loose, sir."

"What?"

"Have a look, sir." Before Filip could finish, Jacek had leapt to the ground and handed him his gloves.

Kneeling, he spotted a dangling buckle. When he ran his hands over it, the buckle wasn't loose, but something about it was off. He drew closer, and Jarosława gave a little grunt and sidestepped. He tugged the cinch to hold her in place, and it pulled away in his hand. As he examined the buckles on the opposite side, an alarm bell clanged in his head. Both had been cut nearly through. When he checked the crupper, it likewise was nearly severed. *Who in God's name saddled her?*

Muttering, he began unfastening the damaged straps.

"Dąbrowski! Are you in this race or not?" Mateusz yelled.

Jacek glanced around; the other competitors were ready to begin.

"Filip!" he hissed. "Find me a cinch. Now!" To Mateusz, he hollered, "A moment, Captain."

"Shall I fetch Marcin?" whispered Filip.

Jacek shook his head. "No time."

His hands were flying over the rigging when Filip returned with a length of thick brown leather.

"Sir," the boy whispered, "the captain seems angry."

Jacek turned his head and glimpsed Mateusz scrutinizing him with a dark look. Jacek worked a little faster, cursing under his breath as he went.

Mateusz barked again. "Now, Dąbrowski, or you're out!"

"This will have to do." With a grumble, Jacek took his gloves from Filip and jammed them on. "Ready, Captain," he announced.

To Filip, he murmured, "Have Feliks bring my other saddle." He nodded toward the cinch and crupper in the lad's hands. "Keep those someplace safe. I'll have a closer look later."

Despite whatever difficulties Jacek had encountered with his gear, he won the race, though without his usual fluid aplomb. Oliwia had cheered him on enthusiastically. Now her eyes riveted on the competitors as they made ready for a test of szabla-wielding skills. Lady Katarzyna had explained the bout pitched each contestant against cabbages impaled on rows of spikes. He was to liberate the cabbages from their posts as quickly as possible with one swing of his blade. The man who dislodged the most in the shortest amount of time won.

With the raucous encouragement of the crowd, Jacek won the match with flair, seeming to revel in slashing the cabbages and scattering shreds of rubbery pale green leaves to the wind.

The horsemen lined up for the next event, which employed what some called a quintain and others called pavo. With blunted lance to hand, competitors were to hit a broad wooden target balanced by a bag of sand. The contraption was mounted on a round wooden post and pivoted when struck. If it was hit cleanly and the contestant cleared it quickly, the device spun harmlessly on its axis. If not, he suffered a blow from the weighted bag.

Oliwia spied Filip wriggling between the other attendants, tightly pressed together to get closer to the participants. The men harassed one another good-naturedly as they awaited their turns and heckled their lord-brothers when each took off toward his target, though Oliwia couldn't make out what they said.

THE HEART OF A HUSSAR

Jacek worked his way to the starting line, and Oliwia stifled a giggle when Filip began bouncing in place beside Marcin, who was reaching for a lance from a stand that held roughly six. Jacek drew up alongside, securing his kolpak before hefting the kopia Marcin handed him. After sliding it into a *tuleja*, a leather sleeve that held the butt end, he tucked it under his arm. The audience grew ever noisier.

"Jaaaa-cek! Jaaaa-cek!" they chanted, then erupted in one wild cheer when Jarosława stepped over the starting line and exploded into a gallop Straight-backed, Jacek held the lance parallel to the ground as the pair streaked toward the target. They were a sight to behold.

Oliwia held her breath, anticipating the strike. The lance shattered on impact with a resounding *crack*; an explosion of wood sent splinters in all directions. An audible gasp rippled through the masses. The lieutenant's momentum caused his body to fold over his pommel, and he reeled as he brought himself back up in the saddle. No sooner was he upright than the sandbag hit him squarely on the shoulder, lurching him to the side. Leaning precariously but still astride, he yanked on the reins and pulled Jarosława away from the offending contraption.

Filip broke into a run, his small legs churning, and reached Marcin's side just as the latter erupted in an explosive string of expletives. This bit of speech Oliwia *did* hear.

"Son of a bitch! Odious heap of sheep dung! Flea-infested, fetid …" Marcin spat.

"What happened?" Filip squeaked.

Jacek appeared beside them both, chest heaving, a dusky scowl on his face. "Marcin! By the Holy Mother!"

Oliwia stood and gasped as Filip wended his small body around the large horse's legs.

Marcin opened his mouth to speak, but Mateusz pulled up beside him. Looking at Jacek, Mateusz laughed mirthlessly. The sound sent a chill down Oliwia's spine.

"Too bad about that last round, Dąbrowski," Mateusz tutted, grinning widely. "You lost." Then he rode off.

Oliwia couldn't hear all of Jacek's words, for they came out in a growl. Marcin chased Filip off, and in his wake she heard the lieutenant arguing with his retainer, using words she had never heard put together in quite that way. She couldn't recall such a tempest in the lieutenant's features before.

With race after race, the afternoon waned, and it was soon time for the final contest, the tilting at the ring. The wind had whipped up, flapping banners and flags as it pushed unending iron clouds before it. Oliwia pulled her cloak more tightly about herself. She, like the rest of the spectators, anticipated the match with immeasurable eagerness. Lady Katarzyna had said timing and precision were mixed with outlandish showmanship, and as the riders ran their laps, the lady's words were proven true. The audience played its part, shouting wild hurrahs or emitting boos at every hussar's pass. The contestants were eliminated with a miss of the ring, while the more skilled—and fortunate—continued to ride.

After many a tall-tale-worthy sprint, the final run came down to a deciding race between the captain and the lieutenant. Both men were neck and neck after the day's trials.

Lady Katarzyna leaned over and whispered in Oliwia's ear. "This is an unusual turn of events. Pan Jacek usually has a comfortable lead by the time this race comes around."

Oliwia's eyes were glued to the starting line.

The purse, the glory, the victor's bragging rights all rested on this race.

Jacek walked Jarosława to the starting line, and Mateusz pulled up beside him. They squared off, and the rabble quieted. Mateusz said something to Jacek and smirked, then surged forward a beat before the signal sounded. Cheers and taunts exploded as Jacek followed. The two men dashed for their targets, Mateusz in the lead.

Mateusz closed the distance to the ring, lance poised to snag the prize. Oliwia bit down on her lip, knowing the captain was about to win—Jacek was too far back.

"Come on, come on!" she urged under her breath.

As the tip of Mateusz's lance touched the metal circle, his horse jerked its head. The motion jammed the lance and snapped it, sending the ring to the ground with a thump and rolling it through the dirt. One track over, Jacek's lance found its mark, and he turned smoothly and thundered across the finish line amid the crowd's exuberant frenzy.

Oliwia jumped up, decorum abandoned, and screamed along with everyone else with every breath in her lungs. Her cheers were swallowed up in the racket.

THE HEART OF A HUSSAR

Chest heaving, Jacek rode before the lord as champion. Behind him, defeated hussars called out myriad colorful insults. He reached up and nimbly caught a jingling pouch Lord Eryk tossed at him, then wheeled and grinned, holding the prize aloft before his vanquished brethren, hurling taunts and insults of his own. He then rode Jarosława the perimeter of the arena thrice before heading toward his retinue.

Oliwia's heart still hammered when Jacek dismounted and strode toward Filip. After loosening the pouch, Jacek distributed coins among all those in his entourage. Filip's eyes and mouth grew as round as the brilliant *złoty* Jacek pressed into his palm. With a laugh, Jacek rubbed Filip's head. He then called loudly to his fellows that he would see them all at the feast afterward, adding they might care to try and outdo him at dancing.

Oliwia lifted her eyes in time to see the captain storm off the field, looking altogether as if a storm roiled above his head.

CHAPTER 17
And Now We Feast

In Oliwia's excitement to get below floors, she nearly forgot to return to her lady's chamber. Now she raced down the passageway, her silk skirt rustling about her.

Her mistress seemed not to notice Oliwia's delay, fluffing and arranging her person while Oliwia—for what was likely the hundredth time—smoothed the deep rose bodice embroidered in colorful threads. The scooped, lace-trimmed neckline exposed her light skin in a flattering yet modest way, while the sleeves pouffed to her elbows, revealing stark white lace draping to her wrists. It was the most beautiful dress Oliwia had ever seen.

As she and Katarzyna approached the great hall, strains of violin music were barely audible above the guests' hubbub. Oliwia's eyes widened at the sight of splendidly dressed men and women pressed together. It was hard to distinguish anyone in the merry mix.

They threaded their way among knots of people who threw about extravagant compliments and raised toasts to one another. Amid the good-humored gibing and laughing, the fête was in full sway.

Oliwia sat at a lower table among myriad guests. She caught glimpses of Jacek, Henryk, and Lesław ensconced at a high table with a number of attractive ladies, including the lovely redhead. The victor's table.

THE HEART OF A HUSSAR

Taking in the scene around her, she reminded herself not to gawk before dipping her spoon into her chicken-and-barley soup. Stuffed goose, capon in wine, and roast venison were served—and of course more mead and wine. After the meal, the tables were cleared and the musicians took up their positions in the gallery. Tonight's ensemble featured not only the usual drum and fiddle-like *suka*, but also a *dudy*—a folk bagpipe. Entranced by the transformation, Oliwia was surprised when a dashing young man asked for the first dance, a promenading *chodzony*.

Katarzyna appeared from seemingly nowhere and now put a reassuring hand on Oliwia's arm. She leaned and whispered, "Let me see how well you have learned the steps. Dance with the young man. He is the son of one of our most distinguished guests. Go and enjoy yourself."

Oliwia opened her mouth, then snapped it closed. Her eyes darted to the nobleman, and she cleared her throat and smoothed her skirts. Though her knees wobbled when he led her to the line of dancers, she acquitted herself well, executing nearly all the steps of the elegant walking dance correctly. Soon she had a queue of partners awaiting their turns. Whenever she caught Katarzyna's eye, the lady simply smiled and nodded.

Begging for a respite, Oliwia extricated herself from her overattentive following and returned to her mistress's side. Lady Katarzyna slipped her hand into Oliwia's and pulled her into a seat.

"You have learned well, my dear, and you've quite a number of admirers. Are you enjoying yourself?" A mischievous smile played across Katarzyna's face.

Oliwia nodded, breathless. "Oh yes, my lady. Everything is so magnificent!"

"The evening is yet young, but be prepared to dance with all the men who received your ribbons today. They will demand at least one dance. No doubt many will want more than just the dance, so be ready for their advances as well."

Appalled, Oliwia turned to her mistress, and Katarzyna laughed. "Do not fret, Oliwia! I am sure your guardians will come to your aid should you need it."

Oliwia was baffled. "My guardians, my lady?"

"Of course. Surely you know some of our garrison keep watch over you, yes? They guard your virtue," she teased. "Look over there. While Pan Henryk and Pan Stefan engage in spirited conversation with those ladies, their eyes always roam back to you. And another of your self-appointed guardians stands there, by the pillar, beside the pretty redhead. Our own lieutenant and champion."

Oliwia craned her head, turning her eyes toward the pillar Katarzyna indicated. When she saw Jacek, she also saw the beauty next to him: the lady from whom he'd secured the favor. Oliwia clutched her armrests in a grip so tight that had she stood, she would have brought the chair up with her.

"She is quite lovely, yes? She is the Lady Izabela. She and the lieutenant have been acquainted for some time now. Do you see the short, bald fellow there, with the gray moustache, talking with Father Augustyn? He is her father, Lord Warszawski, a very powerful man. It is hard to believe such a beauty came from his loins," Katarzyna tittered. She sipped at her cup before prattling on.

"Whenever Lady Izabela visits Biaska, she seeks out our lieutenant and does not let him out of her sight. I daresay she monopolizes all his attention with her ample charms, and she gets away with it too. With no mother and a father more interested in his drink than his daughter's morality, I suspect she does not get the kind of supervision a young lady should—the kind you get." In a conspiratorial whisper, Katarzyna added, "It's not difficult to guess what she and Pan Jacek get up to when they're alone."

The lady's brows suddenly drew together. "Oliwia, are you all right?"

Oliwia wiped her clammy hands and shifted in her seat. Her hammering heart had fallen and landed somewhere near her stomach, and a wave of nausea rose up from the same spot. She swiped at a fine sheen on her cheeks.

"I am fine, my lady. Just a little warm from dancing."

"See you do not overdo it."

Oliwia nodded. "Of course."

"Where was I? Ah! For a time, I thought there was a deep attachment between the two, but I have since decided he is not as taken with her as she is with him. But who can really tell with him? Such a handsome man, but so difficult to puzzle out. He might be utterly mad for her, but I suspect no one would ever know it."

Katarzyna looked around, then dropped her voice. "It would make little difference as she is soon to wed a magnate, a very favorable match arranged by her father, even if the man is as old as he is. Her betrothed has nine children from two wives he has outlived, so he must be quite virile." She laughed primly.

"She is nearly twenty-two, you know. Time almost ran out for her, but I understand she was resistant to suitors. Perhaps it is because she wanted Pan Jacek. But he is the fourth-born, you see, so he will not be a landed lord, and her father insisted on a *good* match. And who can blame him? Strategic unions overcome romantic ones and rule the day." Katarzyna then looked away, engaging with one of her guests.

Throughout the evening, Oliwia watched Lady Izabela covertly as she revolved around Jacek like a celestial body. The woman seemed to never leave his side or allow him to leave hers. Oliwia's heart squeezed with the realization she was nothing like Lady Izabela. This young woman was tall and slender as a willow branch, and she swayed just as gracefully when she walked. Burnished, braided auburn hair wound around her head, held in place with pearl-studded gold pins. Distinctive olive-green eyes were widely set apart. Her unblemished skin was smooth and tawny, and it glowed as though she had been dipped in gold. Her lips were the color of claret and full, as if she wore a permanent pout. She was dressed in dark red satin and ochre velvet. Her slender throat was graced with a gold necklace that held an ornate ruby-and-pearl pendant, and matching earrings hung from delicate, feminine earlobes. The effect was stunning. *She* was stunning.

Oliwia drooped with a silent sigh as she touched her own hair, rebellious as always, fighting its way out of its restraints. In that moment, she knew, no matter how much or how long Lady Katarzyna taught her, she would never achieve the beauty and elegance of Lady Izabela—a true noblewoman, a lady of breeding.

Oliwia was not the only one admiring Izabela. Jacek seemed highly entertained by something the beauty whispered in his ear. He rewarded her with a rare laugh. *What did she say?* The woman fluttered her lashes at him. *Does she have cinders caught in her eyes?* Jacek threw back a cup of something and led her toward a group of dancers readying for a lively *krakowiak*.

A new dance partner invited Oliwia to join him, and soon she whirling in a circle far afield from Jacek and his partner. Lady Izabela kept her eyes fastened on Jacek, her lips enticingly parted with a hint of a smile. When the steps called for her to rest her hand on his shoulder, she invariably brushed her elegant fingers through his hair. They moved together fluidly, as if practiced with one another.

Is that how it's done?

Assessing her partner, Oliwia tried to strike Lady Izabela's pose but merely stumbled over twisted feet, her fingers nearly poking his ear. Men and women broke into separate circles, and Oliwia found herself facing Jacek. He gave her a brilliant smile, and she kept her hands—and feet—where they belonged.

The dance over, Oliwia withdrew and tracked Jacek with her eyes as he walked the lady toward the entrance to the gardens. The doors had been thrown open to the cool autumn air, offering relief for overheated dancers. Jacek glanced toward Oliwia, and she quickly ducked her head, pretending she was fascinated by the conversation between two silly girls beside her. When she darted her gaze back, she caught sight of his straight back heading out of the great hall, Lady Izabela on his arm. His head was turned, and he gifted the lady a beatific smile that wrung Oliwia's heart. In a flash of auburn and ochre, they skirted a clog of revelers, disappeared through the open garden doors, and were swallowed by the night.

Oliwia looked around at a circle of faces. Myriad young men, and old ones too, continually asked her to dance or if there was anything at all they could fetch her. Among them, Lord Eryk's homely, decrepit cousin Lord Antonin was a growing nuisance, constantly trying to pin her against a wall or piece of furniture, or touch her in an altogether familiar manner. Though she did not wish to insult a blood relative of the lord's, her repugnance grew each time Lord Antonin approached.

Between her frequent dodging, she stole glances toward the gaping doors where Jacek and the lady had disappeared. It was cold and dark out of doors. *What is keeping them?*

Nearly an hour had elapsed before Lady Izabela swept in from the garden, looking about furtively. The whole of her face and her throat to her neckline were flushed, and her hair was not nearly as tidy as it had been when she'd left. Her lips were a deep burgundy and plumper than before, as though she'd been stung by a wasp. One earring hung askew, looking as if it might drop off with the slightest brush. Smoothing and re-smoothing her rumpled gown, she scurried away from the doors and melted into the crowd.

Oliwia kept a steady watch of the doors as she feigned interest in the chatter about her. At last, Jacek reappeared, seeming as unruffled as ever. Nothing about his look or his demeanor was out of place. Tugging on each sleeve, he shrugged his big shoulders, the thick fur collar of his *ferezeya* riding up his neck. He scanned the crowd. When his eyes fell on her, he began striding her way, only to pivot abruptly when a slender arm encased in ochre velvet reached out from behind a pillar and tugged him back.

"Oliwia?" Katarzyna startled her. "My dear, fetch me my green wrap. It's in the second trunk."

After securing the shawl, Oliwia hurried, eager to return to the great hall and its booming music and laughter. One flight above the hall, close to the lord's solar in the deserted passageway, she rounded a corner, head down, and let out a yelp when she ran into the captain. He blocked her path and leered through half-lidded, bloodshot eyes.

"Such a pretty little thing. So delicate, so ... You're quite lovely this evening. You could pass for nobil ... nobil ... tee," he slurred, stepping into her.

She darted backward, but he reached out an iron hand and clamped it on her arm. "No, no, no. Mustn't go. I'm a lord, remember ... you're a damned peasant ... of Muscovy." He wagged a finger at her, his eyes appearing to follow his own motion. He leaned in clumsily, his stale, pungent breath wafting over her. She turned her head, but he grabbed her chin and held her face in a viselike grip as he backed her against a wall. A flame of anger rose from her belly, and a few choice words she'd learned from the soldiers whirred through her head.

"Mmm ... so ... soft. I can do much for you ... and you'll do for me, girl."

He lunged at her.

A shadow loomed. "Captain Zalewski?" A hand fell on his shoulder, pulling him back. "Sir, your wife searches for you," a deep voice said.

The captain shot a bleary look over his shoulder at Henryk, who continued to pry him off Oliwia. Henryk offered him a half smile that appeared almost genuine. "Shall I take you to her?"

Mateusz looked at him in confusion. He swayed where he stood, then staggered a step. Henryk hoisted him under his arm and jerked his head at Oliwia, mouthing "go." She scurried past.

After delivering the wrap, she splayed her hand across her stomach and caught her breath beside a cabinet. Looking around warily, she let out a relieved sigh when she saw neither Mateusz nor Lord Antonin. Someone cleared his throat behind her, and she whirled to find Henryk smiling at her.

"Thank you," she said.

He bowed elegantly. "Always at your service, Lady Oliwia."

She raised her eyebrows.

"I don't believe I've had the pleasure of dancing with you yet this evening. There has been such a line of admirers waiting for the chance that I can scarcely believe my good fortune at finding you alone at last. Would you do me the honor?" He held out his hand.

Obligation weighty on her, she joined him reluctantly in a jaunty mazur, followed by a simple reel she didn't know. She wasn't skilled in the steps, but Henryk was an easy partner to dance with, and he deftly masked her awkwardness with his own practiced, graceful movements. He apologized for any mistakes she made as if they had all been his own.

Soon her innards began to settle, and as they did, her movements smoothed out and her limbs loosened. He spun her more vigorously, in and out of the other brightly clad dancers, joining her in abandoned laughter each time they executed a particularly outrageous move. When it came time for the men's dance, he kept his eyes focused on her, smiling the entire time while he spryly went through his leaps and runs. Clapping along with the other women, she suddenly realized she was enjoying herself. Immensely. Dancing with Henryk was the most fun she'd had all evening, and she forgot Mateusz, Antonin, Jacek, and Izabela.

When the musicians stopped to rest and replenish their cups, Oliwia was breathing hard, her hand grasping at a stitch in her side. Henryk fetched more mead—how many drinks had he brought now?—and took her arm. He led her toward the open doors, where the garden beckoned, lively torches breaking up the darkness beyond.

His eyes held a mischievous twinkle. "Come, Lady Oliwia. Let's cool off."

She hesitated at first, but he beamed at her with an irresistible smile that dimpled his cheeks, and she let his charm override her qualms. As they reached the doorway to the night, a wall of cool air hit her. It felt wonderful. She looked up at Henryk, and he brought her hand to his lips and kissed it. For the first time, she noticed his deep hazel eyes were flecked in golds and browns. Giddiness suddenly bubbled in her belly, spreading a wide smile across her face. They had no sooner stepped outside when a voice boomed behind them, and her jollity shriveled.

"Henryk!"

She twisted her head round, but Henryk stood still and exhaled loudly. Jacek stood framed in the doorway, his arms folded across his chest. Oliwia froze in place. Henryk turned slowly and faced his friend.

"What do you want? You have your own, my friend, or have you forgotten so soon? Now let us alone." Henryk sounded annoyed, and he waved Jacek off, but Jacek stood rod-straight and stock-still.

The two men exchanged looks that were anything but friendly. Jacek glanced at Oliwia, then leveled his eyes back at Henryk.

"Lady Katarzyna asks after her charge, and I find you absconding with her. I do not think your roguish behavior would be well regarded by the lady *or* the lord."

Shock waved through Oliwia. She wriggled her hand out of Henryk's and looked at Jacek. "Lady Katarzyna is searching for me?" She turned toward the hall.

Before she got far, Jacek's hand on her arm stopped her. "I will escort you back, Oliwia."

She glanced over her shoulder at Henryk, but he wasn't looking at her. He had folded his arms, mirroring Jacek, and he glared at him. "If you're so concerned, then where the devil were you when the captain had her cornered?"

Jacek scowled. "What?"

Henryk scoffed. "See there? You had no idea, did you? Had you not been so diverted by … I took care of the matter while *you* were busy amusing your—"

"*You're* lecturing *me*?" Jacek snapped. "You have absolutely no idea what the devil you're talking about."

"Oh, I have a very *good* idea!"

"And this idea of yours is what you were about to subject *her* to, wasn't it? Do you forget how old she is?" Not looking, Jacek pointed at Oliwia, who grew more puzzled.

"I'm sixteen," she blurted. "Just today."

Both men swiveled their heads and gave her blank stares. Several heartbeats later, Henryk turned his stare on Jacek.

"Old enough. So, Jacek, why don't you just fu—" Henryk stopped abruptly, glancing at Oliwia.

Jacek smirked at him and grabbed Oliwia's elbow, spinning her toward the great hall. Behind them, Henryk asked, "*Two* in one evening? At the *same* event? Who is the true rogue, Jacek?"

Jacek ground to a halt and pivoted.

Oliwia hadn't understood the terse exchange, but urgency surged within her to report to her mistress, so she picked up her skirts and dashed from both men. She darted a look over her shoulder. In her wake, she left behind two hussars squaring off, snarling at one another about how old was old enough.

For Oliwia, the gala had come to an end, and despite the strange—oftimes discomfiting—events of the evening, it was indeed the best birthday she'd ever had.

Cloaked in the deep pine forest, Romek sat atop his mount and gazed at the brilliant castle on the hill, glowing seemingly from within. But the warm merriment was not for him; he'd been an outsider in this genteel world since leaving his family's estate. He might have outridden, outshot, and outswung every arrogant hussar housed within those walls tonight, but the thought did little to assuage him.

Instead, he fixed on everything wrong in his life, starting with the injury he'd sustained as a boy when an errant limestone chunk had nearly cleaved his head in two—the condition that had brought out his mother's scorn at his "differentness" while bringing out his sister's fierce protectiveness. Bella had mothered him herself, defying their mother's wishes, and she'd suffered for it.

Just as his mother had told him he was unworthy of love, Romek had grown to think her unworthy of any due. The selfish woman's extravagant tastes had forced his father into debt and drink.

Like his father, Romek was driven to earn coin. But alas, also like his father, he seemed unable to keep it, and not for reasons of his own making. Something always seemed to happen as soon as he gained a decent purse.

THE HEART OF A HUSSAR

He let out a frustrated growl as he looked upon everything that should be his. Biaska was the beacon, the symbol of what he'd lost—what his entire family had lost—and what he would gain back. Now that he was in the lord's employ, he would accumulate his earnings. And he'd recruit the best fighters. The lord had been immensely pleased with Romek's plans, which had caused Romek's heart to soar. A bright spot in his wretched existence.

He'd have need of more bright spots, for Bella was dying, and he was powerless to stop it. He owed her everything, and time was running out for him to repay her. The thought filled him with despair, ripping into him with razor-sharp teeth as he bowed his head within the shelter of the forest.

The tournament faded into Biaska's collective memory just as fall faded into winter. Hetman Żółkiewski had entered Moscow and installed a garrison, and Poland had occupied the city since the day after Oliwia's birthday. As Jacek had foreseen, Muscovy was becoming part of the Commonwealth. Zygmunt III's son Władysław IV had been proclaimed Tsar of Muscovy as part of a sworn pact between the boyars and Żółkiewski. It was only a matter of time before Muscovy was absorbed into the Polish-Lithuania Commonwealth. What would it then be called?

Oliwia *should* have given the news of her former country's demise more due, but she couldn't muster it, instead becoming wholly absorbed with Christmas in her new home.

The late afternoon sun threw long purple shadows on the walls of her bedchamber, where she sat at a small table before a bright fire. A multitude of tapers stood on the table's surface, casting amber light on her fingers nimbly twining and tying bits of straw. So focused was she that when a light knock sounded on her door, she jumped. Filip's curly brown head poked through the gap. She waved at him impatiently.

"Hurry! Hurry! Before someone comes."

He slipped in, shut the door, and ran to her side.

He peered over her shoulder. "What are you doing?"

"I'm finishing a gift for Lady Katarzyna," she whispered, as if the lady stood in the corner of her room. She held up a straw angel interwoven with sprigs of dried herbs. "Do you think she'll like it?"

Filip shrugged and plopped into a chair, shuffling through bits of desiccated plant matter on the tabletop.

Oliwia plucked at her creation. "Are you ready for Wigilia?"

His blue-gray eyes flew to hers. "Yes! I'm starving."

"As am I. Fasting all day with all the wonderful smells coming from the kitchens has my stomach rumbling. This Christmas Eve feast will be a little different for us, yes?"

He frowned. "How?"

"Well, we live in a new country with new customs. In Muscovy, Christmas Eve falls on January sixth, but here, it's today, December twenty-fourth. And we eat different dishes. The meal tonight will have no meat, but the soups and desserts are similar. For instance, we start the meal with *kutia*."

Filip licked his lips. "But we still cannot eat until we see the first star."

"True. We wait for Gwiazdka. It will be spotted soon. You are here early, yes?"

"Pan Jacek told me I must visit you while he's away, so I thought I would come now, before Wigilia." He slumped.

She gave him a sidelong glance. "You miss him."

"I don't understand why he has to be gone so long," Filip grumbled, staring at the flames.

Oliwia gathered up her mess and rolled it in a linen cloth. "It's the Christmas season, Filip. He belongs at home with his family."

"But *this* is his home; he even said so himself. And *we're* his family."

"That may be, but he has another family he never sees. His mama and papa, his sisters and brothers. They are family by blood. We get him all the year round." She stowed her bundle in her trunk. "And don't forget, he said he will return right after the Feast of Three Kings."

Filip sighed, then gave her an accusatory look. "You don't care that he's gone, do you?"

"I care. He's my friend too." Softly focusing on the blaze, she added quietly, "In fact, he's my best friend in all of Biaska."

"He is?"

THE HEART OF A HUSSAR

"Yes. Oh, he scared me at first, but he's been kind to me … to us both. He has a caring Christian heart beneath his thick bison hide." Filip crinkled his nose at her. She grabbed his shoulders and turned him toward the door. "Come. Let's go the great hall and admire the decorations."

Descending below floors, Oliwia salivated as the aromas of beet soup, cabbage rolls, and baking apple compote wafted up the stairs. Suspended upside down above the main table was the *podłaźnik*—the top of a spruce tree, festooned with apples, nuts, and paper chains. Boughs of fir hung above the double oak doors and behind holy pictures throughout the hall. She drew in a deep, contented breath while Filip ran toward tables set with white linens. He began pulling lengths of straw from under the tablecloth.

He held them up. "What's this for?"

Beata shook her finger at him. "Young master! Leave the straw where it is. It's placed there to recall Jesus in the manger." She snatched the straw from him and shoved it back under the tablecloth.

He pointed to a corner. "And that bundle of straw there?"

"Thanks for our blessed bounty, and a prayer for fertile soil with an abundant harvest next year," came a deep voice behind them. "You'll be leaving that alone as well."

Oliwia whirled. Lord Eryk and Lady Katarzyna were walking toward them.

Filip's mouth swung open.

A smile quirked Eryk's lips. "Filip, go outside and search for Gwiazdka. I'm famished," he ordered.

Not five minutes later, Filip yelled from the top of the forestairs. Oliwia, along with other eager witnesses, ran to his side. Eryk confirmed the sighting, and the group quickly retreated from the cold. Oliwia sat beside Filip, her stomach aflutter from excitement as much as hunger. Eryk led a prayer, then held up a thin white rectangle—the *opłatek*—embossed with an image of the Christ child. Turning to Katarzyna, he extended it, and she snapped it while the couple exchanged thanks and wishes for a blessed year.

More wishes and prayers followed as the opłatek made its way round. Oliwia's eyes darted to the last empty setting. Who was missing? Her puzzlement must have shown because Katarzyna said, "It's tradition to leave an open setting during Wigilia in case an unexpected guest stops by. 'A guest in the home is God in the home.'"

Hours later, when each diner had sampled all thirteen dishes, the feast remained upon the table should a spirit happen by. Lord and lady stood and made their way to the hearth, where Lady Katarzyna clapped her hands. "Let's gather and sing carols."

Oliwia stepped lively from the table, taking in the wonder of it all like a small child seeing her first snowflake—both for her own delight and to record the new traditions she embraced in her heart—as the group broke into "Praise Be, Lord of Angels."

More thrilling than the feasting, caroling, and happy chatter was the fuss Lady Katarzyna made over her straw angel. Oliwia flushed red and beamed openly. When they clambered into the sleighs that would take them to Shepherds' Mass at the village church, she swore she rode on a cushion of air.

The morning after Christmas, St. Stefan's Day, Jacek sat at a table surrounded by family as he shoveled in cheese, smoked carp, cold cuts, and poppy seed cake.

His mother sat beside him. "How can you eat so much?"

Right after he'd closed around another spoonful, a hand swatted the back of his head hard, driving the implement into the roof of his mouth. "He's still a growing boy, Mama. Aren't you, Wiewiórka?" His oldest brother laughed before leaping out of Jacek's reach.

"Stop calling your brother a squirrel, Daniel," their mother admonished. "He comes home rarely enough as it is, and I don't want you giving him more reasons to stay away." She smiled sweetly and patted Jacek's shoulder.

Ignoring his scraped palate—he was loath to give his brother the satisfaction—Jacek winked at her. "It's all right, Mama," he mumbled around a mouthful of cake. "I will even things up later."

She let out a long-suffering sigh. "Which is what I fear."

A small voice piped up excitedly from Jacek's other side. "Wujek, would you show me how you kill Tatars?"

"Never mind, Gabriel. Leave your uncle alone." This from Gabriel's mother, who was also Daniel's wife.

THE HEART OF A HUSSAR

Jacek poked his finger into Gabriel's bony chest. "Just like that. That's how I do it."

Gabriel's eyes grew round. Soon the child was poking his fingers repeatedly into his squealing sister. A great clamor arose as their mother hauled them both from the table.

Jacek's mother's amused expression became a troubled one. "You should have a wife, Jacek, and children of your own."

He dropped the spoon on his plate and wiped his mouth. "Mama, are we to start this all over again?" He glanced over at his father for aid, but he was engrossed in a chess match with Jacek's older sister.

She smiled at him conspiratorially. "Did Mama tell you who she's invited over today, Jacek? Nearly every noble family within twenty miles—all those with a marriageable daughter, that is."

He rolled his eyes. "Mama, no. I did not return to find a wife."

"But, Jacek, it's time." She pushed his hair off his forehead. "You need someone to round out your sharp edges, my son, to make you happy."

"Don't listen to her, Jacuś," one brother called from the hearth. "Marry, and you'll *never* be happy." The comment earned him a smack from his wife, and he pulled her into his lap with a laugh.

Jacek snorted, overlooking his brother's use of his childish diminutive, then turned to his mother. "Mama, I've told you I will not marry until I've my own land."

"How is that coming, Jacek?" his sire asked, his eyes still focused on the board before him. Though his father had not a note of sarcasm in his tone, Jacek felt the familiar bristling along his spine.

"We had a good campaign, Father. The hetman was there," Jacek said defensively.

"You had more than a good campaign, my son. It will not get you your land, but what the hetman's small force accomplished at Kłuszyn was remarkable. They're writing songs about it."

Jacek reddened, unsure what to say. Compliments, in any form, from his sire were rare. Fortunately—or not—his mother resumed her mission.

"I have invited a few families to stop by today. One has a lovely daughter with a sizeable estate for her dowry."

"Mama, not that fat cow Lady Violetta!" exclaimed Daniel. "Jacek can do better for himself than *her*. Well, not the land, but the woman surely! Jacek, why do you persist? You'll do much better with the right match."

Disregarding his brother, Jacek took his mother's hand in his, masking his exasperation. "Mama, let me do this my own way."

She covered his hand and looked at him with eyes that could have been his own. "I fear you will die an ill-tempered, childless old man if you do not give up this dream of yours and turn your attention to a family while you're yet young."

"He won't live that long, Mama," quipped another brother.

"Mama, please," Jacek replied softly.

She patted his hand. "Well, at least *try* to be engaging when they arrive. You may not live among these people anymore, but we must."

He blew out a great breath and muttered, "For you, I will try."

Oliwia stood on the ramparts, wrapped in a burgundy fur-lined cloak, absorbing the unclouded winter sun's warm pulses as she studied the dormant land stretched before her. Evergreens lined up in the far distance, hiding intriguing secrets within their misted blue-green hues. With a contented sigh, she let the sun lull her into a heavy-lidded laziness. She didn't notice someone approaching until his long shadow fell on her.

She spun and looked up into Jacek's unreadable face as he loomed above her. Her heart skipped several beats. "I heard you had returned."

He held out a long, thin object roughly the length of her forearm.

She dusted off her hands. "What is it?"

"A gift."

"Oh! I've one for you, but not on my person." She thought of the small painting of Jarosława upon her desk.

"No matter. Here, take it." He shoved it at her.

She plucked the rigid article, tied in a length of white linen, and unwound it. She brought wide eyes up to his.

He was grinning. "Do you know what it is?"

"Yes, I think so."

He slid it from her hand. "Here."

THE HEART OF A HUSSAR

He spread it open, revealing a silk fan painted with a colorful scene of ladies seated on a green beside a lake. She stifled a chuckle at the sight of him holding the feminine frippery in his big paw. He handed it back to her.

"But it's wonderful! The painting is beautiful." Delighted, she studied the fan, opened and closed it, fanned herself with it.

"I thought you might like one. Other ladies who attend gatherings all seem to have them."

"It's lovely! Thank you. Wherever did you get it?"

"At a shop my mother frequents." He shrugged. "Will you join me for the midday meal and keep me company? I want to know what I've missed, but I'm famished."

She laughed. "When are you not?"

He smirked, then set off, striding along the battlements. Oliwia hurried after as a red kite screeched overhead.

"Might you stop stalking till I catch up?"

He wheeled, arching a dark eyebrow. Oliwia quickly flicked her eyes away. Thereafter, he slowed his gait, and she kept apace.

"How was your visit home?" she asked, masking her embarrassment.

"I dodged a few dangers, but overall I enjoyed my stay."

She frowned. "Dangers? Like wolves, do you mean?"

He chuckled. "You might call them that."

CHAPTER 18

Cultivating a Warrior

The Christmas season drew to a close, and castle life drifted into cold lassitude. Noblemen at their own estates and garrisoned soldiers alike would enjoy their leisure until the king sent the next letter of array, calling for a return to action in the spring. It was how the rhythm of the seasons had flowed for the past decade: fight from spring to fall, return, rest, and rally to fight again in spring.

Now was the time for warriors to recover, to idle with loved ones, to be nourished, and to grow strong again. Idling did not mean lying about, however. For Eryk's hussars, it meant countless hours of drills.

He stood at the narrow window in Katarzyna's sitting room. When his wife slipped her arms around his waist from behind, he flinched.

"Am I as frightening as all that?" She stood on tiptoe and kissed his neck.

He turned and pulled her against his chest, stroking her gold-silk hair. "Just lost in thought, Kasia."

"And what deep thoughts have set you to brooding?"

He kissed the top of her head. "Nothing to concern you."

"Oh no? Am I not the lady of this estate? Everything that concerns you concerns me." She tilted her head up, resting her chin against his chest.

"Only a very dull business, my love, about the garrison."

THE HEART OF A HUSSAR

She pulled away and tugged his hand, drawing him toward the cushioned oak chairs by the fire. He followed willingly, accepting the goblet of wine she handed him before sitting beside her. She fixed her expectant gaze on him.

He began fidgeting with the pewter buttons of his żupan. "I've been contemplating Jacek's role."

"Is he not proving a good lieutenant?"

"He's doing every bit as well as I expected. Better. He was born to this. I marvel the older warriors defer to him."

"Why shouldn't they?" She swatted at his hand, and he released the button.

Eryk chuckled. "Because he's an unrelenting upstart. I wouldn't enjoy marching in their boots, taking his commands."

"You are the lord, my love. You shouldn't take orders from anyone."

"Anyone but you, I suppose?" He winked at her.

"I've little idea what you speak of." She smirked. "Do the men resent his arrogance?"

"He's not arrogant. If he were, he would do everything his way. He's a good soldier who follows orders. He pushes himself ceaselessly, more so than he does anyone else. He assesses his own strengths and weaknesses and is his harshest judge. The men see it. It's one reason they follow him. Jacek does not swagger, not like ... well, not like some of these peacocks. He's supremely confident."

"Do they obey because they're afraid of him?"

Eryk shook his head and took a drink of wine. He passed the goblet to Katarzyna, who sipped like a small bird before passing it back.

"No, they respect him. Have you watched him fight? No, of course not. I tell you, he would best any gladiator in ancient Rome." Eryk stood to refill the goblet, then grinned. "Fighting with older brothers no doubt toughened him."

"You obviously admire him, my lord, so what is the trouble?"

Eryk handed her the goblet before standing before the hearth, gazing at the dancing red-orange flames. "He has an eye for a battle and a good strategic mind, and he's ferocious. Other warriors—Mateusz, for instance—are equally skilled in the heat of a fight, but Jacek is different. He's methodical. It's hard to describe, Kasia, but his ferocity is thought-out, within his control."

Katarzyna's green eyes were fixed on him, and she flashed him an indulgent smile, so he went on.

"Jacek is an exceptional warrior, and he will soon be a great leader. My trouble, my dear, is if I cannot entice him to stay, he will be lured elsewhere." He noted the look of surprise shifting her features.

"Does that mean you must promote him? Mateusz and Barbara have been here—"

He nodded. "Over three years now. Yes, I know. Jacek has been here nearly seven, and he understands what I want better than anyone."

"So are you considering … What does this mean? What of Mateusz?"

Eryk sighed. How much to tell her? "They don't like one another. I'm not sure what the source of the trouble is. Perhaps it is merely an old bull chasing off a younger one. Does Lady Barbara confide in you?"

"You liken Mateusz and Jacek to bulls, and then ask after Lady Barbara. Are you implying they are *rivals* for her affection?" She stared at him with round eyes.

He laughed, masking his surprise at how quickly she saw through his subterfuge. "No, of course not. I just wondered if … if Mateusz is unhappy at home, he might be inclined to turn it on others."

"You are quite fond of Jacek, yes, Husband?"

"He's a good soldier, Kasia."

"So you said. Eryk, my love, had you to choose between the two, who would he be?"

He glanced at her and bit back the answer that leapt to his tongue. "I could always send Jacek to Silnyród. I trust him to command the garrison and look after my interests there, though I'd prefer keeping him here. Ultimately, I will need to elevate his rank or risk losing him." He paused a beat. "I might convince him to stay with a promise to recommend him to the king for his much coveted land grant, though I'm not sure I curry any favor with the king. His Majesty knows I ally with Żółkiewski, and he does not favor the hetman."

Her expression grew stormy. "But you supported the king against Zebrzydowski's Rokosz! Surely your loyalty means something."

Eryk laughed wryly. "It did not help Hetman Żółkiewski much. The king withholds the title of Grand Hetman of the Crown from him, and he needs Żółkiewski far more than he needs me. Especially with this Muscovy business."

THE HEART OF A HUSSAR

"What of the Muscovy business?"

Eryk let out a long sigh. "The king has changed his mind about the agreement he made to keep his son on Muscovy's throne. Instead, he wishes to take his place."

She blinked. "Is that so bad?"

"Yes!" he exclaimed. "It was agreed Crown Prince Władysław would convert to the Orthodox faith and rule Muscovy. The boyars made a pact with Żółkiewski. Żółkiewski gave his word based on the king's accord. It was all set. Muscovy within our grasp, Kasia. Now not only does the king wish to be tsar, but he insists *Muscovy* convert to *Catholicism*. He is breaking his word ... and making it appear Żółkiewski has broken his."

Her eyes widened in astonishment. She whispered, "What can be done, Eryk?"

He shook his head. "Żółkiewski has not yet told the boyars. He is hoping to convince the king to uphold the bargain, but I fear he will not succeed."

"So the war with Muscovy will continue?"

"If the agreement is cast off, then yes. And who knows where it will end?"

After a pause, Katarzyna ventured in a shaky voice, "Which means you continue to answer the king's call to arms." Sorrowful eyes held his. "Perhaps it's time to stop, my love. Mateusz could stand in for you as your *porucznik*, and Jacek would serve him as captain. Two capable men to lead the company while you remain here."

The notion of sending others in his stead chafed, but Katarzyna would never understand. It was time to leave behind the political talk. "Jacek's young yet," he dodged. "There is still time to decide."

Jacek's quarters consisted of a sleeping area and sitting room, which functioned as a solar. While Jacek could have moved into the late Lieutenant Górnicki's plusher surroundings, he had declined in favor of the familiar. The garrison apartment was tidy, its adornments spare.

Right now, Filip stood in his chamber, his blue-gray eyes fairly bulging at the sight of the wooden sword Jacek handed him. The boy turned it over in his hands.

Jacek sat on the corner of his desk. "It should be the right size to wield."

The boy slashed the implement through the air. He glanced up at Jacek, a grin plastered on his face.

"When do I begin to spar?"

"There are steps you must master first."

The boy brightened. "Like riding a warhorse?"

Jacek folded his arms across his chest. "Not yet. What did I say last time you asked that very question?"

Filip dimmed. "You said I must first learn to ride the draught horses. But—"

Jacek cut him off. "Good. At least you remember that much. In the meantime, you'll continue working in the stables."

"Yes, sir."

Jacek regarded him. The boy was surprisingly determined—not unlike himself at the same age—and eagerly absorbed whatever Jacek taught him. He knew how to groom a horse and feed it. With help, he could dress and saddle it. He had learned to treat the animals with authority *and* reverence.

Filip was ready for the next step, but Jacek held back. His greatest—his only—reason for restraint was the boy's sister. He did not share this with Filip because he knew how he would react. And he wouldn't have blamed him one bit.

Last summer, when he had brought Filip into his world, Oliwia had pleaded with him to keep her brother off the big horses until he grew taller and stronger. Though she'd not repeated the plea, Jacek still deferred. If he pondered it too much, he grew annoyed with himself. A man should not break his own rules.

"Filip, I have a new lesson for you. Get a length of cord, and I'll show you how to rope. Practice every day, and eventually you'll throw it from a horse's back. If you listen and follow my instructions, I will take you out on Gwiazda with me." The horse was a sleek bay gelding named for the white star emblazoned on his forehead.

"Gwiazda? Could we not ride Jarosława, my lord?"

"You are not in a position to wheedle. If you would rather not ride, I will accommodate you." Irritation edged Jacek's voice.

THE HEART OF A HUSSAR

Filip straightened, nearly clicking his heels. "Oh no, sir. I will be happy to ride Gwiazda with you. Thank you, sir."

"Humph. Get the rope, then."

They practiced that afternoon, and the next day Jacek showed Filip how to grip the sword. Though it was mid-winter, the air was still, and a pale sun shimmered off the limestone walls in the bailey.

"Sir, which is your favorite weapon?" Filip practiced a two-handed swing.

"The kopia has a long reach and is very effective, but for hand-to-hand combat, I prefer the nadziak."

"Why?"

"It's a versatile weapon. The hammer head can bash in a helmet or break bones, while the claw will pierce armor. With the spike at the end of the wooden shaft, it becomes a short lance. It will stun and incapacitate a foe or his horse. It will kill."

Filip pointed toward the field. "I saw a soldier use one to tap a stake in the ground."

Jacek laughed. "Yes, there's that too. It makes an excellent hammer. And in times of peace, the spike is removed, the claw is bent down, and it becomes a walking stick."

Filip slashed the wooden sword through the air, nearly dropping it. "What about the szabla?"

"A wooden szabla was *my* first training weapon." Jacek nodded at Filip's sword. "It was so long ago I scarcely remember. Now my blade feels like an extension of my arm. After that, I learned the dagger, pałasz, bow, nadziak, and *koncerz*." He ticked off each one on his fingers. "The koncerz—some call it a tuck—led to the lance. As I grew bigger, so did the lance."

"Which is your least favorite weapon?"

Jacek did not hesitate. "Pistols." When Filip's eyebrows knotted, Jacek continued. "Their advantage is in their ability to wound or kill from a distance, but they're unreliable. If they get wet, they're of no more use than a club."

"But I see you firing at targets all the time."

"Of course. A man should be a master of every weapon he wields."

"Oh."

"Come. You've earned another ride."

Filip bounded beside Jacek as they headed for the stables.

Filip's routine chores and lessons filled his days, just as Jacek's duties did. But in between, Jacek rode with the boy to get him used to the rhythm of the animal's gait and the control of the reins. Oftimes he maneuvered a lance or other weapon. Sometimes he drew and fired a bow. When Filip asked, Jacek demonstrated steering the horse with his knees, though it would be a long while before the boy's short legs had enough muscle and length to mimic the movements.

During their first outings, Filip had squealed so loudly Jacek had halted the lesson and admonished him. "A warrior may use a war cry, but there is no place for joyful shrieks when one is engaged in a battle that will either end his life or his opponent's. Consider also you may scare the wits out of your horse and find yourself at great disadvantage on your backside. Control is your greatest ally."

One morning, they stood together on the battlements, looking at the white-frosted land spreading before them to the horizon. The day was marked by a cold blue sky striped with frozen clouds. Jacek sat on a piece of stone warmed by the winter sun and invited Filip to do the same as he tossed him a wineskin and a wedge of cheese.

"Filip, do you pray? Outside of church?"

Filip opened and closed his mouth like a guppy.

"Perhaps not pray, then, but deep thought, where you focus on solely one thing."

Filip frowned while he nibbled the cheese.

Jacek rearranged his frame. "I'll show you, then do what I do."

He sat, back rigid, his hands relaxed on his thighs. Closing his eyes, he took long, measured breaths. A peek confirmed Filip imitated him, though he squirmed incessantly.

Jacek gave him a sidelong glance. "Have you changed your mind about becoming a great warrior?"

"No, sir. But I don't understand why this matters. A warrior moves and fights. He doesn't sit and … think."

THE HEART OF A HUSSAR

"Are you sure? Putting yourself in a state of deep thought is a way to train your mind, and training your mind is as important as training your body. An accomplished warrior does move and fight, but he must understand *when* to move, when to fight, when not to fight. He must be able to use this quickly," Jacek tapped Filip's temple with his finger, "and for that, he must increase his thinking speed. It could save his life or the life of someone he wishes to protect.

"A warrior observes, calculates, then makes a deliberate choice to take action, hold, or retreat. He recognizes when one action is wiser than another. *And* sharpened senses help him detect telltale signs of weakness in his opponent, so to exploit them."

"What if the opponent has no weaknesses?"

"Everyone does."

Filip cocked his head and drew his brows together. "What are yours?"

"I have none." Jacek chuckled. "When a conflict begins, there's no time for reflection. Do you remember how quickly everything happened during the ambush? One minute was calm, and the next chaos."

Filip nodded.

"Much as a hussar's horse has been trained to perform during a charge, and the hussar has trained his sword arm to deflect a blow, so he trains his mind to react—in half a heartbeat, without having to *stop* and think. Delay, and he—or someone he safeguards—could die."

Filip dug his finger into a crack between stone blocks. Now he looked up at Jacek again, doubt scrunching his face.

Jacek shrugged. "It's an exercise, a drill like any other."

The boy was quiet for a long moment.

"Now tomorrow, we start in earnest. I will awaken you before dawn so we can do this together."

Filip's face fell.

"Discipline, Filip. You can be the strongest warrior in the land, but it will not save your hide if you're undisciplined. A disciplined body and a disciplined mind."

Filip gave him a less-than-enthusiastic nod.

Swathed in fur, Oliwia braced herself against the swirling snow and took determined steps toward the garrison. As she made her way across the ward, a large blur approached in the blizzard, keeping a firm hold of a hat on its head.

Her name spiraled in the wind. "Oliwia?" Jacek was heading in the opposite direction. "What are you doing out here?"

"Visiting my brother," she yelled to be heard above the howling wind.

Jacek grabbed her elbow and turned her back toward the keep. "You shouldn't be out in this weather. Come. I'll walk you back, then I'll fetch your brother."

She waited in front of the hearth, replacing the body heat the short walk had stripped away. A few servants hustled here and there, sweeping floors, arranging fresh rushes, scrubbing soot from floors and walls. When at last two oddly sized bundles appeared, they wound toward her and unwrapped themselves from thick, cozy cloaks and dark-furred kolpaks. Oliwia looked her brother over and approved of what she saw. Though still scrawny, he continued filling out and growing taller. Another tooth was loose, and soon he would shed that one. His hair was styled in hussar fashion, the sides of his head shaven, leaving a mop of curls on top.

Oliwia reached to hug him. He pulled back and stood before her, as straight and tall as his frame allowed, feet splayed and hands clasped behind his back. She had seen the stance many times before, and she glanced at Jacek.

He gave her a sheepish smile. "Filip learns quickly."

She smirked. "I see that. What else has he learned?"

Old habits being what they were, Filip reverted to bouncing in place with excitement. He instantly stiffened when the lieutenant put a large paw on his shoulder.

"Filip, remember what you've learned and maintain control," Jacek rumbled.

Oliwia caught Jacek's eye, and he winked.

THE HEART OF A HUSSAR

"You may embrace your sister. Likely, she needs a hug from a strong warrior like you."

Oliwia felt a flush of gratitude and gave Jacek a brilliant smile. He nodded as she gathered her brother in her arms. Filip hugged her hard, and they held one another until he began to wriggle.

"Liwi! You can let go now."

"Yes, Filip. Now tell me everything you've learned."

Oliwia and Filip sat before the blazing hearth while Jacek excused himself and left.

"I have been practicing with the wooden sabre, and I've even sparred with Pan Henryk! I've used a dagger—Pan Jacek's dagger, the one he's had since he was a boy. He lets me handle it sometimes. He says someday I will have my own!"

She smiled at him indulgently.

"And, Liwi. There is something else." He grinned from ear to ear.

"What is that, Filip?"

"Do you have your sketching things?"

Oliwia reached into a pocket and pulled out a lead pencil and a square of paper, which she unfolded and handed to Filip. Rarely did she go anywhere without a piece of paper and a writing implement, luxuries supplied by Lady Katarzyna. She handed these to Filip, and he stood and made his way to a trestle table. Oliwia craned her neck, curious, and began to raise herself up.

"Stay there," he implored. So she did.

He plopped on a bench and picked up the pencil, applying it to the paper. From his motions, she could tell he was drawing lines and loops. His small pink tongue protruded from the side of his mouth, and his brow furrowed with concentration. When he was done, he grabbed two corners of the paper and walked toward her just as Jacek appeared with warm apple tarts. Filip handed her the paper. Her breath caught, and unexpected tears pricked her eyes. Raising a hand to her mouth, she stood up.

"Filip! When did you learn to write?" She was staring at a broad scrawl that spelled "Filip," and beneath it was "Liwi."

"Pan Jacek has been teaching me to write my name since I moved to the garrison, and he showed me how to write yours too. It was our secret, but he said I could show you. I can't write your whole name yet. Just 'Liwi' for now."

One less letter than his own name. She suppressed a chuckle.

She whirled toward Jacek, who stared at her intently. He fidgeted, dragging a hand through his hair before scratching the back of his neck.

"That's wonderful! Thank you!"

He smiled back, dropping his hand as he let out a breath. "My pleasure, my lady. As I said, he learns quickly. I was afraid you might be angry with us because you hoped to teach him yourself."

"No, this is much better!" she exclaimed. "I am still learning, and you mastered writing as a boy, so he is learning from someone much more experienced than I."

Jacek gave her a dip of his head.

"And, Liwi," Filip bounced again, "I'm learning Latin and math with the other boys!"

Jacek's smile gave way to his scowl. "Filip, remember what we agreed. You will remain still for Liwi."

Her eyes had been fastened on Filip, but the sound of her diminutive falling from Jacek's tongue jarred her. She quickly swung her gaze to him, and he did the most peculiar thing. He stammered.

"I, uh, I beg your pardon, Lady Oliwia. Your brother always calls you 'Liwi,' and I fear I've fallen into the habit when we speak of you—which is often. I meant no disrespect."

She smiled broadly. "I'm not offended, Lieutenant. Since you are my brother's teacher and you are caring for him now, you could be *my* brother. Therefore, I do not mind you calling me the familiar name."

Jacek's eyes flashed, and his mouth moved as if he meant to speak, but he stopped. He stiffened and glanced to the side. Oliwia felt a stab of remorse, though she wasn't sure for what. Jacek handed Filip a pastry and motioned him toward the table.

She peered into Jacek's narrowed deep blue eyes. "I … I'm sorry. Have I said something improper?"

He looked away quickly. "No, certainly not." He swung his piercing gaze squarely back to hers. "I am pleased to be forgiven and invited to address you informally. However, Filip is my page. I would not wish to confuse the arrangement by having him think of me as his brother. I will call you by your proper name, and I will teach him to do the same if you wish it." His tone was crisp.

Oliwia felt heat rising up her neck and hoped the blush didn't show on her cheeks. She shook her head.

"Oh no. It was discourteous of me to refer to you as my brother. Forgive me, my lord."

She followed this up with a quick curtsy, and he took a step back. She fisted her skirts, flustered by her failed attempts to correct her blunders. They only seemed to multiply.

"You've no need of formality where I'm concerned, Lady Oliwia. I will make you a bargain, however." A smile spread across his chiseled face, and his posture relaxed. "If I may call you 'Liwi' as the occasion suits, then you will not call me 'my lord' or 'lieutenant' at any time. 'Jacek' will do."

Still blushing, Oliwia looked up at the tall lieutenant and nodded. "Agreed. That is a fair bargain."

Jacek handed her a tart, and they joined Filip. "How were you able to get these wonderful tartlets?" she asked between fruit-filled mouthfuls. "I have not been able to persuade Beata to spare me even one all week."

Jacek chuckled. "She is protective of her soldiers and hides sweets for them." With a conspiratorial whisper, he leaned close to her ear. "A smile and a kind word got me three, but don't let her know I shared them with you, or she may never favor me again, and we'll both be the sorrier for it. From now on, when you want one, just let me know, and I will see you get it."

Oliwia laughed and thanked him, dispersing the last shred of awkwardness lingering between them. They sat companionably eating the pastries while the snow continued falling in fat flakes outside the keep walls.

One damp winter morning, as the watery sun dappled the practice field, a score of men worked their horses. These were impressive specimens, a combination of Polish and Arabian equine blood, specifically bred for the hussars and newly added to replenish the warhorses lost during the summer campaign.

Jacek had dismounted a sable stallion and stood to one side to observe the riders field-testing the horses. As he tied off the animal, Lesław trotted over to him. Jacek waited, hands clasped behind him. The horse beside him snorted, tossed its coal-black mane, and scuffed the ground with its front hoof.

"These are beauties, Jacek, yes?" Lesław turned when he reached Jacek, looking back at the field with a broad smile.

"Exceptional." Entranced, Jacek repeatedly scanned the animals before him.

Just then, a horse and rider broke into a swift gallop on the far side of the field, turned, and raced back along the drill tracks.

"Izaak!" Jacek hollered. "Keep a tighter grip on the reins if you expect him to do what you want."

Izaak's new horse had stomped all over the outer ring of the turning circle, but the standard bearer grinned in answer.

"Just wanted to see what he could do, Lieutenant," Izaak yelled back.

Filip sidled up beside Jacek as Lesław returned to the field.

"Good day, Lieutenant."

Jacek tousled his curls and immediately chided himself.

"Good day to you, Filip. What are you about?"

"I'm watching the men test the horses so I can learn what to do when it comes my turn," the boy replied confidently.

Jacek looked down at his charge and drew in a sharp breath. "What the devil happened to you?" He bent to examine the left side of Filip's face, which was wine-red and puffy. His left eye was swollen nearly shut.

"Uh, I fell in one of the stalls."

"How?" Jacek placed his fingers under Filip's chin and tilted his head to get a better look.

The boy winced. "I was not paying attention and tripped."

"It looks more like someone cuffed you. Did you fight with one of the stable lads?"

"No, sir, I fell."

Jacek stood up, unconvinced. "Tripped? Or fell? Well, if you were in a fight, I hope you gave as good as you got."

Filip stiffened and looked away. "Sir, I have been here nearly three seasons. When will I start my training on the horses?"

THE HEART OF A HUSSAR

Jacek regarded him for a moment, wondering at the suddenness with which he changed the subject. Nevertheless, there was the same question again. The boy had worked hard, and despite his occasional bursts of unchecked boisterousness, he strove to abide by the commands given him. Perhaps the time had come for his reward.

"Have you been on a horse by yourself yet?" Jacek was certain the boy's experience did not extend beyond the confines of the corral under Feliks's supervision.

Filip vigorously nodded his head. "Oh yes, sir. I've been riding with my sister."

Jacek had turned his attention toward Izaak on the practice field and kept his eyes fastened on him while he addressed Filip. "Your *sister?* And when did she begin to ride?"

"I tried to tell you, sir, that I had been on the draught horses already. Liwi started at the same time as I, not long after we came here. Lady Katarzyna told her a lady should know how to ride, so Pan Henryk has been teaching us," Filip said hurriedly, as if he were a burbling fountain eager to spew its showy sprays. "The horses are old and slow, though, and I would prefer to ride a warhorse—like Jarosława," he added exuberantly.

Jacek's head turned to Filip as if someone had grabbed it with both hands and twisted it. "Henryk has taken you and Oliwia out riding? How did I not know of this?"

Jacek thought he knew all the goings-on at the castle. If this were true, no wonder Oliwia had not lately mentioned her reluctance to let her brother ride—she was as duplicitous as Henryk, which begged a question. Why?

Ignoring Filip's complaint about his mount, Jacek stood dumbfounded—and slightly alarmed. Despite Lady Katarzyna's directive, he suspected Henryk had an ulterior motive behind keeping the lessons to himself. One that had little to do with teaching brother and sister how to ride. In fact, Jacek was sure his true purpose involved only one of the siblings—the pretty one. Jacek was seized by an irresistible urge to thump Henryk.

"We ride when you are away on patrols or meeting with Lord Eryk. Pan Henryk said it should be a surprise, and we weren't to tell you."

Jacek grunted vociferously. He would definitely thump Henryk. "Where does he take you?"

"Mostly to Liwi's favorite spot, down by the lake, on the other side of the wood. It's too cold now, but when we first started, it was warm, and we would swim sometimes. I liked that very much."

Heedless now of all activity on the practice field, Jacek bunched his eyebrows as he looked down at Filip.

"You swam? And what did you wear when you swam in?"

Filip gave him a confused look. "We swam in the lake, my lord."

Jacek rolled his eyes. "No, I mean what did you wear when you swam?"

"Nothing. We always left our clothes on the shore to keep them dry, my lord."

Filip shrugged his slight shoulders as if this were the most natural thing in the world, but Jacek did not think it a natural thing at all.

"*What?* Your sister wears nothing while she swims with you and Henryk?" he blurted.

Jacek's outrage began boiling over—a thumping would not be enough. He once again regretted not pummeling Henryk after the tournament feast. Unbidden, a vision of Oliwia wearing naught but water dripping off her body intruded on his thoughts, spiking his heat and pulse higher still. Though he'd not compared her to Ruta for an age, he still looked on her as something less than a woman, and the vivid image shocked him. He forcefully wrenched it from his mind's eye and stuffed it elsewhere.

Where the hell did that come from?

"Oh no, sir! We have not gone in a long while because it's been cold, but when we did, it was only when she was not with us. Just Pan Henryk and me. Why would we want a naked girl swimming with us? Yech!" Filip was the picture of indignation.

Relief flooded Jacek, and he used all his self-control to restrain the peals of laughter trying to escape him. He would, nevertheless, still thump Henryk.

"All right, Filip. Let's mount you up." Jacek smiled. "Perhaps you can show me this favorite place of your sister's. The first of our lessons—"

Before Jacek could finish his sentence, Filip was off, flying past the practice field toward the stables as quickly as his short legs would carry him.

Jacek called after him, "And make sure it's a draught horse. No warhorses for you." If he let Filip ride a warhorse and Oliwia learned of it, she would thump *him*—of that he was certain.

THE HEART OF A HUSSAR

Jacek followed, leading the stallion beside him. He stopped long enough to call out a few orders to Lesław after arriving at a split-second decision—a decision based on his enlightening exchange with Filip—and rooted in something far from logic.

"You're the field commander, Lesław."

Lesław appeared confused. "But Pan Henryk is the senior towarzysz."

"Not today."

What had Jacek been thinking? Of course Oliwia hadn't been swimming with Henryk unclothed! She would never behave so shamelessly. But Henryk, he would've tried to persuade her, honeyed words dripping off his tongue. Jacek ground his teeth thinking of the clandestine riding sessions and what Henryk hoped to gain. The idea riled him. But tucked behind that thought, nearly invisible to him, was another thought—a rather baffling one. His protectiveness toward her had taken on an altogether more robust, almost covetous quality.

Jacek tethered his careering thoughts, yet he struggled to untangle the jumble. He had spent weeks teaching Filip the necessity of keeping a clear mind—something he was incapable of mastering at the moment. As he walked the stallion the rest of the way to the stables, he blew out a great breath. Erasing the tantalizing image of Oliwia was proving harder than he'd thought.

CHAPTER 19

Campaign

The Lenten season had begun, and Jacek grew restless for news of the next mission. Where would it send him this time? What opportunities would it bring him? His answer came when Eryk called for him and Mateusz. Jacek entered the solar crisply, just ahead of his superior. Eryk sat behind his desk, waving a letter at them.

"Hetman Żółkiewski writes of a gathering Tatar army. They will head north and split into three groups, with one group headed to Podolia. The others are bound for Muscovy. Their force includes janissaries, which means they will carry artillery. Their presence means the Turks have ordered the assault. He's requesting our company join with his army at the southeastern border to repel the threat."

Mateusz settled into one of the carved chairs opposite Eryk's desk. "How does he know this?"

"He hires women spies. They learn much in the bedchamber." Eryk smiled wryly. "The hetman suspects the Turks are emboldened because they believe us preoccupied by our troubles with Muscovy."

Jacek twitched as he pondered the Ottoman Empire's insatiable appetite for light-skinned Christians. Their vassals, the Crimean Tatars, with no economy other than the slave trade, were only too eager to kidnap and sell men, women, and children into bondage. It had been the same for centuries. They devastated towns and villages in the Wild Fields—the steppe—with impunity, leaving no one to rebuild. Fields lay fallow. Settlers stayed away for fear of being enslaved like those before them. The Tatars had been so successful that they'd emptied the Wild Fields, leaving no one to snatch. Consequently, they penetrated farther into Commonwealth territory to capture their prizes.

Mateusz's voice brought Jacek back to the present. "Why not a company closer to Podolia, then?"

Eryk rose, motioning for them to remain seated, and ambled to a window that held the blowing snow at bay.

"The hetman and I have known one another a long time. There's a mutual trust, a mutual pledge to the other. It's one reason I answered the king's call to Muscovy last year, even though the Sejm hadn't approved his action. Hetman Żółkiewski called on me, and I went. Now he needs a larger presence, a show of strength, to reinforce the border against these leeches. Because they are mobile and quick, he seeks cavalry to counter them. And as the hetman so elegantly points out, I too have an estate at the border that may prove vulnerable."

Jacek felt a small jolt of excitement—excitement to be called upon once again. "When do we depart, my lord?" From the corner of his eye, he saw Mateusz yawn.

"We leave in a month," Eryk replied.

"Do we travel to Silnyród?" asked Mateusz.

Eryk shrugged as he looked out the window. "It depends on where the Tatars go. Those jackals are nothing if not elusive. They've taken to bypassing the cities and fortresses altogether, swarming settlements deeper in Commonwealth territory."

Jacek's fists clenched as he reflected upon Tatar tactics. They encircled a village in the dead of night and set it ablaze. When the terrified people poured from their homes, the devils captured them. All of them.

He rearranged himself in the chair, causing the leather seat to groan under his weight. His eyes fixed on the spellbinding snow beyond the window. "During the tournament last autumn, I heard the tale of one town where they found two hundred young children in burned fields, many dead from hunger, cold, or animals." The story had ignited a rage inside him; that familiar flame began flickering again.

Eryk sat forward, steepling his fingers. He glanced at the heavy bookshelves lining one wall. In the ensuing silence, Jacek's mind wandered to the fate of the children the Tatars *did* take. If they survived the grueling march south, they were robbed of their innocence and childhood in short order, boys and girls alike used to satisfy perverse pleasures.

No matter their country or beliefs, Jacek pitied any poor soul who became the Tatars' captive. Many were killed for sport. For every human who survived, four or five died along the way. Those who lived were marched to the northern coast of the Black Sea, to a city like Kaffa—the largest, most notorious slave market in the Crimean Khanate. They were sorted, marked, and branded like so much livestock. Some were shipped to Constantinople and ports beyond, while others languished in the dank dungeons of the fortress city until they were auctioned in a humiliating display.

Jacek surfaced from the abyss of his thoughts when Eryk cleared his throat.

"Jacek, I need an inventory of what we have and what we need."

"Yes, my lord. I will begin right away." Jacek began to rise, the leather under him creaking in relief.

"One more thing." Eryk's eyes flicked to Mateusz, and Jacek stilled.

"I will not be leading this campaign. I am placing you in charge, Mateusz, with Jacek as second while I remain here."

Jacek exchanged a bemused look with Mateusz.

"Is everything all right, my lord?" asked Jacek.

Eryk waved his hand as if impatient. "Yes, yes, fine. It's not so unusual anymore for a lord to stay behind and send his army in his stead, especially as the demands of his estate grow. This is one harvest I shall not miss. And I am sure you two are more than capable."

Mateusz gave him a head dip. "Yes, my lord. I will do well by you."

"See that you do." Eryk signaled his dismissal.

With a smart bow, Jacek departed the solar in Mateusz's wake. His emotions collided and exploded. *Second in command on campaign!* But realization struck him forcefully as he contemplated life on the road without Eryk: control would be under the brute Mateusz.

Jacek shook off the disturbing thought, resolving to take full advantage of the opportunity to acquit himself well in the eyes of the hetman.

THE HEART OF A HUSSAR

That evening, Jacek and Henryk sat in an antechamber adjoining the guardroom. As Henryk tipped a stoneware jug to the rim of his metal cup, Jacek leaned back in a wooden chair, his boots propped on a table.

"So we fight Tatars and janissaries in Podolia," Henryk declared.

Jacek took a sip from his own cup. "A wily cavalry that hates cannon and firearms, paired with a skillful infantry comfortable wielding them. Separately, they are accomplished adversaries. Together, formidable."

"So are we."

Jacek gave him a half smile. "That's why Hetman Żółkiewski requested Biaska's presence at the border, and Lord Eryk could not deny him." He raised his cup. *"Amor patriae nostra lex."*

"Speaking of sly adversaries, have you uncovered aught of the treachery at the tournament?"

Jacek shook his head. "I know who did it, but I've no way to prove it."

"No justice, then." Henryk's chair screeched as he scraped it across the floor.

"Marcin did thump the lad who stocked the lances, though there's no way of telling if the lad was responsible in the first place."

"So what do you do, then?"

Jacek humphed and scratched his cheek. "There's not much to do, is there? If I accuse the guilty party of damaging my gear, it will not go well for me."

"And what of Marcin? Did you thrash him?"

Jacek smirked. "I devised a more fitting punishment. He's had to spar with me. It's been far more satisfying."

With a chuckle, Henryk clinked his cup against Jacek's.

March brought more frigid weather, and with it came the departure of the Biaska chorągiew. Having bid Henryk farewell, Oliwia stood beside her unusually subdued brother in the castle yard as Jacek approached. The lieutenant was dressed in his husaria regalia, from his yellow leather boots to his fur kolpak. Lord Eryk, she'd been told, had ordered the company to display their finest, and Jacek did not disappoint. Over crimson padded żupan topped with armor, he wore his leopard skin, powder horn, and black cartridge box embellished in burnished brass.

Oliwia surreptitiously studied his armor, every piece a work of art. Jacek's breastplate consisted of a solid steel piece with five scalloped lames at the bottom, each adorned with brass rosettes. Two ornate brass emblems—one a knight's cross and the other a raised emblem of Our Lady of the Immaculate Conception—were affixed over each breast. Over top was a gorget, similarly adorned, together with a smaller but no less intricate knight's cross. Completing the armor were gilded pauldrons and arm iron, or *karwasze*.

Grasping two cuffed brown leather gloves in one hand, Jacek bent his head to Filip, his lips moving, his words inaudible. When Jacek brought himself up, he pinned twinkling eyes on Oliwia. Her heart tripped, causing her to look about self-consciously. She gripped her skirts. He gave her a dip of his head.

Amid the clamor of the departing soldiers, he leaned down to her. Surprised, she was unable to take a step back without bumping someone behind her, so she remained wedged where she was. He whispered in her ear, his warm breath caressing her cheek.

"I have arranged for Kasimir to watch over you and your brother during my absence. Should you need or want for anything, you need only ask. I have also ordered Filip to visit you often. I told him you will need his care."

He pulled away and glanced at the forlorn Filip, then chucked him under the chin. "I trust you will carry out your duties while I am away, Filip."

"Yes, sir. I shall." Filip kept his head down and scuffed his shoes in the dirt.

Oliwia gave Jacek a warm smile. "Thank you, Jacek."

"Of course, Liwi. Take good care of yourself."

"May God keep you and protect you, Jacek."

"And you as well." With a small smile and a quick nod, he turned on his heel toward the clog of mounting soldiers.

"Godspeed," she called as he strode toward his big bay.

THE HEART OF A HUSSAR

Filip beside her, Oliwia retreated to the ramparts. The column of glorious red-clad lancers snaked their way over the rise and into the pine stands beyond. Leading them were Mateusz and Izaak, followed by Jacek and Henryk. The chorąży held an enormous red banner emblazoned with a yellow knight's cross. Behind the column were the pacholiks in blue, servants, spare horses, and wagons. The sound of crunching snow beneath horse and wagon reported the company's departure as they traversed frozen ground blanketed in a thick white layer. Oliwia said a silent prayer and crossed herself. Jacek and Henryk grew smaller until they had disappeared from sight, swallowed by the woods. How quiet and empty the castle would be. Unexpected tears stung her eyes.

The company headed south toward Kraków before turning southeast. Fields had transformed into expanses of white crust broken up by clusters of gray-and-brown leafless trees standing like stark sentinels. The trees were at times silhouetted by pale blue skies, and at others, they blended into a gray backdrop. Even the evergreen forests appeared dull and lifeless, and little moved within them, lending them an otherworldly silence.

The crunch of wagon wheels and horse hooves upon layers of snow and ice echoed as they plodded, and Jacek was grateful. Had they left with the thaw, the wagons would have become mired in the rutted, boggy ground and slowed their progress further. Despite the bitter cold, the frozen landscape proved advantageous.

Weeks into their journey, they arrived on the outskirts of Tarnopol on the Seret River. Under a low lid of ominous clouds, they waited on horseback as a contingent from Tarnopol Castle rode out to meet them.

Stationed behind Mateusz and alongside Jacek, Izaak adjusted his grip on the banner. "Lieutenant, have you been here before?"

"No, although I have heard much of it. It belongs to the Ostrogski family, and like many of the fortifications along the border, the Turks and Tatars have attacked it repeatedly. When I was but one, it was badly damaged. I believe they are still rebuilding."

Six men-at-arms and the bailiff of Tarnopol Castle reached them and reined in their horses. The bailiff, a strapping, dark-haired man with an impressive moustache and girth, welcomed them with excessive graciousness, inviting them to encamp within sight of the castle. He insisted Mateusz and the senior towarzysze billet in the castle itself. The bailiff's fawning gave Jacek pause. What ulterior motives did the man have?

It was as the hussars partook of the banquet prepared in their honor that Jacek learned the official fretted the imminent fair weather would bring with it more Tatars. Jacek sat beside Mateusz, privy to conversation between his superior and town officials. The castle and its undermanned garrison, the bailiff explained, could not withstand another attack, even from a small raiding party.

The bailiff gave Mateusz a slippery smile. "We will gladly house you and your company here, Captain Zalewski, through the end of summer or longer, if you wish. And we will provide whatever your men need. We will, of course, compensate you for your trouble." He beckoned a lovely serving girl to refill Jacek's wine glass, even though he had already declined.

Mateusz was distracted by another pretty maid, so Jacek replied for him. "You are very generous, sir. However, we are to report to a staging area west of Kamieniec within the week."

"Bah!" Mateusz set down his empty cup and wrapped his arms around the girl, tugging her onto his lap. "Certainly, we can linger a few extra days. It would be impolite to refuse the bailiff's hospitality." His eyes roamed over the giggling girl.

Jacek bit the inside of his cheek.

The bailiff chuckled and waved a hand at Jacek. "Kamieniec is well protected by its impenetrable fortress and has always withstood attacks from those odious Turks and Tatar jackals. After all, the city is the 'First wall of Christianity,' and its fortress is far too robust to be overrun. We, however, are in need of a strong force of winged hussars."

"No doubt Field Hetman Żółkiewski shares your opinion with regard to his own force, which of course explains why he expects us to report as agreed," Jacek said mildly.

Mateusz darted his eyes to Jacek.

The bailiff erupted in a laugh and slapped a palm on the linen-draped table. "Your lieutenant is dedicated, eh, Captain? A good man to have, no doubt." He leveled his eyes at Jacek. "Our residents are anxious,

THE HEART OF A HUSSAR

Lieutenant. I only have their best interests at heart." With a snap of his fingers, three more maids, prettier than the last one, appeared at Jacek's side while two more flitted to Mateusz. Jacek suppressed an exasperated sigh.

The bailiff was nothing if not persistent, employing every form of bribery at his disposal, and the hussars lingered longer than planned. Jacek abandoned his rich quarters and encamped with the men—someone had to be in charge, and Mateusz had scarcely been seen in days. Though the company was treated like royalty in a near-festival atmosphere, they grew anxious to reach their objective.

Henryk stuck his head into Jacek's tent one morning. "Have you received word of our departure yet?"

Jacek looked up from sharpening his dagger. "Not yet. I've sent the captain several messages without a reply." Then Jacek smirked. "Bored already, Henryk?"

Henryk laughed. "Tarnopol offers very enchanting distractions to be sure—not that you would know—but I feel as though we are Odysseus and his crew stuck on Aeaea. We cannot dawdle here forever."

"Are you Odysseus or one of the pigs?"

"Jacek, you are droll. I expected to find you gnashing your teeth over our delay. But here you sit, making jokes while calmly grinding your blade. It's no doubt so sharp you could shave the hair off your arms by now."

"No doubt. It does little good to gnash so long as Mateusz is afloat in wine and women. While I'm frustrated beyond measure, I am enjoying the respite from his spitefulness. Perhaps I would have more success dislodging him if I sent him a message that Lady Barbara has arrived."

"And is anxious to meet the harem," Henryk chortled, then stepped aside. "Ah, a messenger at last."

A blond man wheezed in the tent opening with a note in his hand. "Lieutenant Dąbrowski?"

"Yes." Jacek stood and reached for the note. His eyebrows shot up as he read, and he looked back at the messenger.

"I am to await your reply, m'lord," the man said.

Jacek stared at Henryk. "It appears we are moving out immediately. Without the captain."

The townspeople of Tarnopol provisioned the banner lavishly, and raucous farewells accompanied the men as they withdrew. The captain, together with a small group of towarzysze he counted as friends, was nowhere to be found. Buoyed by his newfound freedom and the opportunity to lead, Jacek resolved to rule the company as Lord Eryk would.

To that end, he availed himself of Father Augustyn's pious preaching. Reminders that God was ever-vigilant, together with the strict codes of behavior he enacted, facilitated Jacek's control over the conduct so critical to his command. He would direct the company at least as well as his lord. So when a knot of women followed them, Jacek personally sent them fleeing, some of them weeping at his unkind treatment. His mission accomplished, he drew alongside Henryk, who shook his head. The men guided their horses side by side at a walking pace. Today, Jacek rode his gelding, Gwiazda.

They traveled across open, flat ground fuzzed pale green, flanked on each side by dense evergreen forests. Stands of beech, ash, and elm were tipped with promising buds bursting to unfurl. The ground, muddy and springy with the thaw, made the going slow.

Henryk stared ahead, then gave Jacek a sidelong glance. "Tell me something, Jacek."

Jacek looked to the heavens. Wisps of clouds raced overhead, and a chill wind tugged at his kolpak. He grunted in Henryk's direction.

"You chased off that lot following us," Henryk drawled. "All those pretty maids at Tarnopol, and all you did was growl at them. You still *like* women, don't you? I mean, you have been a soldier a long while now, and maybe your fancies lie elsewhere."

Jacek scoffed. "Of course I do! Like women, that is. But a chance like this may never come again. I'm in charge for a short time, and I shall deliver our company to Hetman Żółkiewski just as Lord Eryk would have done: in disciplined, prideful fashion. It has naught to do with what I think of women. That hasn't changed. As for those women," Jacek jerked his head toward the rear guard, now devoid of any female person, "I don't like lying with whores. For that matter, I do not wish to be with women I don't find desirable. Or women I don't know well enough to know whether they're desirable in the first place."

"You make no sense." Henryk's brows furrowed. "And what have you got against whores?"

Jacek stood in his stirrups, stretching his legs. Gwiazda nickered with the shift.

"I cannot help wondering how many have been there before me ... that night, that hour even."

"Forget whores, then. You still make no sense. A pretty woman is a pretty woman. You don't have to talk to her to recognize that. In fact, the less she talks, the more appealing she is." Henryk grinned at this. Jacek merely grunted.

Henryk's face brightened. "Ah! You've grown partial to one in particular, yes? The Lady Barbara! And you're trying to preserve her honor—and your hide. Is that it?"

"Certainly not!" Jacek replied hotly, wincing inwardly at his own duplicitous indignation. While he'd never slept with Lady Barbara, he had been in many a married woman's bed without remorse.

"Then tell me one woman of your acquaintance you *would* bed. One you know well enough to find desirable, that is. Or whatever the hell your measure is now."

The mysterious woman from Jacek's dream chose that instant to appear in his mind, and his heart unexpectedly tripped. "There is no one."

"Is this because Izabela is now wed? You fancied her more than the others."

"Perhaps a long time ago. I don't enjoy her company as I once did."

Henryk chuckled. "Well, it appeared you were enjoying her company immensely while she was at Biaska."

Jacek ignored a sudden stitch of guilt. He shrugged. "She's an old friend, and she was about to be tied to a fat, aged man and a pack of children the rest of her life. I felt sorry for her."

Henryk snorted. "Ah. So you slept with her out of the kindness of your heart. That's as good an excuse as any, I suppose."

The pang of guilt—a heretofore foreign feeling for Jacek—ignited into irritation. He spurred Gwiazda away from Henryk.

"Hey! Where are you going?" Henryk hollered.

"To check the vanguard," Jacek called over his shoulder, dismissing the look of utter astonishment on Henryk's face.

CHAPTER 20

Border

The company neared its destination three days after departing Tarnopol. Five armed men approached from the south, riding hard. One held a three-tailed, rippling red-and-white banner of the Commonwealth. Dressed in mail, all were recognizable as towarzysze pancerni—medium cavalry. Six hussars from the Biaska banner, equally well armed, rode forward to intercept them.

Jacek sat rigidly on Gwiazda, szabla partly unsheathed. Clouds skittered in disarray across a gray sky, driven by a stiff wind that ruffled yellow grasses. Beside him, Izaak gripped the Biaska banner; it whipped and flailed as if in protest to its rough handling. One of the Biaska contingent turned and rode back, leaving those behind him pointing and gesticulating toward the west. Jacek eased in his saddle when his man pulled alongside.

"Commander, they are scouts garrisoned at Kamieniec-Podolski Castle." He jerked his chin toward the small knot of men. "They say a large force is advancing northwest, seemingly bypassing Kamieniec. The enemy objective is yet unknown, but there are many rich fortresses to choose from: Rykhta, Czarnokozińcach, Skała, Żwańcem, Twierdza. The hetman wished to divert us before we reach the encampment at Kamieniec."

Jacek's brows knitted together. "Does he intend confronting the enemy?"

"Not yet. He says they need a larger force. The Kamieniec scouts can better explain."

Jacek's saddle creaked as he swiveled his frame, scanning the company and the terrain surrounding it. They were on a flat piece of ground. Thickets of woods rose to the east of them on Jacek's left, and open ground spread to the south and west. Behind him was a low hill the front line had just traversed. The majority of the company, its baggage, and personnel waited just beyond.

Jacek motioned with his leather budzygan. At the signal, officers sifted through the ranks, breaking into a detachment that ringed him in a semicircle. Horses champed bits, flicked tails, and stamped from hoof to hoof as their riders sat, waiting patiently for the Kamieniec scouts.

The scouts, five in all, were Lithuanians. Their leader, a rugged man with trailing tawny moustaches, presented himself and his fellow scouts, along with a sealed missive. Jacek removed a glove and stuffed it in his mouth while he ripped the message open with his finger. He scanned it quickly.

"We no longer make for Kamieniec. We've been ordered to trail the enemy instead."

The scout leader briefed the hussars, confirming the report of a large Tatar force, with janissaries among them, traveling light and swift. Numbering nearly four thousand, they covered a lot of ground. Among the most vulnerable villages and fortresses lay Twierzda, with a sparse garrison of roughly one hundred.

"Tell me about Twierzda," Jacek said.

"It lies fifteen miles west of Kamieniec. The castle sits atop a ridge above the Zbrucz. The river divides the stronghold from the village on the eastern bank, and a bridge connects the two. The villagers have been warned to take refuge within the fortress walls, but the Tatars weakened the castle's defenses two years ago. Its repairs are still mostly wood."

"What advantage does taking Twierzda offer?"

The leader took a deep breath. "Besides its susceptibility, it occupies high ground, an excellent vantage point and foothold to strike the other strongholds. They can control the confluence of the Zbrucz and the Dniester."

"Then we'll have to stop them. What of the other forces arriving at Kamieniec?"

THE HEART OF A HUSSAR

"A small number of dragoons, infantry, and musketeers are presently encamped. Several bigger estates are sending more troops, though we're unsure when they will arrive. We've two guns thus far. If you've scouts you are ready to put to use now, they can accompany my men. Then you can evaluate for yourselves the enemy's strength, as well as the terrain."

Wind relentlessly buffeted the few tents they erected. It was long past dark when men filtered into Jacek's tent—a round, modest affair of white canvas with a conical roof. By ones and twos, they sat, stood, or perched, crowding the war council as they listened to the newly returned scouts' reports. One scout held up a crude map to orient the others. When they were done, Jacek summarized, pacing the confined space.

"A force numbering nearly *five thousand*. Besides wagons and catapults, the janissaries carry six guns. They skirted Nagórzany and left the village intact. It appears they plan to dig in quickly and besiege Twierzda before we've enough men to counter them."

Jacek paused, raked a hand through his hair, and scanned the faces lit by candlelight. "Has anyone anything to add?"

A murmur ran through the men, and they parted as a messenger entered the tent with a missive. After Jacek read it, he glanced around the room.

Henryk spoke up first. "What is our plan?"

"We head to Nagórzany first thing tomorrow. Hetman Żółkiewski has ordered us to set up camp north of there, between the village and Rykhta," Jacek announced.

"What about striking the enemy now, Lieutenant, *before* they become entrenched?" a voice hollered from the back.

"Just our company? Even including attendants, ours is a small force against five thousand. Furthermore, an attack is an outright disregard of the hetman's order. Is this what you propose, Dawid?"

"Pah!" another hussar spat. "Better odds than Kłuszyn. We could beat those jackals and send them to the devil, Lieutenant."

Jacek ignored the comment. "Lesław, gather a score and escort the messenger to Kamieniec at first light. I will pen a message to the hetman.

I want you to survey their encampment and speak with the quartermaster if you can. I want a report of their resources—troops, artillery, supplies."

Then he turned to a handful of scouts. "You will head to Twierzda. Get as close as you can and report back on the terrain and the enemy's movements. Find out the condition of the bridge. I want to know everything you can possibly discover."

"You," he said to another set of scouts. "Find their supply lines. Check for more troops. I don't want to follow these bastards and find out too late another army is behind us, ready to spring a trap."

In a strident voice, he said, "We're vastly outnumbered, so stay out of sight and do not engage unless absolutely necessary. Understood?"

A chorus of "yes, sirs" sounded, and the men departed the tent, leaving Henryk and Jacek alone. Jacek glanced at his second.

"So? What do you think?"

"I think I'd like to destroy them now before they get breastworks and palisades built and we can't charge them at all," Henryk replied in a bland tone.

"If we were five companies strong, I would agree with you. Those odds would be in our favor, but we would still be defying the hetman's orders. What do you propose?"

"I propose following orders, of course. As much as I would like to attack the sons of bitches now, we are too few, and we run the risk of becoming cannon fodder."

Jacek nodded. "We'll see what the morning brings."

"When is the captain scheduled to rejoin us?"

Jacek put his hands on his hips and blew out a breath. "In a few days. It won't take him long to catch us up in Nagórzany."

"Just when things were going so smoothly."

Within days of their encampment in the fields north of Nagórzany, Jacek was visited by Crown Field Hetman Stanisław Żółkiewski himself. The supreme commander rode into the hussars' camp without fanfare.

THE HEART OF A HUSSAR

A soldier in his sixties, Żółkiewski had intelligent brown eyes set in a weathered, kingly face beneath gray-white eyebrows matching his beard and moustache. Jacek, like so many other students of military strategy, was familiar with the hetman's tactics. The fact that Żółkiewski began his career not as a military man but in diplomatic service had always intrigued Jacek. Perhaps it explained why Żółkiewski was an accomplished statesman as well as a great hetman.

Now, as he greeted the hetman and showed him and his entourage to his tent, Jacek found himself uncommonly awestruck. Despite rounded shoulders and a limp, Żółkiewski's presence was formidable. Jacek masked his nervousness, as well as his delight that Żółkiewski recognized him.

"Well met, Pan Dąbrowski." Żółkiewski lowered himself into a folding chair. "Are you now in command of this unit?"

"Promoted to lieutenant, sir, and only temporarily in charge while our captain is indisposed," Jacek replied crisply.

"Lord Krezowski is no fool. You are an accomplished soldier, and I see a bright future for you. I am glad to see you promoted after Kłuszyn."

Jacek bit back the urge to whoop, thanking him instead, then held his tongue.

The hetman suddenly looked aged. "I'm bound for Muscovy, Lieutenant. The siege at Smoleńsk continues, and the outlook in Moscow is no longer favorable. Our garrison has recently been forced to take refuge in the Kremlin. Before I depart, I wished to greet you personally and introduce you to your commander during my absence." Żółkiewski's eyes fell on a pale, flabby-faced man who stepped forward.

"May I present Michal Sosnowski, the deputy *starosta* for Kamieniec. He's in charge of security while Pan Potocki remains at Smoleńsk."

Jacek scrutinized him as they exchanged pleasantries. Younger than Żółkiewski, Sosnowski had the look of a man used to feasting at a lord's table rather than one hardened by battle. Though not a hussar, Sosnowski was bedecked in metal cladding of the richest variety: karacena armor, resembling a dragon's thickly scaled hide. A large lion pelt, with its enormous maned head still attached, draped over his back plate. The ferocious combination of scale and pelt did little to counter the deputy's foppish appearance. With his nose in the air as if he were stanching a bleed,

Sosnowki sat beside Żółkiewski while Jacek and the assembled men remained on their feet.

Żółkiewski gave the deputy a sidelong glance before resting his gaze on each man in turn. "Let us deliberate how we will eradicate these sons of devils marching across our land as though it were their own."

During a pause in the war council, Jacek smoothed the hair at his nape. "Hetman Żółkiewski, I wonder if we yet know what we face. The army we see might be a spear tip for what's coming, a diversion to pull us *away* from another target."

Deputy Sosnowski looked at Jacek through half-lidded eyes, as if bored. Jacek expected him to yawn momentarily. Żółkiewski cast his gaze to the rug beneath his feet while repositioning his leg.

"Excellent point, Lieutenant, and one you share with my *pułkownik*, Klemens Matejko." The hetman nodded toward a dark-bearded, stocky man in his mid-thirties who gave Jacek a head dip.

"He is also the *strażnik*, in charge of scouting and troop movement. To date, our patrols have confirmed what our spies told us: this is one portion of a larger army. The remainder travels toward Muscovy. Nothing our scouts have observed forewarns reinforcement. Your scouts, Pan Dąbrowski, have not uncovered any other raiders, yes?"

"Correct, sir."

Żółkiewski paused a beat or two. "Henceforth, Pan Dąbrowski, you will coordinate your scouts with Pan Matejko."

"Yes, Field Hetman," Jacek replied.

Żółkiewski slapped his thigh. "Good. I leave you both to the details."

When the hetman stood to leave, he embraced Jacek warmly. "Lieutenant, if you ever grow bored of your soft life on the western border, you are welcome to join my army. I always have need of first-rate officers. God be with you and your men."

And with that, Żółkiewski exited the tent, Sosnowski close on his heels. Jacek bit back the grin threatening to split his face.

THE HEART OF A HUSSAR

A day following the hetman's visit, Jacek tracked infantrymen and camp servants digging into cold, compressed ground, their steaming breaths visible as they carved out entrenchments and built fortifications under the quartermaster's direction.

Mounted on Gwiazda, he surveyed the camp in all directions. Movement on the horizon caught his eye, and he focused on it just as a guard heralded approaching riders. The riders came into view, and Jacek recognized the unmistakable bearing of the man in front. Cursing under his breath, he rode out to meet Mateusz and his retinue.

"Captain," he called as he drew near.

Mateusz reined in his horse and surveyed the camp. "Well, Dąbrowski, I see there's still a lot of work to be done here. I've arrived none too soon."

Jacek looked over his shoulder to where Mateusz's gaze rested. "What seems to be the trouble, sir?"

With a smirk, Mateusz pointed toward dirt mounds skirting the camp. "What do you call those? They'll barely stop a scurry of squirrels, let alone Tatar cavalry." Mateusz then turned a piercing glare on Jacek. "Your incompetence is evident in that pathetic array you call a fortification. My trust was obviously misplaced."

It's good to see you as well, Jacek thought wryly.

Just then, another soldier drew abreast of the two officers. Jacek backed his horse to allow the other rider to pull up.

"Colonel Matejko, allow me to present my superior, Captain Zalewski." Jacek swept his hand between the two. "Captain Zalewski, Colonel Matejko and the quartermaster designed the fortifications and have spent the better part of the day overseeing the work."

Jacek glimpsed Mateusz flinch before the captain recovered himself and cleared his throat. "My compliments, Colonel Matejko. I was just telling my lieutenant what a well thought-out plan you have. It appears to be coming along splendidly."

"Thanks in no small part to your squad, Captain." Matejko nodded toward Jacek. "Lieutenant, they could use your help at the northwest quadrant." Then to Mateusz, he said, "You don't mind my commandeering your second, do you, Captain? I'm sure you're anxious for his briefing, but I will not detain him long."

"Of course not," Mateusz blustered. As Jacek rode away, Mateusz hollered after him. "Dąbrowski, report to me in …" His voice trailed off, then picked up volume again, as if he'd remembered himself. "One hour."

"Yes, sir," Jacek hollered back, then released a huge breath.

Like the Dniester's tributaries, one day spilled into the next, bringing more troops to the Commonwealth camp. The husaria's numbers grew with the arrival of two companies totaling three hundred and twenty, and no additional hostile forces were spotted. The enemy had journeyed past Twierzda, scattering small raiding parties who decimated villages and captured slaves. Commonwealth troops at times thwarted the devils' plundering. At other times, the enemy disappeared like mist, taking their ill-fated prisoners with them to be marched south, lost forever.

After setting up a sprawling encampment, Mateusz held perfunctory meetings with other commanders, usually without Jacek in attendance. In un-hussar-like fashion, Mateusz shared no plans with his company. He did, however, hand off all scouting directives to Jacek and ordered him to lead most daily patrols himself.

The captain enjoyed a robust social life in his lavish camp and village taverns. All the while, the hussars waited. They waited for more troops to join them; they waited for armaments to arrive; they waited for their force to swell so they could attack. Nerves that were keen when the men first reached their destination became jumpy, and a routine of uneasy restlessness took hold. Jacek rotated scouts to give the men a change of scenery, a gallop on their horses, and something useful to do.

One late afternoon brought Stefan to Jacek's tent, fresh from a patrol.

Jacek motioned for him to enter. "What news today? Any more raiding parties?"

Stefan took a moment and caught his breath. "No, Lieutenant, but the bastards appear to be turning back toward Twierzda."

Jacek's eyes widened. "The devil, you say!"

Stefan nodded earnestly. "We watched them for hours. A detachment made for the village."

THE HEART OF A HUSSAR

"Mary, Mother of God! Then Twierzda *is* the target. Are the villagers safely away?"

"I believe so. I left some of our number behind, and we'll soon know more."

Jacek grasped his shoulder. "Well done. Let me know as soon as the rest of your party returns. I will inform the captain. Maybe we've a chance to block them."

The observation team returned and confirmed Stefan's report, but no word came to stop the enemy's advance. Within days, the Tatar army was digging in on the banks of the Zbrucz, appropriating Twierzda's abandoned huts and cottages with impunity. The move vexed Jacek and his men mightily. They were eager to engage the enemy, to strike before they could wreak devastation on the fortress and the people safeguarded within. Itching to deliver a blow before the enemy could wholly fortify itself, Jacek could do little save keep himself and his men sharp while they awaited orders to engage.

Extended days of boredom over top of agitation would eventually lead to an erosion of discipline. Jacek had watched it happen in other camps when soldiers drank too much and fought one another. Following Mateusz's example, half the men drifted to the camp followers and the village, while the other half abided by the lieutenant's edicts—Lord Eryk's edicts.

Besides doubling sentries and escorts for the camp builders collecting raw materials for fortifications, Jacek ratcheted up practices and drills. Where he could, he sparred shoulder to shoulder, boot toe to boot toe, hand to hand, with each of the men. Day after day, he swung his szabla and nadziak as he worked and sweated among them to keep his skills at their peak. But he also subjected himself to the rigor so he might sleep at night. Time spent alone in stillness only invited endless thoughts of what could go wrong.

Every so often, wedged between those worries, Jacek's mind took an incongruous meander to Filip and Oliwia. One night, as he lay on his back, drumming his fingers on his chest, he found himself thinking of them. Certain the boy was fine, Jacek spent little time deliberating him. But he lingered on the girl, wondering if she had grown accustomed to ladyship, to her new religion, to Poland, and if she'd shed some of her gawkiness.

Memories of her conviviality and liveliness warmed him, and he smiled to himself.

Like a bolt of lightning, another thought struck him: without him there to chase the lads away, she was bound to be subjected to an inordinate amount of attention—her fair looks easily erased her awkwardness. What was the likelihood she met a boy whose advances she welcomed? The thought rankled. He had to trust Kasimir would remain vigilant and carry out his orders in his stead.

CHAPTER 21

Emergence

Oliwia hurled herself down the interminable passageway to her lady's sitting room, panting as she went. She'd spent so much time wheedling the recalcitrant Beata into accepting her direction that she was now late. As she ran, she considered the old cook, the frustrating contradiction Oliwia had yet to solve. That Beata adored Lady Katarzyna was clear. Equally obvious was the kindness she bestowed on any soldier who came to her kitchen. But Oliwia was no soldier and hardly a lady herself, and consequently, no matter the layers of sweetness applied, she suffered Beata's thinly disguised derision.

As Oliwia skidded around a corner, mentally spurning the thought of asking the lady to intervene on her behalf, she tripped over a warped board and came down with a hard *whomp!* In a spectacular tumble, she lost all the air in her lungs, smacked her chin on the rough wood, and tore the hem of her petticoat. Gasping, she pulled herself up on her elbows and let out a long, low roar. She smacked her fist against the offending floor, abrading her hand in the process. A door opened, spilling daylight into the passageway and illuminating Oliwia's humiliating sprawl.

"Oh!" came a squeak, then a trill. "I should have known! That racket could only come from a clumsy cow like you, Oliwia." Lady Barbara looked down on her, snickering.

Of all people! Beauty and grace in one malevolent package, bearing witness to Oliwia's mortification.

Barbara was joined by Lady Katarzyna in the doorway, who rushed to Oliwia's side. "Oliwia, are you all right? Barbara! Stop laughing and help me get her up."

Lady Barbara's shoulders shook with mirth, but she made no other movement. Oliwia scrambled to her feet, her chest heaving. "Thank you, my lady, but I've no need of aid."

Lady Katarzyna caught Oliwia's elbow and guided her into the room, looking her up and down in alarm. "Merciful God, Oliwia! Your chin! Your gown! Sit down!" Over her shoulder, she called, "Barbara, get Oliwia a cup of wine, if you please."

Barbara sighed. "Really, Pani Katarzyna, you spoil this oaf of a girl, teaching her music and languages." As she shoved a partially filled cup into Oliwia's hand, her glinting brown eyes roved over her with disdain. To Katarzyna, she said, "It's time I take my leave."

Katarzyna applied a wet cloth to Oliwia's chin, ignoring Barbara.

"How many times have I told you, proper ladies do not run?" Katarzyna chided quietly. "Especially pell-mell through a castle, for heaven's sake!"

Barbara made to leave. "Best save your efforts, Lady Katarzyna. You'll never make a lady out of *that* sow."

When they were alone, Katarzyna tucked a wayward curl behind Oliwia's ear. "Never mind her. She's jealous of all beautiful young women."

Oliwia felt herself flush and let out a small sound that was part-hiccup, part-giggle. Katarzyna examined Oliwia's chin one last time, then bobbed her head in satisfaction. "I suppose we need to work a little harder on your poise, my dear. But we will leave it for tomorrow, yes? Today, we will practice your reading and languages. You will read a poem in Polish and translate into Italian, hmm? Or would you prefer French?"

Oliwia brightened, quickly forgetting her bruised chin and her bruised pride. She had worked diligently on her Polish letters, and Katarzyna had introduced Italian. Oliwia relished the lessons.

"There now! Look how that's cheered you up." Katarzyna smiled as she stepped to a small stack of books on a writing desk. "You remind me of myself when I was younger. I so longed to explore the magnificent places only books could take me that I harangued my father mercilessly until he hired a tutor who stayed at Reczyn until my wedding day. I was an unusual girl in that regard, I suppose, but I'm fortunate I had doting parents who indulged me."

Katarzyna rummaged through the books. "You've a quick mind that grasps ideas with keen energy. Why, even Lord Eryk is impressed by your progress."

Oliwia's eyes widened just as Katarzyna looked up at her. "Well, don't look so surprised! The lord keeps himself apprised of what his wards are up to."

"Wards, my lady?" Oliwia could not quell her astonishment.

"Yes, of course. He is your guardian now and has taken charge of your futures. Surely you understood this at the outset?"

Oliwia hadn't—not the full impact of it anyway. But now, as realization sank into her belly, it spread warm gratitude through her.

Oliwia had felt the shift in the castle's rhythm during the warriors' absence. The underlying current was more sluggish, more serene, like the flow of an indolent river that had begun as a turbulent, silty stream. Meals and dances had lost their liveliness. She missed the quicker tempo and the soldiers who breathed life into Biaska, and most especially she missed the lieutenant's presence. When she thought of him, she pictured him with the rare smile rather than his common scowl. While her new world continuously unfurled like a giant blossom around her, she often prayed for his—and the company's—safe return.

One morning, long after the company had left for Podolia, Oliwia sat, shoulders hunched as she haltingly read a Latin passage from the Bible.

Katarzyna stood before the fire in her chemise. "Come, Nadia. Hurry!"

The young maid scuttled in quick rabbit steps toward her mistress, a heavy load of gold satin and velvet heaped over her spindly arms.

"Yes, m'lady."

The lady's impatience signaled she was having a good day, and Oliwia breathed a sigh of relief. On her bad days, she stood listlessly and shivered until she was fully dressed, or she did not get out of bed at all. But today, she bounced on the balls of her slippered feet, her arms wrapped around her bony torso.

This morning was little different than any other the past month—Nadia tending to her mistress while Oliwia read or listened to Katarzyna's chatter. Today, the lady was eager to begin her day and eager to hear the end of the verse. When Oliwia finished reading, she closed the book and stood to help Nadia.

"Oliwia," said Katarzyna firmly, "you will try the harp again today."

Oliwia's hands stilled for a moment, then resumed smoothing the lady's gown. She glanced at the towering instrument in the alcove, its golden head and taut strings malevolent as it stood regally, mocking her. She hated it.

"Yes, my lady."

"Last time, you played so abominably it sounded as if you had stepped on a cat's tail. Truly, Oliwia, you have been getting worse rather than better. You must practice, practice, practice. Among her many gifts, an accomplished lady plays an instrument." Katarzyna's tone was light, but a sharp edge hinted at irritation.

"Yes, my lady. Perhaps I would do better with a different instrument?"

Katarzyna whirled, freeing her arm from Nadia's grasp. "I do not know another instrument half so well as the harp," she snapped. "It is the one you shall learn."

Oliwia reddened and ducked her head. "Yes, of course, my lady. I meant no disrespect." Inwardly, Oliwia chided herself. Katarzyna's mercurial behavior of late should have kept her on guard.

Katarzyna's stormy expression quickly transformed to one of indulgence, and she patted Oliwia's shoulder. "No, of course you didn't. I know you only wish to please me." Her voice was all warmth now, so different from the harshness she had just inflicted. She sighed long and loud, suddenly looking haggard.

"I tell you what, Oliwia. I have more to teach you about herbs and their uses in cooking and medicine. We will spend our morning in the kitchen garden. Perhaps there are sprouts from your recent plantings, and you can sow the rest of the seeds in their plots before the harp."

Relieved, Oliwia raised her chin and smiled. "Oh yes, my lady."

In the kitchen garden, Oliwia could dig in the warm earth and gently nurture seeds that would become herbs, beans, peas, carrots, flowers. She had squealed like a small child the first time her delicate green shoots had broken through the soil.

"Heavens above!" Katarzyna had exclaimed. "One would think you never grew anything before."

Now a mild, hazy, blue-sky spring day beckoned. "Get your apron and cap, Oliwia. And the gloves," Katarzyna instructed.

As Oliwia headed toward her small trunk, she mused her gardening turned her into a dirty, disheveled girl who alarmed her mistress. Upon seeing her after such an excursion, Katarzyna had rolled her eyes and tsked, "Just look at you! You are completely unmindful that wiping your face and brow covers you in dirt! One step forward but always followed by two steps backward. Oliwia, you must learn a lady is not a ragamuffin!"

From then on, just as she was doing now, Oliwia wore a linen apron and restricted any wiping to that single panel of fabric. Katarzyna insisted she wear gloves, as any lady would, but Oliwia simply removed them when she was out of her mistress's sight—just as she loosened her plaits and shed her cap despite the lady's objections. "Proper maids wear their hair braided and capped!" she would say. But the braids gave Oliwia headaches, and she tugged at them at every opportunity, preferring to gather her unruly hair in a loose binding at her nape.

Today, under Katarzyna's watchful eye, Oliwia resigned herself to braids, cap, apron, and gloves—for now.

Though the tempo was slower, work in the fields, the dairies, the mills, and forges went on as it had for decades. Overseeing it all was Eryk—one man, one lord, for whom the cadence was little changed from a fully garrisoned fortification. He met with estate managers in his solar—the stable master, the hunt master, the winemaker, and a ferret-faced steward named Tomasz.

Besides his management abilities, Tomasz was conversant in eight languages and was an excellent correspondent. Eryk had tasked him with dispatching inquiries about the whereabouts of Oliwia and Filip's Scottish and English relations.

When a letter from Scotland arrived, Tomasz translated and delivered it into Eryk's hands. Eryk immediately sought out Katarzyna. Delightedly, he found her playing her harp, her nimble fingers plucking the strings with strength and confidence. She was backlit by the sun slanting through the leaded window. The light played off her pale golden hair, and he thought he looked upon an angel. His heart swelled. Her eyes were closed as she ran her hands over the strings, and she hummed. When she opened her eyes, they landed on him, and she gave him a smile that radiated like the sunbeams upon her head.

The tune over, she remained seated on her stool by the instrument. He paced in front of her, and he felt her tracking him as he read the letter aloud.

My dear Lord Krezowski,

I write in reply to your inquiry of 22 September 1610 with a heavy heart. The last of the Armstrong lairds has been executed for the grievous offense of leading a raid in Penrith, on English soil, in violation of an edict handed down by the Union of the Crowns. Armstrong Clan members who have not been imprisoned, banished, or transported have abandoned their homes for fear of retribution, without word of their destinations. Therefore, I know no way to locate kin belonging to the children in your care.

I commend you and your lady for the Christian kindness you have shown Sir Alexander Armstrong's progeny. It may comfort you and them to know he is buried beside his wife, Margaret, in consecrated ground at Stobo Parish Church.

May God bless you and keep you.

Your most humble servant,

Father John Carmichael

Tidings of the children's English line brought no better news. Tomasz delivered another letter soon after the first, and Eryk again made his way to Katarzyna's sitting chamber. He found her staring into the flames of a blazing fire, wrapped in a fox-lined cloak. She reclined in an oversized, cushioned armchair, her hand curled around a book.

Eryk moved cautiously toward her. "Are you well, Kasia?"

She raised her soft green eyes and smiled. "Yes, of course. I am a little tired, so I let myself be lulled by the flames."

He caressed her light bronze cheek. Was it her color, or was it the light cast by the fire? Then he glanced down at the hand clutching her book like a claw. "Are your fingers bothering you today?"

THE HEART OF A HUSSAR

She shook her head as he slid the book from her hand. "No. I am fine. Really."

"Well, I'm not convinced just yet, but if you are feeling well enough, I have received a letter from England I would read to you."

She scooted herself upright while he poured two cups of wine. "Oh yes, please do," she urged.

Eryk handed her a cup, which she held without drinking. He sipped from his own and arranged himself in the chair beside hers.

"Carlisle is in Northern England, close to the border, and has been part of the warring and cross-border raids between England and Scotland. Look here. The author of this letter, Bishop Law of Carlisle Cathedral, drew a map showing the locations of Carlisle, Sewell Castle—see, it is here, just to the northeast of Carlisle—and the border." He paused, taking another sip as she looked over the map.

"Because Sewell Castle is a bit isolated, it has been the target of frequent attacks. Lord Sewell defended his considerable estate throughout his life, but he was aging and his health declining. He had no male heirs. With the death of his daughter, Margaret, the lord had no surviving issue at all."

Katarzyna's eyes stayed fixed on the flames. "But he *did* have surviving issue."

"Yes, well, you and I know that, but he did not. This letter states Lord Sewell had known a granddaughter who had been removed at age eight by her parents. They traveled to Poland, where her father hired on as a mercenary. Lord Sewell received letters penned by Margaret from countries throughout central Europe. It says here the last letter came from the Commonwealth, near the Muscovite border. The letters stopped, and he never heard of his granddaughter again. Why he did not know of Filip's birth is a mystery. Nevertheless, the lord presumed the granddaughter, like her parents, had perished.

"He goes on to write about a silver cross, the 'Sewell cross,' he calls it, handed down through generations of Sewell women. He says it is simple in design save a small *SE* engraved in the middle." He glanced up from the letter. "Have you looked at Oliwia's cross closely?"

"Yes, she showed it to me. It has a small mark in the exact spot. I couldn't make it out, but she described it. 'Tis the same." Katarzyna raised her eyes to his. "So Lord Sewell died not knowing he had a grandson or that his granddaughter lived?"

Eryk nodded. "Yes. Furthermore, upon Lord Sewell's death, the estate was seized and occupied multiple times by opposing factions. Bishop Law does not mention what became of it."

"What else does the letter say?" Her faraway look had transformed into something altogether different; she looked as though a fast stream of thoughts flowed behind her light green eyes.

He sighed. "Just that he died alone. Kasia, my love, Oliwia and Filip have nothing to return to. Not anywhere."

"Yet an estate exists in England that should have passed to the descendants."

"It has likely been claimed by the king or another lord. It was long ago, Kasia."

Katarzyna held out her hand, and Eryk passed her the letter. She scanned it quickly, then looked at him, wide-eyed. "Do you not see, Eryk? This letter proves their noble lineage."

"So it would seem, though we cannot be sure."

Katarzyna stood up and walked to her desk, carefully placing the letter in a drawer. She turned to him with a broad smile and light in her eyes.

"I am sure. Think of it! The prestige of an English estate and an alliance with noble English and Scots families—"

"A disgraced, disbanded clan of thieves," he countered.

She threw up her hands. "Then we will leave the Scots aside for now. But the estate! It may hold rich farmland and timber. Villages and towns! Mines even!"

Katarzyna began to pace.

"Katarzyna, stop for a moment," he entreated.

She did stop—just long enough to stare at him. Eryk stilled.

"Kasia, there *is* no family, no estate. Surely you can see that."

She held up her hand as if to halt him. An uncharacteristically hard look twisted her features.

"Eryk, promise me you will do all you can to discover if there's aught we can do to help the children claim the estate."

Eryk gaped at her.

"And I will ask one more promise of you, my love. Promise me a free hand to arrange Oliwia's marriage."

In his eagerness to soothe his Kasia, Eryk gave his promise with little idea what that promise truly meant.

THE HEART OF A HUSSAR

Not far from Biaska, Romek sat beside his sister's bed, dread crawling up his spine. "Bella, you will stay here with this good woman. She will care for you while I am away."

Bella was seated upright, her ravaged body swallowed by the bolsters. She had been watching him with a glassy stare, but now she reached out and clutched at his sleeve, her eyes filled with fear.

"No, Romek. Don't go. I worry for you."

He gently removed her hands and covered them with his. "I have no choice, but it won't be for long. I must seek recruits for the lord. It's dangerous, hard work, and you cannot come with me. I promise you will be fine here. Your every need will be taken care of, and you'll get better. You'll see."

She slumped back against the pillows and squeezed her eyes tight; a tear slithered down her cheek. He brushed it away and kissed her forehead. "I will come back soon, Bella, and we'll have a lively time." He gave her chin a light pinch, and she nodded her head, her eyes still closed.

On his way out the door, Romek turned and deposited a jingling leather pouch in a robust woman's cupped hands.

"We'll look after her, sir," the woman said.

"See that you do, or there'll be the devil to pay," he growled.

That, too, was a promise.

CHAPTER 22

The Tatars

Jacek and a group of hussars set out to scout one restive daybreak as the sun lightened a dull, misty landscape. Six in all, they rode northeast, skirting the southern edge of a deserted settlement. Their path arced north of Twierzda, where they could shelter in the trees and observe the castle upon the ridge and the Tatar camp below.

As the men traversed water and wood, they emerged from the fog into a flat, unfurrowed field. They traveled in the cool air two abreast, three rows deep. Jacek was in the middle row beside Stefan, followed by Izaak and another hussar.

They were moving briskly toward the cover of another dense forest when the lead scout suddenly jerked. So fast Jacek barely sorted it, the man's head snapped back, then flopped to the side as his body slumped in the saddle.

Damn it!

Jacek's heart galloped. His eyes scanned and caught on a blur just as a *whiz-thunk* impacted the earth beside him, followed by three more in blistering succession.

"Tatars!" he yelled, ripping his sabre from its sheath and surging to the front of the line.

Where the hell are they? They were just there! Where in blazes did they go? Shit!

THE HEART OF A HUSSAR

He dropped his reins. Squeezing his knees, he grabbed his nadziak and dug his heels into Jarosława's flanks.

Movement snatched his attention.

He pointed with the war hammer. "Over there!"

Whiz! Thunk!

Whiz! Whiz! Thunk!

Whiz! Thunk!

Christ!

Go! Go! Go!

His men shouted, preparing to attack.

Jesus, God! Stay with me, Brothers!

Horses pounded behind him. No more arrows. No shouts of pain. He regathered his leads. A charge flooded his veins, tautened every muscle, sharpened his vision, his hearing. He thought only of the riders ahead, coming into focus, in the open, going for the trees.

Fifteen? More hiding? We can catch them. Before they reach the trees. They're pulling up! Go! Go! Faster!

A knot of Tatars twisted in their saddles, still galloping. A drawn bow, a fletched arrow, released, flying. A whine came at him, then flew past.

Thunk!

Too close!

His eyes stayed fixed on the enemy. On the periphery, the main body of Tatars careened to the right, heading away.

Twelve there. Three here. Fifteen. We can take them!

The warhorses streaked toward the Tatars at breathtaking speed, flying as though propelled by a gale. The forest was yet distant, but Jacek's men held the advantage on the wide, flat ground. Hooves thundered, flinging great clods of earth into the air. The countryside on either side blurred as Jarosława covered the rises and slopes with ease. An eagle flying overhead would see Tatars galloping in fragmented lines, losing ground to the armored warriors trailing in a shallow V formation, like a small flight of geese with Jacek in the lead.

More arrows flew past.

Almighty God, make them miss their mark!

Jacek's upper body crouched over Jarosława's neck, his heels kicking, digging, thighs burning. Sabre in his right hand. Nadziak and reins in the left.

We're gaining!

He brought himself fully upright as three enemy soldiers stopped and spun, nocking arrows with blinding speed, missing, reaching for their blades. Two hussars on one flank came at them, sabres high, slashing. He caught the flash of a koncerz as it pierced a Tatar chest, ripping fabric, reeling the man backward, howling. Within seconds, the three foes were mortally wounded, one dead in his saddle.

Good!

Jacek and his men dashed toward the main body of Tatars. Ahead, a small group flagged and turned to challenge.

"Get them!" Jacek shouted to the hussars on his right, and they peeled off, away from the fracas about to erupt, chasing the Tatars still riding for the forest.

Jacek, Izaak, and Stefan rode into the band of Tatars fanning out to meet them.

Enemy scimitars rose, deflected hussar sabres. Double-edged blades bit into cloth, into flesh. Glancing blows juddered, metal rang, horses snorted and whinnied.

Jacek swung with a shout, slashing an enemy arm before it could complete its arc. A horse backed into him, pushing him toward another Tatar. Black eyes burned in a fierce brown face screwed in hatred, white teeth gritted between tightly drawn lips, and an arm raised, coming down.

Now!

Jacek swept the war hammer, catching the man in the ribs with a resounding crunch, doubling him over. He swung again, trying to send the man from the saddle, but he missed and sank the claw into his arm. The metal dug into meat. The man sat up, his grimace frozen, then let out a furious yell. Something hit Jacek in the shoulder, hard, shuddering pain down his arm. Fingers numb, he regripped the sabre and swung the nadziak backward blindly. It cut through air, nearly escaping his grasp.

Tangled bodies and weapons, chaos in the melee. Horse flesh smacking horse flesh; blades clanging and crashing; men's savage shouts in different tongues; the coppery smell of blood thickening the air.

Chest heaving, Jacek looked back at the man he'd crushed with his war hammer. He caught a glint. Reflex, quick but awkward, parried the enemy's blow. Then Jacek plunged his sabre into the man's side.

Die already, you bastard!

THE HEART OF A HUSSAR

Jacek kneed Jarosława, and she swung to the left. He glimpsed Izaak's ferocious face, sprayed in blood, as he brought his broadsword down hard on a shoulder without armor. Jacek now faced an enemy back, and he thrust the spike of his nadziak into soft tissue. He felt the body jerk before he yanked the spike out. Swinging back the other way now, his eyes searched for the man he'd been grappling with, but he was gone.

Breathing hard, quickly scanning, calculating. Izaak and Stefan were fighting two soldiers. To the side, the remaining two hussars were taking on five enemy soldiers.

That one's going down! Good!

Now the two hussars dueled four Tatars, and Jacek rode into the fray.

He came between two foes, kicking at one, knocking the blade from his opponent's hand, nearly unseating him. But the man grabbed Jacek's leg and yanked. The other combatant moved off but turned and aimed his blade at Jacek's neck. Jacek twisted and wrenched his leg free, moving just enough to avoid the bite of the blade to his neck, but the edge caught his unarmored thigh as they came together.

Jacek punched the claw of his nadziak into the man's fur-capped head. The impact shot a vibration through his wrist, and metal crunched against bone. The Tatar's momentum carried him, and Jacek released the handle of the war hammer, letting it go with the slumping body.

Wheeling to his right, he drew his sabre across his middle in a backhand stroke, anticipating a blow. The closest enemy was unbalanced, unable to steady himself in time to deflect Jacek's powerful cut to his stomach. Fabric and skin ripped in a long gash, and bright blood bloomed along the slit in the man's coat. Black eyes widened, and he fell forward as he clutched the tear in his body.

Jacek snapped his head up. A lasso flew, encircling Stefan. It tightened around his body, pinning one arm to his side. The Tatar tugged, but the saddle held Stefan in place. The Tatar moved, jerking the rope from the side.

Go! Go! Go!

Jacek sprung Jarosława forward and hacked at the taut rope. Stefan toppled, boot caught in his stirrup. He struggled to right himself. Jacek's heart dropped. His momentum had carried him too far away.

Christ, no!

The enemy swung his blade in a downward slash, cutting a large swath through nothing as Stefan rolled mere inches out of harm's way.

The Tatar with the rope wheeled. Jacek headed to meet him, squaring off.

Can I finish them both before they reach Stefan?

Jacek gripped his sabre and brought it up, riding at the enemy. Boring into his dark eyes, Jacek searched for the sign.

Which way will he strike?

In a heartbeat, he registered it, adjusted, but the shift was not what he anticipated. The man's head pivoted. Jacek's eyes remained fixed on his opponent. The enemy looked back, too late, hissing curses. Jacek swung, and his enemy's eyes widened. Impact. Jacek's blade edge cleaved a gristly neck, releasing a warm spray of blood.

Spinning back, Jacek sought Stefan. Izaak was helping him up, a crumpled, bloody Tatar at his feet.

Jacek halted. His breaths came in quick, rasping heaves. Sweat slicked his face. He glanced around. The other two hussars walked among the enemy. Curses were muttered in a foreign tongue, followed by cries and gurgles. Jacek crossed himself, bent his head, then looked up to the heavens. Blue sky. Small puffs of white clouds overhead. An idyllic morning.

Thank you.

What felt like hours of fighting had been a mere ten minutes from the time they'd spotted the Tatars, if even that. Jacek and his lord-brothers recovered their weapons. With leaden limbs, they gathered up the bodies, relieving them of clothing and possessions. They rolled them into a deep gash in the earth and swept branches, dead leaves, and decayed vegetation atop the corpses.

After they strung together their enemies' mounts, they returned to their downed companion, peacefully laid out in the field. His horse grazed indifferently beside his body. If not for a fletched shaft from the dark hollow beneath his helmet's brim, he might have been resting in the warmth of the sun. The men surrounded him. Heads bent in silent prayer, they crossed themselves before hefting his body across his saddle.

THE HEART OF A HUSSAR

Jacek paced quickly to his tent in preparation for what he expected would be a meeting with Mateusz, the pułkownik, or the deputy himself. As Marcin helped him out of his vambraces, it struck Jacek that his shoulder and leg throbbed. Marcin had been explaining that Mateusz had gone to the village after breakfast and had not been seen since; the pułkownik was at Kamieniec with the deputy.

After scrubbing his hands and face in a basin of water, Jacek looked up at Marcin, assessing the young pacholik.

"I suppose you're here as much to hear the story as you are to help me," Jacek remarked dryly as he dried himself with a clean length of linen.

Grinning, Marcin nodded and began loosening the leather straps holding Jacek's breast and back plates. "I have no secrets from you, sire."

"I want to hear it as well," a voice announced from just outside the tent.

"Can a man have no secrets?" Jacek complained in exasperation. "Come in instead of lurking about my tent eavesdropping."

Henryk ducked his head just inside the tent flap. "It is all the talk, Jacek. I seem to have missed all the fun. Shall I gather up the others? They will need to know."

Jacek exhaled loudly as Marcin unfastened his pauldrons and gorget. "Yes. I had planned to report to the captain. As he's not here, I'll brief the others. Henryk, find Stefan and Izaak. They will have their own details to add."

After Henryk left, Marcin removed Jacek's torn and bloodied żupan. Slipping his breeches to his knees, Jacek sat and dabbed at a four-inch, oozing slice across the middle of his thigh. He ran his fingers along the edges of the cut. "Not so bad. Looks like the hem of the żupan caught just enough of the blade to keep it from doing more damage."

Marcin peered over his shoulder. "Does it not hurt, my lord?"

"Only when I move." Jacek pulled off his boots, untied his linen undershirt, and shrugged it off his shoulder.

"It appears your pauldron did its work, my lord, but the shoulder's bruised. How did it happen?"

"Tatars were trying to kill me. *That's* how it happened." Jacek narrowed his eyes as Marcin's widened.

Marcin bent back to his work. "The shirt is in good condition. There is nothing to be done for the shoulder, but the leg needs tending. I will fetch the barber and a new pair of trousers for you."

By the time the men were assembled in his tent, Jacek's leg had been dressed and he had donned a clean red wool żupan and fresh blue breeches. Marcin had cleaned blood and dirt from his armor and helped him pull it back on again. Jacek was spent, mind and body exhausted. The armor felt heavy, as though driving his feet into the ground, but he held himself straight and began the telling.

His narrative was interrupted when the captain's servant arrived. "Begging your pardon, Lieutenant Dąbrowski, but Captain Zalewski is back and orders you to report to him at once."

Jacek paused a moment and dragged a hand through his hair. "On my way."

After a seemingly endless briefing in the captain's command tent—during which Mateusz took every opportunity to berate Jacek in front of Matejko and the men, criticizing everything from his fighting ability to his leadership and all points in between—the officers were dismissed and dispersed to their camps.

As they headed back to their own camp, Henryk eyed Jacek. "Did you do something special to vex Zalewski, or is this all about his wife?"

Jacek grunted. "He does not discuss his reasons with me."

"He knows, does he not, that you have no interest in her?"

Jacek gave Henryk a sidelong glance. "What he knows and what he chooses to believe are two different matters entirely."

"Nonetheless, try to stay on his good side, Jacek."

"He only has the one side where I'm concerned," Jacek retorted. "At least we have, at last, a promise of swift mobilization. I'm relieved Sosnowski will soon be encamped among us."

THE HEART OF A HUSSAR

Within days of the scouts' encounter, the janissaries began assaults on Twierzda Castle, probing its strength with the boom of their guns. Meanwhile, skirmishes broke out between the Nagórzany troops and the Tatars, with little damage to either side.

One morning, Mateusz ordered a handful of soldiers to dress in Tatar garb to lure the enemy into the woods and commanded Jacek to lead the spy missions. But Matejko overrode him as Jacek stood at attention in Mateusz's tent.

"I won't have you sending in your best officer. Besides, look at him. With his coloring and size, he'll stand out like a bonfire against the night sky."

Mateusz's eyes flicked over Jacek. "Fine, then," he snapped. "His pacholik will go in his stead. That pathetic collection of whiskers he laughingly refers to as a moustache is as straggly as any Tatar's and will make him a convincing Mongol."

The lad had been the subject of frequent good-natured teasing for his attempt at a hussar moustache, which more closely resembled smudges of dirt across his lip with limp bits sprouting at the corners. Marcin's dusky skin and almond-shaped brown eyes enhanced his makeover as Tatar raider, especially when combined with quilted buff coat, brown *sharovary*, black boots, and fur cap.

Though Jacek could not argue the logic, he bristled at Mateusz's appropriation of his retainer. It did little good.

Clashes escalated as days passed. Deputy Sosnowki and his large retinue finally arrived on a bone-chilling morning under leaden clouds that promised rain. His coming preceded the troops marching from Kamieniec, and he lodged himself in opulent quarters. Thusly settled, he summoned the commanders and their senior officers.

As Jacek searched out his kolpak, he called for his retainer. Marcin did not respond. Puzzled, Jacek found a servant who told him Marcin had left on a scouting mission.

Jacek frowned. "But I did not schedule him today."

"He, uh, left of his own accord, sir."

Jacek was stunned. The pacholik had never disobeyed orders, at least not flagrantly. Jacek stalked to Sosnowski's camp, muttering and cursing as he went. Henryk fell in beside him. Jacek shot him a sidelong scowl, maintaining his determined pace. As a few drops of rain bounced off his hatless head, he grew increasingly irritated with his missing retainer.

Henryk smirked. "What has you so vexed? Did the captain dress you down in front of the men again and tell them what a worthless piece of bison dung you are?"

"Pan Sosnowski has called a meeting. Marcin has left, without my permission, to spy on the enemy. The lad has clearly taken leave of his senses. I have no notion if he went on his own or at the behest of another insubordinate soldier, but the fact is irrelevant," Jacek grumbled. "Either way, he will be severely disciplined when I find him. And now this miserable rain," he added with a glance at the sky. A fat, cold drop plopped on his forehead and ran into his eye. He blinked and swiped at it. "You know what we face if the ground becomes too saturated. We'll be charging—more likely sliding—through greasy mud," he huffed. It had been raining off and on throughout the day, and the sullen skies did not appear willing to change. If the storm was to linger, he prayed a cold front would freeze the ground.

"Ah. I'll see what I can discover about Marcin," Henryk offered before peeling away.

Jacek continued his slog toward his commander's tent and slid on a patch of mud mixed with dung. He caught himself, putting his hand in said muck. Upright again, he let out a string of expletives and shook off the slop. A servant sniggered at him.

"What the devil are *you* laughing at?" he bellowed, advancing toward the now slack-jawed, round-eyed lad. "Get me something to clean this mess off with before I throw *you* in that filth!" The sight of the boy covered in manure flashed through his head, and though it would ordinarily be an amusing image, it did little to counter his foul mood.

THE HEART OF A HUSSAR

When Jacek returned to his tent several hours later, his mood was no better. He understood where the men were to be two mornings hence and what he needed to arrange beforehand. In the privacy of his tent, he strode to and fro and let out an anxious breath.

"Jesus," he muttered to himself. "The man is a pompous lunatic."

Jacek was not merely skeptical of the deputy hetman's strategy; he feared it. He didn't think himself alone. Sosnowski, however, had ideas of his own he was determined to implement. Jacek prayed the colonels could sway the deputy toward logic that would save men's lives. His hopes rested especially with Matejko, whom he'd come to respect as a reasonable, intelligent commander.

Jacek called a meeting, dismayed when Henryk was not among his men. He paced with heavy steps, gripping his hands behind his back. The men watched him intently while he imparted information and orders. Some looked at him with questions on their faces, but all held their tongues until they were invited to talk.

Loud scuffling sounded outside the tent, interrupting him mid-sentence. A Tatar was shoved roughly through the flap, stumbled, and landed facedown with a resounding *thud* at Jacek's feet. The man's body seemed to bounce on impact. Following up this impressive display was Henryk, panting as he stepped into the tent. Marcin, dressed in Tatar garb, shook his head and raised himself slowly from the floor, elbows bent. He looked up. Jacek stared down at him, fists on his hips. His gaze jumped between Marcin and Henryk. Marcin attempted a contrite grin.

Henryk held up a hand, then calmly said, "Before you kill him, Jacek …"

"I can explain, sir," Marcin piped up.

"What the devil? Explain *what?*" Jacek stormed. "Why you disobeyed me, or why you're disrupting a crucial briefing? Each is reason enough to throttle you."

A murmur ran through the tent from men suppressing chuckles and shifting to get a better look at the scene unfolding before them. No doubt they wanted an uninterrupted view if Jacek was truly going to kill the pacholik, and they began jostling one another.

"Hold!" Jacek yelled. He visited each man with a challenging glare. They did hold, likely afraid he might murder one of them rather than the current subject of his contempt.

He fixed his scowl on Henryk. "Are you going to tell me what in God's name is happening here?"

Henryk and Marcin began at once. In one swift move, Jacek reached down and yanked the scruff of Marcin's collared *beshmet*. With a loud ripping noise, the fabric tore away in his hand, leaving the man precisely where he was. Jacek looked at the bit he held in his hand before throwing it on the floor in frustration.

"I wasn't speaking to *you*!" he shouted at the prone pacholik.

Marcin kept his head down, seemingly studying the swirling patterns adorning the rug beneath his nose with keen interest.

"May I?" Henryk asked in an even tone.

"Proceed," Jacek growled. He folded his arms across his chest. Officers' heads swiveled from one to the other.

"He did go out on an unassigned scouting mission, one he volunteered for, and was nearly captured for his trouble," Henryk began.

"He volunteered without my permission. Capture would have been merited," Jacek countered.

"I agree. *However,* his foolishness has brought us some very important information about the enemy's movements that may change the deputy's strategy."

Jacek's brows eased a bit, but the scowl was stuck in place. "Such as?"

"Such as they have set up fortifications in a half-crescent: palisades on the flanks with breastworks in front. They have brought several guns across the river to the base of the fortress. The remainder is arrayed behind their defenses. They have traps in the woods and the ground just beyond."

Henryk had everyone's attention now. "They are not reinforcing their back guard with any depth. They appear to be fighting two fronts, as it were. One in defense against us, while they continue their assault on Twierzda Castle. My guess is they're planning to breach the fortress and take up positions within, or they're confident we are too small a force to hurt them and are counting on dispatching us quickly so they can return to their main objective. The guns he saw are light, and their catapults stand ready."

Jacek utterly ignored Marcin, still on the floor. "Henryk, have someone fetch Captain Zalewski immediately. He must hear this."

Henryk nodded before leaving the tent.

THE HEART OF A HUSSAR

Jacek took a step back and addressed Marcin in an icy voice. "You may get up."

Marcin did, dusting himself off as he stood. One side of his face was covered in bruises, and his hand was bloodied. His beshmet was rent in several places, bits of stuffing poking out, and he was without a boot. Jacek took him in but bit back the urge to ask him what the devil he'd gotten into.

A flustered Deputy Hetman Sosnowski burst into the tent, Majetko and Henryk on his heels. He looked from Marcin to Jacek

"Your captain is indisposed, Lieutenant, but I am here for your report." Sounding annoyed, Sosnowski helped himself to Jacek's seat. At Sosnowski's direction, Marcin recounted how he and three others had set out to spy on the enemy camp—making no mention of the fact he had disobeyed orders. They tethered their horses at a distance and crept through the woods, where they climbed trees.

Enemy sentries walked into the woods, and the spies were trapped, stuck high above the forest floor. They sat thusly for the better part of the morning until later when, to the north of their position and out of their line of sight, there came a series of shouts, followed by a woman screaming. The sentries ran toward the noise.

Seeing their opportunity for escape, Marcin and his companions shinnied down and ran. The shrieks stopped, but sounds of metal ringing and men struggling continued. Marcin heard what sounded like a woman mewling. He stopped, and as he turned, his eye caught on a feminine silhouette racing through the woods ten feet away. He ran toward her.

"We couldn't just leave her there at their mercy," Marcin argued despite Jacek pinning him with a withering look. Then he boldly added, "You've done it yourself, sire."

Jacek's posture shifted incrementally, and he quickly masked the look of astonishment threatening to overtake his expression. He had not expected that remark. The deputy shot him a look and arched his eyebrows.

Jacek narrowed his eyes at the pacholik. "Proceed, and be quick about it." He would pummel Marcin later.

Marcin described an impromptu rescue mission, their fleeing from the enemy soldiers with the young woman, and Marcin's leap upon one of the enemy's horses to execute a faster getaway. As they headed for their own mounts, Marcin's borrowed one abruptly stopped at the sound of a whistle, throwing Marcin head over foot. By a minor miracle, all escaped their pursuers, including the woman.

"And where is the young woman now?" Jacek blurted, incredulous.

"We took her to Kamieniec, sir," Marcin answered succinctly.

"You *what?*"

"Well, we knew you would not allow her here, my lord." Jacek was certain Marcin smirked before he went on in one great breath. "We thought to deliver her someplace safe, so we left her in the care of the nuns there. She is a handmaid to Lady Olga of Twierzda. She and two other maids were being escorted downriver from Skała by a small detail of castle knights when they were attacked. They didn't know the castle was under siege. She was the only one to escape. Her name is Joanna." Marcin's face broke into a crooked smile, then quickly went blank.

Jacek suppressed his consternation as Henryk choked back a chuckle with a gloved fist to his mouth. The men stood silent until Sosnowski spoke.

"Well done, lad. Well done! You not only discovered vital intelligence, but you rescued the lady's maid from those heathens while you were about it! I am sure Lady Olga will want to thank you personally when this is over and we've dispatched the enemy."

Sosnowski, who obviously neither understood nor weighed the disregarded orders that had preceded this bold adventure, clapped Marcin on the back and glanced at Jacek.

"I trust you will reward this young man, Lieutenant."

As he exited the tent in a dramatic sweep, Sosnowki added, "I will adjust our strategy. Await your captain's orders."

With that, the deputy ducked his head into the sleet that had been rain just a short while ago. Jacek dismissed the rest, but Henryk remained, arms folded casually across his chest. Marcin stood rod-straight, eyes focused ahead. Jacek scrubbed a hand over his face, pulled it through his hair, and scratched the back of his neck.

"What have you to say for yourself?" Jacek's tone was even, calm. He looked his retainer over coolly, circling him slowly.

Marcin's eyes darted about, and a fine sheen of sweat gathered on his brow and fuzzy lip.

"My lord, I expected to be back before you discovered my absence."

THE HEART OF A HUSSAR

Jacek stopped abruptly and regarded him, mere inches from his face. "And this is what you have to say for yourself? That you did not expect to be caught?"

"Well, no, sir, not exactly. That is, I ..." Marcin stammered. He was not small of stature, but he suddenly looked it in Jacek's long shadow.

"Do you realize the danger you put this camp in? And the Kamieniec camp! You could have led the enemy right into their laps when you took the young woman back there." He stared at Marcin.

Marcin broke his rigid stance. "But, sir, I could not leave her there, and I did not think we should bring her here."

"You should not have been there in the first place, Marcin!"

Marcin's chest, incredibly, puffed a bit. "But if I hadn't been, that poor girl would have been ..." Though his tongue tripped over his words, his eyes narrowed and held steady.

"Yes, Marcin, I know precisely what she would have been. Better one girl than the entire regiment. Your sorry attempt at an excuse does not justify your utter disregard of my orders. You were grievously insubordinate."

"I only did as you would have, my lord. Would *you* have left Lady Oliwia to those dogs, to be used and pulled apart like so much meat?" Marcin protested.

Jacek wasn't sure how or why Oliwia had appeared in this conversation, but he did not like her presence there.

"That was an entirely different situation, and you know it! There was neither a mission nor regiments at stake." His face grew hot.

Saving her and Filip had been an utter aberration, but that was not for this discussion.

"So had Lady Oliwia been in the grasp of those vile bastards, you would have just left her to them? You could have turned your back, walked away, endured her screams?" Marcin's voice rose, along with his bravado. Though he was Jacek's subordinate, Marcin seemed to be invoking his birthright as a nobleman—unadvisedly so.

Henryk had been watching the discourse and now cut Jacek off before he could answer, stepping in front of him and blocking his access to Marcin.

He darted a look at Jacek and took hold of Marcin's shoulder. "Marcin, I suggest you hold your tongue before he thrashes you to within an inch of your life. I would not test God's, or Pan Dąbrowski's, benevolence further."

Marcin opened his mouth, but Henryk resumed, his face stern. "Marcin, consider. These are very different circumstances. Pan Dąbrowski is correct when he points out that recovering Lady Oliwia posed no risk to soldiers, nearby villages, and fortresses. *And* I would also point out he is quite a bit more skilled than you. I wager he would have rescued the girl with none the wiser because he would not have flailed and crashed about in the forest, bringing the attention of the entire camp upon himself."

Jacek's rigid stance eased.

"Your heart and your honor may have been in the right place," Henryk continued, "but your brain was not. You acted foolishly in the first place. You should never have gone. Doing so put many lives at risk."

With that, Henryk released Marcin's shoulder and shoved his slumping frame backward. "I think you had best throw yourself on your master's mercy, my friend. If he chooses to pummel you, none will stop him. He is more than entitled to do so, and I certainly would were you my retainer."

A fleeting look of contrition flashed across Marcin's dark features. For his part, Jacek was in the unenviable position of truckling to a heedless commandant while wanting to whip Marcin for his willfulness. Against this backdrop lay his closeted admiration for the lad—not in choosing to engage in the mission, but in choosing to put life and limb at risk to rescue a helpless girl. He would ponder the retainer's punishment later. Right now, there was work to be done. The time had arrived for combat in the open.

The sleet had given way to a late-spring snow, leaving a thick layer of white crystal over top of the ground during the night, filling muddy cracks and ruts. Jacek was gratified with a resounding *crunch* with each step of his boot heels.

In preparation for battle, weapons were checked, rechecked, and taken to the blacksmith for any needed repairs. Cartridge boxes and powder were resupplied; bows were tested, quivers filled; blades were honed; armor was inspected, polished; mounts were selected, their adornments readied;

saddles and stirrups were brushed and buckled; kopie were examined, hefted, gilded, and graced with pennon; prayers and rosaries were spoken; blessings were sought and bestowed, and confessions given and heard.

In the midst of the activity, Jacek walked the camp after his final meetings with Mateusz and the commanders, his gloved hands tucked under his arms and his nose growing wet from the cold. Mateusz was off to Kamieniec yet again, and Jacek checked on the men to be sure they had what they needed and knew what to do with their wings. Tomorrow, they would be ready to charge, and Jacek prayed the frozen ground would not soften.

That night, he wrote letters to his family, Oliwia, and Filip. He had written sporadically during his time away and enjoyed their letters to him. But tonight's words were especially hard to come by, so his messages were abbreviated, one-page affairs offering little but God's blessings. His task complete, he lay abed, fingering the rosary his mother had given him as a young boy. It was his habit to pray the beads on the eve of a battle. She would likely fuss at him for not engaging in the practice more often. If she knew.

He lay upon his cot, one arm tucked under his head, staring at the ceiling of the tent absentmindedly. It was dark but for the flicker of a flame dancing across the white canvas.

As he slid the smooth wooden beads through his fingers, he repeated his prayers amid thoughts of tomorrow's approaching confrontation.

Our Father, who art in heaven, hallowed be thy name …

Had he thought of everything?

… and lead us not into temptation …

Were they ready?

… but deliver us from evil.

Amen.

Would they triumph?

Hail Mary, full of grace …

Would the fresh-faced young man he'd spotted heaving be an indomitable warrior when the time came?

The Lord is with thee …

Had he instructed them correctly?

Pray for us sinners, now and in the hour of our death.

Amen.

He tucked the rosary away before his last prayer.

Dear God, keep the men safe and lead us to victory over our enemies. Keep me safe that I may return whole. Keep everyone I hold dear safe that they will be there when I do return. Amen.

Jacek was up before dawn and the call to roust. In somber candlelight, he dressed and sat calmly while Marcin shaved him and clipped his hair. Groomed and scrubbed, Jacek veered over icy ground to the cooking tent, where servants set out a watery gruel. Soldiers had consumed a heavy, belly-lining meal the previous night and would have a small helping of the gruel or nothing at all before departing for the frontline.

After downing a few quick spoonfuls of the thin stuff, Jacek joined the soldiers awaiting the deputy's reading of the holy parchment, followed by the Mass to be conducted by Father Augustyn. They stood in a rough half circle, facing a makeshift altar lit with candles and flanked by torches. Soldiers filed in quietly, their armor glinting faintly in the muted light, many with their heads already bowed or looking blankly somewhere distant—a place no doubt filled with images of wives and sweethearts, of children and family.

Izaak stepped beside Jacek, an anxious smile on his young face. Mateusz appeared, and the priest spoke the words that reminded each combatant of his Christian code of conduct and reinforced the behavior expected of him on the battlefield. While he could take a non-Christian enemy's life, and was encouraged to do so, he was not to harm innocents.

Jacek glanced around the sea of faces, recognizing the hard set to their jaws, their steely determination. The less experienced ones showed fleeting fear; he had seen it before, had felt it himself. They knew they might die today, might lose a friend, might take a life or many, might be gravely wounded. He knew it too, so he listened. Focusing on the blessings, he bent his head with the prayers that would absolve him and pave his way to heaven's gates should he have need of it this day. He crossed himself and strode to his own camp once the ritual came to a close.

The infantry and artillery had departed, and the relative quiet in camp was an eerie stillness in his ears. Marcin helped encase him in armor, and when Jacek mounted Jarosława, he smoothed her neck before fitting his helmet on his head. He guided the horse to the gathering area, where he joined an eager Izaak holding the standard. Alongside the young chorąży stood the trumpeters, drummer, and Father Augustyn. Together, they awaited the heavy hussars filing in.

The winged hussars.

The sky, a black, cold canopy frosted with stars, spanned clear overhead. The ground underfoot was a frozen, crusted surface that snapped and popped under the weight of the warhorses and their riders.

"Do you think us ready, Lieutenant?" Izaak's breath clouded the air.

Jacek regarded him. The boy twitched and smiled much too widely, betraying his jitters.

"Yes, Izaak, I do. I believe that, to a man, we have prepared ourselves thoroughly. We *are* God's warriors, and we are the best. We will prevail and vanquish our enemy—God's enemy—today." Jacek's voice was calm and clear, as much to steady Izaak's nerves as his own.

Mateusz at last arrived and joined the assemblage, and by ones and twos the hussars trotted out of the encampment through a gap in its fortified wall. The musicians beat out the signal to ride, and with his budzygan, Mateusz led them to the path they would follow to the battle site. Though few spoke, there was palpable excitement throughout the company—a buzz, a thrum, a crackle.

Jacek looked over the Biaska chorągiew. It was a view he had seen before, and yet he was stirred. A hussar banner in full regalia was always a jaw-dropping sight that could steal one's breath away, but this one was more impressive still.

The Biaska company usually wore wings on the left rear corner of their saddles. The wings were canted back, giving them a flat aspect resembling a winglet, which made them at times barely visible. But Jacek had instructed the men to lengthen and attach each set so it stood upright. To a man, they had toiled over the adornments as they had prepared other parts of their trappings for battle.

The wings had been attached to back straps and plates so they swept above the hussars' heads. Plumage shifted and wavered with the movement of each warrior and his horse. Now a Tatar with a lariat couldn't harness and bring down a winged cavalier so easily. Jacek had struck upon the idea after witnessing the lasso ensnare Stefan during their skirmish.

Each man now rode with a pair of ominous wings sprouting from his back as if he were part of an army of archangels. The spectacle of row after row of straight-backed, hard-muscled, hale and fit warriors was both thrilling and terrifying, and folk gathered to watch in awe as the husaria rode past in the preternatural light on their way to vanquish a reviled enemy.

CHAPTER 23

Winged Warriors

The cavalry, nearly a thousand strong, was a mix of heavy winged hussars and retainers; medium, mailed pancerni; and unarmored dragoons from Polish, Lithuanian, and Cossack forces. They sang as they rode, overtaking their artillery and infantry—the *hajduks*—along the way. As they moved past the foot soldiers, the cavalry continued belting out songs but changed the words to disparage the "wobblers"—as they were wont to call them—while exalting themselves. Jacek chuckled as a group of troopers hailed his squad with colorful insults of their own.

In the still, early morning, the riders arrived in battle array outside a strip of woods dividing them from the battlefield and the enemy beyond. The horizon glowed dully in the east, foretelling the sky would soon be ablaze in light. Wind riffled flags and garb, bringing with it a moldering dampness that chilled the dawn and the men's noses.

Jacek's eyes swept over the thin line of trees, beyond which lay a crusty brown plain stretching to the river. It was there, on that plain, where the Commonwealth and their enemies were fated to clash. But on this side of the wood was another flat stretch where they could establish their own defensive line, and retainers and servants had been toiling, building small earthworks close together.

Sitting rod-straight in his saddle among officers, colonels, and field commanders, Jacek furrowed his brows in concentration as a heated exchange between Sosnowski and Matejko grew louder.

"Begging your pardon, Commander Sosnowski, but we suspect they have traps on their side of the woods. We don't know how many or what variety. If we send in the men without—"

Sosnowski cut him off. "If we send in the men, then we will uncover these supposed traps, will we not?" One of three enormous ostrich feathers attached to Sosnowski's kolpak trembled with his breath, then returned to its droopy aspect from where it hovered over his shallow forehead.

"Who do you propose we send in?" Matejko asked coolly.

"Why, the Cossacks, of course," Sosnowski snapped.

Jacek glanced at Mateusz, but the captain sat impassively in his saddle, unseeing eyes focused straight ahead.

Jacek cleared his throat. "If I may." Matejko and Sosnowski turned their heads, and Mateusz now fixed him with a glare. Before Mateusz could stop him, Jacek said, "Why not send in a small number of hajduks or pancerni to lure them into the woods and a skirmish?"

"Why the devil would they fall for that, Dąbrowski?" Mateusz spat.

Jacek shrugged with a nonchalance he didn't feel. "There is always the chance they won't, but we've much to gain if they do."

Matejko glanced between Sosnowski and Jacek several times. Sosnowski pursed his fish lips, all eyes on him.

"Here is what we will do," he declared. "Send in thirty servants to see if the devil's sons engage."

Matejko's dark eyebrows pulled together in a tight knot. "Why not do as Lieutenant Dąbrowski suggests and put in pancerni or hajduks? Or both? These men are trained soldiers, and if the enemy does engage, they have a better chance of reducing their numbers."

Sosnowski scoffed. "I thought we were trying to discover their strengths and weaknesses."

"We are also trying to neutralize them, Deputy," Matejko said evenly.

Sosnowski flapped a gloved hand. "Yes, of course, Pan Matejko. We all know that."

Matejko darted his eyes to Jacek.

Sosnowski at last gave the order with all the authority of someone who had devised the strategy in the first place and withdrew to his newly erected tent with his retinue. As the officers rode to their units, Mateusz drew alongside Jacek. The captain had barely acknowledged him since he'd arrived from Tarnopol, and Jacek masked his surprise.

Mateusz flashed a mirthless smile. "I know what you're doing, Dąbrowski."

Jacek glanced at him as they guided their horses down a small rise. "Sir?"

"You're trying to show me up in front of the deputy."

"I assure you, Captain, the thought never entered my mind." *Because you never entered my mind.*

"Don't lie, Dąbrowski. You're no good at it. Just like you're no good at warfare. Get back to the men and stay there. Leave the strategizing to the experienced officers." Mateusz clicked at his horse and urged it to a trot.

The sorties accomplished their purpose. A Commonwealth detachment entered the woods and lured the enemy in after them, no doubt aided by the taunts of one particularly vocal and creative young horseman. When the two sides first set eyes on one another, the young lad rode back and forth, hurling one insult after another in the raiders' own tongue while miraculously escaping their projectiles.

The two armies engaged in a number of skirmishes, with few losses. The Commonwealth's two losses came with the unfortunate discovery of well-hidden mace traps in the trees. After chasing the Tatars back to their own encampment, the infantry pulled apart more traps while they pushed through the woods, holding up just beyond its edge.

Jacek was in the shelter of a pine boscage, amid a faction of hussars, when a breathless young soldier rode in.

"Lieutenant? Deputy Hetman Sosnowski requires your presence in his command tent. At once."

"And what of Captain Zalewski?"

"He is with the deputy presently." And with that, the messenger rode off.

When Jacek arrived, Sosnowski was seated at a table, flanked by Matejko and another soldier. Men shuffled as more pressed into the confines of the tent. Mateusz appeared, wordlessly, beside Jacek.

"Good. You're all here," Sosnowki remarked dryly. "Proceed." He fluttered a hand at the soldier beside him.

The man reported on everything that had been observed during the skirmishes. When he was done, a barrage of questions flew at him, but Sosnowski flicked the same limp-wristed hand, and everyone stilled.

"The observations of Lieutenant Dąbrowski's retainer and this brave man"—Sosnowski nodded toward the soldier—"have helped us uncover enemy trenches just beyond the woods. They've dug shallow ditches and lined them with spikes. They have also mounded up short redoubts and put up palisades. Servants and infantry are disassembling the spikes and filling the trenches as we speak, but they've come under fire. Time is running out. We mobilize shortly, so listen carefully."

Jacek's face was placid, shrouding his irritation. *Yes, all thanks to Marcin, the insubordinate mongrel!* In the recesses of his mind, Jacek grudgingly acknowledged Marcin's foray had likely saved countless lives.

When Sosnowski was done outlining his plan of attack—hurling several companies of infantry at the enemy's center, with more to follow if the first waves fell without breaching the defenses—Jacek was sure those countless lives would now be lost.

Harnessing a copious amount of self-control, he hauled himself back from the brink of shouting at the pretender. *He will kill us all!* Mateusz shot him a steely look as he shifted his weight from side to side, motioning him to bend close.

"Not a word, Dąbrowski. If you have something to say, you tell *me*."

Jacek nodded and spoke quietly in Mateusz's ear.

During a lull, Mateusz cleared his throat. "Begging your pardon, Deputy Sosnowski."

All eyes fixed on the captain.

"Captain Zalewski?"

"Yes, sir. Where and how do you plan to deploy the husaria, sir?"

Sosnowski looked annoyed. "I am sending infantry up the center, with pancerni and dragoons divided between the flanks. The hussars will back them up."

Jacek's brows knotted together.

THE HEART OF A HUSSAR

"If I might suggest, sir," Mateusz continued, "why not send your hussars up the middle to break through the enemy's front line, with pancerni and Cossacks right behind? And have the infantry, combined with dragoons, attack the left flank."

Sosnowki glanced at Matejko with bug eyes. Matejko nodded. "It is what the husaria does, my lord."

"And one more suggestion, if I may." Here Mateusz spewed the second of Jacek's strategies.

A long silence filled with palpable discomfort followed. Boots rustled, men coughed, and voices carried outside. Though surrounded by canvas walls, the smell of ever-present horse hide and dung seeped in, mixed with the unmistakable tang of too many men in a confined space.

At last, Sosnowski looked back at Matejko. "Make it so, Klemens. I was going to lead the husaria, but I think it wisest if I remain behind the lines of defense."

A collective murmur, like a sigh dying on the wind, swept through the tent. Mateusz looked up at Jacek, his face inscrutable. "Get our company ready, Lieutenant."

Jacek tore from the tent, dodging artillerymen, horsemen, and infantrymen moving about purposefully. Henryk strode beside him.

"Sosnowski was going to lead us in the charge, Jacek!" he hissed. "What a disaster that would have been."

"Not lead us, Henryk. He planned to hold us back, thereby holding himself back, out of the fray."

Henryk snorted. "As soon as he's told we should be used up front, he decides he's more valuable as a field commander in the rear. Pompous imbecile! And speaking of pompous imbeciles," Henryk glanced around furtively, "Mateusz has not a thought in his head—other than for the widow back in Kamieniec—and uses your ideas as if they were his own."

Jacek's pace did not slow. "I don't give a damn who gets credit. I just care about keeping us all from getting killed. If the captain wants to claim it as his idea, so be it. The result is the same." Jacek stopped, wheeled, and grinned. "And we are right where we're supposed to be. At the front!"

Just then distinct bursts sounded, and the men's eyes were pulled to thick white puffs billowing from the woods, followed by men shouting, running, dragging guns, scrambling for the trees. More shots.

Catching Lesław's eye as he approached the Biaska company, Jacek yelled, "Mount up!"

Rows of hussars led the formations between thin tree trunks onto open ground. Before them were rows of fresh dirt where yawning trenches had been, and low-lying berms that had been mounded as makeshift earthworks to buffer Commonwealth cannon.

They had deployed quickly after listening to a rousing entreaty from Matejko to do God's work, and singing "Bogurodzica" and "O Gloriosa Domina!" Though they were outnumbered three-to-one, they were ready for combat. Of eighteen hundred Commonwealth soldiers, three hundred and fifty were husaria.

Jacek had switched warhorses and sat atop Gwiazda. Beside him, Mateusz gripped a budzygan. Both men's forearms were bared. As he surveyed the field, Jacek took in the ground's undulations, the vegetation, and what little of the enemy could be seen through the haze of cannon fire.

Each side had shelled the other, and arrows had flown from opposite sides of the field. No damage of any consequence had yet visited their side, and it was time to close the distance and get a good look at the enemy. Standards waved and trumpets sounded, and the air was thick with the smell of acrid gunpowder smoke.

As a small group of light cavalry charged, shots rang out from the enemy side. The group retreated, and an eerie quiet settled over the plain. Jacek squinted against the brightness lighting up the dissipating smoke, searching for any telltale movement from the other side yet two furlongs away. And then he spotted spikes bristling in the center of the enemy's line.

Jacek pointed across the field. "Captain? Pikes ahead, with janissaries priming cannon and muskets behind."

THE HEART OF A HUSSAR

Mateusz looked ahead and nodded. "That's where we go."

Jacek adjusted his nose guard and backed Gwiazda, hailing his retainer. Marcin brought him a kopia, which he slid into the tuleja tethered to his saddle. Jacek guided his gelding to the center of the front line, passing Henryk and Lesław, acknowledging the greetings of his lord-brothers. His heart raced and his muscles tensed, but his breaths were deep and even.

Keep the men safe.

Keep me safe that I may return whole.

Ordered into their formations by commanders' maces, two ranks of hussars lined up in front of the breastworks, with two rows of pancerni behind. Servants were also mounted but hung at the back, behind the earthworks, to create the illusion of a greater force.

Jacek looked around. The Biaska husaria stood proudly in the front, painted and gilded kopie held high with their yellow-and-red silk pennons whipping and cracking. Every adornment gleamed, touched by shafts of sunlight piercing ragged clouds. Horses pranced and pawed the ground, eager to break into a canter.

A surge of pride overtook Jacek, and he began shouting to those around him.

"Remember who you ride for! You ride for God, and you ride for your mother Poland! It is they you serve. You are where God has placed you. This is what you have trained for your entire life, to be here, to do His work, and it is in His name that you offer your blood and your life today."

Though he hadn't planned it, his impromptu address seemed to energize the men. They crossed themselves, some kissing hilts, before erupting with a shout. The order came, and commanders signaled riders to close up ranks. Jacek checked his sabre dangling on its swordknot, at the ready. Aligned with other lancers in the front row, he grasped his kopia behind its ball handguard, the butt end snug in the tuleja. Behind him, the second row of cavalrymen held no lances, but they bristled with szabla, pałasz, and koncerz.

"Zlozcie kopie!" Lower lances!

"Dalej!" March!

They took off at a walk, which quickly became a trot. Jacek listened for the signal, and it came, suddenly, when the musicians sounded a different tattoo. Hussar commanders, riding on the outer edges of the formation, gestured with their maces in time with the new call.

"Postój!" they shouted. *Halt!*

As prearranged, the hussars reined in their mounts and lifted their lances as puffs of dense gray-white smoke erupted from behind enemy lines. The enemy's first volleys fell short, and Jacek smiled to himself, picturing enemy soldiers behind fortifications reloading furiously.

Now the commanders cried again.

"Zlozcie kopie!"

"Uderzaj!" Attack!

They restarted the run, once again lowering lances. The horses' hooves thundered and shook the ground. Jacek blocked all sound save his breathing and the drumming of his blood through his ears. He was taut and strong as Gwiazda went from a canter to a gallop. Ahead, pikemen dressed in a blend of earthy grays and browns awaited, kneeling, bracing steady spikes rammed into the earth. He trained his eyes on a target, envisioning where he would thrust the tip of his kopia.

His lower body seemed to fuse with Gwiazda's, and they were as one animal. Smooth, unwavering. They raced toward the enemy in a wide, tight row, lances leveled, parallel to the ground. Faces came into view. The horses' paces fell back to a canter. Jacek's focus tightened on pale gray below a grimacing face where two coal eyes blazed with hatred.

The periphery dissolved. Jacek's kopia slammed into flesh and bone. Shattered. He gripped his szabla. Time slowed. Impacts reverberated. Men screamed. Bodies hurled backward, landing on their fellows behind them. Men impaled on kopie. Shrieks rent the air. Falling horses thudded. Lances splintered. Gunfire popped, whizzed. A cannon roared.

The air was thick.

Waves of riders crashed into pike and artillery. In the middle of the enemy line, a gap appeared, widening as foes scattered. Jacek's momentum carried him beyond, into a sea of enemy. He spun. A musket barrel pointed at him. He sucked in a sharp breath.

Everything happened at once, in the blink of an eye, yet he registered it all. A flash, a cloud of enshrouding smoke, percussion vibrating through his body. A whine sizzled past his head.

Man pulls the trigger, but the Good Lord carries the bullet.

He swiveled his head. The musket was gone.

With his free hand, he snatched up his war hammer. In his right, he still clutched his sabre.

THE HEART OF A HUSSAR

Janissaries were reloading, touching off firearms, thick billows rolling off them. Arrows flew like black eels against the gray sky. A wall of Tatars on foot ran at him, pursued by mounted hussars. He raised his szabla. The musket was once again leveled at him, held by a janissary who suddenly crumpled to his knees. Behind the janissary, a silver blade glistened with blood. The rider grasping the blade flashed a wide grin before wheeling toward another enemy. Jacek would thank Stefan later.

A few turns on the killing field, and Jacek was soon alongside his fellows, slashing, hacking, trampling the enemy. He fought with both hands. Slivers of images, like shards of a mirror, embedded themselves in Jacek's brain between the blows he delivered to the enemy: hussars attacking ferociously, defending fallen comrades, struggling to escape wounded horses, striking at swarms of foemen. Brilliant crimson tangled with earthy hues and janissary *borks*.

The lot they were fighting vanished. Whether they had been felled or had fled, he had little idea. Heart beating like a drum, Jacek steered Gwiazda, gripped his szabla, and took stock. Inside the enemy line, pancerni fought savagely against swarming janissaries and their *kilijes*. The enemy was regrouping, closing the gap, trapping them.

They're cutting us off.

Over the cacophony came high-pitched war cries. He spun his horse. Enemy horsemen erupted from gaps between palisades and barricades, scimitars poised to swing.

Too many. We have to get out!

Movement to Jacek's right caught his eye. An unending stream of Tatars was pouring from behind earthworks and barricades, surging toward the Commonwealth's left flank, swallowing it up. One commander went down; no others were in sight. He swiveled his head again. Chaos everywhere.

"Fall back!" he bellowed.

A fellow hussar was parrying blows from three Tatar cavalrymen, and Jacek charged toward them. A chop to the shoulder neutralized one foe, and a slice through horse muscle and tendon had another tumbling to the ground with his thrashing mount.

"Fall back!" Jacek yelled again, gratified when the order was echoed amid the bloody frenzy. He turned toward the enemy line, determined to break it from behind this time. From out of the fray came other hussars, overrunning the enemy still scrabbling to fortify their line. More of his comrades emerged and fell in, and Jacek's heart lifted.

So many on our side still astride! Praise be to God!

Commonwealth riders scrambled, shouting as they dashed back to their own defensive lines. Shots boomed, and arrows flew after them. Haphazard formations of hussars, pancerni, and Cossacks escaped the enemy camp, but the Tatar cavalry was coming fast on their heels.

Jacek brought up the rear, eyes seeking his men. Two horse lengths ahead, a horse went down, spilling its winged rider from his saddle. Cursing through clenched teeth, Jacek aimed for the fallen hussar.

He slowed as he came alongside him, sliding his boot from the stirrup, and reached his hand down. The hussar stepped into the stirrup and hauled himself behind Jacek. And none too soon. A herd of Tatars was bearing down on them.

Gwiazda chose that moment to dance in a circle. Whether it was the extra weight he balked at or the turmoil, Jacek couldn't say, but the reason mattered little. It was flee or perish.

"The devil's own horse!" Jacek dug in his spurs and jerked the reins.

The charger turned and headed for the Commonwealth side but at an alarmingly slow pace, lagging well behind the rest.

"Gah!" Jacek spurred the horse again and smacked his rump with the flat of his blade to little effect. A projectile flew by, barely missing Jacek and the lumbering load they'd become. He had no need to look to know Tatar horsemen were closer now, firing arrows. One glanced off his passenger's armor, but another pierced the man's knee, and he cried out. A heartbeat later, another raked Jacek's exposed forearm.

Jesus! Only a miracle will save us.

Ahead of him, one such miracle was unfolding. A line of hussars bolted from behind the protection of their earthworks, speeding toward him. More arrows surged through the air, thudding behind him. *Commonwealth archers!* Pacholiks now streamed past him as though he stood still, on their way to reinforce the hussars. When Jacek gained his own defenses at last, he sent thanks to the heavens from the sheltering woods.

THE HEART OF A HUSSAR

Encircled by officers, Deputy Sosnowski sat on a silver-gilded, velvet-padded folding chair quizzing Jacek. Mateusz looked on with a scowl. Jacek plowed ahead with his report *and* his opinion.

Sosnowski gaped at him, his mouth opening and closing wordlessly as if he were a catfish scouring the bottom of a muddy pond.

"You're suggesting, Lieutenant, that we can defeat this army?"

Jacek bit back his frustration. "Yes, Deputy, of course we can, but we must attack soon," he said with fervor. *In for a złoty, in for a pound of gold.* Murmurs of agreement from those around him fortified him like bracing draughts. The casualties he had left behind gnawed at him, and he was anxious to get back before the enemy could finish off the injured.

A pacholik interrupted, urgency evident in his tone and wide-eyed expression. "Deputy, Commanders, there is something you must see."

Jacek emerged from the edge of the woods and looked toward the field. His heart dropped as though weighed down with stone. Scattered on the field beyond their earthworks were disembodied heads, unencumbered of their helmets. In the distance, along the Tatars' fortifications, stood pikes driven into the ground. Atop each one was the severed head of another slaughtered Commonwealth soldier, another man who had lived and breathed and fought beside Jacek this morning.

His eyes caught on a head sailing against the grim sky. His stomach lurched. It thudded in the dirt and rolled before coming to a rest. The head belonged to the young man Jacek had seen throwing up the night before. Smoldering rage deep in his gut caught fire, turning his spine into steel.

Around him, men retched, groaned, raged. Matejko's gritty voice rang out. "Deputy, I suggest we finalize our strategy quickly. That plan will no longer include recovering our injured."

The men had reconvened to prepare the next onslaught. Despite Mateusz's wishes for him to remain silent, commanders had been questioning Jacek, and he offered a strategy based on his observations—observations few in the assemblage had gained firsthand.

"The enemy will reinforce the line we breached earlier with reserves, more pikes, and artillery. Their right flank is weakened, and they expect us up the middle again, so we should attack that side." Jacek pointed at a crudely drawn map. "And once we've penetrated—"

The deputy interrupted. "Are you proposing throwing out your own captain's suggestion to storm the middle again?"

Jacek kept on, as if he hadn't heard the question. "The light and medium cavalry will sweep in here, with hajduks bringing up the rear."

Mateusz stared at Jacek as if he wanted to hurl *his* head onto the battlefield.

Jacek ignored his superior. "We advance and make them think we are committed to a charge up the middle. As before, we wait for them to discharge their muskets and cannon. Once they've launched the first volley, we charge, but we veer to their right flank."

Mateusz scoffed. "And how do you propose to get past the breastworks?"

"They're not as close together as they appear from this angle. When I was behind their line, I got a good look at the gaps. Also, they trampled their own ground when they engaged on that side, and some of those mounds were flattened." Jacek's blood was afire, and impassioned speech had replaced his usual equanimity.

Matejko and several commanders nodded their approval. Sosnowski's eyes darted toward the enemy camp, mercifully quiet.

Matejko tapped the map with a gloved finger. "I agree with Lieutenant Dąbrowski. That is the spot for the husaria to smash."

"But you're proposing trickery, a coward's act!" Sosnowski snapped.

Jacek's shoulders were squared, his jaw set and his body rigid; only his nostrils moved, flaring with each breath. He withheld an exasperated exhale and his growing contempt for the witless commandant.

Another pułkownik cleared his throat. "I think the lieutenant's strategy has a good chance, Deputy." The pułkownik flicked his eyes to Jacek.

Another long pause, and men shifted their weight as they awaited the decision.

THE HEART OF A HUSSAR

"All right, then." Sosnowski reminded Jacek of a petulant child. "Matejko, I leave the execution of the lieutenant's proposal to you."

Matejko addressed Mateusz. "Captain Zalewski, I have need of your lieutenant. I will return him to you when I am done."

Mateusz's eyes bored into Jacek, their intensity easing when he nodded to Matejko. "Of course. He is yours for as long as you need him." His words were brittle, icy.

The day had grown warmer, but the slate skies threatened to pelt them with rain. Once out of earshot, Matejko turned to Jacek, his obsidian eyes twinkling. Somewhere in his beard was a smile that pinked his cheeks and made him look almost jovial.

"You had better watch yourself, Lieutenant. I suspect your captain dreams of seeing your head on one of those pikes, and he no doubt searches for a reason to make it so." Jacek held his tongue, and the colonel continued. "I know it was you and not your superior who suggested the first plan of attack. You have a good tactical mind and an unflinching bravery to use it. I have no wish to see talent wasted. While you are under my command, I will see he leaves you uninjured. After that, I fear you are on your own, but I have no doubt you will survive his rancor."

Jacek thanked him and followed in his wake, snatching bits of conversation between Matejko and the other colonel.

"Lord deliver us from incompetent commandants," Matejko muttered.

"How many campaigns has he led?" the other pułkownik asked.

"To my knowledge, one."

"One? You cannot be serious!"

"Alas, I am all too serious." Matejko let out a sigh. "A small one at that."

"How did he gain his position?"

"He is a relative of Potocki's. His wife's third cousin's son or some such thing. No doubt the assignment was accorded to satisfy the family. Potocki likely never imagined this dandy would be at the head of such a force, against such an enemy," Matejko said.

Jacek reflected bitterly that the Commonwealth colonels had just achieved their first victory of the conflict—against their own supreme commander. The gain, however, meant far more. They were no longer doomed to sure defeat. They might survive the day.

Within the hour, Commonwealth troops were once more arrayed against the enemy. Among the front line, Jacek sat atop Jarosława with charged anticipation. The hussars had executed their feint, and the enemy discharged staggered volleys. The signal came, and the towarzysze took off, followed as before by rows of retainers and lighter cavalry.

A wolfish growl rumbled in Jacek's chest, and a feral smile tugged his cheeks. His line veered to the enemy's right flank, accelerating to a gallop. The move seemed to confuse the janissaries, who began firing irregularly. Tatars loosed arrows before falling back. Jacek and his comrades found their way through the mounded earthworks like a river diverting around boulders, overtaking fleeing soldiers as they went.

Around him, riders fell to enemy shot and arrows. Others tragically found ground traps in which they became ensnared, horses and men falling in spectacular fashion. Commonwealth infantrymen and artillerymen surged, attacking palisades and breastworks, their axes rising and falling. Noise, fire, and turmoil erupted as they coursed through fortifications. All the while, with Commonwealth foot soldiers tangling feverishly in the center of the Tatar camp, more troops and cavalry poured on the enemy's flanks.

Jacek stopped and surveyed the mayhem. Great clouds of dust and smoke hung in the air, obscuring his view.

Izaak reined in beside him, breathing hard, pointing with his szabla. "There they are, Lieutenant."

"I see them."

Jacek signaled, and his line fired into the enemy cavalry.

Into the thick of the battle he burst, as though the decapitated young soldier rode with him. He fought a fierce exchange with two enemy horsemen, using his every weapon and limb with precision. He kicked, punched, elbowed, swung szabla and pałasz, took a punch and roared back.

Combat was swift and vicious, and now came a lull. Jacek circled about atop Jarosława. As he surveyed the scene, he grew heartened by the sight of Commonwealth foot soldiers sweeping over the battlefield, servants on their heels sifting through wreckage. In their wake lay countless bodies—enemy, ally, and equine—and smashed bits of the encampment and its defenses.

He rode to Twierzda's bridge and pulled up, his breathing ragged. He still gripped his pałasz, its shine dulled with crusted blood; his sabre had been forfeited to an enemy body. Now came his first close look at the battle raging across the river. Catapults launched fiery projectiles at the fortress, and smoke rose from its battlements. Janissaries scrambled up long ladders propped against fortress walls while desperate struggles played out along the ramparts.

We must stop them!

Jacek looked about, but no superior officers were in sight. He directed cavalry to follow him over the bridge. Mid-span, dense volleys of arrows loosed from distant barricades fell on them. Save one lone janissary with a sword in hand and something Jacek couldn't make out in the other, the west end of the bridge was deserted.

Jacek held up his fist. "Halt!" he called to the soldiers following him, alarm bells clanging in his head. The janissary knelt by the bridge.

"Retreat! Off the bridge!" Jacek bellowed.

Arrows continued raining down, and pandemonium erupted amid the men and beasts behind him. Pushing Jarosława toward the lone janissary, he unholstered a primed wheel-lock and touched it off. The janissary jerked backward, dropping his sword and a length of rope. As he rolled about, another janissary ran forward and snatched up the rope.

Aiming his second wheel-lock, Jacek fired—only to miss the dodging janissary. The soldier slid down the slope and disappeared. Jacek surged forward and clattered across the bridge. When he reached the other side, he leapt from Jarosława and scrambled under the bridge. Balancing on the steep slope, the janissary was touching the short rope to a cord. Smoke rose, and an orange glow inched along the cord's snaking length toward a barrel affixed to the underside of the bridge. Jacek scanned quickly, taking in five more barrels. The janissary turned and heaved up a kilij.

Jacek felt a surge go through him, and he parried the blade with his pałasz and thrust, connecting, wounding. With a cry, the janissary stumbled, lost his balance, and fell down the slope into the churning water. Jacek grabbed the cord and yanked, but it held fast. Above him, horse hooves pounded on the bridge amid men's shouts. They weren't all clear of the bridge. Teetering precariously, he planted one boot and splayed the cord across a wooden beam. Then he brought his long blade down, but the motion was awkward and only nicked the cord. The fuse continued smoldering.

Jesus!

He thrust the pałasz in the dirt and wrenched his dagger from its scabbard. The ember was advancing, gaining momentum, glowing brighter. Gathering what little slack remained, he folded the cord and sawed, at last severing it. He chucked the lit fuse into the river where it swirled along its surface, out of harm's way.

Gulping in air, he dragged himself up the slope only to be met by the wounded janissary, whose hand was cocked back, fingers gripping a ball.

The janissary jerked, and the ball dropped. The man tumbled slowly, revealing Henryk behind him with a bloody blade. The ball landed upright. A string ran from its top, and it was smoking. Jacek ran at it, shoving Henryk to the ground. The ember on the fuse disappeared into the neck of the ball. Jacek spun on one foot, kicking the grenade away from the bridge. Right before it touched the water, the vessel exploded, hurling wicked shards.

Jacek threw himself atop Henryk, arms cradling his head. All grew quiet. Jacek glanced over his shoulder, then hoisted himself off his friend.

Henryk's wide-eyed stare bounced between Jacek and the river. "What the devil?"

"I was trying to prevent the bridge exploding," Jacek said between panting breaths. "We need to disassemble six casks fixed under it before the bastards can light them. They're full of gunpowder."

"They won't be lighting them, Jacek," Henryk said between heavy breaths of his own. "The battle's won."

Spent, sore, Jacek rolled onto his back and gazed heavenward.

Jacek witnessed little of the final capture save the self-congratulating Sosnowski's dramatic gestures, which he inflicted on the Tatar commander with unrestrained extravagance. *A well-deserved punishment.*

THE HEART OF A HUSSAR

Jacek took inventory of his wounds—muffled hearing, countless gashes and bruises, a fractured finger, and an elbow that throbbed mercilessly. *It will all heal.*

Deputy Michal Sosnowski unabashedly claimed credit for the victory, regaling his tall tales from his sumptuous quarters in Kamieniec. Sosnowski was not the only one to claim credit where it was not due. Mateusz boasted that the tactics had all been his idea, and while he was about it, he had no compunction about reprimanding Jacek before the men.

"You see, Dąbrowski, a *true* leader is one who comes up with solutions," he said loudly amid a cluster of hussars in camp. "You've proven once again you're no more than an everyday soldier meant to follow orders. You may have the size of an ox, but you've also the head of one. You do not belong among those of us directing battles."

Jacek glanced up at Henryk, who stood behind the captain, shooting daggers at the back of his head.

Mateusz regarded Jacek with a wry smile. "You're as high as you're going to climb, and you don't deserve to be even there. Do not make the mistake of thinking you will go farther."

Jacek bit his cheek and rocked on the balls of his feet, his hands clasped behind him.

"I've written the details to Lord Eryk," Mateusz droned, "so he will have the truth. He will know who fought valiantly, who was of great help to me in this victory … and who was not."

Inwardly, Jacek railed. Once again, it appeared no commendation would be forthcoming.

Of minor consolation was Twierzda's gratitude, which was displayed in a lavish celebration to honor the troops—despite its partly charred fortress. The noisy affair began of a morning and spread throughout castle yards. People devoured food and drink, danced, and cavorted with abandon. The captain did not restrain the men in this. Had Mateusz consulted him, Jacek would not have disagreed.

Favoring his elbow, Jacek slouched beside a tall window in the great hall, trying to escape the notice of most everyone—especially a light-haired young woman who seemed to be wherever he was. As he nursed a cup of mead, he scanned the crowd and smiled inwardly each time he spotted one of his fellows partaking of the merriment.

A host of adoring girls thronged Izaak; he looked as though his head might snap off from pivoting it to and fro. The chorąży's exuberant face was fixed with a permanent grin.

Jacek was surprised to see Lesław beside a noblewoman who seemed to be wooing *him*. Cutting a striking figure in his husaria garb, Lesław's darting eyes and jerkiness bespoke his bashfulness, but the smile plastered on his face could not hide his delight.

Jacek was not at all amazed when his eyes lit on Henryk expertly wheedling not one, but four ladies. While Jacek could not hear what tale he spun, his animated expressions and their ceaseless twittering made it clear Henryk's charm was in full sway. Jacek flashed back to the tournament celebration, wondering once more if Oliwia would have succumbed to Henryk's honeyed tongue had Jacek not stopped him. He shrugged the thought away and stared out the window.

On a sprawling green lawn sat Marcin, leaning back on his hands with his legs casually crossed in front of him. Jacek was reminded he still needed to mete out his retainer's punishment despite the deputy hounding him to reward the lad. For now, he watched with a mix of irritation, jealously, and diversion as Marcin wooed Joanna, the lovely brown-haired maid he had helped rescue. Jacek did not envy the pacholik the girl—only that he courted one who seemed to enjoy his advances. Marcin ducked and whispered in her ear. Her irrepressible laughter caught on the air and drifted to the window, clubbing Jacek with an unaccustomed moment of self-pity. His heart hollowed as he considered, for the first time in his life, that no tender beloved worried after him or awaited his return.

The light-haired girl appeared on the opposite side of the hall, looking about, so he bolted through the doors into the spring sun, where children shrieked and chased one another in never-ending circles. Meandering under azure skies amid all manner of folk and tents, his spirits lifted—especially when he paused to witness two young boys squaring off, fists balled and ready, their peers looking on. He cheered on the smaller of the two. No sooner had the little one launched himself at the big one but women swarmed and hauled them off. Jacek resumed his wandering.

Clusters of musicians played, and dancing broke out spontaneously throughout the vast field. So when the young woman materialized beside him, he was less guarded.

"I do believe you have been avoiding me, Lieutenant." Doe-brown eyes held a devilish gleam. She twirled her dark green skirts about herself, revealing snow-white petticoats that skimmed dainty ankles. She was much prettier up close.

"I … No, of course not."

"Perhaps you dodge all the young ladies because you've a wife or sweetheart at home?"

He looked away and sipped from his still-full cup.

"Ah," she said with a triumphant smile. "So you *do* have someone you've left behind. Surely she would not mind if you shared one dance, would she?"

No entanglements.

"I fear my elbow prevents me."

"Then nothing more vigorous than a promenade," she offered.

He looked at her, then told himself twirling with a maid would come to nothing—and it allowed a touch he craved.

He set down his cup and extended his hand. "She would not mind."

CHAPTER 24
Rich Nobleman, Poor Nobleman

Oliwia ambled along a crushed-rock path amid plots and beds in the main garden, clutching her papers. Her heart lifted at the sight of summer's vibrant blossoms arrayed before her. Skimming her hands over tops of blue larkspur and white lilies, she headed to the shelter of linden trees heavy with clusters of yellow blooms. Their sweet honey-and-lemon scent engulfed her. She tugged off her cap, relishing a ruffling breeze on her head.

Trumpet flowers and fragrant honeysuckle interlaced thickly over wooden arbors, offering cool pockets where she could escape the heat. Seeking one such shady haven, she was enveloped in shadow, going deeper into its dappled depths. Eyes still dazzled by the sun, she couldn't focus, though she thought something moved. *A cat on the hunt?*

She sat quietly, soon discovering she was not alone. A pair of ardent lovers occupied the darkest recess, and she froze in the duskiness. Curiosity grabbed hold, overpowering propriety.

As she looked on, her stomach alternately fluttered and clenched, and she wondered what it felt like to be touched as this man was touching this woman. What would it feel like to touch him back? Both seemed to enjoy what they were doing immensely. Oliwia was no stranger to animals mating. She understood how it was done and what resulted, but this was different. Tender caresses, longing stares, and passionate embraces transformed into groping, grappling, and pleasurable moaning.

Apparently finished, they shared more sweet kisses, then stole away. She sat for long moments fanning herself with the cap. Nowhere in her thoughts were the brilliant flowers that had beckoned her here in the first place.

Days later, she returned and plunked onto a cool stone bench. The air pulsated with summer sounds, and she swiped at a hatch of gnats suspended before her. Drawing in a cleansing breath, she loosened her braid and mopped her forehead with her linen apron.

"Now what shall I draw?" she said aloud to a pair of chirping birds.

"A soldier perhaps?"

Oliwia yelped, jumping from the bench and spilling her papers, pencil, and cap. Her heart raced as she peered into the shadows. Something large stirred, and she backed up, her breaths coming fast.

"I'm sorry. I did not mean to frighten you." Oliwia detected familiarity in the gentle male voice. Was that English? With a brogue? A figure loomed, and she took a few more steps back. A man came out of the dark, bent over, and picked up her scattered possessions. A shaft of light caught on a dark copper curl. He rose and faced her.

Several inches taller than she, a young soldier stood, angular and straight, smiling contritely as he offered her the stack he'd collected.

"I am truly sorry, mistress."

Oliwia absently reached out and accepted what he handed her. Tucking the items against her chest, she wheeled from him. A hand clutched her upper arm and whirled her back.

"Please don't go. I fear I've made a poor impression. Might I try again?"

She looked down at the hand holding her, and he released her. When she glanced up, she recognized him as one of Lord Eryk's garrisoned soldiers—one of the Scots—a young man with a handsome, earnest face. He stood immobile as he met her gaze, then seemed to remember himself. He swept her a formal bow.

"George MacMillan at your service, my lady."

"You are ... part of the garrison, yes?"

He grinned. "That I am. Though I've seen you about, we've not been properly introduced."

"I ... am Oliwia."

"Yes. Oliwia of Clan Armstrong."

"How did you …"

He laughed. A warm, nervous laugh. "We Scots are not so many in Poland that we lose track of our own countrymen. Or our women."

Oliwia blinked. The manner in which he looked at her discomfited her, though not in an altogether bad way.

"I … Well, I must go," she stammered.

"Have I frightened you so badly? You usually spend more time here, making your drawings." He pointed at her papers.

Alarm rose within her. "How do you know how much time I spend here?"

He squeezed his eyes shut, then looked at her sheepishly. "I have been here a time or two and seen you sketching."

"I really must go. The lady …" She turned and briskly walked away from him.

He called after. "Might I see you here tomorrow?"

Her heart thudded, and she felt need of the linen to mop her brow once more. She stopped and glanced over her shoulder. He was rotating a deep blue tam clutched in his hands.

"I do not think so."

She thought his shoulders sagged a little as she spun and tore for the castle.

Oliwia did see George MacMillan again. Soon after their first meeting, on yet another glorious sun-drenched day, she strolled toward her shady refuge. George awaited her, a broad smile plastered on his face. She swiveled her head to and fro, hesitated, but at last ducked in and sat rigidly at the far edge of the bench. He took up a position at the other end.

"How old are you, mistress, if you do not mind my asking?"

"I am sixteen, soon to be seventeen. And you?"

"I am eighteen. Only just." An awkward beat later, he said, "Your brother. Filip? How is he coming along?"

"I ... I am not sure I know. I glimpse him from time to time in the stables or at Mass. He must be indispensable in the garrison."

"You are Catholic, then?"

Oliwia coughed. "Yes, though I lived in ... um, along the border. Among the Orthodox."

George gave her an odd look, his brows pulling together. Did he know she had come from Muscovy? An Orthodox, enemy, Muscovite peasant.

"You are Catholic, yes?" she asked, masking her unease.

"Yes, from generations of Catholics. It is very important in my family."

"I do not recall seeing you at Mass."

He chuckled. It was a rich sound. "My practice has been wanting of late. Do not tell my mother." He winked, and Oliwia laughed.

"What brought you here, and when did you come?"

"I came here last spring, long after the company had left for Muscovy. I followed my brothers for an adventure. They moved to Kraków, and I remain here." He shrugged.

Another awkward pause. "I expect you miss them. When I do see my brother, he's with soldiers and their sons. He looks fit and happy, so I try not to fret overmuch. I had hoped to see him more."

"Could I bring him to you?" George offered.

She brightened. "Can you do that? When the company was here, Pan Jacek made sure I saw him regularly. My brother is his apprentice, you know."

George's back stiffened. "You are well acquainted with the lieutenant?"

"No, not so well acquainted. We talk, but he is ... he is a hard man to know."

"A very hard man," George mumbled.

"I did not mean he is a hard man," she corrected. "Just hard to know."

"Is he—are you partial to him?"

"I? Partial to the lieutenant?" she exclaimed a little too loudly. "Oh no. Of course not."

"I, well, I only ask because I hear many a lady *is* partial to him, and ..." George shook his head and looked down at the bench. "I'd best not say."

"Best not say what?"

George leveled his eyes at her, and she realized they were muddy green, ringed in dark amber. "Not say what?" she repeated.

He stared at her as if appraising her, then took a deep breath. "Well, consider, mistress. He is on campaign nearly the entire year, and many of these noble rogues keep ... have ... er, companions along the way." George then leaned over to her, dropping his voice to a conspiratorial whisper. "They may have even sired children. They are different from you and I."

She gaped at him. Her mind flashed. First to the beautiful, swan-like Lady Izabela, who had emerged from a night walk with Jacek, breathless and rumpled, then to Henryk's words: *Who's the true rogue, Jacek?*

Oliwia's throat tightened. George coughed once, twice, and scooted back to his end of the bench. "Begging your pardon, but you are a virtuous girl, and I would hate to see you fall prey to one such as him. He would surely try to take advantage of your, uh, kindheartedness."

Brows knitted together, she twisted her hands in a knot as tight as the one in her stomach.

Oliwia saw George at every Mass thereafter. In the gardens, she met him twice more, alone. They did not speak of the lieutenant again, instead speaking of life in their respective villages. When he recounted stories of his large family, he used animated arm gestures and laughed often, creating endearing sets of creases at the corners of his eyes. She grew comfortable in his company, and the space between them on the bench narrowed.

One afternoon, they were talking quietly when a rather enthusiastic pair scrambled under the cover of a nearby arbor. Oliwia craned her neck for a better look and was stifling a giggle when George reached out and turned her head toward him. His hand lingered on her cheek, then his fingers sifted through a few loose tendrils. He looked at his hand in her hair as if mesmerized.

Then he did the most extraordinary thing. He loudly said, "Are you looking forward to the harvest festival, my lady?"

The shadows erupted, sounding altogether like two large animals crashing through underbrush. Oliwia thought she heard cursing and grunting, and she covered her mouth to hold her laughter back. George grinned at her, his shoulders shaking.

Soon the only sounds were buzzing dragonfly wings and trilling birds. Oliwia looked at George, looking at her, and he was no longer smiling. A few small chuckles bubbled up from inside her. He leaned in and stroked her cheek with his fingertips. Her breath quickened. She bent toward him and closed her eyes. Soft lips pressed hers. Her mind began to whir.

So this is what it feels like? It's not unpleasant, but shouldn't it feel more ... well, more?

He cradled her face, then pulled back and looked at her with a smile playing across his lips. Brushing a thumb over her cheek, he tilted her head up.

"Oliwia," he whispered.

She closed her eyes, and just as his lips touched hers again, she sensed a shadow and looked up.

In time to see a hand descend.

Oliwia jerked backward with a shriek. Towering above her was Kasimir, his swarthy face stormy as he yanked George from the bench and tossed him hard to the ground on his backside.

"Hey!" George yelled.

Kasimir gathered George's tunic in both fists and hauled him up, his dark eyes flicking over Oliwia. "Did he hurt you?"

"No, but *you* frightened me half to death," she retorted hotly.

George grunted, struggling against Kasimir's heavy-handed hold. As if he grasped a hissing cat by the scruff rather than a fully grown man, Kasimir grinned.

"My apologies, Lady Oliwia. Lieutenant Dąbrowski's orders."

"What?" she squealed, horrified.

Kasimir shoved George back down and pinned him with a boot. "Quit your whining," he growled. "Oh, not you, my lady," he quickly added.

He whistled, high and sharp, and several guards materialized beside him. "Take the lady back to the keep." He and another guard wrenched George to his feet.

After recovering from her appalling embarrassment, Oliwia returned to the gardens days later, but she never saw George MacMillan again. When she asked after George's whereabouts, Kasimir simply told her he'd left the garrison. No further explanation.

She hadn't known George well, but she found it odd he never said goodbye. They had been friends, after all. Along with her daily prayers for the swift and safe return of the company, she added a prayer for George's health. She missed their talks and his easy laugh. She did not miss his kisses.

Throughout the summer season, Katarzyna's vigor wavered, and Oliwia assumed more of the lady's duties. As her role grew more familiar, she acquired a flair for the assignment. She even struck a tenuous truce with Beata, though she'd yet to convince the latter to bestow her tartlets easily.

Oliwia relayed her prideful, newfound success in a letter she carefully penned to Jacek, concluding he needed to return in order to filch the mouthwatering treats she so craved.

Her letter-writing was a slow affair, but she faithfully replied to the few he sent her in hopes that a bit of levity from home would be a welcome escape for him—and that he would not forget her. She refrained from asking him about his orders to Kasimir for fear he'd think poorly of her if he learned what she'd gotten up to.

Jacek also sent letters to Filip, each nearly identical to those Oliwia received, describing the drudgery of everyday life in camp. Sometimes he wrote news of other fronts, such as the fall of Smoleńsk to the Commonwealth in June—at last—or the continuing siege of the Polish garrison in Moscow. She found herself applauding the victory at Smoleńsk and fretting for the Polish soldiers trapped within the Kremlin's walls. A turnabout indeed.

Alone in her chamber, Oliwia pulled the hand fan and the short stack of letters from her trunk each night. By candlelight, she reread each one thoroughly, though she knew them all by heart. The ritual ended when she brushed her fingers over his spare, tidy words and lingered on his unexpectedly extravagant signature. As she traced the large loops and whorls of his name, she pondered if a different hand scratched the signature; it seemed more in keeping with Henryk's nature. In the end, she tucked her tiny bundle away with a smile, concluding Jacek filled the page with his name to make up for his brevity.

THE HEART OF A HUSSAR

During summer and fall's warmer months, she busied herself with the harvest festival and a procession of noble guests within Biaska's halls. Among the numerous visitors was Lord Eryk's unctuous cousin Antonin, whom Oliwia avoided as best she could. Upon his arrival, they learned his wife Helena had passed, and he was casting about for a new bride. He'd had the temerity to look Oliwia up and down with his pronouncement, even licking his reedy lips once when no one but she saw. A shiver slithered down her spine, and she envisioned Kasimir tossing *him* on his backside.

At a particularly crowded feast one evening, Lady Katarzyna brightly scanned her guests, then leaned over and whispered in Oliwia's ear.

"Did you see the jewels on Lord Sapieszko's belt? Stunning! He and his son are both handsome. They rather look alike, yes?"

Oliwia glanced toward father and son, suppressing a giggle.

Katarzyna arched an eyebrow. "What?"

"It's just that ... they are *very* much alike. They fancy the same scullery maids."

Katarzyna's eyes flew wide. *"What?"* Her cry drew the attention of several guests.

Oliwia showed contrition while Katarzyna huffed. The lady composed herself and soon leaned back over. "Lord Rybiński is a good dancer."

Oliwia looked around. "Lord Lodziński is also a good dancer."

"Look how round he is," sniffed Katarzyna. "And barely taller than you. He wears his remaining wealth on his chubby fingers. They're all he has."

Just then, a young lord stepped to Oliwia and invited her to stroll. Behind him, Katarzyna pinched her nose and shook her head. Oliwia pressed her lips together and covered her mouth after declining, holding back her laughter. She was pleased to be playing this game with Katarzyna. The lady's particularly pink complexion, together with her sharp wit, signaled what Oliwia hoped would be an extended return to health.

When Oliwia recovered her demure facade, she leaned in to Katarzyna. "Lord Basowicz is pleasant."

Katarzyna's eyes darted about until they fell on said lord. "But that nose! *And* the wart upon it! Have you spoken to him?"

Oliwia shook her head. "No, only danced. He is light on his feet."

"That may be, but he is as thick as our castle walls."

Lady Katarzyna covertly threw out a few more observations, which abruptly concluded with a little jerk. Behind her fan, she whispered, "Lord

Eryk is watching, so I must behave. I do not wish to provoke my husband's possessive nature. He does not show it often, but the last time he displayed his jealous side, it ended rather badly for the gentleman. I've always regretted it." She pulled back and nodded solemnly at Oliwia, a look of regret in her eyes.

The statement shocked Oliwia. "My lady?"

"The young man tried to befriend me to gain Eryk's ear. He misjudged terribly, for Eryk mistook his attentions. The man in question, a mid-ranking nobleman, found himself unable to improve his position or increase his holdings after Eryk was done. For a mere flirtation. I understand he is employed by another middling noble as a mere soldier. I wish I could have prevented it, but my lord would not be deterred."

Oliwia glimpsed Eryk genially engaged in conversation among a group of guests, trying earnestly to imagine the flaring passion that could drive him to such measures. She failed in the conjuring.

A week after Oliwia's seventeenth birthday, the two women sat together in Katarzyna's quarters basking in shafts of morning light, the lady wrestling with a bit of lace and Oliwia industriously working on a rectangle of thick paper stacked atop others.

"What is it you are drawing, my dear?"

"Oh, nothing but a poor sketch of a hussar."

"Anyone I know?" Katarzyna asked.

Oliwia reddened. "Well, yes. Upon his departure, I studied the lieutenant's armor and am now trying to draw it from memory. I fear I do not recall it as well as I'd hoped. It has been so long."

"Here. Let me see." Katarzyna dropped her sewing in her lap and held out her hand. She studied the drawing. "The lord received word of the company just yesterday, you know."

Oliwia's chest compressed. Neither she nor Filip had received any communication from Jacek in weeks. "I … I trust everyone is … well?"

"Yes, aside from the casualties we already knew of. The company is on its way home."

THE HEART OF A HUSSAR

Now Oliwia's anxiety transformed into a full flight of butterflies.

Katarzyna thumbed through a few sketches below Jacek's. Her eyes lit on one, then bounced between Oliwia and the sketch.

"Is something wrong, my lady?"

Katarzyna flipped back to the original image Oliwia had handed her. "No, I just thought … We had a young Scot here for a while, and one of your drawings"—she pointed to Oliwia's stack—"resembles him. Just as your portrait of the lieutenant is a striking likeness of the real man. You have captured his handsome face and the fierce scowl that always overshadows his good looks. I don't know about the armor, though. I confess I have not spent a great deal of time studying it. How is it you were able to?"

"I, well, I just … looked at it when he was preparing to ride out."

Katarzyna's green eyes flew wide. "Do you mean you *stared* at him?"

Oliwia nodded and felt her blush deepen.

"My dearest Oliwia, you cannot just gawp at a man. It is far too obvious."

"What is too obvious, my lady?"

"How you feel about him. *I* am not accusing you of harboring affection for the lieutenant, but if you stare at him, everyone will believe it is so whether it's the truth or not—including the lieutenant. If he notices, that is. If you had stared at Pan Henryk, I am sure *he* would have noticed, but the lieutenant is a slightly different sort. Much more serious."

Oliwia lifted her hand to cover her gaping mouth.

"Yes, well, I see you were quite innocently looking at his armor, after all. But let us say you *were* interested in the lieutenant, and not simply as a study. As a romantic interest, yes?"

"But, my lady, I am not!"

"Good. Even if you were, my dear, the lieutenant has so many women eager to … to accommodate him. Accomplished, beautiful noblewomen, in addition to the girls in the villages who endlessly throw themselves at his feet like freshly picked flowers." She flung her hands in the air, the gesture accompanied by a dramatic roll of her eyes. "He has no doubt amassed a new following in Podolia. He's a young man, after all, not yet wed. And in the meantime … Well, let us just agree Pan Jacek does not lack for female companionship."

The lump in Oliwia's throat prevented her swallowing.

"But all this chatter is beside the point. You, my dear, deserve a much better station than that of a mere soldier's wife."

Oliwia clamped her jaw shut.

"Oh, it's true, Oliwia. The Scot—I don't recall his name—had a charming smile, but nothing more. The girl who marries him will marry only for love as he'll provide little else."

The story of Oliwia's own parents skipped through her mind.

"As for Pan Jacek, he has more to offer than the common soldier to be sure, but he will not inherit his father's estate and will forever be relegated to the status of a petty—and penniless—noble. The best he can hope for is to parley his good looks to gain himself a wealthy wife."

Oliwia winced inside for the man who strove so doggedly to be neither unlanded nor landed by means of an advantageous marriage.

"For you, Oliwia, I see much greater possibilities. You are destined to be the consort of a wealthy, powerful lord—a great lady in your own right. So you must forget about common soldiers." Katarzyna blithely flung Oliwia's sketches into the fire.

Oliwia bit back a protest and willed herself to stay seated while her eyes fixed on the blackening sheets curling in the flames.

CHAPTER 25

Homecoming

A sennight before All Souls' Day, wicked cold gripped the countryside. A raging wind, coupled with impatience for the company's return, had submerged the castle in gloomy agitation. Messengers had arrived days before, proclaiming the company was close behind, yet there was no sign.

Oliwia lingered in the kitchen in the late afternoon, taking in its warmth and aromas, when suddenly the trumpets blared and shots *pop-popped*. Already alarmed, a kitchenmaid further scared the wits out of her when she let out a squeal. The girl ran from the room, her screeches echoing through the passageway to the great hall. Oliwia looked at Beata, whose hands perched on her well-rounded hips, a weary look on her droopy-eyed, lined face.

"I will get no work out of that one for at least a week now." The old cook shook her head.

"Why did she scream?"

"Every day she searches for the pennons; her sweetheart is a pacholik who left in spring. From the growing racket, I venture the company is riding to the gates this very moment. And now I must prepare more food for a horde of hungry soldiers by myself, no doubt. Ack!" She threw up her hands.

Oliwia spun on the spot, following hurriedly in the maid's wake. Behind her, Beata exclaimed, "Tchah! The missing soldiers return, and now all the silly maids go missing."

As she scurried to the great hall, frenzied, exuberant shrieks bounced off the stone walls. Folk surged from every part of the castle like busy ants pouring from their labyrinths after a careless kick caved in their mound. Oliwia was caught in the swarm.

Her heart beating like hummingbird wings, she tore to the battlements as fleetly as her feet would carry her. Others had gotten there before her, and she gleefully shared their joy at the glorious sight: a wave of riders moving over fields toward the castle, ruffling red-and-yellow pennons held high on lances. Tattered, leaden clouds shrouded the countryside, but the cavaliers seemed to reflect an unseen light bursting through the dimness, as if the heavens had opened just to illuminate them.

They rode fast, bringing them closer to Biaska Castle on the thunder of hoofbeats. Soon they were near enough that Oliwia could make them out, and her heart turned over when she recognized the lieutenant out in front with another familiar form. Jacek and Henryk rode side by side, so close their stirrups could have been touching. They urged their horses as though they raced for a heavy purse. She clapped her hands together.

Down the steps she dashed, along darkened hallways, through the massive oaken doors, into needles of sleet slicing down from the iron clouds. Hampered by the burgeoning crowd, she picked her way to the forestairs.

The bailey overflowed with humanity and beasts such that the trailing soldiers struggled to get inside the castle walls. Oliwia stopped and settled her eyes on the commotion, longing to throw herself into the raucous reunion but afraid she'd disappear under a hoof or twelve. Rooted in place, she pulled herself up and squared her shoulders. Inside, she quivered.

Jacek and Henryk were thronged within circles of people, but their statures being what they were, she easily picked them out. Filip pelted through the crowd and narrowly avoided knocking Jacek on his backside when he launched himself at the lieutenant. Jacek picked him up in an embrace, pecking his cheeks thrice before putting him back down on his feet. Filip pointed toward her.

Jacek raised his eyes. He locked on her, his gaze traveling up and down her person. His eyebrows rose, then furrowed, lending him a confused expression that quickly transformed to one of recognition, as if it had taken him a moment to recall who she was. His mouth quirked. Oliwia's smile widened, lifting her cold cheeks. She gripped her skirts. He returned the smile, moved a few people aside, and climbed the steps. Her heart now beat as though an entire flock of hummingbirds darted about in her chest.

When Jacek reached her, she looked up at him towering over her. He scanned her thoroughly from head to foot, and she felt a blush rise up her throat and heat her cheeks. His face was thinner, and a thick, dark brown moustache, like broom bristles, covered his lip. A laugh escaped her. Jacek smiled broadly, saying nothing, looking down at her, eyes shining like polished sapphires. She opened her mouth to speak, and a croak slipped out. Lady Katarzyna materialized, planting herself before Oliwia. Jacek immediately stepped back and bowed. Trying to step from behind, Oliwia was blocked by Katarzyna's slight body, seemingly moving with hers.

"Ah! I am heartened to have you back home again. Welcome!" boomed Eryk. He banged a hand on Jacek's shoulder before embracing him. Behind him, Mateusz stood beside his wife and held one of his squealing children aloft.

"Come. I am sure you have much to tell me, and I am anxious to hear it all." Eryk turned toward the keep doors, and Jacek fell in behind him and Mateusz.

Giving her a sidelong glance, Jacek called out a quick, "How do you fare, Lady Oliwia?"

"I am well," she peeped.

She thought she heard Lady Barbara call to Jacek, but he kept moving as if he'd not heard her. Hugging her arms to herself, Oliwia glimpsed the bulky forms of the men as they withdrew.

"It's cold out here! Oliwia, into the hall." Katarzyna gave her a little push, and she skidded on the ice-encrusted stone. Lady Barbara cackled.

In the shelter of the hall, Katarzyna looked Oliwia over, a frown on her face.

"Is something wrong, my lady?" Oliwia asked.

"Follow me to my chamber. 'Tis time for the harp," Katarzyna said sharply.

Oliwia headed toward the stairs, which in this moment seemed furlongs away. As she crossed the great hall, she considered how she had nearly burst with excitement only minutes before, but now she was chilled and deflated.

As he followed Mateusz and Eryk, Jacek stole a glance over his shoulder. Oliwia had vanished. Nonetheless, her image burned in his brain like a bright bolt of lightning, leaving him thunderstruck. When he'd first laid eyes on her, he'd needed to check the impulse to shake his head lest his eyes be deceiving him, lest she be the wrong girl, lest she change back into the girl he'd left behind. Clearly, she was no longer a girl. While he'd been gone, she'd become a woman. A remarkably beautiful woman. Was it possible she'd looked like that all along and he'd never noticed?

Spirit of God!

He certainly noticed now.

How old was she? Seventeen?

Old enough.

He struggled to corral his wayward thoughts and turn to the business at hand. For a few moments longer, he let the vision linger. Time had enhanced Oliwia; something he could not quite identify had changed. She was no taller. Though he'd not had benefit of the thorough examination he would have favored, he thought she had grown a little fuller, in a way he wholly appreciated. But it was more than that. Her stature, her bearing, her overall air—these had transformed. She exuded more confidence, more majesty, yet her smile had only grown sweeter.

As he entered the lord's solar, he pulled in a great breath and reluctantly expelled her from his thoughts.

The meeting with Eryk consumed the remainder of the day. It was dark when Jacek emerged, tired and grubby, and headed to the great hall for food and drink. After the joyful welcome only hours earlier, the atmosphere was noticeably subdued. Looking around, Jacek reckoned

THE HEART OF A HUSSAR

officers were ensconced in private quarters with their families and would not be seen for days. Soldiers and their ladyloves were behind locked doors, where they would reacquaint themselves. Other towarzysze had already departed for home. Those gathered around the dining tables were weary warriors like he, without sweethearts or wives to lose themselves with.

After the meal, Jacek's unseeing eyes fixed on an empty wooden platter before him. He drummed his fingers on the tabletop while his mind turned over the conversations in the solar—conversations that dispelled the euphoric homecoming and replaced it with the unpleasantness that was Mateusz.

Mateusz had done the talking, recounting *his* version of the campaign. That version shamelessly painted him in the bravest, brightest light as a stalwart commander and strategist, and he availed himself of every opportunity to expound on his false virtues while jabbing at every other member of the company. Jacek had taken most of the blows and had felt Eryk's eyes on him with each slight, as if appraising him. But Jacek's irritation paled in comparison to his outrage over Mateusz's careless, heartless depictions of the fallen.

"He was long in the tooth anyway," or, "He was only a pacholik," or worse, "If he'd been a better warrior, he wouldn't have died." Never mind that they had been part of their brotherhood, that they had sacrificed their lives, or that their loved ones would never lay eyes on them or hear them call their names again.

Lost in his morose meanderings, Jacek jerked when light fingers tapped his shoulder. Oliwia's crystal-blue eyes danced above her hesitant smile, and Jacek was instantly pulled from his morass.

Have her eyes always resembled shimmering aquamarines?

"Oliwia!" He stood at attention, knocking over—and catching—the heavy armchair. Curious faces turned to him, then turned back again. Remembering he still wore his road attire, he dusted his arms and chest.

"I am sorry, Lieutenant. I did not mean to disturb your thoughts. I called to you, but I don't believe you heard me." She covered her mouth with her hand. Despite the effort, her smile peeked out.

"You did not disturb me. I'm glad of the distraction. You've saved me from brooding."

"It was bad, then?" She'd dropped her hand and the smile with it, and she seemed to study him with her wide eyes.

"Not so bad, no. Well, that is"—he cleared his suddenly sticky throat—"the casualties are always difficult to reconcile." He glanced around and noticed Henryk watching him with a peculiar expression.

"Then it's no wonder you brood. I merely wanted to welcome you back and tell you how delighted Filip is to have you safely home again."

And what of you, Oliwia?

Jacek pulled a hand through his hair. "I … It's good to be home," he spluttered. "I look forward to spending time with him again. Of course."

She nodded, a quizzical look on her face. "Did you make many stops on your journey home? Perhaps you visited old friends or familiar towns?"

He shrugged, trying not to stare at her throat, or the exquisite, creamy skin above her modest neckline, or the point where her silver necklace dove under said neckline, just above a hint of cleavage.

He cleared his throat again. "We were all of us anxious for home, so we spent as little time dawdling as possible. With the exception of a few estates and villages where we lingered." He grumbled inside, remembering how Mateusz's dalliances had slowed them up.

Oliwia's face scrunched in a frown, but as quickly as it had overtaken her features, it disappeared. She brushed her fingers lightly over her upper lip and raised her eyebrows. "This is new, yes?"

Only when he raised his fingers to his own lip did he remember the moustache. "Yes, it is. Well, no, not so new. It's … I've had it months now. For a time, I wore a beard."

What an imbecile! Sweet Jesus, what in blazes is wrong with me?

"It's … thick. Does it get in the way when you drink?"

He detected, he was certain, a mischievous glint in her eyes.

"Well, no. No, it does not." Now he was sure he detected disapproval. He caught himself staring at her rosy mouth and pulled his eyes back to hers. "The barber will shave it off tomorrow," he announced on a whim. When her expression didn't change, he suspected she hadn't been looking at him disapprovingly, after all.

As his thoughts spun, so did his innards. People still surrounded them, and he caught stray words in the buzz of quiet conversation. From the kitchen, Beata screeched at a dog.

Oliwia gathered her skirts. "I had best get upstairs and prepare my lady's chamber." She beamed him a beautiful smile. "Again, welcome home, Lieutenant."

He looked around and dropped his voice. "Jacek."

"Of course." She dipped her head. "Jacek."

He watched her glide away. *What an oaf! I didn't ask what she's been doing or what has happened to her in the last eight months!* He resisted the urge to smack his forehead with the heel of his hand.

"Oliwia." He took three quick strides and caught her up. "How have you been?"

Just as she turned, Eryk hailed him. He glanced at his lord and nodded, then looked back at Oliwia.

"I have been hearty and hale, thank you." Turning once more, she headed toward the stairs.

"I wish to hear more," Jacek called.

She stopped and regarded him over her shoulder. Her burnished sable hair cascaded down her back in waves. The curve of her cheek reminded him of something, someone …

Spirit of God!

She snatched his breath away.

A fortnight later, the fully garrisoned castle's familiar routines once more held sway. The cold and wind also ruled, blanketing the castle in frigid lethargy. Jacek glimpsed Oliwia frequently, but rather than hearten him, it unsettled him. Everything about her unsettled him. The attention she garnered rankled, and he brooded as he watched bolder, brasher men than he accost her with a dash he lacked—like Henryk. She seemed unaware of or unimpressed with their overtures, which did little to pacify him. He longed for the easy friendship he'd once enjoyed with her—when he could look at her and *not* see Aphrodite in her stead—so he could talk to her without worry he'd trip over his words.

When Kasimir told him about George MacMillan, Jacek drew no comfort from the rakehell's departure. Instead, he bristled with visions of MacMillan's filthy lips on hers. Could she have welcomed his advances? Absolutely not! MacMillan had forced himself on her. Had Jacek known where the scoundrel went, he would have tracked him down and torn those lips from his face.

While Jacek exhibited naught but decorous, courtly behavior in Oliwia's company, he transformed into a taciturn observer. A wrestling match broke out inside him every time she neared. Through it all, he was unable to utter more than a few inconsequential words—none of them expressing his burgeoning admiration.

As time passed, she seemed to shrink away from him. Sometimes he detected a confused frown or a dark glare he was unaccustomed to seeing on her lovely face. Was he the cause? Worse still, he was convinced she shared a special friendship with Henryk that he was incapable of duplicating.

"Jacek! It's a fine night for a sleigh ride," Henryk hollered at him one evening after the meal. "Would you give us the pleasure of your company?"

Jacek was irritated. Several noble families were visiting Biaska, and it seemed wherever he went, he was confronted by the sight of Oliwia in a knot of noblemen looking her over from head to foot, or a gaggle of giggling girls vying for his attention. Like now. Two noblemen—one of them a weaselly dandy named Jankowski—hedged Oliwia beside a pillar while Henryk stood amid a cluster of ladies by the hearth. Jacek's body was determined to head toward Oliwia, and it wanted nothing to do with Henryk's sleigh ride.

Shoving his wishes aside, he inhaled a deep breath and stalked toward Henryk. Jacek stayed scarcely long enough to exchange pleasantries before excusing himself. When he turned back, Oliwia's skirts were climbing the steps, two disappointed-looking gentlemen watching her go. He glanced back at Henryk, and three ladies smiled and waved at him. He gave them a head dip and quickly left for the garrison.

As he navigated the yard, Jacek puffed his cheeks and let out a huge breath. Not so long ago, he would have found Henryk's companions appealing, and he'd have enjoyed cozying up beside one or two on that sleigh ride. He would have noticed their figures, maybe their eyes. But now he only saw one, an ideal he never before dreamed existed, and he had no desire to waste his time with anyone else. He found himself in the aggravating position of being unable to be in Oliwia's company, nor could he enjoy anyone else's.

THE HEART OF A HUSSAR

Without forethought, Oliwia knew where Jacek was at all times, whether he worked horses in the stableyard, drilled on the practice fields, or strode through the castle. Like now. Though she sat among a group of noblewomen in a salon reserved for the ladies—as part of Katarzyna's ongoing lessons in feminine gentility—Oliwia could sense him a floor below, in the great chamber with Lord Eryk.

Feigning a fascination with her embroidery, Oliwia's attention drifted in and out of the conversations about one tiresome subject after another. Brittle notes being played on a harpsichord accompanied feminine voices in the background. As her mind sought refuge from the inane prattle, it meandered to the change in Jacek since his return. The man habitually glowered at her, as though infuriated. What had she done but show him the same kindness she always had? Though she knew it was unbecoming, at times her fire rose and she glared back—she couldn't help herself.

After the lengthy campaign at the border, had Jacek's more brutal persona emerged and eclipsed the kinder one? She lamented the loss of ease she had once felt in his presence.

The ladies' conversation took a turn, pulling her from her pondering, and she became rooted to her seat.

"So, Patka," a newly married one among them began, "have you discovered any potential suitors among the men of Biaska? One your father would approve of, that is?"

A coy smile curved Patka's mouth, but she said nothing, keeping her eyes glued on an open book in her lap.

"Ah! So you have, I see. And who is the lucky lad? Someone who shares your love of books, I hope?"

All heads turned toward the plain young woman. The only sound was the crackle of the fire.

She looked up and blushed. "Perhaps. He is well versed in the classics, and though I do not play, I watched him at chess and know he is accomplished."

The married woman quirked an eyebrow. "Is he handsome?"

Patka cast her eyes to her lap. "He's the most handsome man I've ever seen."

"Has he a name?" another asked.

Patka's face turned crimson, and she shook her head slightly, bobbing her black curls. Oliwia wondered absently how soon they would twitter behind one another's backs.

"Never mind," the married woman chirped.

The ladies quieted, and Oliwia returned to her private thoughts. Those musings included various excuses she might use to escape their company. Alas, none sounded plausible, and she resigned herself to staying where she was.

She once again lost herself in the enigma that was Jacek. Her reactions to him, she realized, were as puzzling as the man himself, for when he was absent, she was oddly discomfited. It wasn't because she pictured him sharing an intimate meal by a cheery hearth with his bastard children and their mothers. It wasn't because she imagined him holding his szlachta lovers beside him in bed—women like the ones in this very room—or that she missed his fierce countenance. Rather, it was because she felt an inexplicable hollowness.

"Biaska has many appealing hussars," peeped Lidia, the lady at the harpsichord. Oliwia's attention leapt back to the present. "But there is one in particular who is especially tall and muscular—and a very good dancer. I would not mind catching him alone in the garden."

Patka's head jerked up. As did Oliwia's. The other unmarried ladies gasped, and Lidia stopped abruptly.

"Do not pretend you've not considered it yourselves," sniffed the shapely brunette.

"Do you speak of Pan Henryk?" giggled one.

Lidia shook her head, her eyes gleaming. "No, though he is handsome. But he is practically *too* charming; he is never alone. His good friend, however …" she said wistfully.

"Pan Jacek, then?"

Lidia clapped her hands. "Yes! The very one."

Oliwia's stomach curdled, and she locked her eyes on her sewing to keep from revealing what surely must be written on her face.

The women began chattering. "*I* was thinking of him," they seemed to say at once.

"Handsome or not, the man is a petty noble with nothing of value," the married woman scoffed. "Your fathers would never allow such a match, and with good reason. Besides, I doubt he would pay you any mind. He's irascible and says little."

Lidia grinned wickedly. "I wager *I* could loosen that tongue of his."

"Lidia!" exclaimed Patka.

Oliwia stood quickly, her sewing forgotten. All eyes turned to her.

"I … I recalled I am expected, um, expected in … I must go." She hurried from the room without a backward glance.

Compounding Jacek's bad temper was his fruitless year. Though he'd fought hard and received Matejko's personal praise, it was all for naught. The king would not hear of his feats, and his goal was just as remote as it had ever been. Even Lord Eryk had no idea, which brought Jacek to the greatest source of his aggravation: Mateusz, the man responsible for Jacek's accomplishments going unrecognized.

And that wasn't all. The captain's unrelenting provocation had escalated, becoming a festering boil Jacek could not lance.

Treating Filip as his personal boot scraper had grown habitual, but Mateusz was sly and Filip was close-mouthed, so Jacek never knew what transpired until it was too late to intervene. Railing against his superior officer was an unwise strategy, if for no other reason than it resulted in further mistreatment of the very person Jacek strove to protect.

Mateusz did not hesitate to spread his abuse. Even Izaak's retainer caught his ire, and the poor pacholik suffered as much, if not more, than Filip. Izaak was at a loss to stop it. Consequently, Jacek found himself in Mateusz's sitting room. The captain's spacious dwelling, which had been provided by Lord Eryk, resembled a scaled-down manor house sheltered within castle walls.

"What do you want, Dąbrowski? You here to complain about my treatment of your toe-licking whelp?" The last bit Mateusz said in a mocking whine, and for not the first time Jacek pictured his fist in the man's mouth.

Mateusz was seated before the hearth, and though he'd ordered her away with a snarl, Lady Barbara lurked in the shadows, just out of her husband's sight in the passageway. In the dark, her eyes were two glistening pinpoints that caught and reflected light. They were fixed on Jacek, and he thought her lips curled back in a way that revealed a set of gleaming teeth, giving her the appearance of a she-wolf stalking prey.

"No, I'm here about young Rafał."

The captain took a bite of cheese and looked Jacek up and down as he chewed. "What about him? He's a lazy mongrel. Why isn't Izaak here to speak for him?"

"Because I am Izaak's superior, and I told him I would address the beating you gave his pacholik."

Mateusz dusted off his hands. "The boy was insolent, so I taught him a lesson. Just like I taught that brat of yours last winter. Made him behave properly until we left for Podolia, but now he's due for another thrashing if he doesn't watch himself." With a smirk, he poured a cup of wodka and took a sip.

A vivid image of Filip's swollen purple eye and bruised face suddenly flashed through Jacek's mind, and he flared his nostrils. *So it was Mateusz who gave him those bruises!*

"What did he do?" Jacek fought to keep an even tone. He sensed Barbara's eyes still riveted on him.

Mateusz rested a finger on his chin and struck a thoughtful pose. "Let's see. Was it the time he did a poor job unsaddling my horse?"

Heat flushed through Jacek. "He's too small to pull a saddle off a warhorse by himself."

Mateusz drilled him with his blue-green stare. He wore a mirthless smile, his eyes were hardened steel. "Then he shouldn't be passing himself off as a page. Or *you* shouldn't be passing him off as a page. The trouncing was your fault, Dąbrowski. As for Rafał, that boy needs to do a better job mucking out the stalls."

"But he's Izaak's retainer, not a stable hand, and as such, his first duty is to serve his towarzysz."

"I am Izaak's superior officer—just as I'm yours. If I tell his retainer to do something, he had better jump."

"That's not how it works, and you know it." Jacek's voice was low, almost a growl. His clasped hands tightened behind him.

THE HEART OF A HUSSAR

"Ha! It *is* how it works, Dąbrowski. Those in charge make the rules, and everybody else better follow along. I'm in charge here, even though you seem to forget it regularly. As I think on it, I'm none too happy with your retainer either. I think I'll have a word tomorrow. Oh, you don't like that? Why don't you air your complaints to Lord Eryk? He'll be duly impressed to know he appointed a hobbledehoy to serve under his captain. I can't wait for him to dismiss you. And another thing. My wife tells me …"

Jacek detected motion in the passageway, along with the rustle of skirts. Mateusz must have heard it too because he paused and rose to close the door.

"She tells me the brat's sister is whoring with the entire garris—"

"*What?* That's preposterous!" Jacek blurted the words before he could bite them back. Heat rippled through him, tightening every muscle in his body. He narrowed his eyes at Mateusz, clenching his fists at his sides.

Mateusz chuckled malevolently. "Are you accusing my wife of lying? And why do you pretend to be so shocked? The girl's nothing but a filthy Muscovite peasant. What else can one expect of such an obscene creature? That she's bewitched Lady Katarzyna shows the depths she'll sink to, and I won't tolerate her lewdness in *my* garrison. Noblewoman from England indeed! She should have been left where she was, to live the squalid life she was born to instead of spreading lies that she is one of us."

Jacek's jaw flexed from grinding his teeth.

Mateusz guffawed. "Look at you standing there! You want to take a swing at me, don't you, Dąbrowski? Too bad you're not man enough to do it. And if you somehow mustered enough backbone and were stupid enough to try, I'd dance at your funeral. With you out of the way, there would be no one to stop me beating that stripling every day, as he deserves. And the girl?" A wicked smile spread across his craggy face. "Oh, let me tell you what I would do to *her*. First, I'd make her show me *all* her tricks. I wager she has many. Then I'd have her every way possible before I—"

A crash sounded in the hallway beyond the now closed door.

With a frown, Mateusz stood and yanked it open, peering into the hallway. "What the devil?" He looked over his shoulder at Jacek and snarled. "We're done here, Dąbrowski. Get your mangy hide the hell out of my sight."

Fuming, Jacek stalked from the captain's abode, the sound of a man and woman's violent argument echoing in his ears. It brought him no consolation.

Just outside Kraków, seated at a cramped table before a hearth in a rough cottage, Romek sipped a tankard of ale with four Scotsmen. The sky outside had just dimmed black.

"When would we report?" asked their spokesman, a broad man with dark wavy hair and a heavy brow.

"As soon as possible. The estate where you'll be living needs repairs," Romek replied. "As a blacksmith, your skills are in demand, and you'll be well compensated as long as you keep your mouth shut." He nodded to the other three. "Same for carpenters and cartwrights. You'll be expected to divide your days between soldiering and working your trade."

The leader leaned back and crossed his beefy arms over his barrel chest. "And after five years, we get our own land and we're free to work it?"

"Yes," replied Romek evenly. He tossed back his ale and wiped his sleeve across his mouth. "'Twould be an easy life compared to what you're used to. Rather than being on the road as full-time mercenaries, you stay in one place, work your craft."

A woman circled the table, topping off tankards. When she melted into the dwelling's only other chamber, Romek resumed. "And you can bring your women with you. Or not. The lord believes in keeping his men happy, so he'll provide them if you haven't any."

A younger man elbowed the one beside him, sniggering. Romek suppressed a growl of exasperation. *So damned predictable.* The leader narrowed his eyes at the two, and they stopped. Then he turned his gaze to Romek, as if appraising him.

Romek stood abruptly and gathered his gloves. Surprise showed on the man's face. "I would not wait to decide, Machjeld. The lord has men clamoring for this opportunity, and his offer will not stand for long."

Machjeld stood and extended his arm, clasping Romek's. "We're your men."

THE HEART OF A HUSSAR

Romek nodded at each eager face. "Good. We need more men like you. Strong soldiers, willing to work, willing to fight and keep quiet. If you think of others, get word to me."

After Romek returned to his lodgings, he congratulated himself on his growing army. His master would be pleased. As he pulled off his żupan and performed his ablutions, he thought back to his most recent meeting with the lord and smiled. It had gone better than he could have dreamed; he was fiercely proud of what the man had said.

"You are a powerful adversary, Romek, and I am heartened you're on my side. Together, we will drive that devil from our land. It will take time to train and prepare, but all heroic acts do. For such a great reward, we can be patient, yes? Your family's lands will be restored, and you will have your revenge. With the wealth I gain, I will join forces with other magnates and perform illustrious deeds for our country. Krezowski will never know until it's too late."

Romek had been elated.

Immense cleverness on his part—mixed with a stroke of luck—had forged him an alliance with the lord. In a way, Romek's failed ambush had proved fortuitous, for it had driven him to seek out a union with the man. The fiasco had taught Romek he needed more than his own cunning to bring down the House of Krezowski. Much as he'd loathed admitting his shortcomings, and much as he hated partnerships, this new collaboration would yield a much more spectacular downfall—a fitting end for Lord Eryk Aleksander Krezowski of Biaska.

Romek would show his new lord how badly he needed Romek. Perhaps the lord would look at him with different eyes, with gratitude, and be inclined to forge a more personal partnership when they were finally rid of Krezowski.

In time, the lord might return the feeling Romek held dear for him.

CHAPTER 26

Jacek's Command

More and more often, Jacek found himself surreptitiously defending Oliwia's honor. It wasn't just Mateusz's incendiary remarks that got his blood up. It was the garrisoned men deliberating the young beauty as though she were a prized horse. It was visiting nobles trying to outdo one another, performing outrageous feats to gain her favor. She had them all twisted about her fingers—including *him*—and were she aware of her power, she could play them all with the skill of a grand puppeteer.

The notion sat poorly with Jacek. Consequently, he lived with an ever-simmering jealousy—a heretofore foreign emotion. It took little for it to erupt and shake him. Hard.

One afternoon, he strode into the stables, where he came upon a wad of sniggering grooms clustered in a stall.

"It's *my* turn to help her next," one proclaimed. He was shoved for his remark; he shoved back.

"You did it last time. *I'm* next."

So intent were they that they didn't notice Jacek and continued their dialogue of, among other things, the subject's anatomical attributes. Talk then turned to best contrivances for a brush against said attributes while helping her mount or dismount a horse. Jacek paid little attention until he realized *whom* they deliberated.

THE HEART OF A HUSSAR

Something snapped, sending reason in flight. He became a seething, enraged bull taunted with a pick once too often, and he lashed out, roaring and cursing. They scattered through the stall, seeking to squeeze through the gate, jockeying and scrabbling with one another for the best position to bolt. A few miscreants scanned their surroundings as though gauging the most promising escape route. But Jacek would allow no one to flee—not until he was done with them. He used his big body to block their paths.

"You will not dishonor a lady by speaking of her as if she were no more than a common gutter whore. She is a *noblewoman*!" he bellowed.

With this pronouncement, he grabbed a fistful of the closest offender's tunic while he railed at the rest, now pressed against the stall, looking as though they were trying to become one with the wood. Releasing the one he had hold of, Jacek shoved him into a corner, where he stumbled and landed in a heap, resembling a listing sack of grain.

One groom held his hands up in surrender, squeaking, "I've never touched her. It was the rest of them, I swear it. And I would have stopped their talk, but …" He trailed off.

Jacek was not mollified. Rather, his fury bloomed. Seizing the man's throat, he drove him against a solid wood post. "You didn't speak up! You did nothing! You're *worse* than they are!" He waved his clenched fist before the man's ashen face.

Surveying them all, he growled, "If ever there is a next time, you will throttle any man who utters a vulgarity against her or dares touch her. If you don't, you will answer to *me*! And I promise you, unlike today, I will not go easy on you."

The men nodded vigorously. The man he held, whose face was now a deep shade of pink, tried to nod. Jacek released him. Crumpling at Jacek's feet, the groom gasped on his knees, filling Jacek with grim satisfaction.

The lightning that had sizzled in his bloodstream began to ebb. Brushing off his żupan and breeches, he straightened his belt and turned to leave, only to be startled by Henryk leaning against the opposite stall, arms folded casually across his chest. Henryk's expression was unreadable, though his usual playful grin was nowhere to be seen.

Jacek tugged his cuffs over his wrists. "How much did you see?"

"I witnessed the entire extraordinary affair. I daresay it was not a fair fight. There were only six of them."

Jacek grunted, pushing past his friend on his way out of the stables.

Henryk pulled alongside him as he stalked across the bailey. "What started it?"

Jacek came to a sudden stop and glowered at his friend. Henryk took a few steps back. "They insulted one of the ladies of the castle," Jacek spat, then resumed his march.

Henryk nodded. "Ah. I see. Well, then, they deserved what they got, yes? I expect they'll behave from now on. If they recover from their fright, that is."

Logic and reason had not fully returned, and Jacek stormed away, hollering, "The devil piss on you. Leave me the hell *alone!*"

But Henryk wouldn't leave him alone, instead matching Jacek's determined strides. Jacek couldn't shake him.

"Why don't you tell the lady of your affection for her?" Henryk asked. "I wager she has no idea."

"What in blazes do you know?"

"More than you think I do."

They reached a row of abandoned shacks tucked in a corner between a curtain wall and the main tower's stone base. Jacek wheeled abruptly, scattering two wayward chickens that clucked at him belligerently. He glared at Henryk.

"I am not an imbecile, Jacek," he said mildly.

"What is that supposed to mean?" Jacek snarled.

"It means, my friend, that you have had a burr up your backside ever since we returned from Podolia, and that burr festers every time a certain dark-haired, blue-eyed lady is in your line of sight. So naturally, I have asked myself what it could possibly mean, and I have come to a conclusion. Shall I tell you what it is?"

Jacek turned his back to Henryk and began relieving himself. *Just go away!*

Henryk joined him.

"It explains so much, you see, such as why you ignore every other female. It explains why you goad your men into fights, *especially* those who dare glance at said lady. It explains why you no longer speak of becoming commander, which will not happen if you continue provoking your men. They will mutiny."

Jacek snorted.

Both men adjusted their trousers and stepped away from the wall. Henryk folded his arms across his chest.

THE HEART OF A HUSSAR

"Admit it, my friend. You are smitten. Utterly, unreservedly besotted. So much so that it renders you witless," Henryk drawled. "Just answer me this. How is the girl supposed to know you care for her if all you do is scowl at her?"

"I do not scowl at her."

"Oh yes, you do. She probably thinks you'd rather tear her limb from limb than kiss her. She's innocent, unlike the women you're used to, mind, and that look of yours likely terrifies her."

Jacek pushed past him. "Always diverting listening to your drivel, Henryk."

Henryk called after him, "Don't concern yourself! The men merely think you wish to impress the captain at their expense. They will never hear the truth of it from me."

Jacek didn't bother acknowledging him.

"Oliwia!" called Henryk after the evening meal. Turning her head toward him, Oliwia curved her lips in a dazzling smile. Jacek also turned his head to Henryk, his knotted brows as far from a smile as he could possibly get.

Henryk sauntered toward her and took her hand, kissing it extravagantly as he pulled her from her seat. In a corner of the great hall, the fiddler tuned his instrument while the piper positioned himself.

"Dance?" Henryk invited. She nodded.

As he led her away, Henryk winked at Jacek and mouthed, "Watch." Jacek felt an irresistible urge to throw his clenched fist into Henryk's jaw.

By Christ and all the saints, it would feel good!

Henryk snaked an arm around Oliwia's waist, pulling her much closer than necessary. He grinned at her, and she let out a musical laugh.

Christ!

Jacek glowered at him. Henryk gave the musicians instructions before bending close to Oliwia's ear. *What the hell is he trying to talk her into now?* Jacek imagined the heat rising from her body, intermingling with her fragrance, and Henryk pulling it all in. Jacek wanted to throttle him.

The music began, and Henryk gathered Oliwia in his arms, scandalously moving face-to-face with her across the stone floor. *They're dancing a weller, for God's sake!* Jacek threw back his cup of wine, rose abruptly, pulling his frame to its full height, and began walking toward them. Other dancers appeared, executing more proper reels while they tittered. Jacek dodged them. Henryk pivoted his head, looking as though he sought a clear path of escape.

As Jacek drew near, he overheard Henryk say, "I just remembered something I must do." Then he gave Jacek a smug smile, still speaking to Oliwia. "Why don't you finish the dance with Jacek? He looks as though he could use the cheer."

Henryk twirled her right into Jacek's arms and hurried away.

She looked as surprised to find herself in Jacek's hold as he felt having her there, and she let out a nervous laugh.

"It appears Henryk was seized by a mysterious urgency," she offered.

Jacek narrowed his eyes on Henryk's retreating back. "I venture he was concerned about his health."

He shrugged when she gave him a puzzled look. Though he'd never practiced the steps, he suddenly found himself quite in favor of the weller.

Eryk pressed his finger to his lips when the door opened and Nadia's white linen-capped head appeared. Her eyes flew to his, and he motioned to Katarzyna's frail form in the middle of his bed. Nadia squeezed herself into the chamber and crept up beside him.

"Lady Katarzyna had a bad night," he whispered. "See that you or Oliwia are with her when she wakes. I will be in my solar."

"Of course, my lord."

Releasing a heavy breath, Eryk descended the stairs. Jacek stood at attention beside the solar door. *Prompt as usual.*

Eryk led him into the great chamber and signaled for him to sit. "A messenger arrived last night from Pan Zebrzydowski. Zebrzydowski seeks our help."

THE HEART OF A HUSSAR

Jacek looked around as if expecting someone. He arched his eyebrows when Eryk handed him a folded piece of paper. "Shall I wait to read this until the captain joins us, my lord?"

"Mateusz will not be attending this meeting." Eryk paused, taking in Jacek's curious look. "As you can see in the missive, Zebrzydowski asks Biaska to intercept a band that's been plundering villages along the western border. They don't just take the peasants' property. They brutalize them, kidnap their women, and burn villages."

Jacek scanned the letter. "The raiders are soldiers?"

"Mercenaries. Danes, Swedes—three-hundred strong. Read farther down. They banded together on the southern coast of the Baltic, and they've been looting their way southwest."

Jacek shrugged. "Why does Pan Zebrzydowski not got after them himself? Or leave them to the Austrians?"

"We're closer. The court fears they'll turn toward Kraków and disrupt trade routes." Eryk pointed at the paper. "The king wants them stopped immediately."

Jacek raised his head.

"Frankly, Jacek, after siding *against* Zebrzydowski's rebellion, I am more inclined to answer his call, to mend relations between us."

Jacek nodded, and Eryk cleared his throat. "I will not be leading this endeavor. Nor will Mateusz." He waited a beat, taking stock of Jacek's puzzled expression. "You have executed your duties well, and I am needed here. The choice is logical."

What Eryk didn't tell Jacek was that this was a test, a competition of sorts, to see if the young lieutenant was capable of commanding on his own. Eryk had felt every bit of his waning youth, as his back now reminded him. The siren's call to glory no longer seduced him, and he needed a replacement—a competent, trustworthy officer. He reckoned he had two good candidates; the most steadfast of the two sat opposite him now.

"Gather the men and provisions and hunt these sons of devils down before they make any more trouble."

Jacek stood and handed back the missive. "Yes, sir."

Jacek led a squad of eighty hussars and dragoons, along with one hundred attendants, across the drawbridge and pressed to the west.

Daily, scouts fanned out like spokes in a wheel, but their quests turned up nothing about the enemy company. Two weeks into the mission, just as sunset's deep oranges and pinks limned the horizon, the last scout rode into camp hungry and empty-handed. The aroma of charring wood and roasting roebuck rose from cooking fires, and Jacek sent him off to supper before retreating to his own tent, where his war council awaited. Here he took up his place amid a half-dozen officers.

Henryk sheathed and unsheathed his sabre repeatedly, grumbling, "We're chasing our tails."

"Maybe they've gone home," Stefan offered.

Jacek raised his eyebrows.

Stefan hooked a thumb in his belt and shrugged. "One can pray."

Lesław clapped him on the back. "And perhaps God smote them all with one lightning bolt, and their bodies rot until we recover them. How convenient!"

Jacek stroked his newly sprouted beard. "We will look elsewhere. Tomorrow, we turn southeast. Lesław, increase the scouts in that direction and add two pair to sweep. Henryk, don't despair. You'll be home by Christmas."

Days later, as they drove farther southeast, a fast-moving rider approached from the company's rear, snow swirling behind him like glittering clouds. The rearguard turned and bolted toward him and soon surrounded him.

Jacek sat in his saddle, his back rigid, waiting for the rider's face to come into view. He gripped his holstered pistol, his other hand resting on the hilt of his szabla. As soon as Jacek recognized him, he eased his hold of the pistol stock and called Henryk and Lesław over.

Breathless from the ride, the soldier drew up beside him and panted, "Several hundred heading our way, Lieutenant, less than a day's ride."

"Are they the enemy we've been chasing, Dawid?"

THE HEART OF A HUSSAR

"Yes, sir. We got close enough to observe them. They're coming up on our rear right flank, moving through the forest. They will cross the meadow, then encamp in the next clump of woods." Dawid turned in his saddle and pointed behind him. "Kasimir stayed behind to track them."

Jacek appraised the brown-haired young man. "And how do you know this?"

Dawid grinned. "We overheard two of their men standing sentry by the bushes where we hid. They were grumbling about the wodka tasting like piss. They're moving on Krzyszkowice, counting their spoils already."

Jacek looked up at the clear blue sky, mentally backtracking across the terrain they had just crossed. The sun was slung low, but it was a bright day. The squad had not yet had its midday meal. The timing was perfect.

"Then I look forward to upsetting their plans. We attack now, while they're caught in the open and the sun is at our backs, so we need to move quickly. I want to gain the top of that rise before they see us." He pointed to a wooded knoll.

Jacek felt a familiar thrumming inside him. Excitement over the upcoming battle. The upcoming *conquest* of their enemy. "Gentlemen, prepare for battle," he announced coolly.

Jacek's force prepared itself and struck out. Hussars, dragoons, and attendants alike were now primed to meet the raiders. He allowed himself a satisfied inward smile; it had taken less than an hour.

His vantage point was under cover of fir trees atop the ridge, and he surveyed an expanse of thigh-high brown grasses dotted with dark evergreen thickets. The advancing corps lumbered around wagons grouped together, as though protecting them. They were out in the open, exposed. A strategy decided, Jacek gave commands, and cavalrymen organized into formation.

Hussars, backed by pacholiks and dragoons, gathered and arranged themselves along two precise lines. Jacek inspected his troops, his neck prickling at the sight. Armor on straight bodies glinted in the slanted winter afternoon light as it pierced the veil of trees. To a man, the hussars had attached their wings. With the showy plumage atop their helmets and kolpaks, they appeared larger than they were.

A charged quiet hung over the force. Even the horses seemed to be holding their snorts and stamping hooves. Jacek took two long breaths, in and out, then a third. He turned Jarosława and faced his men. Behind him, the enemy was now less than a half league away.

Anticipation shot through him as though lightning pulsed in his blood. His breathing was shallow but steady. In this moment, he wished to be nowhere else but atop his warhorse in the crisp afternoon air, looking into each warrior's eyes as he imparted strength and calm. In return, the grim set of each man's face revealed his determination. They were ready.

Trotting the length of the line, he paused, encouraging and rallying, his voice strident and strong. "Gentlemen. God has called us here, to this place, to vanquish His enemy, our enemy. We answer His call with honor, that we might do His bidding. His blessings are upon us, so let us ride with Him and finish what we came here for."

A motion of his budzygan, and men tightened up and gripped weapons. One more gesture as he rode beside them, and the hussars began walking in unison, out of the trees, down the shallow rise, before breaking into a charge.

They shook the clearing with an ominous, pounding rhythm. Their adversaries were caught by surprise, sparing no time to arrange defenses, reducing them to drawing blades. Some foes discharged firearms wildly only to scatter like cockroaches exposed to light. The hussars streamed around the wagons, cutting them down. Men were trampled, speared, hacked. Some mounted a feeble counterattack, while others fled the carnage on foot. But there was little they could do against the hussars' deadly efficiency, and they were quickly overrun.

Jacek backed up for a better view. The scene was a mass of noisy confusion—mostly the enemy's—blurred by men, smoke, and debris. The ground had transformed into a furrowed field of mud, churned by frantic hooves.

His men battled the enemy's corps on horseback, on the ground, often two against one of theirs. Escaping foes raced from the mayhem toward the trees, doggedly pursued by dragoons riding like devils on their tails.

Here, Dawid wrenched a combatant from his saddle. There, Lesław chopped one's shoulder, nearly cleaving the arm. Henryk hefted his bloody

THE HEART OF A HUSSAR

szabla and spun on his horse, slicing one before turning on another with blinding speed. Izaak swung his sabre with feral ferocity. The chorąży had not shied from fights in the past, but had fought with the caution of the inexperienced. Not so today. He easily overpowered his opponent.

With grim satisfaction, Jacek turned his attention to servants capturing horses and finishing off the fallen.

No quarter.

Just as they showed the defenseless villagers no mercy.

Images of small bodies, broken and bloodied as they lay strewn about a burning village, flashed through his mind. *What sort of evil could commit such atrocities against mere children?*

Jacek detected a cranking noise, but before he could pinpoint it, it stopped. Alarm bells clanged in his head, and he wheeled. A foe leapt upright from the bed of a wagon. The man pressed his cheek against a wooden crossbow and took aim.

With a flinch, Jacek braced for the impact. The man lurched backward. His arms jerked, and he glanced down at an arrow embedded in his chest with detached curiosity. A solid *thwack*, and another projectile sprouted from his shoulder. Bewildered, he looked up. A third arrow struck his forehead, snapping his head backward. He dropped back into the bed of the wagon and lay still.

Jacek quickly patted himself down, but found no bolts in his armor, clothing, or flesh. Bemused and breathless, he narrowed his eyes and spotted Izaak, astride his horse, a cocked bow alongside his cheek. A beat, two, and he lowered his bow and grinned at Jacek, then jabbed his forefinger toward a loaded crossbow on the ground beside the wagon. Jacek tapped his heart and dipped his head in thanks. Izaak answered with a silent nod. Jacek would find a way to thank him properly, in front of the entire squad.

Before he could give the matter another thought, Izaak's horse screamed and crashed forward. Everything happened with blurring speed. Izaak hit the ground, landing at the feet of a huge man gripping a broadsword in one hand and a Dane's axe, bright with blood, in the other. Snorting furiously, the wounded horse flailed and dug at the ground, trying to stand, only to fall back again, landing squarely on Izaak's chest.

Jacek surged Jarosława toward them, sabre firmly gripped. Arcing the blade like a scythe, he rode at the man poised to deliver a death blow to the trapped standard bearer. The man dodged at the last second, and Jacek missed his mark. He spun and dashed back, nadziak in his left hand. The foeman cursed at him and brought up his long-handled axe, swinging at Jarosława's chest. Jacek yanked on the reins, turning her as he kicked out, deflecting the blow. She reared and pivoted. Jacek reeled in his saddle. The axe flew from the man's grasp, but he grabbed Jacek's leg, jerking hard, pulling Jacek down on top of him. The mare peeled away.

The enemy soldier had lost his breath and his broadsword but recovered both. Jacek had dropped his weapons in the fall. He scrabbled in the dirt for his nadziak and closed his right hand around its haft. Broadsword to hand, the man lumbered toward him. Jacek rolled, snatched at his sabre with his left, and leapt to his feet. The man came at him, and Jacek slid a few steps back, his movements spare. They squared off. The foeman was large. Jacek stepped back again, drawing the man away from Izaak. They circled one another in a deliberate, appraising dance. The combatant's eyes blazed in a beet-colored face streaked with blood. Teeth bared, he growled in an unrecognizable language and teased Jacek's blade with brisk taps. Jacek waited patiently, stepping smoothly. He had played at this many times before.

A prickling sensation rose from his belly, spread through his chest, down his arms and legs. His breathing, deep and even, slowed, matching the whooshing cadence in his ears. He locked on his opponent's eyes. Bright blue. Against white. Blond eyelashes. A wild look. Sweat dripped on the man's eyelid.

A flick. A blink.

Another tic, eyes shifting right.

In a blur, the man brought the broadsword up and lunged at Jacek with a grunt, coming at his left. Jacek was already pivoting a quarter turn to his right, and the stroke missed him. With a yell, he thrust the szabla into the man's left flank. It pierced soft tissue, and the man's weight dragged against it. Jacek jerked the blade out, and the man groaned, then staggered. Jacek swung the nadziak backhanded and caught him in the gullet with the hammerhead. The man's hands flew to his throat. He dropped to his knees, rasping. Jacek raised the sabre. The man's eyes snapped wide.

Muscles taut and strong, Jacek brought the blade down on his enemy's neck with savage power. The man thudded to the ground chest first, then lay motionless. His blood, thick as syrup, spread slowly and soaked into the dirt beneath him.

Jacek swiveled his head round, but no one moved. Familiar faces. Faces of his brethren. His chest heaved, and sweat rolled down his face into his beard. He wiped his brow with the heel of his hand and shook droplets from his head. He heard someone say the fight was over.

Staggering back a step, his eyes lit on two kneeling hussars paces away. His strides ate up the distance. Izaak lay helmetless beside his dead mount, face-up on the ground between Kasimir and Dawid. Blood leaked from his mouth, and he gasped for air. His eyes slid back and forth, panic evident in them, but when Jacek bent over him, he fixed them on Jacek's face. He moved his lips. A peculiar wheezing sound escaped him.

"He's been asking for something, Lieutenant," Kasimir said quietly. "We cannot make him out."

Jacek grabbed a discarded fur cap and placed it under the young man's head. "Izaak, no talking now. There will be time enough later." He gently squeezed the chorąży's shoulder and felt more than saw him shake his head weakly from side to side. Izaak clenched his arm fiercely, and Jacek checked the impulse to cross himself.

"Lieut ...," he gasped. "Must..."

Jacek bent closer, nodding as he locked eyes on him. He spoke softly. "What is it, Izaak?" He hovered his ear by Izaak's mouth.

"Mama ... please ..." His hand traveled up to Jacek's breastplate, and Jacek grasped it in his. It felt like a block of ice with fingers.

"Shall I tell her you love her?" He lowered his head again to listen.

"Esss ..." Izaak hissed like a punctured bellows bag.

Jacek looked into the young man's face.

"I will. I promise. What else can I do for you? Does it hurt?"

Izaak shook his head feebly. "Cold," was all he said, and Jacek pulled off his leopard skin and draped it over the young hussar. He tucked one of Izaak's hands under the pelt and kept a firm grip of the other in his own warm hands.

"Pray ... bless." Izaak's eyes began to glaze.

Jacek cradled the young man's face and peered into his eyes. He wanted to shake him, wanted to shout, "No, no, no!" but there was no time. So he made the sign of the cross over him, and in a steady, strong voice, he said, "I vow to you I will see you get a proper Catholic burial. I will tell your mother how much you love her, and I will tell your family how bravely you fought. I will tell them how you saved my life, that I am indebted to you. They will be very proud, Izaak. We are all very proud."

A light flickered in Izaak's eyes, and he stared up into Jacek's face. A single tear slid from the corner of his eye. Then his mouth slackened, his eyes dulled, and one last, long gasp rushed out of him. Jacek kept hold of his hand, sat back on his heels, and hung his head. He crossed himself and didn't move for long minutes.

"Lieutenant, you're needed by the wagons," a voice called.

"A moment," he rasped, swiping tears from his cheeks.

"We will take care of him, Lieutenant," Dawid said softly.

Jacek pulled himself up, gathered his kolpak, sabre, and nadziak, and mounted Jarosława. He stroked her neck, telling her in soothing tones how magnificent she was. Her ears flicked, as if she acknowledged his words. They trotted to Lesław.

"We've dealt with most of them. The servants are in the woods, looking for any who escaped. The man you killed over there," Lesław jerked his chin, "I am told was their leader."

"Were any of ours lost?"

"None other than ..." Lesław's voice caught, like fabric tearing on a nail. He cleared his throat. "Six injured and two horses dead. They've got a problem with the wagon over there." Lesław pointed toward a small group of wagons.

Jacek rode over and drew alongside Stefan. "What is it?"

Two dragoons peeled back a canvas cover, revealing a bed of frightened, filthy women and girls clinging to one another. Covered in lacerations and bruises, each one displayed signs of abuse. A woman cradled a partially clad girl of no more than eight who stared at Jacek glassy-eyed. He suddenly felt weary, heavy, as if he had been battling for days on end with no respite— as if he were weighted down with boulders and sinking in a cold pond.

Scanning the disheveled group, he drew in a breath and doffed his kolpak.

"My ladies, I am Lieutenant Dąbrowski of Biaska. My men and I are at your service. No harm will come to you while you are in our care." He pointed to Stefan. "Identify yourselves to my officer. He will help sort you so we can return you to your villages and families."

THE HEART OF A HUSSAR

As he was turning Jarosława, a woman stood abruptly. Trembling, barely audible, she said, "Lieutenant Dąbrowski, God bless you."

CHAPTER 27

Jacek's Folly

The hussars returned to Biaska Castle, lines of captured horses and wagons in tow. One wagon carried Izaak's body. Despite his grief, Jacek could not prevent his heart accelerating at the guards' heralds. He rode with an energy he shouldn't have possessed after the costly, heartbreaking journey. Scanning the silhouettes on the parapets, he tried to pick out Oliwia among them. Seeing her was what his spirit craved.

As they approached the drawbridge, the excitement at their homecoming grew apparent. People ran along the ramparts, and a horde poured into the bailey. He spotted Filip tearing down the stairs, caught in the rushing crowd like a leaf on a brook. But Oliwia was nowhere in sight, and disquiet spread up his spine. *Where in blazes is she?*

Jacek dismounted and handed Marcin his reins. Filip was beside him now, yelping his welcome.

"Have you been behaving yourself, Filip?" Jacek patted him on the shoulder.

The boy nodded and grinned. "Oh yes, sir. I've been working hard."

Jacek took in a breath and blew it out, pretending a nonchalance he didn't feel.

"I've no doubt. And your sister? How is she? Is she inside with Lady Katarzyna?"

"She is well, my lord, and no, she went to the village with some lords and ladies."

Jacek raised his eyebrows. "Which lords and ladies?" His mind whirred through a list of her possible companions.

"Pan Jankowski, his sister, and his cousin."

Heat rose from Jacek's belly at the mention of Jankowski's name. So the skinny scoundrel was back, likely hanging about Oliwia like a buzzing fly alighting on a sugary confection.

"Jankowski? When did he arrive?"

Filip furrowed his brow and glanced to the heavens as if calculating. "A few days ago."

Jacek smacked his gloves against his palm. "I must report to Lord Eryk." He stalked to the forestairs, climbing them two at a time.

His strides expelled some of the nettles inside him, but his mind wasn't sharp when he entered Eryk's solar. It was muddled with thoughts of Oliwia and Jankowski. Oliwia and anyone. His mood plunged further when he spotted Mateusz seated in front of Eryk's desk. The lord greeted him with a smile, but the captain radiated pure hatred.

"Well done, man! Come! Let's drink to you, the men, and your success, for another menace has been wiped from the earth," Eryk said jubilantly.

"My lord, I, ah …" Jacek cleared a clog from his throat. "I have sad tidings. We lost our chorąży."

Eryk's jaw dropped, and his dark brows drew together. "Izaak? How? What happened?"

The men sat solemnly, hands wrapped around cups of mead, as Jacek unwound his tale. When he'd finished, he held up his drink and proposed a blessing to Izaak.

After the briefing, Jacek trod the yard, lost in ruminations. As commander of the mission, another weighty burden had fallen squarely on Jacek's shoulders: he would soon deliver wretched news, together with Izaak's belongings, to loved ones whose hearts would be torn apart with his words.

Merciful God, help me! It's nearly Christmas.

He was unaware of Mateusz until the man called out to him and caught him up.

The captain matched his strides. "So, Dąbrowski, I suppose congratulations are in order. The lord seemed duly impressed by your little skirmish. I daresay it worked out well for you, didn't it?" Mateusz smirked.

Son of a jackal!

Jacek stopped in his tracks and turned slowly, deliberately, to face his sneering superior. "I wouldn't say it worked out well, no. Especially not for Izaak and his family." A vision of Izaak's face, split with a sunny smile, beamed into Jacek's brain before shifting to his last memory of the young man—his desolate death mask.

"Nice touch, raising your cup to him," Mateusz chortled. "Eryk seemed moved by the gesture. But I had to ask myself, 'Why bother?' He didn't die honorably. He let his horse *fall* on him, for Christ's sake! What kind of a hussar lets that happen? Not a real one, certainly. More's the pity about the horse. It was a beauty and worth more, I'm sure, than its pathetic owner."

A sizzle entered the crown of Jacek's head, coursed through him, and exploded from every finger and toe. Lesław appeared by his side, his hands fisted; he scowled furiously at Mateusz. Henryk sidled up to Mateusz and shot Jacek a warning look. As Jacek opened his mouth to speak, Mateusz glanced beyond him, the smirk firmly planted on his face.

"Ah! And what have we here? Our fair *lady* returns with her witless companions who seem to have forgotten the difference between their noble stations and hers."

Henryk and Lesław looked over at the same time, and as he spun, Jacek caught Oliwia's musical laugh. She rode amid a group of well-dressed men and women, looking every bit as if she belonged among them. When her eyes fell upon him, they lit up—he was sure of it. Her smile widened, and she nudged her horse toward him.

"Jacek! Henryk! Lesław! You are safely home," she cried. Then she seemed to notice Mateusz, and her brilliant smile shriveled.

Henryk deftly grabbed her reins, turning the horse's head, as Jankowski looked on. Jacek couldn't hear what Henryk said when Oliwia leaned down to him, and for a breathless moment his heart lifted at the sight of her. She wore a pewter brocade travel cloak, with lush sable edging the wide collar, and gray leather gloves. Her mahogany hair fell in two long braids down her front, and on her head sat a kolpak trimmed to match the cloak. At the center of the cap's cuff was a simple silver pin embellished with three rounds the size of pearls that held a single pheasant feather.

THE HEART OF A HUSSAR

She was stunning.

Henryk turned her horse, walking her toward Jankowski, and she shot Jacek a rueful look over her shoulder. Mateusz cackled and muttered, "*Another* Muscovite impostor—just like the False Dmitrys claiming to be tsars," loud enough to merit a Jankowski glower. Was that the best Jankowski could do?

Impotent milksop!

Before Jacek could square himself, Mateusz walked away, snickering. Oliwia pivoted and called, "Lieutenant, will you and your men join us for roast goose tonight?"

He nodded dully.

Jacek growled to himself while that son of a devil Jankowski fawned over Oliwia in the great hall. She was holding the fan Jacek had given her, he noted with pride and a measure of warmth. As to Jankowski, Jacek didn't care how rich his family was; the imbecile was not deserving of her. He was a twig of a man incapable of safeguarding her if the need arose. Could he even grow a beard? Jacek sized up the girth of his neck and reckoned he could wrap his hand around it. Twice.

Though Jacek couldn't brawl with him as he did others, he could call his honor into question. How well could Jankowski handle a sabre? Jacek stroked his now smooth chin, envisioning challenging the puny maggot to a duel. A feral grin tugged the corners of his mouth as he imagined the exquisite feel of running him through.

And what did Oliwia think of his attentions? The pompous dolt slobbered over her hand so often that she likely needed an extra cloth just to mop it up. Jacek was studying her when Henryk materialized beside him.

"Shall I trounce him for you?"

Jacek swiveled his head. "What are you talking about?"

Henryk snorted. "It's written all over your face, Jacek, even as you lurk behind the pillar. Admit it. You'd like nothing better than an excuse to throttle the man."

Jacek followed Henryk's gaze, humphed, and folded his arms across his chest. "You do him a favor, and the rest of us a disservice, by calling him a man."

"I reckon you're right about that." Henryk glanced over at Oliwia and her admirer. "I wonder if she feels affection for him? His family is well-placed, nearly as high up as the Zebrzydowskis. They are very political and very wealthy."

Jacek dragged his hand through his hair. Oliwia smiled at Lord Jankowski. Not her full, dazzling smile. A small one. As if she were indulging a child. The same smile she wore when she listened to Filip blather about armaments.

"Perhaps she's blinded by his gold," Jacek said absently.

Henryk scoffed. "Surely not. Why, if that's all she cared about, she would never pay you or me any mind. As it is, we enjoy a large share of her attention." He grinned. "Especially me."

"If not gold, what else, then? She's never shown interest in politics or status. If she doesn't care about him, then why the devil is he here? And why the devil does she let him hang about?" Jacek huffed in exasperation.

"Didn't you know? Lady Katarzyna invited the family back and instructed our Oliwia to entertain the young lord."

Jacek frowned. "*Our* Oliwia?"

"Well, she belongs to no one yet, so I deem her ours." Henryk paused a beat. "I've seen enough, as I'm sure have you. Shall we rescue *our* Oliwia from the boor? I'll see to her, and you do whatever you wish to him. I'm sure you've already worked out how long it will take to snap his neck."

Jacek's mouth quirked. Leave it to Henryk to invent an amusing distraction.

"I'll even take that sister of his off your hands," Henryk said.

"Lady Lidia? Sweet Jesus, please do before I do something I will forever regret."

Henryk smirked. "Do you mean bed her?"

"Merciful God, no. I'm likely to thrash her along with her brother."

THE HEART OF A HUSSAR

Jacek had lost track of Oliwia during the celebration of the squad's victory. Every time he tried to dance with her, she was being whisked away on another man's arm or he faced another young woman eager to dance with him. Now she was in the garden with a handful of eager escorts, and he was caught in Lady Lidia Jankowska's powerful tentacles, unsure how to extricate himself from her ceaseless chatter.

Slick as goose grease, Henryk appeared beside him and extracted her hand, bowing as he lifted it to his lips. He straightened, glanced at Jacek, and raised an eyebrow. "I've not yet danced with Lady Lidia."

Jacek raised an eyebrow right back, suppressing the urge to hug Henryk. "Please. I've monopolized her enough." He gave said tentacled lady a quick bow, pivoted on his heel, and hurried to the garden.

His blood boiled when he found Oliwia strolling the crushed path, surrounded by avid suitors drooling over her like dogs waiting for a juicy bone. Stalking toward them, he drew himself up straight and gave in to the urge to puff his chest like a crowing rooster. Through tacit intimidation, he encouraged them all to leave her side, gratified Jankowski at least had the good sense to appear nervous.

Jacek thought her smile had brightened as he'd approached, but he had observed Henryk vivify her in much the same way when she was in *his* company—which was more often than Jacek cared for.

Easing beside her, Jacek took her elbow. It was just the two of them.

"Thank you." Oliwia let out a sigh. "They had become quarrelsome, and I was trying to guide us all back to the great hall. Now they are gone, I will breathe easier."

"Of course. Anytime anyone troubles you, come find me." *And I will thrash them soundly.*

Their ensuing conversation, as was often the case, centered on her brother and insignificant prattle about the goings-on at the castle.

Her eyes fixed on his. "Has Filip told you…"

"Told me what?"

She glanced away quickly. After a lengthy pause, he asked again. "Has Filip told me what, Liwi?"

She laughed nervously. "How strong he's getting? Why, he hoisted a saddle onto the back of a pony only last week."

"No, he failed to mention it. I'll try to catch him at it so I can praise him."

"He would like that very much."

Jacek pounced on a lull, steering the conversation in a different direction.

"Are you pleased Lord Jankowski and his sister have come to visit?"

She peeked up at him. "Well, I …"

"So you're not pleased?" he prodded.

"It would be unkind to say so."

He nodded. "I understand many young ladies have set their caps at him."

She shrugged. "I would not know."

He took a quick breath. "You are not one of those young ladies?"

She stopped, twisting from his light grasp, her bright eyes flying to his. "Of course not!"

Relief loosened his shoulders, which had crept upward to his ears. "Why not? He's from one of Poland's best families."

"You sound like Lady Katarzyna!" she laughed. "I've no time to consider such things, not while Filip is still young. Besides, what would someone like him see in someone like me?"

"Unless he's utterly blind," Jacek blurted, "beauty, grace, intellect, and amiability … at the very least."

Her lips parted, drawing his gaze, then pressed together. Darting her eyes from his, she started down the path once more. They ambled in awkward silence, she holding her skirts and he holding his hands at his back. Voices carried on the night air as revelers entered the garden.

"Has anything changed since your return?" she finally ventured. "That is, after your first command?"

"No. It is much the same."

"I expect your family is very proud. Have you told them?"

They were close to the garden wall, where torchlight played on her face. She tilted her head and smiled up at him.

What the devil did she just say?

He cleared his throat and rolled his neck, popping it. "I beg your pardon?"

She let out a giggle. "You seem awfully distracted this evening. I asked if your family knows of your recent success."

"I expect so. I wrote my mother. And of course I will be with them soon."

THE HEART OF A HUSSAR

"So you will return for Christmas?"

"Yes," he sighed.

"Are you not eager to see them?"

"I'm not eager to endure my mother's incessant matchmaking. She is convinced I will fall into an irretrievable state of petulance if I am not encumbered with a wife and a passel of children. So she will parade an endless string of marriageable noblewomen before me as if they are horses at market."

"Oh. I see," she said quietly.

Christ! Rein yourself in!

A stilted silence followed, then they both rushed to speak at the same time.

"Please. Go ahead," he invited. *Heavenly Mother, yes, and keep me from continuing to make a fool of myself.* He contemplated ways, pleasant ways, to prevent himself talking. Unfortunately, an image of George MacMillan kissing her burst into his mind and rattled him.

"I take it you have not changed your mind about ... about marriage and family. You find no value in it. For yourself."

Her comment snapped him back to the present, and he reacted by shaking his head spiritedly. "No. I still have too much to do."

"You are determined to get your land grant. Is that the reason, or is there something more?"

They had reached a sheltered part of the garden where couples retreated for privacy, and he glanced around. "No other reason. I'm not averse to marriage, but I will not compromise on my objective. Until I attain it, there's no room in my life for anything else. It is of the utmost importance to me."

She smiled faintly, and his eyes met hers. The cold, the shadows moving in the garden, his annoyance with most everything—especially himself—melted away. There was naught but her, facing him, and a secluded corner a few steps away. Her mouth was moving, but he heard nothing she said.

"Pardon?"

"I said it is admirable to have such a clear purpose." A few beats later, she added, "Shall we go inside?"

"In a few minutes."

Small talk had never been his strength, and he furiously searched his brain for something to say to keep her there. It occurred to him this was the very spot MacMillan had cornered her. He'd done his own fair share of cornering, and suddenly the place felt all wrong for what he had in mind.

She seemed to shiver.

"Are you cold?" he asked.

"A little."

He shed his fur-lined cloak and whisked it about her slight shoulders; the hem puddled on the ground at her feet. She clutched the garment about herself. It resembled a large, furry sack hanging on her petite frame and evoked a powerful surge of protectiveness in him. Protectiveness boding entanglement.

"Perhaps we should get you inside," he said.

After delivering Oliwia to the great hall, Jacek returned to his quarters. He heaved himself on his cot and stared at the wooden ceiling, chiding himself for his clumsy attempt at wooing her in the garden. And why woo her at all? She'd made it clear she had no time to consider suits, and he *certainly* didn't. Even if he broke down her defenses and she were receptive to his advances, then what? Complicated attachments were extravagances he could little afford at this juncture, no matter how much she beguiled him. His honorable voice, echoed by his pragmatic one, told him he'd best stay away.

Thinking on it hurt his head. His only consolation was that for the first time in a long while, he dreamed of his deity that night. And this time, he knew who she was.

CHAPTER 28

The Porucznik

Jacek reined in Gwiazda and dismounted briskly in the stableyard.

Feliks took his reins. "Welcome home, Lieutenant."

Jacek unfastened his belted blades and bow, handing them to Marcin. "Thank you, Feliks. It's good to be back." He swiveled his head, his eyes searching out a familiar form.

"You were away a shorter turn this time. I trust you had a joyous Christmas season?"

"I did." *Until my father and brothers started in about my quest for land. Until my mother began the prospective brides procession. Until craving Oliwia's company became unbearable.*

Jacek began a single-minded march toward the keep, only to stop short when her cries pierced his thoughts.

"Jacek! *Jacek!*"

He pivoted. She was running toward him from the garrison, tears coursing down her cheeks. Her unbound hair streamed behind her, and she wore no cloak against the chill. His heart seized. Meeting her partway, he grasped her shoulders and steadied her.

She was gasping. "Filip!"

"What's wrong with Filip, Liwi?"

"He's been beaten! His arm … I think it's broken … He can scarcely move. And his face! It's … Oh, dear God, he's …" she wailed between heaving breaths.

Gently squeezing her arms, he peered at her. "Who did it, Liwi? Who beat Filip?" His voice was even, calm. For her.

She glanced behind herself, then raised frightened eyes to his. Tears continued to spill down her face.

"It was the captain," she whimpered. "He's done it before, but this time … I should have told you sooner."

He released her and streaked to the garrison.

When Jacek saw Filip's small form on his bloody pallet, rage flared white-hot in his belly. The boy was covered in welts, bruises, and cuts. His arm rested awkwardly across his stomach. A healer stooped beside him, and he winced every time she touched him. Oliwia knelt by his feet, her hands screwed tightly in her lap.

Worst of all was his unrecognizable face. Swollen, bloodied, and covered in dark reds and blue-purples, Jacek wouldn't have known he was the same child. He looked as though he'd been stung by hundreds of bees, slashed a multitude of times, then painted with berry stain. His slitted eyes leaked, and he clenched his teeth between puffy, oozing lips. Jacek looked around at plaintive soldiers and gaping boys.

"Take him to my quarters and put him in my bed," he barked at Stefan and Kasimir. To one of the boys, he said, "I want his pallet scrubbed."

Then he addressed the healer. "Gather up your salves and care for him there. Send a boy for the physician if he hasn't already been called."

Softening his timbre, he turned to Oliwia. "Go with them, Oliwia."

A fearful look marked her features. "What are you going to do?"

"That's not your concern. Your brother is your concern. Go with him," he repeated, making it clear he would brook no argument. He was relieved when she rose and left with the others.

He scanned the stifling chamber. "Who can tell me what in God's name happened?"

THE HEART OF A HUSSAR

Henryk jerked his chin at a boy shrinking into a corner. "He's the only witness."

A soldier's lad, he looked to be Filip's age. The boy glanced at one of the soldiers, who gave him a grim nod.

"He is your boy, Otto, yes?" asked Jacek.

"Yes, Lieutenant. Gustaw will tell you what that son of a bitch did to Filip."

As if he were rapidly unraveling a ball of twine, Gustaw recounted how Mateusz had instructed Filip to retrieve his warhorse from a thicket beyond the practice field. The large charger headbutted Filip as he tried to gather his reins, sending him sprawling before moving off. Mateusz had stormed over, hauled him to his feet and slammed him with the handle of his war hammer. Filip went down again. Yelling and cursing, Mateusz struck more blows with a horse's whip.

"He stood over him, shouting, 'Now get that accursed horse or you'll get more!' When Filip didn't get up, he kicked him. I ran over, but the captain said he'd beat me too. I ran quick as I could for my sire." Gustaw's eyes were as big as saucers.

Otto said, "By the time I reached him, the captain was walking off the field with his devil of a stallion. When I asked him what happened, he said Filip had disobeyed and he'd had to 'teach him a lesson.' Those were his exact words, Lieutenant."

"I followed shortly after," Henryk added, "and helped Filip off the field. I suspect more than the arm is broken."

Jacek looked at Gustaw squarely. "Lady Oliwia mentioned other beatings. Is this true?"

The boy bobbed his head. "Yes, sir. But Filip didn't want you to know. Said he'd get in even more trouble. I think the lady found out."

Men shifted, coughed in the packed room.

"What's your intention, Jacek?" Henryk asked.

Jacek's voice was coated in steel. "I'm going to pay Captain Zalewski a call."

Jacek exploded from the garrison and stormed across the yard to Mateusz's home, fists clenched so tightly his forearms vibrated. It took all of Atlas's strength to keep his fury contained in his body. He pounded on the captain's door. It swung open, revealing Lady Barbara. She looked Jacek up and down, the hint of a smile curving her lips.

He glared at her through narrowed eyes. "Where is your husband, Pani Zalewska? And do not think to test me."

"I'm right here, Dąbrowski," the captain called from behind his wife. "Barbara, leave us."

She turned, and Mateusz's eyes tracked her out of the room before he sauntered to the doorway, wiping wet hands on a linen cloth.

"You here to apologize for that urchin of yours? I'm still getting the blood off my hands. Christ, that boy's a bleeder!"

Jacek's tautened muscles bunched. "No. I'm here to do what he could not."

Mateusz's eyebrows rose to his hairline. "Oh, really? Ready for your own beating? You don't have the stones to do it, so be off. Go play in the yard with your friends." With a snicker, he jerked his chin to somewhere behind Jacek.

Jacek glanced to the side and caught sight of a ring of men in his periphery. He'd had no idea the garrison had followed him.

"Or did you bring them with you to do what *you can't*?" Mateusz taunted.

"I didn't bring them. I don't need their help."

Mateusz rolled his eyes and placed his fists on his hips, striking a bored pose. "Apologize for the brat, and I'll let it go this time."

"No, Zalewski. I'm not leaving until we settle this. Man to man, not man to boy."

Mateusz threw his head back and laughed, then riveted bloodshot eyes on Jacek—blue-green swimming in spidery red. "It can't be man to man, Dąbrowski, because you're not a man. When will you get it through your cracked head?"

Then he raised his hands and looked past Jacek. "You all heard, yes? My subordinate challenges me. And for what? I taught his impertinent shaver a lesson! You are my witnesses."

A voice called out from the crowd, "Brave man, Zalewski. Beating a child with a nadziak."

THE HEART OF A HUSSAR

"He had it coming!" The cords in Mateusz's neck stood out. "He needed to be taught who his masters are. *He* wouldn't do it," he pointed at Jacek, "so I had to."

A murmur waved through the crowd, and Jacek turned toward the commotion. Someone stepped out of the throng. Too late, he caught the blur by his right eye that was Mateusz's cocked fist wrapped around something hard. Blindsided, Jacek dropped to his knees. Wet, warm, sticky blood flowed from his brow into his eye, eclipsing his sight. He swiped at it with the heel of his hand, his head exploding with stars against a black backdrop.

Jacek pulled himself up, and his eyes dropped to a stone pestle in Mateusz's fist. Mateusz snarled, "That brat had it coming. And when I'm through with you, I'll go see his sister and show her what it's like with a real man." He licked his lips. "After she's had a taste of *me*, she'll want nothing to do with you."

Jacek vaulted at Mateusz, wrapping his arms around his middle, driving him into an outer wall. He grasped Mateusz's wrist and smashed it against the wall. The pestle dropped to the ground. Mateusz grunted, then shoved his knee into Jacek's gut. Dragging air and the rank odor of alcohol into his lungs, Jacek held Mateusz to him a few beats, then propelled himself backward. Mateusz pushed off the wall and came at him warily. Jacek wiped more blood out of his eye. They squared off and began circling each other.

From a back corner of his mind, Jacek heard the crowd buzz. Dogs barked. A woman gasped. Chickens squawked. Men cheered and jeered. A silver button glinted. Warm rays bathed moist spring leaves with light.

He pulled in a breath.

Wild eyes flashing, Mateusz threw a punch that sliced air. The momentum brought him forward, and Jacek jabbed his breastbone hard. The strike didn't stop Mateusz, but it slowed him. Jacek kicked out, landing a heel just above his knee. Mateusz roared, staggered backward, but stayed upright. He dove for Jacek. Jacek sidestepped him, pounding his back with steely forearms. Mateusz's shoulder rammed his hip, and he pulled Jacek down.

Mateusz sprawled in the dirt facedown, shaking his head. Jacek sprang out of reach, fists at the ready. A bottle flew from the crowd and landed by Mateusz. He seized it and leapt to his feet, breaking off the bottom against a wooden post.

Gripping the neck of the bottle, Mateusz came at Jacek with the jagged glass. He lunged. Jacek grasped the wrist holding the bottle, keeping it away from his body. They came together. Chest to chest, they strained against one another, grunting, growling, grappling, heels digging in, fighting for purchase. Jacek shifted his stance and managed to wedge his knee between Mateusz's legs. Mateusz broke Jacek's hold on his wrist, but Jacek pressed his weight against Mateusz's inner thigh, and Mateusz stumbled backward, Jacek crashing on top of him. Mateusz's hand flew open, and the bottle rolled harmlessly out of reach.

Jacek scrambled to his feet, crouching, while Mateusz heaved to his side. Before Mateusz could recover, Jacek cinched his arm in the crook of his elbow, pinning his other wrist to the ground. He leaned on him with all his weight, one leg straddling his lower body, digging his heels into the dirt. He tightened his grip on the arm. Mateusz cried out. Jacek clamped down harder.

"Enough!"

Jacek jolted at the sound of Eryk's voice, pushing himself off Mateusz. He stood apart, heaving in breaths, his hands pressed to his thighs. Eryk stood beside him while Mateusz stirred on the ground and cursed.

"This is done, Mateusz. He defeated you. Gather yourself and report to me in ten minutes." Eryk pivoted, and Jacek watched as his retreating back parted the susurrating crowd.

A woman screamed.

Jacek was already in motion as a glint in Mateusz's hand caught his eye. But Mateusz wasn't coming for him. He raced at Eryk with murder in his eyes, the broken bottle in one hand and a dagger in the other.

Oliwia had harbored a clenching fear since learning her brother had been hurt. Horrified by the sight her eyes beheld when she reached Filip, she'd been running to the keep for the physician—anyone who could help—when Jacek's tall form had caught her eye like a beacon. Letting her panic spill over, she'd torn for him blindly. *He* could help. Only when he'd laid his warm hands on her arms could she begin reeling her terror back.

THE HEART OF A HUSSAR

Now Oliwia paced Jacek's small anteroom just outside his smaller bedchamber while the physician checked Filip. To distract herself, she scanned the austere room and nearly let out a laugh. Jacek's solar was neater than her small trunk, and his furnishings were as spartan and practical as he. Other than the painting she'd given him the previous Christmas, there were no decorations. No superfluous adornments to clutter the space. Nothing to distract her.

Sighing, she wandered to the chamber's only window. As she peered through the occluded pane, her fingers brushed the tops of a short row of books precisely lining a shelf. She looked down at her fingers absently; they held no dust. A small leather-bound volume caught her eye, and she plucked it out.

When she opened it, the cover cracked as though the volume had never been opened. She looked upon a pristine book of poems. Delicately, she peeled back the front page, and a small rectangle of paper fluttered to the floor. Ruffled, Oliwia picked it up quickly and inserted it where it had nestled. As she did so, she recognized Jacek's sweeping signature. She glanced around, then scanned the note:

Christmas, In the Year of our Lord 1611
For Liwi,
A singular book for a singular lady.
May God hold you in his good protection always,
Jacek

She reread her name several times. It truly was *her* name. Or was he acquainted with another Liwi?

"My lady?" the healer's soft voice called from the bedchamber, startling her.

Oliwia snapped the book shut, nearly dropping it. "Coming."

Like a thief soundly caught, her hand shook as she tried to fit the book back in its tidy space. Hastily, she crammed it home.

"He's been given a sleep draught," the physician said. "He will recover, but he must rest. The healer will tend him a while longer. While she does, take a respite."

Oliwia felt a sudden urge to flee the confined space, her brain muddled with thoughts of her brother, thoughts of her discovery. As she emerged from Jacek's quarters into bright daylight, a commotion drew her attention. Walking toward the ruckus, she spotted a wall of men—soldiers, servants, stable hands—arranged in a semicircle as though watching a performance. A performance staged in front of the captain's dwelling. She raced toward the throng, panic welling in her anew, sending her heart careening against her ribs. Murmurs, punctuated by shouts, rose from the crowd.

"Get up!"

"Watch out!"

Wriggling between men too distracted to notice her, she swam her way to the front and stopped cold. In the dirt patch before the captain's house, Jacek was lumbering up from his knees, his hand covering his eye. Was that blood? As he rocked on his feet, a deranged-looking Mateusz stalked toward him, clutching what appeared to be a pestle in his hand. Jacek raised both forearms, his hands fisted. Blood covered one side of his face, dripping off his jaw, and he blinked rapidly. She gasped.

"Get her out of here," Eryk's disembodied voice ordered.

Iron arms encircled her middle. She flailed as Henryk hauled her out of the fray.

"This is no place for you, Oliwia," he warned. "Go back to the keep."

She wrenched herself from his arms and stood defiantly. "Jacek's fighting him because of me, because of what I said," she cried.

Henryk looked at her sympathetically—or condescendingly, she wasn't sure which. He planted his fists on his hips. "This has been a long time brewing, Oliwia. It's not about you or anything you said. Now go." He waved his finger at her, as if flicking a fly from the table. Her color rose up her neck and fired her cheeks.

"Go!" he commanded in a very un-Henryk-like manner.

Muttering between clenched teeth, she turned on her heel and paced toward the keep, arms pumping furiously. She stopped and turned, then dashed to the side when Henryk's back melted into the crowd. Carefully picking her path through the thicket of men, she heard Eryk's voice boom. All about her, men yelled and jostled. She wedged herself into a sliver of space. Eryk stood beside Jacek while Mateusz twitched in the dirt.

Eryk has stopped it!

Relief flooded Oliwia's body. Now she could expel some of the unbearable guilt she felt for dragging Jacek into her distress—for being the cause of his bloodied face and hands. She should have told him of the beatings when they'd strolled in the garden, but she'd stopped when Filip's pleas had replayed in her head.

THE HEART OF A HUSSAR

"No, Liwi, you mustn't tell him! He'll be angry with me, and he'll fight the captain. Then Lord Eryk will punish him!"

Will Eryk punish Jacek now?

Bent at the waist, Jacek was hauling in breath when Eryk walked away. Her eyes were on Jacek, but something bright caught her eye. Mateusz stood upright, clutching a broken bottle like a sword. He sprang into a run. She screamed. Bodies moved with blurring speed. Mateusz ran at Eryk. Jacek ran at Mateusz, shouting, "Zalewski! Your fight's with me, not Lord Eryk!"

Mateusz stopped, spun, and slashed the wicked points at Jacek's face. Jacek jumped back. Mateusz advanced, a long knife in his other hand.

"I *will* finish you, you son of a whore," Mateusz snarled.

Mateusz came at Jacek in small steps, backing him up with short jabs. Eryk yelled, but Mateusz seemed not to hear. The crowd pressed forward. Jacek inched backward, his hands empty. He was backing into a wall. Someone yelled, "He's unarmed!"

Mateusz lunged with the knife.

Oliwia held her breath, images bounding through her head. The book of poems. The word "singular." Jacek's extravagant signature. His long strides. His smile. Dancing with him. Apple tarts. His large hand holding the dainty fan. His warm breath caressing her neck. The tingling his nearness always triggered. Stammering the first time he called her "Liwi." His unwavering loyalty. Beautiful sapphire eyes twinkling at her.

Merciful God, let him live!

Urgency took her, and she squirmed between the bodies, angling to pitch herself between the two men. Hands restrained her.

"Let me go!" she shouted in frustration.

Her restraints tightened. "No!" Henryk barked in her ear.

Powerless to break Henryk's hold, she watched as the blade caught Jacek's forearm and he sidestepped, faltered, stumbling backward, colliding with the wall. He put a hand out as if to catch himself. Mateusz pounced. The crowd gasped. Jacek flung something, and Mateusz's head was engulfed in a cloud of dust. Mateusz spat and shook his head. Jacek rushed him. Both men crashed to the ground.

Images flashed through Oliwia's brain. A fist gripping a knife, arms, elbows in a tumble. A hand holding a wrist holding the bottle. Grappling for the glinting knife.

Everything happened at blinding speed and yet was so slow that she saw it all unfold. The bottle struck a cobble and shattered. Mateusz raised the knife and plunged it into Jacek's shoulder, inches from his neck. Jacek's head jerked, and his emerald żupan darkened with blood. Grunting, boots and bodies scrabbling in dirt. Jacek slammed his knee on Mateusz's arm, the knife still embedded in his shoulder. Mateusz spat and struck Jacek's chest with his forearm. Jacek's breath whooshed out of him, then transformed into a savage growl. Mateusz reached up, grasped the dagger's handle, driving the knife deeper into Jacek's shoulder. He clamped his hands about Jacek's throat, cutting off his pained cry. Jacek's body juddered, his face locked in a grimace, reddening as he straddled Mateusz. Jacek thrust his hand into the clutter of glass shards.

Jacek cocked his arm back. He punched a slice of jagged glass into Mateusz's neck. Mateusz released his hold. Jacek dragged the wicked shard across his flesh with a throaty, visceral roar. Mateusz's body spasmed, the gash at his neck disgorging rivulets of blood. He reached his hands to his ruined gullet. His mouth fell open, and he spluttered as his wide blue-green eyes darted back and forth.

Jacek hovered over Mateusz's twitching body, taut, immobile, as if frozen. Mateusz at last sagged into the ground.

Simultaneously ecstatic and horrified, relief and unspeakable anguish swamped Oliwia. All had fallen quiet, Jacek's ragged breathing the only sound. He yanked the knife from his shoulder and cast it in the dirt, rising from the corpse and crossing himself, his eyes fixed on the body at his feet. A wail came from behind him, and all eyes shifted to Lady Barbara. She tore to her husband and dropped beside him, sobbing wretchedly, hugging herself. Two small, wide-eyed children looked on from the doorway.

His face wilted with sorrow, Jacek reeled backward. While folk rushed to the widow's side, Oliwia broke free and ran to Jacek. He looked at her as though he didn't know her. Wrapping her arm about his waist, she tugged him away from the devastating carnage.

THE HEART OF A HUSSAR

Under cover of a moonless night, Romek stepped into the dimness of the lord's quarters.

The lord threw the bar across the door. "Did anyone see you?"

"Of course not." Romek pulled off his cowl and looked around the cluttered chamber. Had it grown dustier and more derelict since his last visit?

The lord poured out two cups of wodka, handing Romek one. Romek raised it and smirked. "A toast. To Biaska's lieutenant killing its captain and making our job easier."

The lord gave him a hard look. "Not so hasty, Romek. My spy tells me the lieutenant is far more dangerous than that fool of a captain. It would have been more advantageous the other way round."

"Well, then, I'll see to it the lieutenant follows his superior to hell." Romek grinned wickedly. He tapped his grubby cup to his master's.

"Here's to the fall of Biaska."

Jacek sat rigidly in Eryk's solar one frostbitten February afternoon on the eve of Lent. His shoulder twinged, but he dismissed the ache.

Eryk eyed him. "I am pleased your injury was not more serious." With a mirthless smile, he added, "I understand Filip has nearly recovered despite his sister's cosseting."

Jacek nodded, staring with unseeing eyes out the window. "He'll have a few scars, but the bruising has faded, and his bones are mending." Hands resting on his knees, he brought his attention back to Eryk.

Eryk pursed his lips. "Mateusz ... He was responsible for his own undoing. You saved my life and will forever have my gratitude. It might comfort you to know Lady Barbara and her children will be escorted to her family's estate tomorrow morning."

Jacek nodded, his limbs leaden, numb. Even after all these weeks.

Eryk held a sheet of paper aloft. "We must deliberate the garrison. I lead the Biaska chorągiew back to Podolia in a month, and I need a captain."

When Jacek departed the solar, the sun had submerged in a gaudy fuschia-streaked horizon, and he was no longer the lieutenant. He was the captain, soon to embark on another mission to the border as Lord Eryk's second. Campaigns Eryk elected not to lead would be Jacek's to command—he would serve as porucznik. Two months before reaching twenty-four, he had attained a pinnacle few men older than he had reached.

It was a hollow victory.

Since he'd arrived at Biaska, he'd anticipated this moment nearly as much as he'd envisioned standing upon his land. Where he'd expected effervescence popping in his bloodstream, infinite emptiness was his companion. Achievement had come at terrible cost. He'd killed a lord-brother—a husband and father—and now took his place. That the man wasn't worthy of his regret didn't wash away the bitterness.

Jacek pulled his kolpak over his ears and walked to the garrison, picking his way through mud. The wind drove stinging sleet into his face, tugging at his cloak and chilling his skin anywhere it found an unsecured bit of cloth. Pausing, he watched a squat man lead horses to the stables. Aromatic smoke wafted from clustered cottage chimneys, disappearing into the gray curtain of rain. The everyday did little to soothe his tattered conscience, so he resolved to entomb his morose thoughts and do what he'd always done.

He would lose himself in war.

CHAPTER 29

Gifts

Jacek raised the war hammer above his shoulder in a two-fisted grasp and brought it down hard. The blow was parried by the shaft of his opponent's nadziak, and the vibration shuddered up his arms to his neck. He felt the wound in his shoulder give and sticky warmth ooze into his linen shirt.

His adversary shoved him hard, knocking him on his back in the slick, frosted grass. Jacek swung the hasp across his chest, every muscle tense as he prepared to deflect the next strike. Instead, his challenger extended his hand and laughed.

"By all the saints, I defeated you again!" Henryk cried triumphantly between heaving breaths.

Jacek batted his friend's hand away and pulled himself upright. He dragged an arm over his face before grabbing his shoulder. "The *only* reason you stopped me is this infernal shoulder."

Henryk gave him a smug smile. "Believe it if you must, but *I* know the truth of it. I am stronger and more cunning, and you can no longer best me."

"Ha! Believe *that* if you must, but when my shoulder has fully healed, our sparring will go as it always has, and I will trounce you each time. Your victory will be short-lived." Jacek rotated his shoulder slowly and winced.

"Victories," Henryk corrected.

Before Jacek could spit out the next rejoinder, he heard his name. He squinted, looking across a swath of stiff brown grasses bending under a biting March wind.

"Marcin!" Henryk called before Jacek recognized his own pacholik. "Have you come to rescue your master?"

Marcin drew alongside, his normally light expression sober. "No, Lieutenant Kalinowski. I have come to fetch Captain Dąbrowski for my Lord Eryk. He has requested your presence in his solar, sir. Without delay."

Captain. The word sounded strange. Jacek nearly checked his surroundings for the ghost of the man who had, until weeks ago, held the title. The man he had killed. Ignoring the squelching in his stomach, Jacek looked up at Marcin. "I will report shortly."

Fifteen minutes later, in a fresh yellow brocade żupan over a clean white shirt, Jacek took the short flight to the solar.

Eryk waved his hand. "Have a seat. Tell me about the preparations for the mission."

Jacek sat, his back rod straight. "Towarzysze report with their retinues daily and join us in drills. Supplies are being gathered and wagons packed. We'll be ready to march in two weeks' time."

Eryk pursed his lips and nodded. "Good." Then he heaved in a great breath and looked up at the dark wood-beamed ceiling for a beat before swinging his gaze back to Jacek. "I have changed my plans, Jacek. I am not coming. This will be your first campaign as my porucznik. 'Tis a big undertaking to lead the company so soon after becoming captain, but you will be in familiar terrain, among familiar superiors—Hetman Żółkiewski and Pułkownik Matejko."

Bemusement—coupled with excitement—swelled inside Jacek. "Yes, my lord."

"I have no doubt you will perform your duties with your usual competency."

"Thank you, sir. I will do my utmost."

"I know you will. That is all." Eryk gazed out the window, and Jacek withdrew.

Wending his way through the passageway, Jacek pondered this surprising turn. Here was his chance to finally prove himself! Nothing—and no one—stood in his way now. He sprang down the stairs and came

THE HEART OF A HUSSAR

to a stop on the landing, nearly toppling Oliwia. Her crystal-blue eyes startled wide.

"Please excuse my clumsiness, Jacek," she breathed when she'd recovered.

"I believe I owe *you* the apology. And not just for running you over. I, ah, have not been a good friend of late, I fear, but I hope to do better." He began rummaging around in his ferezeya for the book of poems he'd wholly overlooked until recently, when he'd tidied his antechamber. Reconciling his conscience to Mateusz's death had blotted out most everything else—at times even Oliwia.

She frowned. "You have had a rather difficult time. How is your shoulder?"

"Better, thank you. It should be completely healed when I leave several weeks hence." Extracting the small volume, he cleared his throat. "I have been meaning to give this to you since my return, but somehow …" He thrust it at her. "Here."

Her hands unfolded like petals of a flower, accepting the book. Graceful fingers carefully prized open the stiff cover and slid out the note he had written. He held his breath as she scanned his words. She looked up at him, her face brightening like the sun cresting the morning horizon.

"It's beautiful, Jacek." She held the book against her chest. "Thank you. I will treasure it."

He scratched the back of his neck, his shoulders easing. "You like it, then?"

"More than you know."

"Liwi, I just learned I am to lead the company," he said, biting back his giddiness. "It's a chance to distinguish myself."

"And get your land," she said softly. "How wonderful for you, Jacek."

"Yes! Exactly." He suddenly remembered himself. "May I walk you somewhere?"

She shook her head. "No. I am on my way to my lady's apartments to plan the farewell feast. You will be there, yes?"

"I will not miss it. You will save me some dances?"

"Of course."

GRIFFIN BRADY

A fortnight later, Jacek hunted through the solitary wooden chest in his chamber. *There it is!* Lifting out a dagger, he sat on the edge of his cot and pulled a sharpening stone from a drawer in a side table.

He held the blade up to the meager light, inspected it, then expertly manipulated the stone along the dagger's steel edges. As his hands worked the blade, his mind worked on Oliwia. She'd been so taken with his trivial gift—thanking him repeatedly and reciting each poem to him from memory—that he was inspired to give her one far more memorable. The action flirted with recklessness, but he'd be gone by week's end without worry of his heart enmeshing him in a thorny liaison. In the meantime, the knife would help him mend any schisms his brooding over Mateusz's death had created between them.

The sharpening completed, Jacek placed the stone back in its resting place, seated the dagger in its scabbard, and wrapped it in a soft woolen square. He headed to find Filip.

A half hour later, Jacek leaned against the door frame of Oliwia's bedchamber, watching Filip squirm as she hugged him joyfully. The boy's eyes darted to Jacek, and his face was bright red.

"Liwi, stop it!" Filip wriggled in her arms. "Great warriors do not get hugged by women!"

She beamed, a single tear sliding down her cheek. Jacek felt an urge to brush it away, to kiss her soft cheek, to kiss a trail to her beautiful mouth. He longed to taste her cerise lips. Checking himself, he winked at her before arching an eyebrow at Filip. "Filip, warriors *do* get hugged by women. It's one of the many advantages of being a great warrior."

Filip screwed his face as if he'd bitten a lemon. "Yech!"

Oliwia swiped at the tear, then let out a lyrical laugh. Jacek suppressed a chuckle at Filip's indignation, folded his arms across his chest, mustered a stern air, and looked down his nose at the boy. "Filip, enough."

Filip snapped to.

"That's better. Now wait in the passageway while I have a private word with your sister."

THE HEART OF A HUSSAR

Filip shot him a puzzled look before taking up station in the hallway within sight. Jacek watched him retreat, then faced Oliwia, blocking Filip from her view. He had been holding the knife, which he now carefully unwrapped, revealing an ornate hilt and scabbard encrusted in ruby-red-and-pink gems. The two pieces nestled together so perfectly that they appeared to be one. The gems were mounted in six-petaled gold flowers, and intricate silver-and-gold filigree surrounded each flower in swirls and diamond designs. Rows of the jeweled flowers ran the length of the scabbard and hilt, and each row was offset from the other so the pattern seemed to undulate.

He felt her eyes fix on it as he uncoupled the assembly, sliding out a burnished metal blade. He presented her the glinting handle, and her eyes traveled the length of the dagger. The blade was as exquisite as the scabbard and hilt. It was fashioned of steel, and as he turned it in his hands, he revealed detailed, exotic loops etched on each side. She looked up at him wide-eyed, and her mouth formed into a perfectly round O, but no sound came out.

"Do you like it?" He masked his apprehension. He'd never thought to give a woman such an extravagant gift before. Not even Izabela.

"It's beautiful! I have never seen anything like it. Where did you get it?" Her fingers hovered over the hilt, but she didn't touch it.

"I took it off a janissary I ki—" He straightened and cleared his throat, then bent back down to her. "I acquired it in my travels from a Turk. I didn't think … That is, he no longer had a use for it."

Her eyes flicked over the weapon, and her face lit up, causing elation to fizz within him. "It's a fine example of Turkish craftsmanship," he continued, "and what you see on the blade is Turkish writing. I'm not sure what it says, but I am told these are blessings for the person who carries it."

She stood still, staring.

He lifted it to her hand, still floating just above the hilt. "Touch it," he urged.

She ran her fingers over the knobby hilt. "The stones. They're so smooth, so cool," she whispered.

"Here. Hold it, like this." He wrapped his hand around the hilt and bent his elbow in a plunging aspect. He offered her the handle once again.

"See how it fits you. The hilt doesn't have much girth, and it gets lost in my hand. I thought it might fit yours nicely." He encouraged her with a smile and a nod. "Go on. Take it."

She lifted the weapon from his palm and grasped the hilt as he had demonstrated. It seemed long and awkward in her small hand, and she fumbled it. He reached out to catch it, but she recovered in time.

Turning it over in her hands, she said, "It's heavier than it looks." Her fingers barely closed around the stone-studded handle.

"There, you see? It fits you."

She offered the hilt back to him, but he shook his head.

"No. I want you to have it."

"What?" Oliwia sputtered. "I cannot accept such a precious gift. It would not be right." She thrust the hilt at him, but he stepped away and clasped his hands behind his back.

"What's not right? I cannot use it, and I would like you to have something with which you can protect yourself."

Her brows knotted, and he took a step toward her.

"Rest assured, Liwi, you are in no danger here, but it's wise to have a weapon with you at all times. After all, you're not very big, and you could easily be … That is, while you are a spirited fighter, you could be overpowered by any blackguard. You should have some way to defend yourself."

She stared at the hilt suspended between them.

He pointed at it. "It was likely a ceremonial blade, but it's an excellent piece of steel, and I've just sharpened the edges. It will serve you well should you need it. Besides, it's a pretty thing." He shrugged. *Like you.*

She stood mute. Jacek lifted the hilt and slid the dagger back into its scabbard. He pushed it into her hands before she could utter another protest.

"I must go, but I will see you tonight." He turned and walked toward the doorway. When he reached it, he stopped, wheeled, and took her in. She stood in the same position, as if she were a statue, holding the glittering object in her hands. She raised her head.

Spirit of God, but she is beautiful!

THE HEART OF A HUSSAR

Oliwia smoothed her new teal-and-gold velvet silk gown while Nadia tucked a wayward tendril under the beaded headband. *Everything must be perfect.* The company would depart in two days; Oliwia planned to leave an indelible impression on its porucznik.

As she descended, said porucznik stood at the foot of the stairs, as if waiting for her. He held out his hand and guided her to the landing. The touch of his warm, rough hand shot a thrill through her. When he offered her a cup of mead, she readily accepted and sipped. It tasted especially good this evening, and it calmed her twitchiness. Soon she accepted more.

She drank throughout the meal, nearly forgetting to eat the morsels on her plate.

Jacek frowned beside her at the table. "Are you not hungry?"

"No." She shook her head happily. "You may finish my portion, if you wish. But I *would* like more mead. Is it time to dance yet?" She swiveled her head in search of the musicians. The motion left her dizzy.

Time was forgotten. Oliwia floated on a stream of bubbles, dancing in Jacek's strong arms. Then came another dance partner and another cup of mead. Soon she was lost to the color and the music enveloping her. A man laughed—was that Henryk?—as he walked her in a promenade. Another grabbed her familiarly about the waist and was shoved away. Somebody gripped her arm and steered her from the whirling revelry despite her protests.

A glower was screwed into Jacek's dark brows. "Oliwia, how much mead have you had?"

She brushed the back of her hand across her nose. Something tickled it incessantly. "I'm not sure."

Objects blurred, and she stared at one silver button on his chest to sharpen her focus. The action made her sway on her feet. He uncrossed his long arms from said chest and took her elbow, shaking his head.

"Where are you taking me? I've yet to dance with everyone," she argued. They were climbing the stairs.

"You are not going to dance with everyone. In fact, you're not dancing any more this night. You, my girl, are going to bed."

Though he muttered crossly, a warm, slow tingle began to spread from her toes to the tops of her feet, unfurling itself slowly, deliciously up her calves to her knees before curling up her thighs. She looked up at him as he dragged her along, taking in his back, his broad shoulders. Her eyes dropped wantonly from there, but the skirt of his żupan hid it all.

She imagined what he'd look like—or tried to—beneath the layers of clothing. The muscles along his shoulders and back would stretch, long and smooth, then flex and bunch if he picked her up. She pictured his forearms, their cording defined under fine golden-brown hair. What did his skin feel like? Her imagination now in full sway, the warmth continued to ooze and spread to her belly, stretching exquisitely across the entirety of her chest and up her throat.

A little voice yelled inside her head. "Oliwia, you wicked girl!" She swallowed, then scurried to draw even with him.

"Where are you taking me?"

"I told you," he huffed. "To bed."

She giggled, and he stopped and wheeled, looking altogether scandalized. "Dear God, you are utterly sotted! I am *putting* you to bed, then I am leaving. You will remain there, by yourself, until you're sober—which may take days, judging by your condition."

Confusion fuzzed her mind. "Am I so … unappealing?" Her tongue suddenly felt thick. It didn't seem to work properly.

He humphed and tugged her along again. "You are in no condition to have this conversation."

"I'll have you know I am perfectly conditional, er, conversational." She giggled again.

He threw open the door to her bedchamber, pulling her in after him before stepping away. She turned ever so slowly, resolved to keep her balance. His frame filled the doorway, and he stood poised with the latch firmly in his hand. Facing him, she yanked off the infernal headdress before fumbling to liberate her hair. She was partly successful. Her cheeks pulled up in what felt like a smile, but the lines and shadows between his dark brows only grew deeper.

"You're behaving like a cat in heat!" he scolded.

THE HEART OF A HUSSAR

She should have quaked in her slippers, but her brain was too muddled to get the message to her lower extremities. Instead, she rested her fists on her hips and stuck her chin out.

"Cats in heat are indiscriminate. I am not." She was quite pleased she'd gotten out the whole bit without tripping over her words. In a less indignant tone, she asked, "How does a woman go about seducing a man anyway?"

Jacek appeared flustered—a most unusual look for him. He flapped his hand at her. "It takes very little. You look at him the way you're looking at me."

She grinned and took awkward steps towards him, the prim voice screeching somewhere in her head; she squelched it.

His eyebrows shot up to his hairline. "No, no, no. I didn't say *I* could be seduced with such a look. But if you look at any other man that way, you will surely succeed. Which is precisely why you're staying here."

She stood before him now, staring at the indigo flecks in his azure eyes. They brought to mind slender threads of deepest blue drifting on an ocean. He straightened, but he didn't move away. Somewhere in her foggy head, another voice told her to close her mouth, that it wasn't polite to gawk.

Rising on tiptoe, she placed her hand on his arm for balance and brought her lips to his ear. He smelled of Scots pines after a cleansing rain, of finest leather, and spiced wood smoke. It was a heady, masculine scent. A distracting scent.

She began giggling in his ear. "I've utterly forgotten what I was going to say!"

He pulled back and looked at her, an odd expression replacing the scowly one. She smiled; he did not. Before she could register the motion, he'd walked her back and shut the door, cradling her face in his big hands. Then his mouth was on hers, soft and warm. Her fingers crept up his arms of their own volition and dug into hard muscle under a layer of textured silk.

Even in her addlepated condition, she felt the full force of the kiss. This was nothing like kissing George MacMillan. It was like being caught in surging waters when a river roars through a clutter of boulders. It took her by storm. Not just the fact of it, but because it was all gentleness and succulent pliability and not the hardness and steel she'd imagined of him. He kissed her slowly, thoroughly. On some level, the sensation of his tongue exploring hers shocked her. On an entirely different level, one deeper down, it triggered all manner of strange tingling in rather illicit parts of her body. She gave herself over to it and savored the taste of him, spice and wine in a muddle, so foreign yet so delicious. He ended the kiss, leaving her bereft of his lips and his warm breath. She fluttered her eyes open to find his fiercely fixed on hers. Brushing his thumb over one corner of her mouth, he gently tugged her lip down and lightly nibbled it before engaging the whole of her mouth in another mind-melting kiss, sending jolts of pleasure from her neck to the very tips of her toes.

As he kissed her, he splayed his hands across her back, drawing her to him along the length of his torso. She leaned against him, molded herself to him. Everywhere his body touched hers was scorching heat. Her hands glided to his solid shoulders, relishing the feel of the sinew beneath her fingers. Unbroken kisses grew demanding and deep, urgent, and she felt an intensity well up in her that rivaled his.

He pulled away abruptly and stared at her, his breathing noisy and ragged. He frowned. Dazed, a sinking feeling seized her. She must have done something wrong. Gently grasping her arms, he set her apart from him, leaving chills where the heat of his body had been.

"Bar the door behind me, Liwi." His voice was gravelly, rough, but he didn't sound angry. He then bounded into the passageway without a backward glance.

Jacek tore down the hall, grasping at shreds of self-control.

Jesus! What the hell got into me?

One moment he'd been exasperated with her, and the next, he couldn't stop himself kissing her. And those kisses had rocked him. Leveled him. Devastated him.

He needed to move, get away, put distance between himself and the tantalizing temptation behind him. His body, however, had ideas of its own, commanding him to retrace his steps, close and bar the door, and carry her to the bed. It didn't care that she was befuddled with drink, that she was innocent, or that he wanted no intricate entanglements. All it cared about was the feel of her, and it craved more.

I can't be seduced with her look, indeed! It had taken one beguiling smile, no more, to inflame him and make him lose his wits.

He stopped and pivoted, looking down the long, dim passageway. Had she closed the door? Barred it against him as he'd instructed? Maybe he should check. He took a step, then another. Clenching his fists, he dug his nails into his palms. A war raged inside him. There would be no stopping if he went back. *She* wasn't likely to stop him, and he'd be unable to haul himself back from the precipice of his want—and his recklessness. For it was reckless—and reprehensible—to bed her now, like this. The thought doused a modicum of his desire.

Something rustled on the steps, and he pressed himself into an alcove. Nadia flitted by. He heaved in a breath and waited. Like it or not, Oliwia *was* an intricate entanglement, though his logical mind saw no reason to make it worse. Better to hasten from the lure of her soft lips, her intoxicating taste, and the provocative curves of her body—sensations he needed to expunge if he hoped to remain tethered to sanity—and honor. He would go—as soon as Nadia left.

Dampness leeched from the limestone wall into Jacek's back, but it had done little to cool the fever blazing inside him. After Nadia's departure, he'd placed himself at sentry on the landing to ensure Oliwia didn't get herself into trouble, though he'd had to seek refuge in the alcove repeatedly while he dodged servants. For hours, his thoughts had spun wildly. Oliwia's fragrance had infiltrated his clothes, filling his nose. The taste of her honeyed, supple mouth lingered on his tongue. The feel of her lush, yielding body crushed against his taunted him, incessantly pulling his eyes down the passageway. Far too many layers had separated them, yet he envisioned tracing his fingers over every bare contour.

No one had ever affected him as she did. He was stirred up, out of kilter. His thoughts remained stubbornly fixed on her.

He exhaled a frustrated breath and shifted on the hard-planked floor. Though her door wasn't in his line of sight, his strides could carry him there in a mere second. So close. Raking a hand through his hair, his thoughts turned to her asleep in her bed. He pictured her on her side, her curves outlined by the counterpane. Her back would be to him, her mahogany hair in a loose spill behind her; her alabaster shoulders, clad carelessly in thin white linen, would flutter with each breath she drew. He pictured himself sliding against her back, pulling her to him as he cradled her in his arms. The warmth of her skin would spread through her chemise, over his chest, down to his groin.

He shook himself back to the frigid blocks he leaned against. Dropping the back of his head against the wall, he thumped it repeatedly. Suddenly, he realized he'd never checked if she'd barred the door. He sprang to his feet and crept down the hall. Hand on the latch, he put his ear to the wood but heard nothing. Slowly, carefully, he released the door and cursed under his breath when it creaked out a rusty groan. It gave; she hadn't barred it.

Footfalls sounded from the landing where he'd just been, and his heart leapt in his throat when a shadow grew in the torchlight illuminating the wall. He pushed the door open and slid inside, securing it behind him. His hand found the bar, and he noiselessly slipped it into its bracket. Heart pummeling his ribs, he leaned his back against the door and listened as someone shuffled past.

He darted his eyes toward the bed and waited for them to adjust to the gloom, lit by one lonely taper. Oliwia wasn't posed as he'd imagined. Instead, she was on her back, one arm flung to the side and the other bent across her chest. Her hand rested on the bare skin above the sweeping neckline of her pale nightdress, trapping her silver chain beneath it. He sucked in a breath.

Her head was turned away. The soft curve of her porcelain cheek rose above the tangle of her dark hair. The coverlet rode low, scrunched around her hips. Her legs, outlined by the bedclothes, were bent as though she sprinted in her sleep. Everything about her looked soft, inviting. His eyes traveled across her body, resting on one rounded breast draped in gauzy fabric. Mesmerized, he stared at its rise and fall with her deep, even breaths.

The handle rattled at his back, and the door strained against the bar, sending a jolt through him. He pressed his weight against it. The clatter stopped. Oliwia sighed and rolled onto her side, facing him, eyes still closed. She licked her lips and let out a soft moan, sending a fresh jolt through him, straight to his loins. He tried to swallow, but his throat was parched. The handle shook again. A succession of raps followed. Oliwia lifted up on an elbow, peering into the shadows. He shrank against the door and held his breath.

Sitting up, she swung her legs from under the counterpane, exposing bare skin from her small feet to her thighs. She rose, the fabric drifting down her shapely legs and floating around her ankles.

"What is it?" she mumbled in his direction. She glided toward the door and him standing against it, her eyes cast down. His jaw clenched. She seemed to suddenly fix on his boots. Her gaze shot up, and at roughly his mid-chest, she gasped.

With lightning speed, he threw his arm about her shoulders and pulled her to him. Her mouth landed in his cupped hand. Her eyes, wide and wild, fastened on his. He lowered his mouth to her ear. "Shh! 'Tis I, Jacek." He held her there, unmoving, for several beats. At last, she nodded.

"You will not give me away?" he whispered. She shook her head, and he carefully released her. Her silky throat moved as she swallowed.

She leaned her cheek against the door. "Who ... who is it?"

"Nadia, m'lady. Just checking the fire, but your door is barred."

Oliwia's eyes darted to Jacek's face. Utterly at a loss, he shrugged and grinned idiotically. He wasn't in the habit of stealing into ladies' bedchambers uninvited—or getting caught.

Oliwia rested her hand against the door. "All's, uh, well, Nadia. You may retire."

"Very well, m'lady. Until morning, then."

"Until morning."

They both held very still while Nadia's light footsteps receded down the hallway. He let out a huge breath and slumped against the wall. But he wasn't out of danger. Oliwia whirled, hands on her hips, a little storm breaking out over her lovely features.

"What are you *doing* in here?" she hissed.

He snapped to attention. She retreated toward the bed, gathered up her dressing gown, and pulled it on. *Damn.* This wasn't going as he'd planned. That, of course, presumed he'd *had* a plan at the outset. Well, one part of his body had a plan, but it was operating of its own accord, ignoring the orders his rational mind was busily, and ineffectively, blathering.

Scratching the back of his head, he faced her frown. "I, uh, was worried, and, uh …"

She crossed her arms. "Worried about *what?*"

He took a few steps toward her. The stronger light here illuminated her, and he saw the tight furrow between her dark brows. She backed up until her legs bumped the mattress.

"I wanted to safeguard you," he said feebly.

"By skulking about my bedchamber as I slept?"

"What better way?" he offered, but she wasn't amused.

He cleared his throat. "Begging your pardon, but you were rather intoxicated, and it was my fault. I hadn't paid attention."

Her hand suddenly flew to her temple, brushing back a tress. Her expression grew appropriately contrite.

"How are you feeling now, my lady?" He bit back a laugh at her ruffled appearance. It only added to her appeal and tugged him closer.

"I, uh, my head feels as though it was trampled by a dozen horses." She winced. "And my stomach feels no better."

"Yes, well, I believe you consumed an entire barrel of mead on your own. You shamed at least ten warriors who could not keep up with you."

She narrowed her eyes. "I thought you hadn't paid attention."

He drew a little closer. What could it hurt?

"Did I … do anything unseemly?" she asked.

"You behaved perfectly. Do you remember my walking you back to your chamber several hours ago?" He locked eyes with her.

She darted her gaze. "Very little. Did I … um …" She sidestepped him. "Did I kiss you?" she whispered harshly.

His eyebrows shot up. "You don't remember? How disheartening. Apparently, it didn't leave much of an impression."

Her hand rushed to cover her round mouth. Her eyes grew just as round.

"Oh, oh, oh!" was all she said.

Chuckling, he took her hand. "I might have been the one who started it. It was very pleasant, at least for me." He planted a kiss in her palm, and she wrested her hand away. The light might have tricked him, but he thought her face was stained the color of beet soup. Undaunted, he gently took her wrist and drew her toward him. Encircling her in his arms, he brought her closer still. She placed her hands on his chest, holding him away.

"You should not be here," she reproached.

His eyes drifted to her mouth. "I'll go, but before I do, perhaps you'll deign to let me try a more memorable kiss." With a long, slow sweep, he ran his hand up her back and entwined it in her tresses.

She eased and tilted her face up, giving him her parted mouth, sweet and soft. He tightened his hold on her, and she melted against him. One hand held her head, lost in the silk of her hair, while the other wound under the dressing gown and caressed her back, clad in the whisper-light fabric. She shuddered against him. God, she felt wonderful! Kissing a trail from her lips along her throat, he breathed in her scent—like the nectar of honeysuckle blossoms—and tasted her skin, salty yet sweet. She released a long, musical moan, sparking a wildness he fought to reel back. The more he savored her, the more ravenous he grew.

She wrapped her arms about his neck, plowing her fingers through his hair. Shivers rippled along his spine. He roved his hands over her back, her hips, whatever he could reach. Cupping her bottom, he snugged her to him, but his trousers and żupan insulated the feel of her.

He picked her up and brought her head level with his. She let out a strangled sort of giggle.

"What?" he whispered against her lips.

"My feet are completely off the ground!"

He grinned. "As are mine."

Hoisting her a little higher, he wrapped her leg around his waist. She lifted the other and locked her ankles together. Deliberately, he lowered them both to the mattress, laying her alongside him. Their lips came together again in a slow meld, but his measured movements belied his racing heart. It occurred to him, dimly, that he hadn't been so nervous since he'd been sixteen. Dimmer still was the notion he shouldn't be doing what he was doing. When she moved her body languidly against him, all further conscious thought, dim or otherwise, fled.

The fire crackled quietly, and a light wind soughed through the window. Her lips brushed his neck, and he quickly unfastened the top of his żupan and his undershirt. She skimmed her fingers over his skin, her moist mouth following with sweet kisses, leaving gooseflesh in its wake. Sweeping his hand under her shift, he stroked her hip, her ribs. When he reached her breast, he covered it, filling his hand fully. Then he circled his fingertips around her contour, mapping every inch of glorious flesh until he reached her firm peak, its shape like a pearl. She drew in a sharp breath.

While he continued touching, stroking, relishing the feel of her, he kissed her forehead, then her eyes, and wound a line of kisses along her cheek, her jaw, her neck, until he reached the top of her nightdress. Gathering a ribbon between his teeth, he pulled until the neck gave way, then slid the garment off her shoulder. He nipped her skin, ran the tip of his tongue along it, nibbled his way down her chest. When he guided her nipple into his mouth, she let out a choked sort of wail. Wrapping her hands around his head, she pressed him closer.

As he suckled her, licked her, grazed his teeth over her, he rolled her on her back and pulled the chemise and dressing gown off the other shoulder. He caressed her other breast, and she bucked slowly, her hums and breaths echoing in his ears, wreaking all manner of havoc in his body. She ran her hands under his collar, over his back, digging her fingers in his flesh. Nothing else existed in his world but her soft sighs, her warm, fragrant skin, and the powerful effect all of it inflicted on his cock.

He sucked a light path to the other breast, and as he drew that one in his mouth, he explored her soft belly, the point of her hip, and the unbearably smooth skin along her thigh.

Somewhere a door closed, and she stiffened. A distant voice echoed along the passageway. She wriggled backward and sat up. Jacek flicked his eyes over her. Very little of the nightdress covered her, the sight intensifying the torturous throbbing in his member.

"I shouldn't be doing this," she said breathlessly, tugging the chemise over her shoulders and legs.

He stared at her for a beat, then dropped his forehead, stifling the urge to pound his head into the mattress—or grab her ankles and yank her under him.

"I must stop, Jacek. If I keep ... I shouldn't ... I can't. I am ... I'm sorry."

Of course she shouldn't. And I know better.

He let out a long, low breath and remained prone on his stomach. The mattress shifted, and he glimpsed her standing up. He captured her arm and hauled her back as he pulled himself upright.

THE HEART OF A HUSSAR

"You did nothing wrong, Liwi. I'm the one who must apologize. For being here, for carrying things too far."

You make me a bit daft.

He pulled her into his lap and retied her nightdress. Cradling her in his arms, he nuzzled her neck and stroked her head, her hair. She nestled against him. Her hand found the opening of his shirt, and she rested it against his bare chest. Her touch felt good. As he held her, he pulled her sleeve over her arm and caressed her warm skin through the fabric. Thusly entwined, they remained in one another's embrace for how long, he could not say. Instead, he thought how easy it would be to remain this way. He imagined seeing her first thing when he wakened of a morning and reaching for her. The thought warmed him.

At last, she stirred and softly asked, "Do you think poorly of me?"

His answer came without hesitation. "No, never." He cradled her cheek and kissed her temple.

She slid from his lap. Reluctantly, he rebuttoned his żupan and stood. He traced his finger along her cheek and kissed her lips tenderly once, twice. Interlacing his fingers with hers, he drew her to the door. "Beware the scoundrels, Liwi. Bar it this time," he said with a wink. He kissed her wrist and stepped into the passageway. When he heard the bar drop, he left for his own cold cot.

On the eve of the company's departure, Oliwia's hands trembled, fumbling the clasp of her cloak. Jacek had asked her to walk along the ramparts, and she hurried to meet him. Since their encounter, they'd not had a private moment together. *Likely for the best lest I throw myself at him shamelessly.* As she'd done endlessly, she pondered her surprising, wanton reaction to his touch, and her cheeks blazed. Then her stomach fluttered precariously.

When she arrived, he was waiting for her, and he extended his arm. She hugged his solid bicep, and they began ambling. The night was heavy with moisture. He covered her hand with his; it was rough, warm, and completely engulfed hers. She felt safe, protected.

"How will you occupy yourself during our absence, Liwi?"

She shrugged. "The same as always. And you?"

"The same as always."

She felt a familiar, discomfiting stab. *How many lovers along the way? With how many will he do the same things in the dark? How many will allow him to finish what he begins, unlike me?*

"You seem troubled," he remarked. "Is everything all right?"

She glanced up at him. "I'm sad to see the company go."

He smiled. "Anyone in particular?"

"Well … you … of course," she stammered. "And Henryk." His smile fell a little. She hurried on. "And I am preoccupied with Lady Katarzyna. 'Tis unlike her to have missed the feast."

He stroked her hand. "I will pray she recovers soon."

A drop of rain, then another, plopped on her cheek. He pulled her under a covered portion of the walkway. "It seems nature conspires against us tonight, Liwi."

He stood near—so near she felt the heat radiate from his body and his warm, moist breath on her cheek. He'd wrapped up her hand in his and held it against his chest. Her insides, already squelchy, began to quirk in earnest with thoughts of running her hands over said carved, smooth chest.

"You will write me often?" he asked quietly. "Bring me news of what you're doing? I will miss … I will miss home."

She could feel his intense stare, but she kept her eyes glued to the base of his neck as rain fell on the ramparts.

"Yes, of course I will write. And I hope you will do the same."

"As much as the enemy allows." He tilted her chin up with a knuckle. "Liwi, I should be back mid-autumn." He kissed her cheek softly. She checked the impulse to turn her mouth to his. "I would like to believe you'll be waiting for me when I return."

"Yes," she whispered right before their lips met.

Jacek hit his open palm with his gloves repeatedly, his eyes sweeping the keep façade. His heart lifted when Oliwia glided down the forestairs, stepping into the yard where the company now gathered. He walked briskly toward her. When he reached her, she raised her crystal eyes to his. He was so close he could have leaned down and kissed her rosy mouth as he'd done last night for far too short a time—before she'd breathlessly pulled away and said she couldn't stay. Then his mind flashed to kissing other parts of her, and his loins stirred.

Chiding himself with an inner curse, he caged his amorous thoughts. Her infectious glow—usually brimming from her like morning light spilling through an open window—was missing. She looked as though tears might spring from her eyes at any moment.

"Liwi, are you well?"

"Yes, Jacek." She swallowed. "I am well. I am … dismayed to be saying good-bye."

He cast his gaze to his gloves and nodded. Raising his head, he pinned her eyes. While he didn't wish to see her unhappy, something inside him leapt for joy knowing she would miss him and would be here, waiting, when he returned.

"Captain! Sir!"

Jacek looked to the overcast heavens, squeezing his eyes shut. *Christ Jesus! Now what?*

A breathless, grinning Filip drew up beside his sister.

"I have come to wish you farewell and to assure you I will uphold my promise to carry out your orders while you are away."

Jacek squeezed his shoulder. "Knowing you are here, looking after your sister," he said as he winked at Oliwia, "I shall rest easy while I am gone."

The boy reddened, and his chest swelled like a bellows bag. Oliwia smiled beside him.

The bailey grew louder, overflowing as soldiers mounted up and sent clouds of dust into the shimmering morning air. It was time to go. Oliwia's hands dangled at her sides, and Jacek covertly took one in his.

"Liwi, I—"

"Captain?" came a trill.

Releasing Oliwia's hand, Jacek wheeled. A woman stood before him with a wide smile. Where had he seen her before? "I've a token for you." She pressed something into his hand.

Flummoxed, he looked at an intricately embroidered garter festooned with dainty blue satin ribbons. He thrust it back at her, scowling.

"I cannot accept this."

She held her smile. "But I embroidered it myself and wore it only this morning on my way here, just for you. A keepsake to remind you of our … special friendship." Before he could point out they had no friendship—he couldn't even remember her name—she sashayed away and melted into the crowd.

He exhaled a great breath and turned slowly, his jaw muscles bunched. Oliwia looked from the garter in his open palm to his face. Her expression was unreadable, but her smile had vanished. He opened and closed his mouth, holding the garter away from him as if it might explode.

Filip frowned and pointed at the frilly article. "Why did she give that to you?"

"It's … ah … a trinket, a gift. For good luck. Apparently." Not knowing what else to do with it, he tucked the offending item into his sash.

Oliwia stepped back and gave him a dip of her head. "Godspeed, Captain. I wish you and the company a safe return." She turned and, with a swish of her skirts, was gone.

Only later—when he was well away from Biaska and remembered the woman was a tavern maid he'd scarcely spoken to—would Jacek drop the token in the dirt and chastise himself for not having done so while Oliwia looked on.

CHAPTER 30
Katarzyna's Plan

One frosty morning after Easter, Eryk quit the great chamber and wound his way to his quarters. Suddenly his eyes misted, and a lump the size of an egg lodged in his throat. Dread had seeped into his bones as he lay cradling Katarzyna last night, trying fruitlessly to quiet her tremors. But she was so thin that he'd not slept for fear of crushing her. A heavy weight had congealed in the pit of his stomach and remained there.

Her illness seemed to consume her. When she wasn't at prayer, she slept. She drank little and ate less. Gone were her rosy cheeks and lips, replaced by a complexion that resembled graying wood. Eyes that had been such a vibrant green and full of life were now sunken and dim. He feared she was slipping away from him, and there was absolutely nothing he could do. No longer young at thirty-four years, he did not think he would recover if Katarzyna passed. She was the true reason he had not led the company, though he'd told no one.

Checking himself, Eryk cleared his throat and tiptoed into the bedchamber. She slept soundly—praise God for small blessings—with her head turned from him and her silky hair feathered across the pillow like a gauzy golden veil. Oliwia perched at Katarzyna's bedside, sketching what, he knew not. She raised her eyes, and Eryk waved her away. She crept away, latching the door behind her.

Katarzyna stirred, rolled onto her back, and fixed her eyes on him. "Hello, my love." She smiled.

God, how he loved that smile.

He was lowering himself onto the mattress when she abruptly sat up and looked around. Alert, her eyes shone, and she transformed into his lovely Kasia again.

"Where's Oliwia, my love?"

"I sent her away. Do you need her?"

Katarzyna shook her head, then took his hands and tugged him down beside her. A flirtatious glint lurked in her eyes—it had been an eternity since he'd seen that look. He caressed her cheek with the back of his hand and pushed a few strands from her face.

"I love you, Eryk, you know."

"I never doubt it, my love. And I love you."

He planted a tender kiss on her cool, dry forehead. His heart skipped. Could she be recovering again? Katarzyna wrapped her arms around his waist and pulled herself close, tucking her head under his chin. She sighed as he caressed her hair.

"Make love to me, Eryk."

He froze.

"But you are not well, Kasia. I may hurt you."

She peered up at him. "When have you ever hurt me? Even at your most passionate, you have never hurt me."

They both laughed.

Katarzyna began to urge him in her special way, and he put up scant resistance. When had he last lain with her? His heart began to race, and urgent need overtook him. And so they made love as they had in the beginning—with affection, with tenderness, with abandon.

Eryk held her close when their coupling was done. Drifting off to sleep, he could not imagine anything sweeter than this.

Later he awoke, and Katarzyna had donned a dressing gown. She sat on the edge of the bed, staring at him in an unnerving way that brought to mind a terrified waif. How long had he slept? He sat up quickly.

"What is it, my love? Are you all right?"

"No, Eryk, I am not all right."

His stomach clenched. Any remaining sleepiness took flight. "What is it, Kasia? What can I do for you? Would you like me to fetch Oliwia?"

"After you hear what I have to say."

He opened his arms to her.

"No, Eryk. I will stay where I am. I want you to see me clearly when I speak."

Panic rose, sending its icy tendrils through his veins. This woman, the one looking at him, was not his sweet wife. He shuddered.

"Eryk, you know I have not been well."

He nodded, girding himself.

"I am dying, Eryk. I have been on death's doorstep a long while now, and my time has come, I fear. I pray I am destined for the kingdom of heaven."

Though he had braced himself, he was not in the least prepared for the jolt her pronouncement sent through him.

He opened his mouth to protest, but she leaned in and pressed her fingertips to his lips. "I am sorry to leave you so. Would that I could stay with you forever, my love," she said.

Tears welled in her eyes and slid down her cheeks. Despite his thundering heart, Eryk remained completely still, utterly devastated as he looked at her.

"Eryk, I want a promise from you before I go."

Eryk swallowed hard, his heart shredding. "Anything. What is it, dearest love?" he choked.

"Promise me you will marry within the year after I am gone."

He stared at her, leveled by her words. She stared back, her gaze unwavering. He shook his head vigorously.

"Eryk, listen to me. You should have divorced me years ago and—"

"We said we would never speak of it again, Katarzyna," he gritted out, his voice a warning.

This again? She'd spoken of it several times, and they'd had terrible rows until she'd finally bent to his will and abandoned the ludicrous notion. Yes, he had the right to divorce her after years of barrenness, but his heart allowed him no such choice—he loved her too much.

"My greatest regret is I was not able to give you an heir."

"I don't care!" He flung his arms in frustration.

She went on calmly, steadily. "You must care, my love. It is your duty to your people, to your father and forefathers. To me. You must beget a legitimate heir."

Eryk leaned against the wooden backboard and gaped at her. "You ask too much, Kasia." Still trying to digest the words "I am dying," he was neither prepared to lose her nor to contemplate another.

She rallied on. "Eryk, I have selected someone to take my place, to be your wife."

Eryk transformed from agape to aghast. "I don't want anyone else. No one can replace you, Kasia."

She must be mad!

But no, she was lucid and clear, focused—more than she had been in a long time. Her intense light green eyes pierced his, and her fingers curled liked bony claws around his hands.

"Oliwia is my choice for you, Eryk."

Impossible! Eryk groaned. "No, Katarzyna! How can you ask this of me? Of her? Have you spoken to her?"

"Not yet. Husband, do you not see how perfect this is? She's of two noble lines, neither of them Polish. Your heir will reap the benefits. The great house of Krezowski will be strengthened by the connection."

She rushed ahead. "I saw it when you received the letter from England. Since that time, I have groomed her for you, taught her everything I know. She will take over effortlessly when I am gone. She is young, vibrant, and strong. She will give you an heir and many children besides. God sent her to us for this very purpose."

"Kasia," he pleaded, "you must not ask this." *I do not want her!* "What if she has a young man, a sweetheart she favors?"

"No!" she hissed, yanking her hands away as if his held hot embers. "I have transformed her for *you!*" Her voice dropped to barely a whisper. "Doing this, for you, is a vast comfort to me. You will break my heart if you do not fulfill my final wish."

Eryk didn't move. *This cannot be happening.* He had just made love to her, and now she was imploring him to marry a mere girl, one young enough to be his daughter, his niece—one he looked upon *as* a niece. It was unthinkable.

The spark that had lit Katarzyna's eyes before their lovemaking was extinguishing. She seemed to shrivel before him. "Bring her here so we may tell her together."

THE HEART OF A HUSSAR

Fear supplanted disbelief, and Eryk hurriedly pulled on his garments. He tore from the chamber, his heart pounding, and he paced the halls in a frantic, desultory search for Oliwia. What would he say when he found her?

Oliwia found him before he had regained the sense to find her. "Lady Katarzyna is failing, and she would speak with you," he said.

Panic spread like spilled ink, eclipsing Oliwia's heart with darkness. She scurried in Eryk's wake. When they entered the chamber, Katarzyna rested against propped pillows, a crucifix clutched in her frail hand. Bluish lips and ashen skin contrasted starkly against the pale gold of her lank hair. Her dull, half-lidded eyes tracked Oliwia as she rounded the bed to her side. Katarzyna reached out her hand, and Oliwia grasped it and held on fiercely.

"My lady!"

"Oliwia. I haven't much time. I must have a promise, yours and my husband's, so I might pass in peace," she rasped, seeming to drag in each ragged breath.

"Of course."

Eryk stood immobile beside the bed, his face pale, and he gripped the bedpost as if to hold himself upright. His eyes were fixed on his wife.

To Oliwia's horror, Katarzyna told her, between wheezes and rattles, what that promise was. Oliwia desperately sought succor in Eryk's face. *Say something! Tell her no! Tell her anything! Do not let this happen!* But he said nothing. Wet, vacant eyes lent him a look of utter defeat.

"Oh, my lady, you ... cannot die." Even as she uttered the words, Oliwia recognized their impotence. Naught would hold death at bay.

Her thoughts spun, colliding and shattering into fragments. Had she the right to refuse? Would her lord be affronted and cast her and Filip out? Could he force her into marriage—any marriage? What was she to do? She had no say.

Did she?

Oliwia rose, slipping from Katarzyna's skeletal grasp, desperately searching an escape from this trap. Pain reflected in the lady's features. She seemed to disintegrate before Oliwia's eyes. Eryk drew in a sharp, choked breath and sank beside his wife. He reached to hold her, but she shook her head.

"Promise me," she beseeched.

She looked from Eryk to Oliwia and held out the cross with a trembling hand, her eyes pleading and terrified. A force seemed to clutch Katarzyna, tugging her from this life into the next. Steadily. Inexorably.

Her voice came out a harsh croak. "Avow it before God. Swear it on everything sacred."

Tears coursed down Eryk's cheeks freely. Oliwia's belly churned, drawing bile into her throat. She observed the scene as though apart from it.

"You have never denied me anything, Eryk," Katarzyna rasped. "Don't deny me now, my love."

He kissed her hand, dappling it with tears. Then he took the crucifix and swore his oath. Katarzyna sighed back into the pillow and turned her watery gaze to Oliwia, who stood rooted in place. If only she could move her feet, she would flee the room.

"My husband is my gift to you, my dearest Oliwia. This oath will be your last gift to me. Consider it repayment of your debt."

Katarzyna's words pummeled Oliwia's chest like rocks, forcing the air from her. *Repayment of my debt.* She owed the lady everything—she had welcomed her, taught her, nurtured her, been her mother and sister when she had no one. If there was any way to repay Katarzyna, and this promise was it, how could Oliwia deny her?

Oliwia couldn't breathe. The trap was sprung.

So did she place her shaking hand on the crucifix and swear the terrible promise—all the while praying she would never have to keep it.

Not long after, Katarzyna was placed upon a fur on the floor. She faded in and out of consciousness throughout the day and into the next. A candle was placed in her hand, a scapular about her neck, and Father Augustyn administered her last rites. Windows were opened throughout the castle so her soul could fly.

A pall shrouded the castle as its inhabitants sang and mourned.

As that day faded into night, Katarzyna came to, brightening like a shooting star. She grasped Eryk's hands. "I've been so blessed, my love. You were the great love of my life. I will love you always, dearest husband." While Oliwia hovered nearby, Eryk cradled his wife's wasted body in his strong arms, hugging her to him as he whispered to her and stroked her hair.

Then she sagged against him, her limbs limp. With a choked cry, he kissed her temple. He held her head to his and sobbed. Oliwia retreated quietly, swiping her cheeks with the heels of her hands. Nothing would ever be the same.

Nadia poked her head into the kitchen garden. "Lady Oliwia, Lord Eryk requires your presence."

Oliwia yelped. "Why does he wish to see me?"

The slight maid's eyes darted, as they often did. She looked down and stammered. "I … I do not know, my lady. He said … um … That is, he asked me to find you and send you to his great chamber."

Oliwia's gut had been coiled since Katarzyna's death, and now it wound tighter. She'd dashed Jacek a hasty letter, omitting any mention of the terrible oath. She would find a way, somehow, to tell him. Right now, she wiped her hands, smoothed her bodice, and threw her shoulders back as she departed the garden's sanctuary.

Her heart hammering, Oliwia paused at the heavy wooden door. It was ajar, and male voices drifted from the chamber. She knocked.

"Oliwia? Come," Eryk said.

She entered to find him surrounded by the priest, the tailor, the carpenter, and his new manservant Ludwik.

To her relief, Eryk barely looked at her. "Join us. We're discussing preparations for Lady Katarzyna's funeral, and you are part of the planning."

He then turned to the carpenter. "You have the coffin portrait? The one depicting Lady Katarzyna in her riding clothes? She is on the most important journey of her life now."

The carpenter nodded, and Eryk then turned to the tailor. "And the livery for the staff?"

"Nearly complete, my lord. Everything will be ready for the procession," replied the tailor.

"Good. Now for the food and wine for the guests …"

And so did Oliwia take up the duties of the lady of the estate, just as she had been trained. Never had she dreamed her first task would be the burial of her mistress.

Katarzyna's body lay in the elaborate castle of mourning, the *castrum doloris*, in the village church. Untold numbers lit candles, sang, and looked upon an oval portrait at the head of the coffin where the lady's face might have been. The image had been painted when she'd first arrived at Biaska at the peak of her vitality, and it recalled her beauty and grace. The coffin was eventually escorted before a vast, snaking line of singing mourners to the castle's chapel—her final place of repose.

Now as Oliwia looked about the great hall, the wake was in full sway, a subdued celebration in the heavy gloom cloaking the castle. Oliwia watched Eryk covertly. How did the man remain standing? He received everyone graciously, thanking them for their words of comfort. Surely somewhere within him yawned an unfillable pit he kept tightly covered, hidden from the well-wishers surrounding him.

Merciful God, please do not let him call upon me to fill that hole.

Guilt over her own selfishness followed this prayer.

As she studied him, Oliwia realized Eryk's expression was vacant, unchanging during the weeks of funerary ceremonies. His usually animated amber eyes were vacuous, as if no living spirit inhabited within. He subsisted, breathing in and out, his heart pumping as his body moved through its everyday business. But his soul had taken flight. She wanted to weep for him, but all her tears were for herself.

Romek stood beside the freshly mounded earth, clutching his kolpak as if he might tear it apart. The priest and few paid mourners had left long ago, leaving Romek alone at Bella's graveside as the advancing night wreathed him like black smoke.

"I failed you, beloved sister," he choked.

He stood for hours, unmoving, and let his sorrow wash over him. His tears spent, a bottomless void remained. It imploded and rose like a blazing phoenix, transforming into white-hot fury. He had to feed it, fill it.

He crushed the kolpak on his head and stalked from the church graveyard. *Krezowski will get his due when the time is right. But the worthless bitch I entrusted Bella to? Hers comes tonight!* His rage would be visited upon the woman, and she would feel its devastating lash. For one shining moment, she would be his sister's shrine. She would become the carcass upon which his furious beast feasted.

He allowed the first real smile in weeks to creep up his cheeks.

CHAPTER 31

Walking in Shadows

Jacek sat before the table in his tent, rereading Oliwia's letter. Her missive was brief, yet its very brevity communicated much. He was smoothing his beard when Henryk entered.

He waved Henryk in. "You've no doubt heard?"

"Yes, the whole camp has." Henryk's face was somber. "I knew she hadn't been well, but this ... How does Lord Eryk fare? And Oliwia?"

Heaving out a sigh, Jacek held up the letter. "She writes only that he is composed and nothing of her own state of mind. I wish I could offer her comfort," he mumbled.

"Oliwia's a strong girl, Jacek. She's likely marshaling the entire castle *and* telling the garrison what to do as we speak."

When Henryk departed, Jacek's mind drifted to the disordered girl from two years ago who had been afraid to talk to the stable master. He smiled to himself. Awkwardness had been replaced by the power to bewitch; she could sweetly coax a bear to share its pilfered honeycomb if she chose to.

Raking a hand through his hair, he pondered how he'd fallen under her spell. It had likely happened long ago, unfolding so gradually that discovery came far too late. She had stolen into his heart like soft moss nestling in every unguarded chink in a stone wall. Though she had adopted a highborn deportment, an earthiness simmered just below the surface, and the combination enthralled him. She thought independently, rationally—likely born from necessity. Forthright when prodded but never shrill, she demonstrated logic that matched his. She was quick-witted. He reckoned it explained why he was often off balance in her presence. Though crafted of tough steel, she was softhearted and generous. She laughed easily, but she was no tittering fool. Achingly beautiful, she didn't ply her beauty to further any ambitions. Though he would admit it to no one, the fact she challenged him—sometimes with just a look—exhilarated him.

And then there was the way she felt in his arms, the impassioned way she kissed him, the fire she stirred inside him. In that moment, his estate faded from his mind, supplanted by a far more compelling purpose. Its name was Oliwia.

With the mourners departed and the heavy adornments packed up, Eryk barricaded himself in his quarters, allowing only Ludwik in his chamber. Eryk neither asked for nor acknowledged her, setting her adrift to manage the castle—the entire estate, really—as best she could. While she worked side by side with Tomasz, grappling with the stewardship of Biaska's affairs, she grew alarmed at Eryk's seemingly scant concern for his enormous dominion. After all, wheat and barley had to be harvested; timber had to be cut and shipped; soldiers had to patrol and fortify. And yet Oliwia was relieved. Eryk's lack of attention allowed her to exist in an otherworld where the deathbed oath didn't exist, where she wasn't bound to a man whom she viewed as an older brother, a protective uncle—never as a husband or lover. The thought turned her stomach, so she discarded it and submerged herself in the duties of the lady of the estate.

"Mistress," Beata called to her one day, "I fear our supplies of meat are running low. Will you be ordering more sheep slaughtered? And we have need of more kitchen servants …"

Like Beata, other staff sought Oliwia out, and she discovered she was capable. To her surprise, draping herself with the ponderous mantle of management buoyed her. Soon the castle's thrum ran at a wholly predictable tempo—all without Eryk's input or knowledge.

Each morning, as Eryk wallowed in his apartments, Oliwia's thoughts revolved around what needed to be accomplished that day. Time spent considering him waned and nearly disappeared. So it was in this suspended state of reality that Ludwik surprised her one summer day in the kitchen garden as she babied her beloved plants.

"Lady Oliwia! Lord Eryk demands you come at once." His arms flapped about as if he were a stork preparing to take flight.

Always on guard the rare times Eryk called for her, Oliwia's alarms clanged as stridently as the bells that had tolled during Katarzyna's final procession. In her calmest voice, she said, "What is it Lord Eryk requires?"

"He requires *you*!" the man squawked. "He has drained his second bottle of wodka this morning and just threw a pewter platter at me. With food still on it! He yelled for Lady Oliwia, and I did not stand about to find out why."

Oliwia splayed a hand across her belly and inhaled a deep breath as she dropped gloves and apron on a nearby bench. "Coming."

The bedchamber door stood ajar when she arrived. Eryk's plaintive voice carried through the crack, turning her blood to ice.

"Oliiiiiwiaaaaa!"

With a deep breath, she steeled her spine and stepped through the opening. All was dark, and a foul odor assaulted her. When her eyes adjusted to the gloom, she detected motion on the bed.

She paced toward a window, pulling back a tawny velvet curtain. Light flooded the room and lit the bed. "My lord?" Kneeling on the mattress, in naught but a stained linen undershirt, Eryk flung his forearm over his eyes.

"Gah! Shut that damned thing!"

Shut it she did, instead lighting a taper. As she approached him, her shoes crunched over bits on the wooden floor. His arm still over his eyes, he slumped against the bolsters, muttering, "Watch out for the crockery." Then he added, "A jug of piwo slipped from my hand."

That explained part of the odor.

When she reached the bedside, she realized the other part of the odor was the reek of his body. Anger flared as she thought of the feeble Ludwik, who had allowed his lord to flounder in filth.

As if he'd read her mind, Eryk huffed, "Do not allow that witless manservant in here again. From now on, I will only tolerate you or Nadia."

THE HEART OF A HUSSAR

After tidying his chamber and leaving him in drunken sleep, Oliwia entered the passageway, where she spied Nadia. She glanced around, then propelled the maid along its length until they were far beyond Eryk's quarters. In a conspiratorial whisper, she said, "No one save us enters Lord Eryk's chamber. I will instruct Pan Lesław to place two sentries outside his door."

And so it was that Lesław, the garrison's temporary captain, ordered a rotating detail to guard the lord's apartments. Few knew how often Eryk howled his despair, hollered obscenities, or destroyed the more delicate contents of his chamber in a drunken rage. All believed he was sick with grief; it did not occur that he lived in abject madness.

After Ludwik's demotion, Oliwia's shoulders would tighten as she braced herself for what awaited whenever she entered Eryk's domain. A darkened chamber certainly; a drunken lord most likely; a collection of empty flagons; a rank odor marking the long passages between clean clothing.

Oliwia dragged herself to the lord's chamber one morning—would he be waiting for her bleary-eyed and combative, or blissfully unconscious?—where she encountered Nadia exiting with a tray.

"How is our master this morning?" Oliwia inspected the tray heaped with untouched food and empty bottles.

"Sleeping like the dead, m'lady, but he ate nothing yet again. I don't understand. Beata prepares his favorite foods, but he does not touch them."

Oliwia sighed. "But he does touch the drink, yes?"

"What can be done, mistress?"

"I have little idea."

The rare joyful moments in Oliwia's world were days she received Jacek's letters. She and Filip had each received a small bundle and sat together one afternoon sharing Jacek's news, which, weeks later, was hardly news but welcome nonetheless.

Filip excitedly waved a page about. "I also have one dated June 12, Liwi. What does he say in yours?"

"Let's compare. I believe they say exactly the same thing. He likely makes duplicates and addresses them differently." She scanned the missive. "This one is little different from the others. He recounts how something is brewing farther south involving a different army—one that belongs to Pan Stefan Potocki, whoever he is—against Moldavia and the Tatars. But this conflict so far does not involve the Biaska company, so they sit. He grows tired of the tedious days in camp."

Her mind leapt to how he occupied himself during the tedious nights, and she squashed a flare in her belly. His letters did little to counter her apprehensions, for truly they were nearly identical to Filip's: a bit of discourse about camp, the countryside, and the weather, but little to indicate he thought of her specially. With a sigh, she broke the seal on a different message.

"This one is dated … hmm, the next day. June 13. He must have been *terribly* bored to write so much in such a short time," she laughed. As her eyes moved across his words, she stopped laughing and suddenly flushed.

"What does he say, Liwi?"

"Um, nothing really. He, ah, had left out a few things and added them the next day before the messenger collected the letters."

Filip gave her a puzzled look. "Like what?"

She cleared her throat. "Some nonsense about horses and how he won at dice. That's all."

When Filip left the chamber, she scattered the letters and plucked the one, carefully unfolding it. She looked about furtively, as though someone stood over her shoulder, before reading it aloud.

13 June, In the Year of our Lord 1612

My dearest Liwi,

I have been remiss, for I have not told you how much I miss your sweet smile. I think of you daily. Hourly, in fact. Only last night I dreamed of you and the last time we walked together on the ramparts. Do you recall it rained that night? I confess I had little idea, for your bright countenance outshone the heavens. Had the moon and the stars dared showed themselves, you would have put them to shame.

I look forward to seeing you and walking beside you once more.

Your devoted friend and servant,

Jacek

THE HEART OF A HUSSAR

Holding the letter to her breast, she stared through the window's rippled glass with unseeing eyes, imagining him scratching out the words by candlelight in his tent. She sat at her table and dipped her quill. Her hand hovered above the fresh sheet of paper while her mind hovered over what to say, how much to say. She'd lost count of the messages she'd begun only to crumple into balls she fed to the fire. How to tell him about the oath? Would he be angry with her? Would he think her presumptuous? After all, they had made no promises to one another. They'd shared part of one tender night and now one affectionate letter. No more.

She scrawled "Lord Eryk" and continued with a description of his occasional emergence from despair and his fleeting moments of lucidity amid his ugly tirades fed by drink. From there, she scribbled a sentence about the vow and stopped. One hasty review and she wadded up the letter and cast it into the hungry flames. *Wastrel!*

In the end, she did pen a letter, painting a shining picture of life at Biaska, making only the lightest reference to Jacek's special letter, thanking him for thinking of her. Then she secreted his letters away.

Jacek sat atop his mount, watching gray clouds boiling on the horizon. They would soon turn charcoal and race across the sky, scourging the earth with rain. As he scanned the horizon, he pondered a different sort of scourge: the Tatar vermin. Day in and day out, he waited with the rest of the army for the enemy to retaliate after Stefan Potocki's aggression against Moldavia. That Potocki's seven-thousand-strong army had been devastated by Stefan Tomża and the Moldavians—aided by Khan Temir's Tatars—was not enough. The enemy sought to exact a higher price, a greater revenge.

So Jacek and his men bided their time, awaiting Hetman Żółkiewski's signal to defend against that revenge. *Another idle, dreary day.* He sighed as he headed back to camp. A group of hussars, six across, trotted in his direction.

Lesław hailed him. "Jacek, we're off to the village. Join us?"

Jacek shook his head. "Not today."

"Why bother asking?" Henryk scoffed at Lesław. Nodding toward Jacek's crotch, he added, "Take care it doesn't shrivel and fall off from lack of use."

Jacek nudged Gwiazda. "Your concern is touching," he retorted as he passed his fellows.

Back in his tent, he pulled Oliwia's letters from a small chest and sat on his cot, fanning them over top of his blanket. He pinched one and unfolded it, read it, and tossed it aside with a humph.

"Well, you dolt, what did you expect?" he muttered aloud. "Christ, you can't even decide what the hell it is you want."

He lay back on the cot, atop the scattered letters, and crossed his ankles and hands. He stared at endless white canvas. Somewhere distant, men shouted good-naturedly, and the whipping wind foretold of pelting rain. He exhaled. At the pace this campaign dragged, he would return home no closer to his reward, and Oliwia would be eighteen.

A thought had been poking at him for months now, and he'd managed to hold it at bay. But for the first time, he openly deliberated whether he needed the land before marrying. Would the expectation he *would* get it be enough? Need anything stand between him and his brimming desire for Oliwia? She could do worse—much worse—than a twenty-four-year-old captain of a revered husaria banner. Jankowski flashed in his mind, reminding him she could also do far better.

As he bounced his thumb pads together, his mind drifted to familiar, pleasing images. Oliwia's burnished, mahogany hair, her lively crystal eyes, the curve of her berry lips when she smiled. She gamboled through his thoughts ceaselessly no matter how earnestly he willed her away, and the distraction was at times unbearable. When had he stopped thinking of her as an entanglement? Now she was a fixation—one he ached to conquer and possess.

And yet … He could do so much better by her if he could snatch that last golden ring.

Nowhere in his myriad thoughts was the inconceivable notion she might deny him.

THE HEART OF A HUSSAR

The months lumbered on unendingly, and melancholy echoed through Biaska Castle's cold limestone halls. Oliwia, now eighteen, had received occasional letters from Jacek, the most recent one telling her Hetman Żółkiewski had successfully thwarted a joint attack without a single battle and had signed a peace treaty at Chocim with the Moldavian leader, Tomża. Jacek's missive said nothing of returning home, nor did he include more tender verse, setting her imagination and agitation to bubble incessantly. *The mission is over. What holds him back? Is he beguiled by a new lover?*

Lord Eryk continued his self-indulgent behavior barricaded in his quarters. His drinking had decreased somewhat, and so had the episodes when he raged at her and Nadia or fell down dead-drunk.

One night, Oliwia let herself into his chamber to remove the debris of the evening's excesses. As was her habit before retiring, she slinked in to retrieve empty bottles that invariably littered the floor. But this evening, only one bottle stood empty, another half-depleted. Full bottles remained on the tray undisturbed, and some of the food had disappeared. When she glanced over at him, Eryk was sprawled across the bed, illuminated by candlelight. Most evenings he thrashed, and he sometimes yelled at her when she entered, driving her to grab up what she could before hurrying from his chamber.

Quiet was not what she had expected tonight, so she ducked in for a closer look, slumping in relief when she saw his chest rise and fall. She had begun a silent retreat from the chamber when he roused.

"Oliwia?" He peered into the gloom, and she froze beyond the pool of light. "Oliwia? Nadia? Who's there?"

She hesitated a beat. "It is Oliwia, my lord."

"Good. I'm pleased it's you. Come here."

When she didn't move, he waved a hand in her direction. "Put down whatever you carry, Oliwia, and come here," he ordered.

She squelched her astonishment—and dread. "Yes, my lord."

He struggled to sit up, battling soft pillows. "Straighten these for me. I wish to sit up."

"Yes, my lord."

She fluffed and propped, and he fell against the pillows, sighing as he scrubbed a hand across his pinched face. He smelled of sour alcohol, and his hair hung long and lank. He was shirtless, the coverlet pulled partway up to a dusky patch of hair on his chest, revealing his thin, ravaged body. In better times, Eryk was not a bulky man, but neither was he lean. Rather, he was heavily muscled and broad-chested, robust—very unlike his current state.

"Oliwia, you read, yes?" he asked brusquely.

"Yes, my lord."

"Good. My eyes are tired, and I have difficulty reading in this weak light. Sit and read to me." He waved to a small book on the night table. "You should easily find where I left off."

Oliwia slowly lifted the book, turning it over in her hands. "Il Tesoro Della Sanita," she said aloud. *The Treasure of Health*. She looked at him.

He sighed. "Katarzyna kept at me to read it ... before she passed." He coughed and darted his gaze to the hearth. "She, uh, said I must learn to take better care of myself, to live a healthful life, in the event I found myself ..." He trailed off.

"I am familiar with the book," Oliwia said softly.

His eyes flicked to hers, and one corner of his mouth twitched as if trying to curve into a smile. He glanced around himself. "I don't suppose I'm doing a very good job of it, am I?"

Wordlessly, Oliwia lowered herself into the chair and fanned the booklet to find his mark, a mere two pages in. When she hesitated, he nodded to her.

"Begin, Oliwia. Let us both discover how I am to gain this wholesome life."

Oliwia read while Eryk rested his head against the pillows and stared up at the dark-wooded canopy. A quarter hour later, his eyelids drooped closed, and his head lolled. Oliwia closed the book, slipped from the chair, and stepped back stealthily. Eryk startled, bellowing once more. "Oliwia!"

"Yes, my lord." She jerked in place and tried to shrink into the shadows.

He pointed at an earthenware jug. "Bring me that bottle over there before you go."

She fetched it and left the room, tray in hand, willing herself to walk calmly rather than tear through the door.

THE HEART OF A HUSSAR

The next morning, Oliwia entered the chamber to find the curtains tied back, the dull morning light illuminating motes every place it touched. Awake and propped against pillows, Eryk sat clear-eyed, swathed in a red silk dressing gown. He gazed out the window to a slate-gray sky, where a stiff wind chased and tossed dry leaves in the air. The bottle Oliwia had given him the night before stood on the nightstand where she'd left it.

"I have asked Nadia to have a bath drawn," he said. "I'm also in need of a shave—this beard is scratching me beyond sanity—and my hair could use a generous trim."

With a chuckle, he continued. "Lady Katarzyna always saw to such things. I suppose that's your domain now." He resumed staring wistfully beyond the window. Moments later, he turned his gaze to her.

"Choose some servants to help me with my daily ablutions. And after the midday meal, I will hear you read again. You've a soothing voice. Perhaps something livelier this time, however. I've been meaning to read *The Dismissal of the Greek Envoys* by Kochanowski."

After he released her, Oliwia scampered down the passageway, a fine sheen of sweat along her hairline. The thing had hung there in his chamber, lurking as it grinned at her obscenely. The thing—unseen, unheard, unwanted—had reared its vile head today after she had managed to ignore it these last many months. Her oath, *their* oath, waited to be brought out of the dark into the full glare of light. He had said nothing of it, but it was there, palpable and undeniable. She could no longer pretend it wasn't.

Oliwia read to Eryk every afternoon. Sometimes she read in Polish, sometimes in Latin, occasionally in French or Italian. He was more coherent and stayed awake longer, seeming to ease with the relaxed rhythm of the reading. The volume of drink decreased in counterbalance.

One afternoon in his bedchamber, Eryk surprised her when he asked, "What of your sketching? And music? I know Lady Katarzyna taught you, but I do not believe I have ever heard you sing or play."

She bent to the hearth, poking at a log with an iron rod. "I am accomplished at neither, sire."

He scoffed. "Surely you're being modest. It's been far too long since I've heard the sweet sound of music. Kasia," he paused, resting a fist against his mouth for a beat, "Katarzyna would play her harp for me, and she always arranged for the minstrels. I long to hear a melody."

He stood at the window, his profile to her as he gazed into the distance. She busied herself gathering up platters and cups. Without looking at her, he said, "You will tell Tomasz to meet me after the midday meal tomorrow in my solar. You will join us there."

She clutched the tray. "Of course, my lord."

Oliwia readied to leave, but Eryk narrowed his eyes at her. "See to it no more drink is brought to my quarters. And from now on, I will take my meals in the great hall as before. I am also dismissing the guards outside my door."

And with that, he excused her, but not before giving her the first genuinely warm smile she'd seen from him in a very long while.

Time stood on the brink of winter when the Biaska husaria returned from its lengthy campaign. Despite the day's chill and the somber, drizzling sky overhead, Oliwia thrilled to the sound of the heralds. She felt as though frogs leapt about her innards as she dashed down the forestairs and into the yard. For so long, she had anticipated Jacek's return and how she would tell him, rehearsing speech after speech. But for now, she let giddiness sweep over top of anxiety; she would need to hold herself back to keep from jumping into his arms.

Craning her neck, she scanned the warriors, her hands twisting together. Henryk strode a straight path toward her, his expression unreadable.

The flutters in her stomach became one enormous knot. "Henryk, where's Jacek?"

"He did not return with us, Oliwia."

Her heart plunged. "Is he all right?"

Henryk nodded. "He was hale last I saw him. He has gone to Żółkiew Castle and plans to return before Christmas. He gave me this letter for you."

THE HEART OF A HUSSAR

Her limbs went numb, and a lump swelled in her throat. Henryk was regarding her with sympathetic hazel eyes when Filip appeared beside her.

"I, ah, thank you, Henryk," she whispered as a wave of nausea rippled through her. "Um, the company ... Is everyone all right?"

"What is it, Liwi? Where's Pan Jacek?" chirped Filip.

"We are all well, Oliwia," Henryk replied. "Filip, come and help me. Leave your sister for a bit, yes?"

Henryk guided Filip away, and Oliwia tore to her bedchamber, barring the door behind her.

15 November, In the Year of Our Lord 1612

My dearest Oliwia,

By now, you will have seen Henryk and know I have gone to Żółkiew, at the invitation of the Field Hetman himself. He welcomed me to remain the entire season, through Candlemas, and while I have not yet devised a way to leave such polite company without slighting my generous host, I plan to arrive at Biaska in time for Christmas.

As you know, though I commanded the company in this year's campaign, there was no opportunity to demonstrate worthiness for recommendation. So when the hetman offered his hospitality, I seized the opportunity. In this manner, I am able to ingratiate myself with two superiors, for Lord Eryk enjoys an abiding friendship with the hetman and will no doubt be pleased with my decision. I know you understand how important this is to me, for all the reasons we have discussed, etc.

I pray time flies quickly and I am soon reunited with you and Filip.

Your devoted servant and friend,

Jacek

Christmas. Not so far away. Eryk had made no overtures, no mention of the promise. There was a chance all would be well when Jacek returned. And yet Oliwia had never felt more alone.

CHAPTER 32

A Promise to Keep

Jacek stood stiffly in a candle-brightened great hall, questioning the veracity of his mission for the hundredth time since his arrival. Everywhere he looked, men in fine brocades revolved about perfectly coiffed women bedecked in every bauble imaginable. Though he belonged among them, he was far more comfortable in a battlefield camp than amid the lavishness that defined a magnate's court.

Stark amid the frivolity was his dismay over news of the Polish garrison's surrender in Moscow, accompanied by horrendous stories of starvation which led the soldiers to eat saddles, offal, and each other. After the surrender, half the garrison soldiers were slaughtered as they departed. Jacek's certainty Muscovy would be absorbed into the Commonwealth, with Crown Prince Władysław IV seated upon Muscovy's throne, lay in fragments.

As he brooded, a woman sidled up beside him and in a sweet voice said, "I do not wish to seem forward, but you look most uncomfortable, hussar."

Startled, he glanced down at a pretty, plump, blond woman with steel-gray eyes. She raised her gaze to his. "Am I wrong?" She gave him a beguiling smile.

THE HEART OF A HUSSAR

A servant with a tray of full goblets materialized, and Jacek unfurled his long arms and snatched two. He offered her one. With a ring against his cup, she said, *"Na zdrowie!"* and tipped the glass to her lips.

Peering at her over the rim, he took a tentative sip of his own. "Why do you call me hussar?"

She looked him up and down with a mischievous gleam. "You're here, yes? Further, you have no belly, and your hands are used to work. By the way you hold yourself, you are clearly a soldier. You would not be dressed as you are unless you were szlachta. Therefore, you must be one of the great gentlemen of the horse. A lieutenant, I'd venture, though you are rather young for such a rank. Have I got it right?"

He smiled. "Almost. Porucznik to Lord Eryk Krezowski of Biaska and Silnyród, Jacek Krzysztof Dąbrowski at your service." He gave her a formal bow. "And you, my lady?"

"Magdalena von Rohan, my lord."

"You are Austrian, then?"

"Yes. I am a distant cousin of the king's mistress and a courtesan at his court," she said nonchalantly.

Jacek's eyebrows shot up to his hairline, and she laughed, small lines creasing the edges of her mouth and her bright eyes.

"I see I have shocked you, Pan Dąbrowski. On account of the king's mistress, or that I am a courtesan?"

He took another sip of his wine, trying not to choke. "That you speak Polish so well."

She chuckled. "I have been in your country many years now. I followed the king's favorite, Pani Urszula Meyerin, when I was widowed. I found Polish court highly diverting and stayed. Did you know"—she leaned in conspiratorially, engulfing him in the cloying scent of rose water—"King Zygmunt employs the most Italian musicians of any court in Europe? The performances there have no rival."

"I had no idea."

"So you are not one of the hetman's hussars. Pray, are you here to court his daughter?" She snapped open her fan.

"Katarzyna Żółkiewska?" He shook his head. "I'm merely an inconsequential guest."

"Pity for her. Tell me, are you married, Pan Dąbrowski?" Her lips curving in a playful smile, she scrutinized him.

"Not yet, but I shall be by spring." That is, he planned to be. Hoped to be. Suddenly, he grew uncomfortable. Whether it was the subject or the way the lady blatantly appraised him, he couldn't be sure.

"You have picked a bride, then. Tell me, are you faithful to your betrothed?"

"Yes." He gulped his wine. *Why the hell do I feel compelled to answer Lady von Rohan's impertinent questions?*

"A shame. Many find me irresistible, you know." She winked.

"I have no doubt."

"Actually, you may be able to provide me an invaluable service." She placed her hand on his arm, and he glanced down at it. She left it where it was. "I am in need of an escort to the Royal Castle in Warszawa. I must arrive by Christmas. You would be well compensated, I assure you."

"The only compensation I desire is an introduction to His Majesty."

"He's begun his retreat from Moscow. Stay as my guest through the Christmas season. If the king returns during that time, I pledge you will meet him." She batted her eyelashes from behind her fan.

"When do you leave?"

Two days after Christmas, Oliwia received a letter, together with a small bundle, from Jacek. She plopped on her mattress, opening the letter with unsteady fingers.

7 December, In the Year of our Lord 1612

My dearest Liwi,

I trust you had a joyous Feast of St. Nicholas. I wish I could have joined you. While I had every intention of returning beforehand, a chance arose I cannot refuse. Tomorrow, I leave for the Royal Castle to escort Lady Magdalena von Rohan, a member of the court and close friend of His Majesty. Lady von Rohan has offered an introduction, with an invitation to stay the entire season. I am humbled by this opportunity and pray I will gain the king's notice.

I am dismayed to be away from you at Christmas, but I hope you will accept this gift in the spirit it is intended. Lady von Rohan took pity on me and helped me in its selection. I confess I relied on her exceptional taste and hope we chose wisely.

THE HEART OF A HUSSAR

Your devoted servant and friend,
Jacek

A thousand steely stabs could not have have pained Oliwia's heart more than Jacek's words. She squeezed her eyes shut, holding back the flow of tears. Would that she could mount a horse and ride on the wind to Warszawa! With a defeated sigh, she untied the small package and beheld a silver hair comb, as wide as her palm, affixed with pearls and ice-blue gemstones.

It was beautiful. Jacek's companion had exquisite taste.

Oliwia let out a wry laugh. *Of course the lady has exceptional taste. She picked Jacek, didn't she?*

She stared at the glittering object a few beats before flinging it and the letter to the floor. "Dismayed indeed!" she yelled aloud. "Dismayed to be escorting *Lady von Rohan,* or to be endlessly attending pageants and parties, cavorting all night with beautiful ladies? Just so the king might favor you with a silly patch of earth!" Try though she did, Oliwia could not obliterate an image of Jacek snuggling with a perfect, well-heeled woman in a coach, walking with her arm in arm as *they* chose *her* gift, dancing and laughing with her every night, kissing her in the dark.

She dropped her head in her hands. *What does Jacek's eventual return even mean?* He hadn't asked for her hand—he'd never mentioned marriage. Ever. Her ridiculous hope had been pinned on naught but an illicit, stolen night. If she wrote and explained about the oath, she would grant him greater reason to leap into this woman's bed—assuming he hadn't already—or any number of courtiers' beds. Oliwia couldn't decide which was worse. Through it all, she was stuck like a horse in a bog, promised to a lord who'd made no mention of their vow.

Mary, Mother of God, what am I to do?

Eryk at last emerged from his self-willed purgatory, though his soul was forever scarred. As he put muscles to use once more, his vitality returned. Physically, he felt as he had before he'd plunged into, and clawed his way back from, the nadir of sorrow. He spent time once again among his people on the estate or riding through his holdings, buoying his spirits. But at night, the unavoidable ache of his loss pressed on him as he lay in his bed, smoothing his hand over cold sheets.

He had just dismissed Tomasz and was penning a letter to a Kraków merchant when the blazing hearth sent out a loud pop, pulling his attention to the hypnotic flames. He stared absently, thinking back to his most recent visit to Maławieża, a fortress a mile distant. A small smile—tinged with guilt—tugged one corner of his mouth. A sumptuous meal had been lavished on him, and he had partaken heartily of his host's hospitality—and the bright company of another guest, a lively widow from a nearby estate. Being charmed by her had come surprisingly naturally, and for a little while, he had been free of his grief.

He lifted his head at a light knock. Oliwia entered the chamber, her cheeks polished like ripe apples and her light blue eyes sparkling as she smiled at him shyly. She wore a brocade gown, the color reminding him of summer leaves—deep and lush. Two thick braids spilled down her front, accentuating the profile of her bosom. Tearing his eyes away, he cleared his throat.

"Ah, Oliwia. I have just been with Tomasz and made some decisions that affect your domain. Be seated."

Much as he had done with Katarzyna, Eryk reviewed household details with Oliwia, although she had managed so adeptly during his bleak time that these meetings proved needless—like this one, which was coming to an end far sooner than he wished.

"Oliwia, have I ever spoken to you of my manor house?" He stood up and began rifling through a stout cupboard.

"Now where did they get to?" he muttered. "I abandoned the plans long ago. Katarzyna wanted no part of it, so I put them away and ... Ah! Here they are."

He pulled out a dusty set of yellowed rolls that he blew off and carefully unfurled on the desktop. They crackled as if complaining of being opened after so long a rest. Waving his hand as he spoke, he indicated numerous points on the renderings, and his long-forgotten exhilaration with the discarded project came to life. "The design was drawn up by an Italian architect who visited the estate years ago, a student of Santi Gucci himself."

Following an hour of explaining the engineering of walls and the placement of timbers, he at last relinquished Oliwia. As he watched her go, he realized he had underestimated her—hadn't estimated her at all, really—and her fresh perspective surprised him. Delighted him, in fact. Though he did not consider her an equal by any measure—she was a woman, after all—he trusted her confident counsel in all things domestic and even heeded her advice from time to time.

Alone, he rolled up the plans and sat back down at his desk, resting his chin on his steepled hands. The small thrill he'd felt when he first recalled the widow had diminished, usurped by the recollection of a pair of light blue eyes.

One late morning, as the sun made a rare appearance and sent shafts of light into the solar, Eryk glanced up absentmindedly, catching sight of Oliwia, her back to him as she drifted toward the bookshelf. He treasured his books and opened them often, leaving them scattered about for someone else to put away. Today, that someone was Oliwia.

Something about the way she moved grabbed his attention, momentarily enthralling him. He'd heretofore noted her beauty unfolding gradually, but now he evaluated her appreciatively. The more he looked, the more stunning she grew. Her skin had always glowed like smooth ivory, but now he also noticed she was dainty-footed and delicate-boned. Her striking crystal-blue eyes were large, oval-shaped, and peeped from beneath lush, dark lashes matching her cascading curls—curls loosely pulled back with a simple ribbon he could so easily undo.

Eryk had never minded Katarzyna's lack of contours, but he found himself mesmerized by Oliwia's curves. She moved smoothly, deliberately, like a sleek, sauntering cat that casually sweeps its tail in languid waves. She possessed an ample bosom that, in his active imagination, strained her bodice and begged to be freed of its constraints. He admired the flare of her hips—hips that swayed her skirts enticingly as she moved about the chamber. Though she was trim, she was generously endowed in all the places a woman should be.

Abashed, he shook himself from his lustful reverie. This was Oliwia, his ward, a mere girl, he reminded himself.

He cleared his throat. "Oliwia, how old are you now?"

She glanced at him over her shoulder, the look a fetching one. "I turned eighteen autumn last, my lord."

"Already! I hadn't realized."

Oliwia quickly dashed her eyes away. Her movements seemed to speed up.

Eighteen. A fully grown woman.

Perhaps Katarzyna's plan had not been so outrageous, after all.

Oliwia rotated toward him. He cast his eyes down and muttered as if searching for something while he shifted in his seat. By the time he'd completed his fidgeting, she stood at the doorway like a deer ready to bolt from a predator. He dismissed her, and after she'd left, he admonished himself. His healthy appetites were asserting themselves and growing more raucous.

With a quiet exhale and an ample serving of contrition, he considered his choices. He could take a mistress to assuage his urges. A very pretty castle maid with bouncing red curls often caught his eye, bestowing him with inviting smiles. He stopped himself short. No, certainly *not* one of the castle maids. Katarzyna would never have sanctioned it, and he would serve her memory poorly with such indulgences.

He glanced at the closed door, pondering the choice blessed by the woman who seemingly still ruled him, albeit from the grave. If he upheld his oath to Katarzyna, he would need to remarry, but the guilt over bedding another would be blunted. And there was the newly resurrected hope, steadfast and strengthening: an heir for Biaska.

A fortnight after entering the halls of the Royal Castle, Jacek stood in the ballroom, having just escorted a lady from one of the king's favorite entertainments, a polychoral concert. It seemed he'd been talking politics, attending performances, and dancing endlessly since he'd left the border; he questioned how much more he could endure.

"Have you an empty spot on your dance card for me, Captain?" a familiar voice sang behind him.

THE HEART OF A HUSSAR

He turned to Magdalena, bowed, and brought her hand to his lips. "I would be delighted to dance with you the rest of this evening, Pani van Rohan." Though Magdalena was eight years his senior and no great beauty, Jacek understood why men found her enchanting. Were his heart not already bound, he might have counted himself among them.

She tapped his shoulder with her folded fan. "Your flattery will get you anywhere you wish, my lord." She gave him a wicked smile.

Jacek smiled back, shaking his head.

"Satisfy my curiosity, my lord. This lady of yours, if she is as beautiful and sweet-tempered as you've described, do you not worry other men will try to steal her away? You are no doubt the most handsome and valiant man of her acquaintance, but you have been gone for … how long now?"

A familiar uneasiness crept up his spine. "Pardon?"

"Present company excepted, men are like a pack of dogs fighting over a scrap of meat where such a prize is concerned. Look over there, for instance." With her fan, Magdalena indicated a cluster of men surrounding a young woman on the opposite side of the splendid chamber. "She is pledged to an officer who's away, and those men know it. One, in fact, is his closest friend. And look at her smile, the coquette! She feasts on their adulation."

"Oliwia's loyalty is without measure. She would never …"

Magdalena arched a blond eyebrow at him.

He darted an unseeing gaze to the gilded ceiling.

"When did you last write her and profess your undying love?" she asked sweetly.

He shrugged.

Magdalena's gray eyes widened. "You do not write daily telling her she's constantly in your thoughts, that you pine for her? A woman longs to hear such words. And if you do not utter them, another man will fill her head with tender verse and steal her from under that stony chin of yours." Magdalena humphed and whacked him with her fan.

Henryk flashed through his mind, and the flame of jealousy ignited.

Magdalena leaned in and whispered. "Look now. The king approaches our aspiring lovers. They will scatter in the face of a more powerful rival."

An impeccable man attired German-style, with a sweeping dark moustache and pointed beard streaked with gray, made his way toward the knot as all eyes tracked him.

"His Majesty cannot intend wooing her?"

Magdalena scoffed. "He is the king! And as long as Pani Urszula is not about …" She swiveled her head and grabbed Jacek's arm. "Come! I shall introduce you."

"Now?"

"Yes! His Majesty will be intent on the lady and therefore disarmed and possibly amiable. He's usually neither." She fluttered her eyes at him. "Simply show him the same steadfastness—and charm—you've shown me, and all will be well."

CHAPTER 33

Choices

Eryk had summoned Oliwia to his chamber earlier than usual. With foreboding, she rapped softly. Jerking the door open, he ushered her in with a broad smile. Freshly trimmed and shaved, he was outfitted in his lordly finest, as if greeting a high-ranking dignitary. He wore an intricately embroidered gold silk ferezeya trimmed in sable, beneath which was a cardinal brocade żupan with gilded buttons in a neat row the length of the garment. He stood back, roaming his eyes over her. Feeling a flush surge up her throat, she darted her gaze to a table and frowned.

"My lord, I see no books. Shall I retrieve one?"

"No, Oliwia." His voice cracked, reminding her of a twelve-year-old pubescent boy. He cleared his throat. "I wish to discuss something of great importance with you. Please sit down. May I pour you a cup of wine?"

"Please." As she sank into a chair before a bright blaze, her heart rate accelerated; she knew how a rabbit in a snare must feel. He handed her a full cup and settled in the leather seat facing hers. She stared at the flames, feeling his eyes on her.

Eryk gulped a mouthful, then drew in a breath. "Oliwia, we've spent a great deal of time together these many months. You have helped me through a very difficult time and have become invaluable to me. I will forever be grateful."

"It has been my honor, my lord."

"You are happy here, yes?"

"Yes, my lord."

"And Filip. He is thriving and happy as well, yes?"

"Yes, my lord."

"I have been considering," he said, pausing for a sip. "That is, I have been reflecting on the future of the estate and have come to a decision. It is time I take a new wife and sire an heir."

Oliwia's heart plummeted like a rock hefted from a cliff, and the hand holding the cup trembled so that a wave rippled over the surface of the wine. She wanted to drink deeply but fretted her stomach would only hurl it back up. She cast her eyes down so he would not see the dismay surely creasing her face.

"I shall honor Kasia's ... Lady Katarzyna's wish and uphold my holy oath. I shall wed the person she chose for me, to whom she gave her blessing. Do you understand?"

Oliwia understood only too well. Her throat and chest constricted. Nodding her head numbly, she focused on a minute speck of lint in her lap. She thought she'd braced herself for this, but the blow was a savage one and nearly doubled her over. Eryk captured one of her hands in his.

"You will be the lady of the land, Oliwia. Think of Filip and the countless opportunities he'll be afforded that he could never have otherwise." He paused, then continued softly. "It is time you were married. Of utmost gravity is that we *both* uphold our vow before God while honoring Katarzyna's dying wish. Anything less would be a sin."

Fingers under her chin, Eryk tilted her head up so she met his gaze. His amber eyes searched hers. Oliwia's mind whirred furiously, digging once more for a reason to escape the promise.

"Oliwia, I want you to come to me willingly. I want you to *want* to be my wife."

She swallowed hard. He frowned. In a halting voice, she said, "But my lord, I am ..."

Eryk's eyes narrowed. "Do your affections lie elsewhere?"

She nodded feebly. He released her and stood up.

"Who is he?" His voice was low, tight. He began pacing, his face growing dusky.

THE HEART OF A HUSSAR

Lady Katarzyna's voice roared into Oliwia's consciousness. *The last time he displayed his jealous side, it ended rather badly for the gentleman.* Fear hobbled her tongue.

"Is it Henryk?"

She shook her head. Eryk stopped abruptly, his face twisting in an expression she'd never seen, not even during his worst drunken tirade.

"Jacek, then."

The name jolted her, and she must have given herself away, for he nodded. His eyes blazed, and a muscle in his jaw jumped repeatedly.

Dear God, what have I done?

"You realize your devotion is misplaced, yes?" His tone had grown sardonic. "You are just one among many." She stared at him, her tongue still glued in place by dread and doubt. He resumed pacing. "I've observed Jacek a long time now. He has his pick of women, and he takes full advantage at every opportunity. If he's told you any different, he's lied to you. Why do you suppose he's never married? I'll tell you why. He has far too many diversions."

Familiar stabs of pain lanced her heart. She ransacked her brain for images of Jacek, but the one where a young woman gave him a garter to honor their "special" friendship became stubbornly wedged. Then she flashed to lying with him atop her bed, and a wave of shame washed over her. *Stupid little fool!*

Eryk's gruff voice wrenched her back to her present misery. He stood still now, his hands behind his back, leveling his eyes at her under dark, rigid brows. A shiver snaked up her spine. This was not a man she knew. "If you truly care for him, he had best stay away, for I promise it will not end well for him. Do not forget I am the law here. I've the power to grant him what he most wants, or withhold it. I've also the power to destroy him, just as I've the power to send Filip far, far away. If you pursue Jacek, or he you, make no mistake, you will regret it, Oliwia. And then you will live with the consequences of your imprudence."

"What of wanting me to *want* to be—" she blurted, her voice pitched high.

"Then you'd best convince me becoming my wife is what you desire."

"I have no dowry," she countered futilely.

His features softened, and the sudden shift was nearly as discomfiting as the flaring of his temper. "But you do have a dowry—of sorts. It's an allegiance Katarzyna longed for, between Biaska, England, and Scotland. There's a small chance your English grandfather's estate could be claimed on Filip's behalf. I will work tirelessly to see Filip gets it once you're my wife."

A fresh shock waved through her, upending her tender stomach. "Estate?"

"After exhaustive inquiries, I learned everything your mother wrote you was true. I also learned the Sewell Estate is abandoned. There's a chance it will come to your brother."

"But no one told me," she whispered, stunned.

"No, because there was nothing to tell. I thought it best to wait until there was substantial news. I did learn where your parents are buried, and I will take you there once we're married, if you wish. We'll bring Filip."

"How long have you known?"

He shifted his weight. "Over a year now."

Oliwia couldn't breathe. Her eyes darted about as she tried to sort her tangled thoughts. She was trapped, like a bird tethered to its perch, flapping its wings desperately but unable to take flight.

One inescapable fact bloomed in her head, as though a bright, blinding light shone in her eyes. She had made the promise, and he was claiming it whether she agreed or not—and he was willing to use those she cared about against her to his end. Whether his accusations about Jacek were true or false, he was prepared to undermine the man who had served him unwaveringly for years. Any hope she'd had of evading her fate was dashed at her feet like shattered glass.

Eryk sat back down, easing into his chair. A ponderous pause lasted for what seemed hours, filling the dead space in the cavernous chamber. The cheery fire crackled and spat, but she grew chilled. The wine had left a sour taste in her mouth and burned her belly. She clasped her hands tightly to keep them from quaking while his gaze rested on her. Her life was about to change forever—not in a way she desired—and she saw no way to prevent it.

And what of Filip? Eryk had so shrewdly pointed out what this union meant for her brother. As her status was elevated, so would his be. This solitary advantage to the match was one small spike on which she could hang her future happiness.

Stay strong for Filip, Oliwia.

THE HEART OF A HUSSAR

Slowly, as if turning her gaze to him would end her life as she knew it—and she wished to savor every last second—Oliwia locked eyes with Eryk.

"I will marry you, my lord. Willingly."

Oliwia had closed the lid on herself and driven the last nail into her own coffin.

Jacek sat at the writing table in his chamber, pondering Magdalena's counsel. When he'd argued that Oliwia surely knew his deep affection for her, Magdalena had scoffed. "Is she accomplished in divination, then?" He chuckled to himself, then stared absently at the blank paper before him. Wind rattled the panes and whistled in the chimney. He dipped the quill and began to write.

An hour later, he reflected that this rectangle of paper held his heart and his soul—both of which he was preparing to hand over. He twisted in his seat; he'd never felt so exposed. But he reckoned he'd been as patient as he could possibly withstand. Both patience and self-control had given way to yearning and overpowered his qualms. Drumming the corner of the desk, he reviewed his missive.

26 January, In the Year of our Lord 1613

My most beloved Oliwia,

At last, I have met King Zygmunt III. Lady von Rohan was kind enough to make the introduction last evening. Though it was the briefest of exchanges, it was salutary. I cannot hope for more.

The true purpose of my letter, sweetest Liwi, is to tell you how ardently I long to be with you. I have taken far too much time away from you and can endure no more. I will remain just long enough for civility, not a day later, and leave for Biaska the morning after Candlemas.

When I do return, I wish with all my heart to make you my wife. Though I have little to offer while you have your pick of suitors, I vow to make you a loving, faithful husband who will worship you until the end of our days for the goddess that you are.

Lord Eryk compensates me well, and I can provide for you and Filip comfortably. When I return, I will take the captain's dwelling. There is room enough for we three, and children as they come. I hope you want many, as I do, though the size of our brood is, of course, in God's hands. You will be the most excellent loving consort and mother. I well imagine a trail of children, like goslings, following you. I pray one will be a beautiful girl like her mother, with eyes that shine like aquamarines.

I promise you an easy life, which you so richly deserve. I will continue my quest for an estate of our own, which, after my service has ended, I am confident I will gain.

Most cherished Oliwia, I never imagined losing my heart as I have to you. It is irretrievably forfeit to me and abides with you forever. If you will not have me, I shall not recover. For me, there is no equal. So I entreat you not to deny me the privilege of waking up beside you every morning for the rest of our lives.

I adore you.
With all my affection and devotion, your friend and servant,
Jacek

Blowing out a breath, he stood and pulled on his ferezeya. Before he could head for the door, there came three quick raps. Yanking it open, he was pleased to see the manservant he'd been assigned.

"Ah! I was on my way to find you. See this gets to a messenger."

The man bowed and handed him a letter in exchange. "A man's just brought this for you, m'lord. I will see he gets this straightaway."

Jacek's heart nearly leapt from his chest when he recognized Oliwia's handwriting. *At last!* Without a backward glance, he mumbled his thanks to the servant and tore the letter open. He quickly scanned its brief contents. The heart that had soared moments before now crashed to his knees.

Shaking his head, he reread it. Brilliant explosions of vivid crimson and searing white burst against the black backdrop of his mind. Lightning snapped and popped throughout his body in volatile flashes, every nerve ablaze. He paced a circle, then another, like a caged lion.

He stalked to the writing table and grasped the desk, hurling it, the chair after it. The inkwell smashed, splattering black ink. Wood splintered and sprayed as the pieces clattered together and landed with resounding thuds. Jacek held himself rigid and read the letter a third time. Oliwia would wed Lord Eryk. His lord, his commander, his brother.

His rival.

His *foe*.

Jacek gritted his teeth. Thoughts of crushing Eryk with his bare hands, of tearing his throat from him, crowded together in his head. He let them come. Grasping a porcelain statuette, he envisioned Eryk's head and squeezed it until it disintegrated in his hand, slicing his palm. He felt no pain. Blood formed a line at the base of his thumb and ran to his wrist, trickling scarlet drops to the thick carpet under his feet while he watched with curious detachment.

A gasp had him turning to see the manservant, agape and ashen, in the doorway. "Is everything all right, sir?"

Jacek stared at him, his mind a dark, bottomless whirlpool. In that abyss, he had just been impaled on a kopia, dead center, and hoisted up, twisting round and round on its axis. He faltered toward the wash basin and heaved. And heaved again. And again. His body hollow, he spat and dragged a cloth across his mouth while the agitated servant hovered.

"Fetch my letter back and find my retainer," Jacek rasped. "I leave at once."

An hour later, he was freshened, bandaged, and packed. The room had been straightened by a battalion of servants. Even the desk and chair had been replaced.

Magdalena appeared in his doorway. "What has happened?" Worry etched her features.

"Something ... unexpected calls me to Biaska."

Jacek gripped Oliwia's letter, together with the one he'd penned. Numbly, he tossed both into the hungry flames and watched the paper blacken and curl.

Magdalena stood beside him. "Is it your young lady? Is she unwell?"

"No, she is very well." He faced Magdalena and canted his head. "Your instincts were quite insightful, my lady."

He caught Magdalena's shoulders and kissed her cheeks. "Your friendship has meant a great deal, and I am indebted to you."

"You will not stay? But Candlemas is mere days away."

"I will not." He spun on his heel, leaving the stunned woman in his wake.

During the next days, Jacek barely noticed the weather, riding hard with Marcin through the frozen landscape as though the very devil chased them. They stopped at inns after dark and were gone before sunrise. He said little as they traveled, and if Marcin had questions, he had the good sense to hold his tongue.

Jacek's churning mind alternated between shock, disbelief, anger, and misery. One question continually bubbled to the top of his roiling thoughts.

Was he too late?

With each dawn since she'd promised herself to Eryk, Oliwia's spirit sagged incrementally. Soon it would lie in a hopeless puddle about her feet. This morning, after yet another restless night, her eyes fluttered open and she looked up at the canopy, remembering where and who she was. And just like every other morning, she squeezed her eyes tight and imagined she was anywhere but here. Eventually, she dragged herself out of bed to face the inevitable.

When she arrived at his chamber, Eryk held his arms out to her. Her feet wanted to run the other way, but she forced herself to step toward him and accept his embrace.

She backed out of his arms. "You wished to see me?"

"You look enchanting this morning, my love," he said.

She felt anything but enchanting—wan and constricted, perhaps. He came to her and lifted her chin, unsettling her when his lips touched hers. She tensed and pulled back. He stroked her jaw with his thumb and gazed into her eyes.

"Oliwia," he whispered, "you must get used to my touch. You will soon be my wife, and I will be kissing you often."

The muscles in her neck strained from holding her head back. His hand fell away just as she urged herself to relax. She suppressed a gasp of relief.

"I wonder, were I Jacek, would you be so reticent?"

Heat rose, blazing from her chest to her scalp.

His amber eyes fixed on hers. "You will have to do better convincing me that your devotion has taken a turn, my love. Frankly, if I thought you still harbored …"

Strident alarm bells clanged in her head. "If you thought I still …"

"If I thought you still cared for him, I would eliminate the threat," he said with a wry smile.

Shivers rippled up and down her spine. Eryk drew her close, caressing her cheek.

THE HEART OF A HUSSAR

"You are mine, Oliwia. If *any* man touches you, it will be the last thing he does. Now close your eyes." She squeezed them shut, feeling altogether like a poppy drawing its petals up for the night.

He feathered a soft kiss on her lips and drew back slightly. She opened her eyes.

"That wasn't so bad, now was it?" he said.

Oliwia shook her head in short, jerky movements.

"Let's try that again." He smiled at her indulgently, his hand spanning the small of her back. She couldn't escape. "Close your eyes."

He bent his mouth to hers, landing a lingering kiss. Wrapping his arms fully around her, he drew her against him and stroked her back. Her hands dangled lifelessly at her sides. Releasing her, he pulled away. She snapped her eyes open and peered at him.

"I prefer to marry during Shrovetide," he declared, "but with Lent upon us, time is too short. So I've decided we will wed after Divine Mercy Sunday. That span of roughly nine weeks allows you ample time to prepare the castle *and* yourself."

She nodded listlessly.

After one last kiss, he dismissed her. She hurtled pell-mell down the passageway to the landing one floor below. Breathing heavily, she skidded to a stop and rubbed her sleeve furiously over her lips. She wanted to spit, but her mouth was as dry as a newly fired clay pot. Bile crept up her throat.

How will I ever get through this?

As she charged down the next set of steps, her brain tore itself apart, whirling in different directions simultaneously. She was incapable of putting two coherent thoughts together. Taking the next flight, Oliwia barreled heedlessly around a corner and collided with a soldier. Before she could fall, he grabbed her elbows and righted her. She grasped his muscular forearms to steady herself, glimpsing his bandaged hand. She looked up to thank him and gasped.

"Jacek!"

His blue eyes widened.

Oliwia ripped herself from him and fled toward the kitchens, but he dashed after her, catching her up before she could plunge through the scullery.

He grabbed her upper arm forcefully, spinning her toward him. "Oliwia!"

She smacked her free hand against his chest as she tried to twist away. "Let me go!" she hissed.

He released her, and she ran from him blindly with one thought: Escape! She steered toward an arched doorway where a hefty oaken door stood ajar. *Sanctuary.* She slipped through and yanked the door shut behind her. The space, a high-barrel-ceilinged buttery, was neatly stacked with crates, racks, and kegs. A veil of dust hung thick in the air. Looking around, she panted, one hand to her forehead and the other to her belly. *Think! Breathe!* Bracing her back against a cold rock wall, she slid to the chalky floor in a heap of skirts and swiped at her cheeks.

Jacek, here! She tried to reconcile his presence.

To her dismay, said presence pushed through the door and thudded it behind him, then took up station against it. Scowling, Jacek welded his arms in place across his chest. Briskly picking herself up, she brushed dirt and cobwebs from her clothing and faced him, her heart galloping anew.

"Oliwia," he said evenly. "What has happened? Has someone harmed you? Are you ill?"

Her attempt at a smile resulted in something akin to a grimace. "No, Jacek, I am unharmed. I apologize for my behavior. I was … taken by surprise."

From a tight, drawn face, his blazing sapphire eyes drilled into her. "You did not expect me." It wasn't a question, but a statement tinged with tetchiness. "We must speak," he added in the same tone.

"Does Lord Eryk know you've returned?" she blurted.

He arched an eyebrow at her. "I just arrived. He does not yet know, though he soon will. I came to you first."

She discharged a relieved breath. Carefully placing one foot before the other, she headed for a shelf holding a row of jugs.

"When did you arrive?" She unstoppered a flagon and filled wooden cups with a trembling hand, feeling his eyes tracking her every movement. He accepted the cup she offered, his fingers lingering on hers and skittering her heart for a beat.

"Less than an hour ago."

She gulped wine, furiously gathering her thoughts. "What happened to your hand?"

"An accident when I received your letter five days ago."

"And you got here so quickly?" Astonishment made her squeak. "Did you ride through the dark?"

"And the snow." He took a sip and set his cup down. "I came to find out if it's true."

She dropped her eyes and brought the cup to her lips but didn't drink.

"Is it true, Liwi?" he gritted out.

She didn't look at him. *Couldn't* look at him. "It is true I am to wed Lord Eryk. In two months." Though she knew the exact count, nearly to the minute, she withheld it. Jacek would mistake her for an eager bride rather than a prisoner measuring her last hours of freedom.

He picked up his cup and took a long pull, watching her over the rim. "You said you would wait for me. I thought you and I … After what passed between us, I thought we had an understanding."

Oliwia's head jerked up. "You've been gone a year, Jacek, leaving me with a few kisses and letters. You never spoke of a permanent arrangement. We made no promises." Helplessness flooded her as she scanned his face.

Astonishment lit his eyes. "A few kisses? That's all it was to you?"

A flame flickering inside her caught fire. "That's all it was to *you,* yes? Just one more in a string of conquests."

His eyes narrowed and darkened, churning and tossing like an angry ocean in a winter gale. "What in blazes does *that* mean?"

"Lady Izabela, the maid with the garter," she countered, flinging her hands in the air. "Your letters! The dancing, the sleigh rides, the endless revelry, Lady von Rohan 'taking pity on you.' You must think me a naïve child!"

"Because you're acting like one!" he stormed.

She clenched her jaw. "You write me letters identical to Filip's, then I receive a gift from you, picked out by your … your … whatever she is to you. Your own words! Tell me how I might have distinguished myself as a special acquaintance."

Jacek exhaled an enormous breath, his chest seeming to deflate as he did. He dragged a hand through his hair. "Liwi." He looked away a moment, then swung his eyes back to hers. "Liwi, I have done you an injustice. I've done us both an injustice, if I led you to believe … Magdalena von Rohan *did* take pity on me, and I'm grateful for it. The place was intolerable. She's a stout matron who's a close acquaintance of the king. Without her generosity, I would not have come to his attention. As for the comb, I asked her to approve the gift I selected for you. I wanted it to be perfect. I have little experience with such things. The aquamarines ... They reminded me of your eyes, and the pearls of your skin." He sighed. "As for the girl with the garter, she was mad. I'd scarcely spoken to her."

His gaze intensified. "Liwi, there have been no 'conquests.' None since I returned from Twierzda in 1611 because, since that time, I've had no desire to be with anyone but you." He scrubbed his hand over his stubbled chin.

Oliwia hugged herself. "Why did you say nothing?" Her voice was a near-whisper, her heart tearing itself apart.

He glanced at the stone ceiling. "Because I'm a clodpole who only recently admitted it to himself. Being away from you, I realized how much I ..." He looked at her, his eyes imploring. "Liwi, I assumed you would wed *me* one day, but I wanted something more to offer you than my name. 'Tis the only reason I went to Żółkiew and Warszawa."

She closed her eyes and turned away, fighting the logjam in her throat that threatened to strangle her. "I would have welcomed your name, with naught but you in the bargain, and gladly."

He stepped to her and took her hand in both of his. "Then I will speak with Lord Eryk and explain—"

"No!" She jerked her hand from his.

A fresh look of surprise overtook his features and was soon replaced by an expression she'd only seen on his handsome face once—after he'd killed Mateusz. Regret.

"Are you determined to wed him, then?"

She nodded, and the clog broke apart, rimming her eyes in tears. She pressed her lips in a tight line to keep them from quivering.

He took another step toward her. "Then why do you cry?" One warm, rough hand recaptured hers while the other tilted her chin up. "Liwi, look at me. I've been a damned fool, but it's not too late."

"What of your dream, your estate?"

One side of his mouth quirked. "'Tis a curious thing. As much as the land meant to me all these years, it means naught without you on it. And I can still pursue it after we marry. With you beside me, I will have it all, Liwi."

Eryk will see to it you have nothing.
Not even your life.

THE HEART OF A HUSSAR

Jacek cupped the back of her head and kissed her forehead tenderly, then snugged her to him. She wound her arms around his waist and pressed her hands into the channel along his broad back.

"Dear God, how I have missed you," he breathed. "Like a parched man without water." He rested his cheek on her head. "I will talk to Lord Eryk now. Or not, if that is your wish. But come away with me. I'll take care of you and Filip."

"Do you know what you're saying? Eryk will destroy you."

He pulled back and looked at her, a savage scowl in place. "He may try, but he will not stop me." His expression left her with no doubt.

Ferocious words from a noble warrior's heart.

A warrior marching to battle blindly.

Were Eryk to spare Jacek's life, he still possessed the power to deliver Jacek's prized estate. He also held the power to withdraw it and crush any hope Jacek had of ever attaining it. Images of Jacek beaten, turned out, forever to serve as no more than a magnate's mercenary—like her father, who had lost everything—swirled through her head. And could Jacek live with betraying Eryk? For a while, he'd be happy with her—a few weeks, a few months—but what then? What a high price Jacek would pay for such a fleeting duration.

Oliwia's heart splintered, scattering in millions of irretrievable shards as she understood the power *she* held—and how she must wield it. She rested her head against him. Squeezing her eyes tight, she took a long inhale, pulling in his scent, clinging to him. She memorized the feel of his strong arms about her, his hands warm on her back, his hard chest under her cheek, the feel of his proud heart thumping beneath it. Then she disentangled herself and took several steps back.

She drew herself up and tilted her chin. "I cannot go with you, Jacek."

Incomprehension spread over his face. "Why not?"

She dug her nails into her palms.

"Is it his wealth?" he asked, sounding incredulous.

"This is not about riches, Jacek."

"Then tell me what it *is* about," he bellowed. He huffed a contrite breath. "Liwi, tell me you love him, and I will spare you any more of my foolishness. But if you don't, then say you're mine and I'll take you with me this instant, and we'll wed. He cannot harm us."

"I'm sorry, Jacek, but I do love him. I am eager for this wedding." She nearly choked on the bitter lies. *God forgive me.*

Jacek's expression gave way to sadness that tore at her heart. "Is this what you truly want, Liwi?"

"It is."

Glancing at the floor, he nodded his head. Then he leveled a cold, steely gaze at her. "I see. I took too long … yet I was too late before I started."

He let out a wry laugh and scanned her from head to foot. "You have done well for yourself, my lady, especially considering where you came from. My congratulations to you."

His words hit her as though he'd connected with his meaty fist. She willed her face to remain a mask, her spine to keep her upright. She bit her lip while Jacek stalked to the heavy door, wrenched it open, and banged it behind him as though it were no more than a wooden platter.

As a wellspring of tears overflowed in Oliwia's eyes, she crumpled to the floor. His dark sapphire glare, the contempt it held as he'd hurled his last words, would forever be emblazoned in her memory. In Oliwia's desolation, the only comfort she could cling to was knowing he would remain alive, whole, and free to chase his dream.

Jacek bolted from the buttery, and emotions that had coiled in him unwound whip-fast. Rage flowed through him, scorching him. As his innards boiled with jealousy and betrayal, he envisioned ripping Eryk limb from limb, feeling life drain from his body.

Maggot-infested piece of sheep dung!

Ruttish hell-spawn!

Fucking son of a bitch!

Nor was Oliwia spared Jacek's formidable wrath. Even as she'd readied to cast him off, she had let him hold her, given him hope. He'd offered up his quivering, wholly unfettered heart, and she'd stomped it into cruel oblivion. As he wove his way to the stables, his arms and legs pumping, jagged bits of their exchange sliced into his thoughts. "I do love him," she'd said. "I am eager." And to think he'd ridden through winter's hell to reach her! What an extravagant idiot he'd been.

He marched into the stables, barking for his horse. A pimple-faced youth jumped and ran to the stall, tripping over his own feet.

"Begone! I'll do it," Jacek growled. He grabbed Jarosława's harness, and she shied from him. He exploded in a string of expletives, some of them aimed at the mare; she was female, after all. After more trouble than it should have been, he saddled and mounted her, and tore through the yard, scattering stable hands, soldiers, and dogs in equal portions. Someone yelled his name, but he ignored the call and flew through the postern gate and rode.

And rode.

Time, like the frosted countryside, blurred and flew past. The lather on Jarosława's neck and haunches finally made him pull up. He led her to water and dropped to the ground beside her, elbow on his knee and chin in his hand. He realized he had a clear line of sight to the castle. The view from a distance had always lifted him, but as he looked upon it now, he saw only its unsightliness, every blemish exposed.

Like its lord, he mused bitterly.

When he thought of Eryk's hands on Oliwia, he rose to his knees and pummeled the earth until his knuckles ached.

"The devil piss on them both!" he bellowed. Jarosława jerked her head.

His stomach rolled like a boat being thrown between cresting waves in a storm. With an extended sigh, he allowed a shred of sanity to reassert itself. Oliwia had betrayed nothing; she didn't deserve his scorn. His lack of action made him culpable. Mooncalf that he was, he'd never declared his affection during the long, forgettable year. *Is she accomplished in divination, then?* Nor had he extracted any understanding from her. In this, Oliwia had been right. He'd made far more assumptions than he had express overtures. Had he changed a few words in his letters, been more forthright sooner ...

Would it have mattered?

How could she fall in love with another—a man old enough to be her father, for God's sake!—when she's always been meant to be mine?

I see, he'd said in a steady voice that had surprised him when it escaped his lips. He'd felt anything but the steely composure he'd manifested. And he hadn't seen. At all.

Flopping on the ground, he ignored the icy dampness seeping into his back and closed his eyes. Unbidden, her face floated before him. She was still the most beautiful thing he'd ever seen. His desire for her had not flagged in the slightest; it had only grown stronger, binding him, cursing him. Now her fragrance, a vague scent of citrus and something fresh, like newly picked rosemary from the garden, filled his nose.

What remained of his rage crumbled under the weight of anguish; he dropped his arm over his eyes.

CHAPTER 34

Anyone Will Do

"Jacek, enough! Hold!" Henryk gasped, lowering his weapon. "Who is it you seek to kill today? If it is indeed I, tell me what offense I've committed, and I will stop it at once!"

Henryk's tone was light between his heavy breaths. Jacek stilled his sword arm and glared at him, then dragged his other arm across his drenched forehead and repositioned himself.

"I think I know what is bothering you. We need to find you a soft woman who will help you cast out whatever demons chase you."

Jacek raised his pałasz once again. Fulminating with fury, he crashed his arm down in a slashing arc, barely missing Henryk—the momentary focus of his rage.

"I. DO. NOT. NEED. A. WOMAN!"

Henryk gawked at him.

Jacek fought to catch his breath. Gripping the hilt, he looked at Henryk remorsefully and dropped onto the damp ground, checking the bandage on his hand. Dusk edged in, and they were the only two fool enough to spar on the slick, frosted field. In spite of the cold, damp air and being clothed only in boots, breeches, and shirt, Jacek's body struggled to cool itself. Maybe he was sick. Maybe he had a fever. Likely both. But he knew of no cure.

Henryk chose a patch of grass and eyed him curiously. "Are you going to tell me what's happened?"

Jacek began tearing tufts of dead grass from the earth. "You'll learn soon enough."

"If I am to know soon enough, why not tell me now?"

Jacek's heart rate finally slowed. "I learned …" Jacek swallowed hard before continuing. "Lord Eryk is to remarry."

Henryk raised his eyebrows. "And who is the lord to marry?"

Jacek sucked in a breath and looked at him squarely. "Oliwia."

Henryk jerked upright. "*What?* Impossible! How the devil can he do that?" he spluttered. "Why Oliwia?"

Taken aback by Henryk's heated reaction, Jacek eyed him closely. "Why *not* Oliwia? Were you hoping to have the lady yourself?"

"*Of course not!*" Henryk bellowed. "She is not for me. She is for you!"

"She is for Eryk."

"Does *she* desire this union?"

Jacek felt a stab of misery. "Yes."

Henryk sighed. "Will you stay here?"

"I cannot." But where would he go?

After a momentary silence, Henryk grasped Jacek's shoulder. "Ah, by Christ, Jacek. I'm truly sorry."

They pulled themselves up from the damp ground, donned their garments, and headed for the great hall. Jacek caught sight of Oliwia's silhouette moving toward the stairs. His heart lurched. Only a year ago, he'd escorted her up those stairs, and …

He had little idea where to go, but he could not stay. Not like this. He would petition Żółkiewski to serve in his army. He'd be welcomed there. Suddenly, a familiar, high-pitched squeal bore down on him.

"Sir! Captain! You are back! My sister is to marry the lord!"

Filip's shrill voice preceded his slight body which was running full-out the length of the great hall, dodging people and hurdling greyhounds as he went. Any sentient being present who did not heretofore know of the nuptials certainly knew now. Jacek stood tall, his arms folded across his chest.

"Filip! Have you forgotten a true warrior does not run through the great hall yelling at the top of his lungs? Display some decorum." Until that moment, Jacek hadn't realized how much he'd missed the boisterous

THE HEART OF A HUSSAR

brown-headed boy—and how much he would miss him once he left for good.

Rather than give in to his self-pity, Jacek scowled at Filip, who fidgeted in place.

"Stand at attention, Filip, and lower your voice. What is it you wish to say?"

"Liwi is betrothed to the lord! She will become the Lady of Biaska, which means I will become ..." He trailed off, confusion scrunching his features.

"Which means you will become the brother of the Lord of Biaska," Jacek finished for him, a little harshly.

"Yes, my lord. And I am to become a hussar, like you! It is exciting, yes?"

Excitement reverberated through the castle in preparation for the wedding. People bustled and chattered, but Oliwia was not among them. In her chamber, she stood impatiently on a stool, subjecting herself to yet another fitting. She hated her gown and let everyone in attendance know of her displeasure. Truth was she wouldn't have liked any garment they fashioned for the occasion.

Nadia gushed, "Oh, m'lady! The silver brocade is beautiful on you. The color shows off your skin and your eyes, and the neckline accentuates your lovely bosom. I am sure my lord will love looking on you in this."

Oliwia was taken aback. Nadia was voicing an opinion, but she was picking the very worst time to spread her wings. Oliwia picked up the skirts and stomped down from the stool. She thrust her face several inches from Nadia's and snarled.

"Well, I do not care *what* my lord will like! I will not wear this dress as it is!"

She began pulling it apart, sending several of the ladies flitting about the room, tsking and wringing their hands. One seamstress caught the dress after Oliwia wrangled it off her body and threw it as hard as she could. The fabric was light, and the dress fluttered, robbing her of the satisfaction of a solid *thud*.

"My lady," one seamstress said haltingly, "we will add some pearls to the neckline, and I think you will be pleased."

Another cleared her throat nervously.

"Yes, what is it?" Oliwia snapped.

"The *czepek*, my lady. Would you like to try it on?"

The czepek. The cap. Oliwia shuddered at the mention of it. It was Polish custom to unbraid the bride's hair, hack it off, and stuff a cap on her head. As if the guests were too stupid to comprehend, the tradition announced she had transformed from maiden to married woman. The ridiculous czepek the woman held now merely served as a symbol of all Oliwia would lose: her freedom, her tresses, and her maidenhood to a man she did not want.

She frowned at the quaking woman. "I don't care what the vile thing looks like on me."

With that, they all scurried away, but for the quivering Nadia, who remained the only attendant to catch Oliwia's wrath. When Oliwia looked at the girl's face, she dissolved.

"I'm sorry, Nadia. I don't know what got into me." She squeezed her hand.

"You need not be sorry, m'lady. I should not have said anything. If I may, I think you are just an anxious bride," Nadia stammered.

Oliwia was about to argue with the girl, but she realized it would do her absolutely no good whatever, so she ordered her to help her get dressed in a sturdy woolen gown, boots, heavy gloves, and fur-trimmed cloak instead.

"Will m'lady be walking in the gardens on this chilly day?"

"No, your lady is going for a ride—a very long ride," Oliwia announced tersely.

"Oh, m'lady. Is that … is that …"

Oliwia glowered, and the girl held her tongue. When she was dressed, Oliwia departed the room and hurried to the stables. As she swept into the entrance, several stable boys jumped from their perches. She barked at the first one she saw.

"You! Boy! What's your name?"

"I am Piotr, m'lady." He bowed deeply, hand over his heart in a very sweet gesture that gentled her temper.

THE HEART OF A HUSSAR

"Piotr, I would like my horse saddled at once. Do you know which one it is?"

The boy nodded vigorously. For their betrothal, Eryk had given Oliwia her very own Polish-bred mare. She was as handsome an animal as Oliwia had ever seen, with a glossy reddish-brown coat, a white elongated splotch on her forehead, and two white stockings on her front legs. She was younger and smaller than the other horses in his considerable stable, and he had selected her specially. Oliwia loved the animal, but she'd had little opportunity to ride her. She would change that today. In her present mood, she needed to do *something*, and racing across a meadow was the something calling to her.

"And Piotr?"

"Yes, m'lady?"

"You are to tell no one. Not even Feliks. Do you understand?" She gave him her sternest look, and he nodded once more before scampering away.

Oliwia huffed in place, raring to be free and streaking over the ground. After what seemed an eternity, Piotr emerged with a fully saddled and bridled horse. Oliwia eased when she saw the majestic animal, and she climbed atop with Piotr's help.

Proceeding out of the stableyard, Oliwia fixed her gaze on the postern gate and the horizon, aware of nothing and no one. From seemingly nowhere, two cats streaked across her path. The horse whinnied and skittered, then reared, its front hooves flailing at air. Panicked, Oliwia pulled on the reins, but the horse jerked its head, and they flew from her hands.

"Hold on!" a voice urged. Suspended mid-air, Oliwia reached for the pommel right before the thrashing horse thudded back to earth. Askew, Oliwia fought to stay upright. Someone shoved her roughly back up, and she fell forward, her head nearly colliding with a furry kolpak. Jacek shouldered the beast, its harness firmly secured in his gloved paw.

"Easy does it." He spoke in a soothing tone to the animal he grappled with.

Oliwia was nearly as astounded to see him as she was by the catapult she was astride.

"Where did you come from?" she gasped.

"From the shadows, my lady." He calmly pulled on the mare's restraints and turned her toward the stables, stroking her neck as he did so. A contingent of stable hands stood like a palisade.

"What are you doing?" Oliwia yelped.

"Returning your horse—and you."

How dare he! "Why?"

Jacek stopped and glanced up at her with a frown, then continued walking as if he hadn't heard her. Eryk pushed through the wall of onlookers and strode briskly toward them.

"Oliwia! Are you all right?" he demanded.

She snapped right back with a curt, "Yes."

"Thank you, Jacek, for collecting my headstrong bride." Eryk did not look pleased. He took the leads from Jacek.

To Oliwia, he said in an exasperated tone, "My dear, have we not discussed this? You cannot ride alone. You must first check with me. An escort will be arranged at *my* direction, with *my* permission. It's too dangerous for a woman. Look what nearly happened!"

She bounced her gaze between Eryk and Jacek, trapped between them, without hope of escape. Mustering her anger, she addressed Jacek tartly. "How did you know?"

"It's the captain's job to know who comes and goes," Eryk interjected. "Jacek did his job correctly and protected you. That is all you need know."

Oliwia reddened like a chastened child. Eryk kept hold of the leads.

His tone softened. "I will arrange an escort and ride with you when I am done, Oliwia."

"I will ride in the courtyard," she said frostily, trying to reclaim the reins.

He held them fast. "I think not."

Jacek stood by and listened keenly to the exchange. He couldn't disagree with anything Eryk said. Not only had Oliwia thought to ride alone, but she'd nearly been thrown. What addled thoughts knocked about her brain? Her expression was set like carved stone, but her face and neck glowed blotchy pink, giving her away. She stared straight ahead, her chin tilted upward, her lips pressed tightly together.

Eryk reached up to help her down, but she ignored him, so he handed the reins to a groom and watched as she was led away. The mare's tail flicked, nearly catching both men with one energetic swish. *Obviously, horse and rider have a connection.* Eryk perched his hands on his hips and frowned. Jacek strode toward the keep to thank Nadia for alerting him of Oliwia's reckless impulse. He'd taken no more than three steps when Eryk caught him up.

"Jacek. She must be safeguarded despite her unruliness. And while I am grateful to you, I think it unnecessary for you to guard her personally. You have more compelling duties."

Jacek scrutinized Eryk for a few heartbeats, trying to decipher the entire message lurking behind his terse words. Coupled with this puzzle was a twinge of sadness. While Jacek pinned nearly all his troubles on Oliwia, unruliness was not a word brought to mind when he thought of her. Determined, perhaps, but not unruly. And truth be told, although he would never admit it aloud, he found her pigheadedness diverting.

He was jolted back by Eryk's mirthless laugh. "Oliwia requires a steelier hand and more instruction on a noblewoman's proper behavior, to go hand in hand with reining in her willfulness. I have selected a corps of trusted guards to watch her movements so you need not bother."

He gave Eryk a blank stare. Why in blazes had he not been told of these *trusted* sentries—he was still captain of the guard, after all—and where the devil had they been when she'd nearly slipped away just now? He swallowed both questions.

A sudden thought struck him. Oliwia was like a beautiful, lively horse being handed to a master intent on spurring it into submission. For the first time since Jacek had learned of her impending marriage, a sliver of compassion surfaced from the scattered bits of his heart. Reminding himself she'd visited this upon herself, he buried the sentiment deep down.

Jacek prepared the garrison for the gala during the day and drank in taverns at night, circumventing the burgeoning revelry at the castle. In Henryk-like fashion, his friend made it his mission to bring Jacek cheer.

"Here! You've earned this!" Henryk banged a glass of wodka before Jacek on a scarred wooden tabletop. They were several miles from Biaska, in a crowded tavern in the town of Łac.

Jacek glanced up at him and smirked as he clutched his tankard of piwo. "Henryk, I do not think—"

"Bah! Lent's nearly over, so drink up." Henryk looked around at their fellow hussars, raising his own glass. "We toast Muscovy's newly elected boy-tsar. To Michał Romanov, may he and his country go to the devil! *Na zdrowie!*" Cheers erupted throughout the overflowing establishment. Henryk swallowed his drink in one gulp and threw his glass to the floor, shattering it.

Jacek shook his head, then threw back the vessel's contents before smashing it.

"Another!" barked Henryk.

Tavern maids sprang toward the table with smiles and another round. Henryk leered at them all. One let out a loud giggle when he grabbed her backside, and he winked at Jacek. "See what you're missing?"

Jacek tried to ignore him, but Henryk plopped down and elbowed him. "Drink!"

"I've had enough. Besides, it tastes like goat piss." Jacek pointed to a fresh glass. "Give it to Stefan. He *likes* this shit."

Henryk sighed in exasperation. "Jacek, the wedding is but a few days away. Goat piss or not, I advise you start drinking now and not stop till it's over. You're going to need it, my friend. Every last drop." Henryk brightened. "Besides, the more you have, the better it tastes."

He picked up the cup, waved it under Jacek's nose, set it down, and walked away. Jacek nursed his piwo as the crowd grew louder and bawdier. Soon Henryk wove his way back, his arms around two tavern maids. One looked familiar and caught Jacek's attention. She was rather pretty.

"One for me, and one for you," Henryk announced. The familiar one sat beside Jacek, squeezing close. She lifted his arm and draped it over her shoulders so his fingers brushed the top of her breast.

"Hello, Captain," she cooed.

He looked down his nose at her. "Where have I seen you before?"

THE HEART OF A HUSSAR

She giggled. "I gave you my garter before you rode out last year. I thought you might have sought me out to return it. Do you keep it still?"

He hastily reclaimed his arm.

"You said it was to remember our friendship, but I don't even know you." His voice dripped with indignation.

Undaunted, she slipped her hand under the table, slithered it beneath the hem of his żupan, and boldly stroked his wool-clad inner thigh. Leaning in close, she breathed in his ear, "You can get to know me now." She licked his earlobe.

Cheeks flaring, he knotted his brows together, grabbed her hand, and dropped it in her lap. Her eyes widened, then narrowed, and her lips drew together in a grimace. She shoved his chest with both hands. "How dare you!"

The place hushed, all heads turning to them.

He stood abruptly. "How dare *you*! I never asked for your damn—"

Something hard whacked the back of his head, and pain exploded in his skull. He blinked rapidly but saw only bright bursts before him. A pair of beefy hands hooked him under the armpits and hauled him off the bench, and a ruckus broke out all around him. People shouting, wood cracking, crockery smashing.

Blurry-eyed, he grasped the hands holding him and twisted. A man grunted and slammed into his back, jarring the needles stabbing Jacek's head. Jacek roared and cursed, digging his heels in for purchase, hauling himself upright. While he struggled with the man behind him, his world came into focus. And what a riotous scene it was. Fists and objects flew. Bodies grappled and rolled. Blood and drink ran down faces, ears, arms.

Jacek slipped. His combatant hauled him back down and cinched his arm about Jacek's neck, choking him as he spewed rules of chivalric behavior. He clawed the man's arm. Someone grabbed his ankles, and he kicked out viciously, connecting his metal boot heel with soft tissue. A man groaned, doubled over, and rolled away. The man he fought eased up, and Jacek dragged air into his lungs, bellowing a curse. The man tightened his hold once more and began pummeling the back of Jacek's head. Jacek pulled his dagger from his belt and jabbed it into the man's forearm. The man fell away with an angry yowl.

Bounding to his feet in a crouch, rasping in breaths, Jacek swept the dagger in front of him. A boot connected with his wrist and sent the blade flying. White-hot pain radiated from wrist to shoulder, numbing his arm. He stumbled after the knife, but it was grabbed up by a man whose back was to him. The man turned partway, revealing his profile just before he pulled up a hood. He looked familiar.

Jacek poised to vault himself at the thief when he was slammed face-first to the floor. His breath rushed out of him in one big *whoosh!* Gasping, he pulled himself upright and scanned the ruined tavern. The man with his dagger was gone. The fight was mostly over, the sounds of destruction giving way to groans, grunts, and retching.

Henryk wrenched his arm, marshaling him away. They rushed outside, and Jacek dragged in cool night air. Reins were stuffed into his injured hand, making him wince.

"My dagger!" he yelled.

"To hell with your dagger! Let's go!"

He began to protest that he'd had it since he was a boy, but he bit back his words and mounted, falling in line with the rest of his companions. They rode a few miles through dark, deserted countryside and pulled up before a dilapidated house. As they dismounted, Jacek's eyes flicked over the building. "Is this wise?"

Henryk clapped him on the back, and pain shuddered to his aching head and his tender wrist. "A bordello is the perfect place to end the evening! Try not to start another brawl, eh, Jacek? At least not till we're done."

"I didn't start it. Whoever bashed my head in started it." Jacek reached up to his scalp and flinched as his fingers roved over an oval lump.

He followed his troop inside a dimly lit, wood-walled salon scattered with tables for cards and drinking, shabby chaises and armchairs for appraising, and alcoves for carrying an encounter beyond appraisal. Above the parlor was a railed gallery surrounded by doorways. Some were covered by tattered curtains, others by solid doors, while a few yawned open. Judging by the sounds, every room was in use.

They sat down at a warped table with cups of wodka and several prostitutes. Before long, Jacek's companions drifted upstairs with the whores, leaving just him and Henryk.

"This place is in the middle of the wood. How the devil did you discover it?" Jacek asked.

Henryk laughed. "I know them all! What in blazes made you shout at that girl, anyway?"

THE HEART OF A HUSSAR

"She ... Never mind," Jacek grumbled.

"For Christ's sake, Jacek! *You* may not enjoy a barmaid on each knee anymore, but don't ruin *my* chances with them!" Henryk chuckled and eyed two women in bedraggled dressing gowns descending the narrow, creaky stairs.

"Then stop throwing them in my lap." Jacek fidgeted with his empty scabbard.

"How'd you lose it?"

He shook his head and abruptly stopped. It ached like the devil. "A man picked it up. He was there one minute, gone the next. He looked familiar, but I couldn't place him."

Henryk glanced over his shoulder at the two women now leaning against a worn bar. He wiggled his eyebrows and raised his cup at them. "Everybody's familiar in a tavern."

Jacek grunted and downed his wodka. "Jesus! This stuff is worse than the last place. It tastes like goat piss watered down with dog piss."

The two women sashayed to their table. Henryk opened his arms, and one made herself at home on his lap. The other, a blond, set down a tray of drinks. Henryk looked her up and down and winked at Jacek. Jacek grabbed a cup, threw it back, and wiped his hand across his mouth before reaching for another.

He awoke on his back, his head pounding mercilessly. Only one eye worked; the other seemed glued shut. As he roved the eye around, he couldn't place where he was. Blurry, wan light shone in the shape of a frame. As it came into focus, he realized he looked at a window covered in oilskin with moonlight leaking around its edges.

He brought his hand up to his forehead and let out a groan. Something huddled against him, pillowy and warm, then shifted with a small squeak. Definitely feminine. Taking inventory, he realized he was clad in shirt and trousers under a threadbare blanket.

Snapping the second eye open, he looked around a tattered room with a few rough pieces of furniture—a table, a chair, a trunk, a frayed bit of fabric tacked to a wooden wall. Embers smoldered in a sooty hearth. The place reeked of tallow, cologne, stale liquor, and vomit. He glanced at the body beside him. A fleshy bare back and tousled blond hair.

Jesus Christ and all the saints!

Gingerly, he lifted himself from a cot barely big enough to contain the woman in it and swayed a moment, woozy. His belongings were heaped on the chair. He pulled on his boots hurriedly. As he was shrugging on his żupan, the woman stirred. He grabbed up belt and sabre and tossed a few coins on the tabletop.

"Leaving so soon, love?"

Damn!

He turned, recognizing the woman who'd brought the drinks. She sat up, and the blanket slipped to her waist, exposing surprisingly small breasts when taken in with the rest of her. Unabashed, she grinned at him.

"I wouldn't want you to feel cheated, m'lord. I can oblige you proper now."

Puzzled, he stared at her.

She shrugged. "You and your friends had a grand party. I brought you up with me. Tired, you said you was, so I put you to bed. I tried waking you up several times, but you wouldn't have none of it. Now you're rested up, though …" She gave him a cheeky smile.

Relief began unbunching his muscles. "Nothing happened?"

She shook her head. Curls on one side bobbed. The hair on the other side was plastered against her head like a disordered nest.

"You see what I mean about cheating you." She raised her chin at the tabletop where the coins glinted.

He flapped a hand at her. "Keep it. You shared your bed. You should be paid for the trouble."

Chemise to hand, she stood, stark naked, and walked toward him. "You should get what you paid for, love. I don't mind. You're much nicer looking than what I usually get. Cleaner too."

He thought something crawled up his back and checked the urge to scratch himself. "There's no need." When he glanced down, he noticed a dark round spot resembling a button between her breasts. She shrugged and pulled on the chemise.

"What's your name?" He surprised himself.

THE HEART OF A HUSSAR

She helped fasten his żupan, a sly expression on her face. "Gryzelda. Going to ask for me next time, love? You won't be sorry." He'd thought she was older than he, but on closer inspection, he reckoned she was no more than eighteen.

"Next time." Moving stiffly, he added another coin to the pile.

"Aw, putting down a deposit, are you?" she trilled. "We'll have a grand time, love. Come see me soon." She patted his chest and winked.

He lurched from the room, down the rickety stairs, and out the door into the waning night. In the barn, Gwiazda stood among a number of familiar horses while a lad sat on an upturned bucket. When he saw Jacek, he sprang up.

"Everything is as you left it, m'lord. Shall I saddle him for you?"

Jacek raked his eyes over the horse's trappings; all seemed to be in order. "Get them all saddled. My companions and I are leaving." He flipped a coin into the boy's cupped hands.

Soon they were all mounted, his lord-brothers grumbling over the indelicate way he'd rousted them. Despite his thundering head, aching wrist, and queasy stomach, he broke into a gallop, leaving the grubby place behind. The stench, however, followed him doggedly.

Several days later, Jacek entered Eryk's solar. "You wished to see me, my lord?" A small mink-faced man clad in a black żupan stood.

"Jacek, this is Witold Bilicki, Pan Zebrzydowski's deputy starosta. He's on an errand from Łac and has some questions. Deputy Bilicki, my porucznik and second, Captain Jacek Dąbrowski."

After abridged pleasantries, they sat. Bilicki faced Jacek.

"Captain Dąbrowski, I understand you accompanied your men to the tavern in Łac two nights ago."

Jacek confirmed the statement.

"And that you had a row with one of the tavern maids," Bilicki said evenly.

"It wasn't a row."

Bilicki peered at Jacek over wire-rimmed spectacles straddling a thin nose. "What would you call it?"

"She was a bit too familiar, and I took exception."

"Familiar with whom?"

"Me."

Bilicki stared at him. "I understand she was attractive. You don't enjoy attractive women flirting with you, Captain?"

"What do you mean 'was' attractive?" Jacek darted his eyes to Eryk, who sat impassively, his fingers steepled against his chin, gaze fixed on Bilicki.

Wordlessly, Bilicki reached into a satchel at his feet and brought out an object wrapped in wool. He unwrapped it and held it out to Jacek.

"My dagger!" Jacek cried. "Where did you find it?" Dread suddenly prickled his spine.

"How do you know it's yours, Captain?"

Jacek pointed to a small mark on the butt. "Those are my initials. My father had them engraved when he gave it to me."

Eryk straightened, drawing both men's eyes to him. "Perhaps it's time you told Pan Dąbrowski why you're here."

Bilicki stowed the dagger and gave Jacek a hard look. "The maid you argued with was found dead in the stables. Her throat and …" Bilicki paused and pressed a cloth against his mouth. "She was butchered. Your bloodied knife was beside the body."

Jacek leapt up. "*What?* I had nothing to do with it! Someone stole my knife during the scuffle. She was alive when I left." He turned to Eryk, who merely blinked.

"Witnesses have confirmed that, but you could have returned. She wasn't found until first light."

Jacek felt a small rush of relief. "I didn't return, and I can prove it." He sat back down. "I was at a brothel the rest of that night."

Bilicki's head snapped up. "Which brothel?"

"I don't know. It was my first time there."

"What did you do there?"

"It's a whorehouse! What do you think I did? The girl will vouch for me."

"Do you remember her name?"

Jacek exhaled noisily and looked at the ceiling, biting back his frustration. "Gert … Gracja … Gryzelda!"

THE HEART OF A HUSSAR

Bilicki's black eyes seemed to sharpen. The man reached into his satchel, extracted a piece of paper, scanned it, and tucked it away.

Bilicki continued. "Can you describe her?"

"Chubby. Blond. Young."

"Any unusual characteristics?"

Small tits, Jacek refrained from adding, but it sparked a thought. "A large mole here." He pointed to the center of his chest.

The room was quiet for several beats. "I'm afraid she won't be able to help you, Captain. You see, she was found strangled in her room that same morning."

The blood in Jacek's veins turned to ice. His stomach rolled when he thought of the pitiful girl.

"For the last year, prostitutes and tavern maids have been turning up dead northeast of Sandomierz, murdered just like this young woman from Łac." Bilicki directed his bland comment to Eryk. "Their shoes are always missing. It's curious, yes? It would be interesting to inspect your captain's quarters. I'd also like to know his whereabouts the last twelve months."

Jacek felt a band tightening about his neck. "What about the stable lad at the brothel? He saw me leave."

"What lad? Perhaps you'd like to accompany me, and we'll find him together," Bilicki offered.

Eryk stood abruptly, fisting his hands on his desk. "He's answered your questions. He'll not go anywhere with you, nor will you inspect his quarters. He's szlachta and therefore untouchable until you've a decision from a court of law. If you believe him guilty, get your decision, *then* come see me. Until then, you will not enter my castle again," Eryk growled.

Bilicki repositioned his glasses, grabbed his satchel, stood, and bowed. "Of course, my lord."

Once he'd left, Eryk turned to Jacek. "A strange coincidence, yes? These other murders and your two women?"

Jacek gripped his armrests. "They weren't my women."

Eryk arched a dark eyebrow. "Nonetheless, Bilicki believes it so, *and* he believes you're involved. 'Tis understandable. Look at the similarities: all harlots, same area, no shoes, all horribly butchered."

"Not the prostitute," corrected Jacek.

"But her connection to the other wench is *you*. Bilicki no doubt supposes she saw some damning evidence, or you said too much while you were clipping her, and you killed her to cover your tracks."

"Suppose the real killer is the one I spotted in the tavern snatching my knife, and he followed me and committed these murders to make it appear I am the guilty one?"

"To what purpose?"

"Revenge? Hatred? Amusement? He would not be the first to wish me harm."

Eryk nodded. "Possibly."

A fresh worry popped into Jacek's head. "Surely you do not think me responsible, do you?"

Eryk gave him a hard look. "It doesn't matter what I think. These murders occurred outside my jurisdiction."

But it does matter—to me!

Eryk continued, his voice even but for a hint of frost. "Your service, however, *is* within my jurisdiction. I've a plan which will serve us both."

Stuffing away his disquiet over his lord's demeanor—and lack of faith—Jacek squared his shoulders. "My lord?"

Eryk pursed his lips. "I've need of someone capable to fortify Silnyród. I can think of none better than you, so you will take a detachment and leave immediately after the wedding."

Jacek clamped his jaw to prevent his mouth dropping open. "How long am I to remain?"

Eryk shrugged. "For the remainder of your service to me. I will name Henryk your placeholder here, your *namiestnik*. In the event you return to Biaska, the position will still be yours."

Merciful God, he's exiling me to the border! How can he believe I had anything to do with—

"Jacek, this move may seem like a punishment, but it's for the best. I trust no one else for this mission as I do you, and it will separate you from Bilicki and his suspicions. As recompense, I will petition the king on your behalf and see you get your land when your turn with me is done. But I require an oath from you."

Jacek sat rigid, staring dumbly at the lord to whom he'd dedicated his fealty these last nine years.

THE HEART OF A HUSSAR

"In exchange for my patronage," Eryk continued, "you will swear that should anything happen to me, you will return and safeguard Oliwia and any children she bears me."

Though all manner of thoughts skittered through his head, Jacek replied promptly, "I vow it."

"Furthermore, while you remain here, you will stay away from her."

Jacek had concealed his uneasiness in Eryk's company since his return, but something unidentifiable had been building. It had just crystallized.

He knows.

CHAPTER 35

She was in a Wreath and Comes in a Cap

The night is so fine, the moon is so bright, that one might carry off another man's wife~Polish proverb

Lord Eryk Krezowski's wedding drew guests from every corner of the county. Vivid flags in an array of bold colors flapped proudly from the gates and battlements, and the castle grounds were awash in a festival-like atmosphere. The castle's limestone walls radiated an ethereal glow.

Busy folk careened around one another in disarray while the kitchens overflowed with people and food. The great hall had been scrubbed, and the lush tapestries had been beaten clean, renewing their vibrant threads. Chairs and tables were polished, tableware and utensils burnished. Hothouse herbs and greens adorned tables, and garlands hung throughout the huge chamber.

Belying her anxiousness, Oliwia acted the perfect chamberlain, accommodating guests as they appeared. Among them was Lady Lidia Jankowska, chosen by Eryk to serve as Oliwia's maid of honor, and her awkward cousin Patka as bridesmaid. When Eryk's sisters, their families, and entourages arrived, the women embraced their brother joyfully, then Oliwia as if she were one of them. Their chatter swept her away.

THE HEART OF A HUSSAR

"We will supervise the baking of the *kołacz*. Your wedding bread will be flawless, sister! Oh! And we will help with the blessings and the unveiling, of course."

Oliwia's heart should have rejoiced with this newfound family. Instead, it constricted with the wicked wish Jacek were beside her, and they greeted *his* sisters.

While her exterior façade was one of unflappable grace, inside, her roiling emotions devoured her bite by bite. The lovely gown and accoutrements did nothing to lift her. In fact, they sapped her spirit further, for they embodied the ties that would soon leash her. She girded herself with reminders she did this for Filip and Jacek; the union would launch the former into a world he would otherwise never reach and protect the latter from being expelled from it.

Eryk plied her with words of love, but she wanted none of it. When he reached for her, she recoiled. When he kissed her, she froze. His growing frustration was palpable. She would have to unwind herself somehow, for soon he would own her.

As she rounded into the kitchen on the eve of the wedding, she heard a string of very unladylike expletives. She stopped and peeked around the corner. With hands on hips, Maria, Eryk's eldest sister, stood beside the younger sister, Sylwia, and was raining her wrath upon a harmless golden pastry while Beata and Lidia looked on.

"'Tis the second to crack, Beata! What is wrong?" Maria wailed.

Oliwia entered, and four sets of startled eyes darted to her. Beata grabbed the steaming bread and tucked it behind her, her arms moving as she juggled it.

"Beata, put it down lest you burn yourself," Oliwia said. For the first time since she'd known her, Beata reddened—a sizeable feat, considering the cook worked among steaming pots and banked stoves the day long.

"May I see it?" Oliwia might as well have asked to flay Maria alive.

Brows tightly knotted, Maria flapped her hand wildly. "'Tis only a small crack, I assure you, caused by my clumsy handling." Maria then turned to Lidia. "Time to begin the maiden evening, yes? Take her from here so we may finish our baking."

Slipping her arm through Oliwia's, Lidia led her away. "Come, Lady Oliwia. We will find Patka and begin making your maiden wreath, yes? The last one you shall wear. I brought myrtle from my own garden, and Patka has some rue from her hothouse. We will make you a splendid headdress."

As they left the kitchen, Oliwia tried to chase the sight of the failed bread from her mind. If she could forget it, perhaps the omen would not bear out.

Cracked bread, cracked marriage.

The ceremony was a blur. Images flashed through Oliwia's mind: the women cooing as they dressed her and placed the wreath upon her head; Eryk's sisters blessing them; people cheering as they climbed aboard the carriage headed for the church; oats and wheat grains raining from the sky; Filip's colossal smile; a forest of fluttering hussar wings; "Te Deum" being sung by a choir; her trembling knees at the altar; Father Augustyn's kind, pudding face as he recited the vows; Eryk sliding a sapphire-and-diamond ring on her finger; flickering candles on the altar, and gasps when Eryk's inexplicably went out.

Now she and Eryk stood just inside the great hall before his sisters, their husbands, Filip, and Father Augustyn. Maria was talking, holding something up. Oliwia felt heavy-limbed, dazed, as if she might fold over and sleep at any moment. Maria and Filip presented them with bread dipped in salt while Father Augustyn blessed it and spoke of prosperity and bitterness. Oliwia nibbled at it, but it tasted like ashes in her mouth, so she choked it down with wine. Soon they were ushered toward raucous wedding guests eager to begin feasting.

Oliwia had barely eaten when, many hours later, she was escorted to a seat. As guests gathered round, Eryk, his brothers-in-law, Jacek, Henryk, and other familiar male faces stood in a row before her. She stared straight ahead, not daring to look at Jacek's large frame crowding a corner of her eye. Beside her, Lidia and Patka removed the wreath; she was no longer a maiden. Filip's small fingers unwound her braids, tugging out the ribbons. He laughed while the women told him what to do, urging him on with cheery chatter. Oliwia felt as though she existed on a different plane than the one the revelers occupied.

THE HEART OF A HUSSAR

Her hair loose, Filip pecked her cheek and whispered, "Are you ready, Liwi?" She couldn't talk, couldn't breathe. Only nod. She swore a belt had been wound round her chest and was being cinched tighter and tighter. Tears burned her throat and stung her eyes. A shearing sound, tugging, then lightness as her brother cut her hair away. Around her silence shimmered, punctuated by quiet gasps. She dared not look at the tresses drifting to the floor.

Filip's small hand patted her shoulder, then Maria placed the czepek on her head and pulled her up. She had become a married woman. With candles in their hands, the women presented her to the guests and sang:

"Everyone take a look, she was in a wreath and comes in a cap."

Then they danced with her and turned her over to Eryk. He gripped her hand and kissed her cheek. "You are a beautiful bride."

When their dance was finished, he invited Maria's husband, Teodor, to dance with Oliwia, followed by the rest of the menfolk. The people, the noise, the color all dissolved together like spilled pots of dye in the rain.

Jacek's men had done everything he could wish of them. They had ridden proudly, in perfect time with one another, and they had sparkled from wing to spur as they escorted the wedding party's carriages to and from the church. When the celebrating began, words such as "Magnificent!" "Breathtaking!" "Amazing!" buzzed in his ears. The revelers spoke of the glorious Biaska banner, and it brought him a small inner smile and a large slice of pride. He sorely needed both.

Twilight turned to night, and the great hall and castle yards overflowed with merry guests lost in eating and rejoicing. Jacek had also lost himself, but not in rejoicing, though he mimicked the part. Copious amounts of piwo, mead, and wine had passed through his gullet. Weaving his way through the celebrants, he avoided any line of sight to the wedding table. Instead, he grabbed a cup of something and threw it back with a rumbling *"Na zdrowie!"* directed at no one in particular.

Despite the drink, he couldn't block out the fact he must appear before the happy couple with his blessings. But first, another dance and more fortification. He gulped the wine offered him by yet another guest eager to congratulate him on the show.

"Ah! The *good* wine!" Jacek exclaimed, garnering a refill.

The liquid slid down his throat. Maybe it would dissolve some of the bitterness moldering in the pit of his empty stomach.

He scanned a cluster of women. One gave him a wily smile, and he strode to her.

"Lady Lidia!" he cried, then looked around. "Is your brother here?"

"Alas, Pan Jacek, he was unable to come."

"Pity. But then, I'm not here to dance with *him*." He winked at her and led her to the dance floor.

After the dance, she asked him to take her for a garden stroll, and he obliged her, relieved to escape the frivolity. A deep velvet sky was sprayed with shimmering stars.

Lidia took his proffered arm and clung to it possessively. "The bride is lovely, yes?"

Jacek nodded. He had spent the day trying *not* to look at the bride and congratulated himself on his fairly even success.

"He seems quite taken with her. Did you see how he looks at her?"

Jacek shook his head.

"They make a handsome couple. I expect they'll be quite happy," Lidia said.

"I expect so." A twinge of sadness threatened to undo him. *Think of anything else.*

They'd come to the darkened corner, and Jacek pulled Lidia into the deserted shadows with him. He drew her into his arms, and she slid her hands to his shoulders. Angling her head, she met his lips partway. As he kissed her, he warred with thoughts of Eryk kissing Oliwia and what they would soon do together in their wedding chamber.

Lidia responded eagerly, but it was all wrong. Perhaps he hadn't imbibed enough. He wanted to lose himself with her, but his mind remained fixed on how Oliwia had felt when he'd held her against him, how she had tasted when he'd kissed her, and the fire he'd fleetingly discovered smoldering inside her. Did the same depth of passion blaze in her for Eryk?

Jacek broke the kiss. Lidia gave him a puzzled look. He shook his head to dispel the images flashing through his mind.

She caressed the side of his face. "Are you unwell?"

THE HEART OF A HUSSAR

He pulled her hands away. "I, uh, had best escort you back." He offered her a stiff arm and concentrated on slowing his gait lest he bolt. When he delivered her inside the noisy hall, he abruptly excused himself and went in search of a bracer. Just then Eryk beckoned him, so he pivoted toward the dais and drew in an enormous breath.

Eryk was beaming. Beside him, however, Oliwia looked just as glum as she had during the excruciating *oczepiny*. It had taken all of Jacek's might to stand beside Eryk during the capping ceremony.

"I was beginning to think we'd already lost you to a bevy of lovely ladies," Eryk said with a broad smile.

Jacek winced inside. "I apologize for the delay, my lord. I have been attending to duty."

Oliwia kept her eyes cast down while Jacek heaped pretty words and blessed wishes on them both. When he had concluded his rehearsed, exceedingly polite speech and believed escape was imminent, Eryk offered him Oliwia's hand.

"I've not yet seen you dance with my bride, and you've but a few chances remaining before the final dance."

Startled, Jacek froze in his boots. Oliwia raised her eyes to him, her grim expression mirroring his thoughts. It was the last thing either of them wanted to do.

Oliwia began to protest. "My lord—"

"Come, both of you! I wish to see you together." Eryk's lips twitched as if he held back a smirk.

Jacek squelched an overpowering urge to pound the smirk into Eryk's teeth. Instead, he numbly extended his hand and helped Oliwia to her feet. She didn't look at him, merely glanced at his chin when she needed to gauge her steps. Eryk's eyes tracked them, and they danced woodenly, awkwardly. It was less of a reel than it was a series of cumbersome steps. The worst of it came when they twirled with their arms about each other, or danced face-to-face, his arm wrapped around her and her hand on his shoulder. Her fragrance invaded his senses, tormenting him. The nearness was unbearable.

Partway through the dance, the drink seized him, and he surrendered to the impulse to fasten his eyes on her. *The devil piss on you, Eryk!* Teal flecks reflected in her luminous eyes. Normally a clear, crystal blue, today their grayness matched the dress. He took in the wedding cap covering what remained of her hair. On her, the czepek was surprisingly fetching, highlighting her delicate cheekbones and the fine curve of her ivory face. The ever-present silver chain lay against her chest and plunged under her gown, reminding him of a time long ago when she had been a cheeky girl in his care.

For not the first time, he considered resorting to bride-stealing.

Oliwia kept her eyes hooded lest she look into Jacek's and see his contempt; or worse, lest she give herself away under Eryk's vigilance. She felt Jacek's eyes boring into her and a stain creeping up her neck, no doubt shining like a beacon against the silver of her dress.

Don't look at me like that!
Dear God, when will this dance be over?

As if in answer, the reel came to an end, but her distress merely compounded when Eryk materialized. "Last dance. I will take my wife now."

Jacek nodded, then melted into a throng of guests who gathered and applauded Oliwia and Eryk as they danced. When the music stopped, the groomsmen appeared beside them. Teodor faced the crowd and held up his hands.

"Lord Eryk and Lady Oliwia thank you all for being here and for witnessing their sacred vows before God this day," he said stridently. "But my brother is impatient to begin wedded life with his beautiful bride—and who can blame him?—which is why—" He was interrupted by loud laughter and bawdy remarks. Oliwia's stomach turned over. "Which is why the oczepiny has taken place the same day as the ceremony." Now guests booed good-naturedly. "But fear not! Simply because the capping is done does not mean the celebrating ends *this* time. The bridegroom, your most generous host, has asked that you carry on your revelry after he and his lady take their leave."

Cheers erupted.

The bridal party escorted Oliwia and Eryk away from the celebration, lewd comments and blessings chasing them up the stairs. Oliwia's legs shook as though she climbed to the gallows. Teodor preceded the small group to Eryk's bedchamber, tonight recast as the bridal chamber.

Teodor stepped through the door and inspected the room. The rest of the party, including Filip, filed in and voiced their approval. Groups of candles burned and shed amber pools of light from different corners of the room. The fire had just been stoked, and the blaze glowed warmly from the hearth. The fragrance of burning wood mixed with sweet beeswax floated on the air. A tray of cheeses, fruit, and fresh bread stood on the table before the hearth, together with a jug of Hungarian wine and a pair of gleaming silver goblets encrusted in colorful gemstones.

Oliwia darted a look at the bed. The covers had been turned down, revealing an expanse of white linen under the high wooden canopy.

To her horror, Teodor stretched out on the bed and grinned. "I am simply warming it up, my dear Oliwia." The women clambered up and took turns jumping upon it, fluffing the pillows with shrieks of laughter. Filip joined them. From the courtyard below came hoots and ribald serenades.

Teodor cleared everyone, including himself, from the wedding chamber. Oliwia was guided by her attendants to Katarzyna's old chamber, where they removed her wedding garments and dressed her in a sumptuously embroidered white nightdress and lapis silk dressing gown. Flustered by the preparations, she continually twitched and reached for hair she could no longer twist, disquieting her further. After they had dabbed her in fragrance and brushed the tresses skimming her shoulders, they led her down the connecting passage to her husband's door with suppressed giggles.

The lamb had just been delivered for slaughter.

Too nervous to sit or stand, Eryk had been pacing the room, his green dressing gown billowing around him as he moved. What he had cleverly hidden was that he had experienced all manner of jitters today as he'd considered his young, voluptuous wife entering his chamber tonight. Those thoughts were interspersed with ones of his late wife.

For more than a decade, Katarzyna had been the only woman he'd bedded here. Would thoughts of her seep in and lie between him and Oliwia? Would he see Katarzyna's face when he took Oliwia? Amid the waves in his belly were inescapable feelings of betrayal and guilt—his betrayal of his beloved Kasia and the guilt it brought.

Now Oliwia stood in the doorway, on the brink of entering his chamber. The light behind her obscured her face, and he walked slowly toward her with his hand extended. As he drew near and she came into view, he quietly sucked in a breath.

"Come, my love," he said gently.

He left behind all thought of his late wife at the door's threshold.

Oliwia stood in the doorway as Eryk came toward her, looking everywhere but at him. Everything was perfect.

Except she faced the wrong man.

He guided her to the fire and poured them each a cup of wine. Her hands shook. She sat and quickly quaffed the contents of her goblet, fixing her eyes on the dancing flames. Soon she swallowed two more. Each went down easier than the one preceding it and enveloped her in a fuzzy sort of softness. Eryk took the empty vessel from her and placed it on the table before lifting her to her feet and into his lap.

"You continually twist the ring. Is it uncomfortable, my love?"

"I, ah, I am simply not used to it." She twirled it again before she could stop herself. The skin beneath the ring burned, feeling as though it blistered. "The wine is delicious. Might I have more?"

He gave her an indulgent smile. "I know you're nervous, Oliwia, but I would prefer it if you were conscious."

Wrapping her gently in his arms, he pressed soft, lingering kisses along her throat.

"You smell wonderful," he mumbled against her skin. "And you taste wonderful too."

Sitting on his legs woodenly, she willed herself to relax. The wine was not as helpful as she'd hoped. She squeezed her eyes shut and pressed her

THE HEART OF A HUSSAR

lips tight; her chin hovered above his head, where he couldn't see her taut face.

Pretend.

"You are so beautiful," he whispered against her ear.

He ran a hand through her loose hair. Tugging a fistful, he pulled her head back so she could do naught but look at him.

"You are my wife now, Oliwia, and I promise I will take good care of you."

The sound of men singing drifted from below. She sent a silent prayer heavenward.

When Jacek had relinquished Oliwia to Eryk, he'd spurred a quick path out of the great hall to the stables, where he groomed Jarosława, crooning to her to shut out the singing from the courtyard.

"I cannot do it," he said to his mare as he worked. "If I were going to steal her, I should have done so long before now. Besides, she does not want me, and the church would never recognize the union if she were unwilling."

When the vulgar regales at last died down, he left the stables and found Henryk and his lord-brothers spilling down the forestairs.

"Ah! Look what the dogs dragged in," Henryk hollered.

"Why are you out here?" asked Jacek.

"We were spurned by the fair ladies for being too drunk. Imagine! So we shall hold our own celebration." He threw his arm around Jacek's shoulders, pulling him away, and shoved a full bottle in his hand. He lowered his voice. "You look as though you could use this, my friend."

Jacek tilted the wodka to his lips.

"I will miss you—and Lesław," Henryk said with a note of soberness.

"We leave for Silnyród two days hence. The day after I turn twenty-five."

Henryk nodded. "Well, you'll finally have what you've always wanted. Your own command and soon your own estate, even if it is far from home."

Not everything I've always wanted.

Jacek gulped down more wodka. "Podolia will be my home now. And you, Henryk, are the namiestnik—you are in charge here."

Their companions shouted toasts, clinked bottles, and began singing. Henryk smiled and shook his head. "I vow I will look after Filip—and Oliwia."

Jacek looked him in the eyes. "For Filip, I thank you. On her account, I care not."

In a murky stand of woods outside a mean village in Sandomierz, Romek submerged his naked body in the freezing stream and scratched blood from his skin and hair with dirty fingernails. Pulling his bundled clothes from a tree branch, he dried himself and dressed. His eyes continually flicked to the glistening heap propped against a tree trunk, and he felt warm satisfaction ooze through him. Tonight, he'd celebrated Lord Krezowski's wedding in his own way. His urges should have been sated since his foray into Łac—an unguarded risk he hadn't been able to resist when he'd witnessed Dąbrowski argue with the tavern bitch—but strangling the second whore had left a surprisingly gaping void. He so preferred using the blade.

He chuckled to himself when he considered the irony that he and Dąbrowski shared a commonality. He hated women putting their hands on him too. Hopefully, it would take Dąbrowski a long while to wriggle out of his trap, if he even could.

Humming, Romek painstakingly cleaned his knife with sand and water. He smiled, reliving his latest victim's last moments: her terrified pleas for her worthless life, her promises to give him anything, her wide-eyed horror when she realized she had nothing he wanted. What a merry chase she'd given him after he'd taken her shoes and given her a head start. She'd muffled her panting and footfalls better than any of the others had.

He patted his saddlebag where her shoes were stowed, then picked up a burlap sack that dribbled a bit when he tied it to his pommel. With one last longing glance over his shoulder, he rode away. Five more miles and he'd reach the hog pen and toss in the bag. They'd eat well tonight. A month, maybe two would pass before the spark flared and consumed him again. The only consolation from Bella's passing was he need no longer snuff it out. In the meantime, no one suspected. He'd been far too clever for the witless fools.

Romek continued riding and finally pulled up at an abandoned, decrepit cottage on the outskirts of Biaska. His heart leapt when he saw the familiar horse, and he hurriedly dismounted. Holding his excitement in check, he slowed his steps and pushed open the flaking, splintered door.

Moldering dampness and decay hung thick in the air. His eyes began adjusting to the gloom. "My lord?"

A broad-shouldered form moved from a shuttered window, exposing a lit candle.

"Romek. Well met. The celebrating continues, so I haven't much time, but here is the installment. I daresay I am pleased with the army's progress." The man dropped a hefty leather pouch in Romek's open palm.

"With my new lieutenants in place," Romek said, "the training has improved tenfold. And more join our numbers as they hear of the opportunity from their brethren."

The man clapped him on the shoulder. "Keep up the good work." Romek could not stifle his smile.

The man brushed past him and turned in the doorway, chuckling. "Lord Krezowski was jubilant as he exchanged vows with his lovely bride and is no doubt enjoying himself in his marriage bed as we speak. I cannot wait to see his expression when I demolish all he holds dear."

"'Twill be sweet indeed, Lord Antonin."

A radiating, dull ache lingered, but she hadn't bled terribly. Eryk had been gentle and considerate, and she didn't fault him. Now she was naked, exposed, and she felt sullied. She folded her arms over her chest to cover her breasts. Had she still the hair, she could have pulled it into place to hide herself. Eryk peeled her arms away and gathered her to his side. As he held her close, her body went rigid, and she fought the urge to shrink away from him. Waiting for what seemed an interminable time, she finally spoke.

"You are likely very tired, my lord. Shall I leave you now?"

He cocked his head and looked at her, then ran his fingers through her hair, pushing it back from her face. "No, Oliwia. You will not leave my bed. You will stay here at my pleasure and go only if I allow it." Smelling of wine, his warm breath brushed her hair and face. It wasn't unpleasant, but it didn't matter. She wished to be anywhere but here.

After he had satisfied himself a second time, Oliwia lay in the dark, tense, waiting for him to drift off. His heavy, rhythmic breathing signaled sleep had finally taken him. She inched away, her back to him, hugging the edge of the mattress and drawing the coverlet tightly over herself, tucking it firmly under her chin. Shame crushed her, the stain on her soul indelible.

Katarzyna, why did you make us promise this?

Oliwia's heart fractured in the dark as she lay in her wedding bed. She wept quietly long into the night while her husband slept blissfully unaware beside her.

Jacek, forgive me.

The hussars sang vociferously and danced with one another in a drunken stumble that became a shoving match and near-brawl. Jacek had no idea how much time had passed when Henryk grabbed him by the shoulder and wagged his eyebrows, a mischievous grin lifting his face.

"We go to Kobietasklep. Stefan says they have some new girls. Come with us and forget your troubles. I'll wager there's at least one dark-haired one you'll fancy among the lot."

Jacek shook his head. "I've had my fill of women."

After they'd left, he stood alone in the courtyard. A breeze ruffled his hair, carrying strains of music and laughter from the great hall. Looking up at the massive stone keep, his heart dropped. The windows of the lord's bedchamber, fully visible at this angle, were dark. Clearly the bride and groom were abed. Though he'd told Henryk he would leave days from now, he couldn't withstand another moment. He would find Marcin; it wasn't too early to pack.

Pulling a glossy shorn lock from his sash, he held it to his nose, inhaling the familiar scent. He brushed the silky mahogany strands along his cheek before stowing it under his żupan, tucked against his heavy heart. Heading for his quarters, he took in the comforting sights that had embodied home for so long, etching each in his memory.

He now trod an unknown path toward a future he'd never foreseen, but he was resolved to shoulder it.

And then he would conquer it.

End of Book 1
To be continued in *A Hussar's Promise*, coming November 2020

Thank you for reading *The Heart of a Hussar*. I hope you enjoyed it as much as I enjoyed writing it.

Reviews are crucial for indie authors, and I would be so grateful if you would leave one on Amazon, BookBub, or GoodReads. It doesn't have to be long to make all the difference.

Thank you so much!

Glossary

Beshmet – outer coat worn by Tatars

Bogurodzica – (Mother of God) Polish knight's hymn before battle, from the Battle of Grunwald in 1410

Bork – (also "börk") a janissary's headgear

Buzdygan *'Booze-de-gun'* – mace, usually wielded by a higher-ranking officer

Cham – a peasant, a lowborn person; calling a Polish nobleman a cham was an insult

Chodzony *'Hode-zoneh'* – early name for polonez, a walking dance and Poland's national dance

Castrum doloris – Latin for "castle of grief;" a decorated structure within a church that shelters a bier and holds candles, flowers, epitaphs, coats of arms, paintings, allegorical statues to honor the deceased

Chorągiew *'Ho-rongev'* – company, banner, usually between 100-200 men

Chorągiew Husarka – a hussar banner or company

Chorąży *'Hoh-ronje-ah'* – a standard bearer; usually a young, promising towarzysz selected by the commander

Commonwealth – short for Polish-Lithuanian Commonwealth; a term that refers to the United Kingdom of Poland and Duchy of Lithuania

Crown – the Kingdom of Poland

Cuirass – metal breast and back plates; armor for the torso

Dalej! – March on!

Elear – a member of a regiment that rode for the adventurer Aleksander Lisowski; also known as "Lisowczycy," meaning lost men, forlorn hope

Ferezeya *'Fair-ah-zay-ah'* – a nobleman's overcoat, worn over a żupan or kontucz; sleeveless and often fur-lined

Gorget – metal neck piece; armor worn at the neck

Hajduk – foot soldier of Hungarian or Turco-Balkan background used by the Polish infantry from the 1570s to the 1630s

Heavy lancers – see husaria

Hetman – general

Husaria *'Hoo-sah-reeah'* – heavy cavalry; Polish winged hussars

Husarski *'Hoo-sahr-ski'* – another word for husaria

Hussar – another word for husaria

Il Tesoro Della Sanita 'The Treasure of Health' – a handbook for healthy living, written by the physician Castore Durante and first published in Rome in 1586; the handbook was printed in many languages and was a popular work found in many a nobleman's home

Karwasz *'Klah-dah-vash'* – arm iron, vambrace. Plural: kawarsze *"klah-dah-vashah"*

Kilij – a Turkish sabre

Kołacz – traditional Polish wedding cake or wedding bread

Kolpak – aka 'calpac;' a man's fur hat

Koncerz *'Kone-sesh'* – a tuck; a thin four-foot blade with a triangular or square cross-section used like a short lance to punch through armor

Kopia – long, hollow lance wielded by a hussar, between 13-20 feet long

Łan – fief; typically 15-30 families per fief

Letter of array – military conscription; a call for a nobleman to fulfill his military duty to the Crown

Mazurka – aka mazurek; an up-tempo Polish folk dance

Muscovites – Russians

Muscovy – Russia

Na slawa! – To glory!

Nadziak *'Nahd-jack'* – war hammer with a hammer head on one side and a claw on the other

Namiestnik *'Nah-mia-sneek'* – placeholder; an officer/lieutenant who fills in while the regular is away

Pacholik *'Pahk-ho-leek'* – a retainer or squire; serves a towarzysz

Pałasz *'Pa-wash'* – a hussar's broadsword

Pallash – see pałasz

Pan – Lord, sir; title for a nobleman

THE HEART OF A HUSSAR

Pancerni – medium cavalry; armored in chain mail
Pancerz – chain mail
Pauldron – shoulder armor
Piwo *'Pee-voh'* – beer, ale
Poczet *'Poe-chets'* – retinue; 2-5 men (servants and retainers) who serve the towarzysz/hussar
Porucznik *'Poh-rootz-neek'* – a commander's second, the lieutenant
Postpolite ruszenie *'Pos-polite roh-shanya'* – noble host, or levy of knights
Ród – clan
Rotmistrz – aka 'rotameister;' commander of a company of towarzysze
Sharovary – baggy trousers
Starosta – mayor, official in charge of security
Strażnik – great guard or field guard (field guards were found on the eastern borders); officer in charge of scouting and troop movement
Szabla Husaria *'Shah-blah hoo-sah-reeah'* – a hussar's sabre; highly valued and prized. Next to the kopia, the favored weapon of a hussar
Szlachcic *'Shlahth-cheets'* – Polish nobleman
Szlachta *'Shlahth-dah'* – Polish nobility
Szlachta cząstkowa *'Shlahth-dah chonse-ko-vah'* – nobility with fractional land ownership
Szlachta zamoża *'Shlahth-dah zah-moja'* – propertied nobility
Szlachcianka *'Shlahth-chiankah'* – noblewoman
Towarzysz *'Toe-vah-jez'* – literally a "companion" in Polish; a hussar; a nobleman of wealth, with his own armor, horses and retinue. Knight class
Towarzysze – plural of towarzysz
Tuleja *'Too-lay-ha'* – a cup or tok mounted on the right side of a hussar's saddle into which he slips the butt end of the kopia; acts as a sleeve
Weller – an early version of the waltz; sixteenth century; scandalous when it first appeared
Winged hussars – heavy hussars; heavy husaria; heavy lancers
Wodka – vodka
Wujek *'Voo-yeck'* – uncle
Żupan *'Jzo-pahn'* – a man's outer garment; resembles a long coat with a high collar; buttons down the front; normally worn over trousers and a shirt

Historical Figures

Batory, Stefan
King of Poland, Prince (or Grand Duke) of Transylvania, elected King of Poland and reigned from 1576 until his death in 1586. Batory was responsible for forming the winged hussars in the iteration for which they became famous.

De la Gardie, Jakob
Commander of the Swedish army at Kłuszyn.

Dunikowski, Samuel
One of the Polish commanders at the Battle of Kłuszyn.

Dmitry (False)
A pair of bad actors who sequentially sought rights to the Muscovite throne by claiming to be the long-lost son of Ivan the Terrible, Tsar of Muscovy. Ivan died in 1584. He left two sons, Feodor, who took the throne, and Dmitry, who was exiled and murdered in 1591. Feodor died in 1598, and Boris Godunov ascended the throne, only to die in 1605.

The First False Dmitry, claiming he had escaped death, appeared in 1604 and was crowned in 1605 after Godunov's death, only to be murdered and his remains fired from a cannon in Red Square. Tsar Wasyl Szujski IV became tsar and was challenged by another False Dmitry who, with an army consisting of Polish adventurers (Aleksander Lisowski among them), Cossacks, and Russian boyars, besieged Moscow in 1609, only to fall back.

Lisowski, Aleksander Józef
A Lithuanian nobleman and soldier who led a konferacja (a legal rebellion) for unpaid wages. He also took part with the rebels against the royalists in the "Zebrzydowski Rokosz" (Zebrzydowski Rebellion) in 1607-1609. Lisowski eventually became the leader of a band of mercenaries that fought on behalf of the Commonwealth. They took their pay in the form

of pillage. Lisowski and his men were opportunistic, often preying on their own countrymen. Because they were skilled, fearsome fighters, the Crown looked the other way. Lisowski's men adopted the name "Lisowczycy," which means lost men, forlorn hope, or chorągiew elearska (company of elears), after his death in 1616. They were eventually hunted down and executed and later officially disbanded by the Sejm (the lower house of Polish Parliament).

Potocki Family
Powerful, influential Polish magnate family. Stefan Potocki was part of the Moldavian Magnate Wars and was defeated with his army July 1612. He later died in Ottoman captivity. Hetman Stanisław Żółkiewski wrote in his memoirs that Jakub Potocki (Castellan of Kamieniec) was ordered by the king to prepare ladders for the assault on Smoleńsk and became one of the first men up on the great fortress's wall before it was breached and taken by the Poles on June 11, 1611.

Szujski, Dymitr
Brother to the tsar, and commander of the Russian army at Kłuszyn. Captured and died in Poland 1613.

Szujski, Tsar Wasyl IV
Tsar of Muscovy from 1606 to 1610. Stanisław Żółkiewski delivered Wasyl IV to the King of Poland in Warsaw after the Battle of Kłuszyn in 1610. Wasyl IV died in Poland two years later.

Vasa, Władysław IV
Son of Zygmunt III, was elected Tsar of Russia July 27, 1610 at the age of fifteen. Because Zygmunt coveted the throne for himself and consequently lost the support of the boyars who elected his son, Prince Władysław never assumed the throne, though he held the title until he relinquished it in 1634. Władysław followed in his father's footsteps and became King of Poland/Grand Duke of Lithuania from 1632 until his death in 1648.

Vasa, Zygmunt III
King of Poland elected in 1587 and reigned until his death in 1632. Zygmunt was born in Sweden to King John III and his wife, Katarzyna Jagiellonka of Poland, while his parents were held captive. He was raised Catholic and remained so throughout his life. He held the title of King of Sweden until 1599 when he was deposed by his uncle, King Charles IX Vasa, though he would not give up his claim to the Swedish throne. In fact,

he went to war with Sweden to reclaim his crown. The Polish-Swedish War would continue intermittently until 1629 (the term "Polish-Swedish Wars" is a broad term that includes a series of wars between the two countries from the sixteenth century until the eighteenth century). Zygmunt III was criticized for his Swedish ambitions at Poland's expense. He was also criticized for warring with Muscovy (the Polish-Muscovite War, also known as the "Dymitriads") during his reign.

King Zygmunt attempted to institute a number of reforms which the Polish nobility (the szlachta) viewed as a threat to their power and their "Golden Freedom." Conflict between the King and nobility led to the Zebrzydowski Rokosz (Zebrzydowski Rebellion).

Zebrzydowski, Mikołaj

A Polish magnate from Sandomierz and the Palatine of Kraków. He led a rebellion of nobles against King Zygmunt III known as the "Zebrzydowski Rokosz" (Zebrzydowski Rebellion) in 1607-1609, in which Aleksander Lisowski also participated on the rebels' side. The rebellion stemmed in part from the king's attempts to expand his power, which the nobility viewed as an erosion of their own power. The rebels were defeated at Guzów by the king's forces and later pardoned without suffering loss of privilege or assets. The conflict was deemed a stalemate, with neither side making any advances. The rebels were unable to wrestle power from the king, and the king was unable to usurp any of the nobility's power over the monarchy.

Żółkiewski, Stanisław

A Polish magnate and diplomat who was lauded as one of Poland's most brilliant generals, best known for victories such as the Battle of Kłuszyn. He served as Crown Field Hetman, and in 1613, the king appointed him Grand Hetman of the Crown, Poland's highest military ranking and a lifetime position. Żółkiewski had an uneasy relationship with the king (many thought he should have been awarded Grand Hetman of the Crown far sooner than 1613 and that the king withheld it from him purposely). Żółkiewski had negotiated an agreement with the Muscovite boyars and entered Moscow in 1611 prepared for King Zygmunt III's son, Prince Władysław IV, to take the throne. The king thwarted this plan, which ultimately lost Poland the opportunity to gain Muscovy's throne. Żółkiewski penned his memoir, *Expedition to Moscow*, explaining events as he experienced them—some say in an attempt to tell his side of the story.

THE HEART OF A HUSSAR

Żółkiewski would continue his brilliant military career engaged in numerous campaigns on the Commonwealth's southern and eastern borders, eventually losing his life at the Battle of Cecora in 1620. He was in his 70s.

Author's Notes

1. The Polish-Lithuanian Commonwealth came about as the result of the Treaty of Lublin, signed in 1569, which united the Kingdom of Poland and the Grand Duchy of Lithuania. The Commonwealth was one of the richest, most powerful, and most populous countries in Europe at the time. It existed until the Third Partition of Poland in 1795.

2. Poland was one the great powers and a center of culture in Eastern and Central Europe for two hundred years. Memories of its former greatness were methodically erased during the Partitions of Poland in the eighteenth century. Russia, Austria, and Prussia carried off Poland's books and treasures and disseminated propaganda that its might and influence had never existed.

3. Golden Freedom, or Golden Liberty, refers to privileges enjoyed by the Polish nobility (the szlachta). It conveyed religious freedom and declared all nobility equal, regardless of rank or status. It also gave the nobility extensive legal rights, including assigned private jurisdiction, protecting them from being arrested or having their property seized without a conviction from a court of law. In addition, it limited the monarchy's power. The szlachta made up the two-chamber legislature/Parliament: an appointive Senate and an elected Sejm. The king was chairman of the Senate. The szlachta filled the legislative seats, wrote the laws (often for their benefit), and elected the king. In short, they wielded a great deal of power. The *Liberum Veto* conveyed the power of veto on a single member so, quite literally, one man could bring voting to a halt.

4. With the advent of the Golden Liberty, formal titles were banned. All noblemen were to refer to one another as "Pan" ("Sir" or "Lord"),

whether they were a lowly noble or a powerful magnate. Loopholes did exist, however. For instance, noblemen who signed the Union of Lublin with their titles were allowed to keep them.

5. Noblemen were granted the right to bear coats of arms. However, coats of arms worked a little differently in the Commonwealth. Noble families adopted those belonging to others, fitting themselves under an "umbrella," if you will. While there were over forty thousand noble families, there existed approximately seven thousand coats of arms (and variations). Thus it wasn't uncommon for two noble families to share the same coat of arms.

6. During the time the novel takes place, Poland was fighting Muscovy, Sweden, and the Ottoman Empire. The conflict with Sweden was a series of intermittent wars that spanned two centuries. King Zygmunt III Vasa was Swedish and had been King of Sweden until his uncle, Charles IX Vasa, who had been ruling in Zygmunt's place, took the crown for himself. Zygmunt was deposed in 1599 but never gave up his claim to the Swedish throne.

   At times, Poland was allied with Sweden against Muscovy, and at other times with Muscovy against Sweden. For instance, Poland and Sweden signed a truce in 1611 that lasted until 1617, when full-on war broke out again between the two countries over, among other things, possession of Livonia and domination over the Baltic Sea.

7. The conflict with Muscovy arose during Russia's Time of Troubles (1598-1613), when that country was in the midst of a leadership crisis. The conflict has several names, including the Dymitriads, the Polish-Muscovite War, the Polish Invasion, and the Polish Intervention. The conflict ran from 1605 to 1618, though Poland's real involvement began in 1609 when Muscovy and Sweden signed a treaty, with Sweden pledging some of its military force to Muscovy. Poland had been seeking to federalize Muscovy and saw this union as a threat. The King of Poland acted, marching on and besieging Smoleńsk with a small army. The Commonwealth would eventually take Smoleńsk in 1611. Poland did take Moscow in 1610, occupying it until 1612. The king's son, Prince Władysław, was elected tsar by the boyars in 1610, but the king sought to change the terms of the agreement with Muscovy, and

the boyars became alarmed. The agreement unraveled, Władysław did not take the throne, and the conflict continued.

8. To the south, the Ottomon Empire and its vassals, the Crimean Tatars, threatened the Commonwealth and Christianity. The Commonwealth was often referred to as the "Bulwark of Christendom," and indeed was a deciding factor in turning the Ottomans back when they were set to capture Vienna in 1683. Of the two, the Tatars were deemed the greater threat because they raided annually, pillaging, burning, and carrying off countless captives to be sold in Turkish slave markets. It is estimated that in all, the Tatars took over one million Poles captive. Their raiding was equally, if not more, devastating in surrounding countries, such as Muscovy.

9. The Moldavian Magnate Wars were a series of conflicts spanning from the late sixteenth century to the early seventeenth century. Amid ongoing cross-border raids by Cossacks into the Ottoman Empire on one side and Tatar raids into the Commonwealth on the other, a semi-permanent war zone existed. In this hotbed, magnates from the Commonwealth began interfering in Moldavia's affairs in order to extend the Commonwealth's influence, which upset the Ottoman Empire. Wallachia, Transylvania, Hungary, and the Habsburgs were also part of the mix. Stefan Potocki, a powerful magnate, sought to re-establish the head of Moldavia and led an army of seven thousand into battle against Moldavia and the Ottoman Empire. He was defeated in July 1612 and taken prisoner. He later died a captive in the notorious Fortress of the Seven Towers (Yekidule Fortress). Months after Potocki's defeat, Żółkiewski negotiated a treaty without further bloodshed. However, the conflict would continue until the Battle of Cecora in 1620, where Żółkiewski lost his life.

10. The Thirty Years' War began as a war over religion. The conflict lasted from 1618 until 1648 and involved the Holy Roman Empire and nearly all of Europe. For the most part, the Commonwealth stayed out of it, aiding the Holy Roman Empire indirectly. For instance, Zygmunt III sent ten thousand cavalrymen to help the Habsburgs. A number of hussars, perhaps adventurers, are said to have joined the fight on the side of the Holy Roman Empire, hiring on as mercenaries. Sweden's

THE HEART OF A HUSSAR

engagement overlapped its war with the Commonwealth, teaming up with Muscovy, who sought to recover Smoleńsk.

11. Biała (also known as Bely) was a fortress where a Polish garrison came under attack in the weeks prior to the Battle of Kłuszyn. Żółkiewski was marching his troops to Carowa-Zajmiszcze when he diverted to rescue the garrison. Biała was one of the locations where he divided his already small force prior to the battle.

12. Carowa-Zajmiszcze was the location where the vanguard of the Muscovite army was garrisoned, and it was here Żółkiewski traveled after leaving Biała. The Muscovites withdrew the week prior to the Battle of Kłuszyn. When Żółkiewski received news of the approaching Swedish-Muscovite army, he further divided his troops and marched his small force from Carowa-Zajmiszcze to the battlefield near Kłuszyn.

13. The main character, Jacek Dąbrowski, is promoted and replaces his slain lieutenant, making Mateusz Zalewski his immediate superior. In the book, Mateusz is the captain, but he would have actually been the lieutenant (the porucznik), and Jacek would have become deputy or second lieutenant. Hussars did not use ranks that translate to those we are accustomed to. Since they were all equals, they were all designated "junior officers" under their commander (the rotamaster or rotmistrz). For the sake of facility, the designations of lieutenant, captain, and colonel (pułkownik) have been applied to this story.

14. There were two top generals in Poland: the Crown Grand Hetman and the Crown Field Hetman, with the Crown Grand Hetman being the highest ranking of the two. Both were offices assigned for life. Lithuania had its own separate, equivalent designations for generals.

15. The main character fights with a nadziak, a war hammer with a hammer head on one side, and a claw on the other (also known as a horseman's pick). The distinctive term "nadziak" wasn't yet established at the time this novel takes place. It might have been called a "czedan," which is a similar weapon but with an ax blade in place of the claw.

16. Miles used are English miles, not Polish miles, which were longer.

17. The layout of Biaska Castle is loosely based on Ogrodzieniec Castle in the Eagles' Nests fortifications in the Polish Jura. Its geographical position would, however, more closely resemble that of Bobolice Castle.
18. The Eagles' Nests fortifications are a series of castles along Poland's western border that King Kazimierz the Great (Kazimierz III Wielki) ordered built in the fourteenth century to secure Poland's western border against its aggressors. As time went on, the fortifications were no longer necessary, and many fell into disrepair.
19. Twierzda is loosely based on Kudryntsi Castle, which was not built until the early 1600s.
20. Hetman Żółkiewski was likely not in Podolia in the spring of 1611. His memoirs place him in Mogilev, Moscow, and Smoleńsk.
21. Placing Hetman Żółkiewski at his home during Christmas 1612 is merely my supposition. He was, however, in the area in October of 1612 when he negotiated a treaty with Stefan Tomża of Moldavia at Chocim. Likewise, King Zygmunt III's presence in Warszawa, after departing Muscovy, is supposition. Jacek's friend in these scenes, Magdalena von Rohan, is a fictional character.
22. The novel uses a variety of English and French terms. While perhaps not historically accurate for the story's place and time, I chose terms I felt would be easily recognizable to the modern reader.
23. A number of historical locations and figures were referred to by different names and had various spellings. Where possible, I opted for names recognizable today, in their Polish spellings.
24. In my research, I discovered many rich Polish Christmas customs and traditions, though not all are incorporated in this story. I also found a variety of references to the number and types of dishes served at Christmas Eve supper (Wigilia). I chose a historical source which stated that an uneven number of dishes were typically served. In wealthier homes, that number ranged from eleven to thirteen, which is why thirteen were served at Biaska, the fictional castle in this novel.

Timeline

Date	Event
Jul. 1, 1569	The Union of Lublin treaty is signed, forming the Polish-Lithuanian Commonwealth
Jan. 28, 1573	The Confederation of Warsaw is instituted, granting religious freedom throughout the Commonwealth
May 1, 1576	King Stefan Batory is crowned king, reforms army, and organizes the husaria
Apr. 17, 1577	Battle of Lubieszów, the first of many hussar victories
Dec. 12, 1586	King Stefan Batory dies
Aug. 19, 1587	Zygmunt III Vasa is elected King of Poland
1593	The Moldavian Magnate Wars begin
1595	Fire breaks out in Wawel Castle (Kraków), destroying the royal quarters
1596	King Zygmunt III elects to move his court to Warsaw
1598	Death of Fyodor, Tsar of Muscovy; beginning of Muscovy's Time of Troubles
1600	Beginning of Polish-Swedish War
1605	Beginning of the Dymitriads, the rise of false claimants to the Muscovite throne
1605	King Zygmunt III marries Austrian Archduchess Constance, sister of his late wife
Sep. 27, 1605	Battle of Kircholm, a hussar victory over Swedish forces
1606	Zebrzydowski Rebellion begins

Jul., 1607	Battle of Guzów, where the Zebrzydowski rebels are crushed
1608	Zebrzydowski Rebellion ends
1609	Polish-Muscovite War begins
1609	Siege of Smoleńsk by Poland
Jul. 4, 1610	Battle of Kłuszyn, led by Field Hetman Stanisław Żółkiewski, a hussar victory over combined Muscovite and Swedish forces
Aug., 1610	Field Hetman Żółkiewski marches into Moscow; Poland begins its occupation
Aug. 27, 1610	Muscovite boyars sign a treaty wherein King Zygmunt III's son, Prince Władysław, is elected Tsar
Jun., 1611	Smoleńsk falls to Poland
Jun., 1611	King Zygmunt III sends Field Hetman Żółkiewski to Moscow to relieve the Polish garrison
Aug., 1611	Field Hetman Żółkiewski is driven off by the Muscovites; returns to Poland
Sep., 1611	King Zygmunt III moves into the Royal Palace at Warsaw
Oct., 1611	Field Hetman Żółkiewski presents deposed Tsar Wasyl IV to King Zygmunt III
Jul., 1612	Magnate Stefan Potocki leads his army into Moldovia where he is defeated and taken prisoner
Oct. 22, 1612	The Polish garrison is driven out of Moscow
Oct., 1612	Field Hetman Żółkiewsk reaches agreement on behalf of the Commonwealth with Ștefan II Tomża of Moldavia
Feb., 1613	Michał Romanov, founder of the Romanov Dynasty, becomes Tsar; the end of the Dymitriads
1613	Żółkiewski given title of Great Crown Hetman
Oct. 7, 1620	Great Crown Hetman Żółkiewski dies at the Battle of Cecora in Moldavia; end of the Moldavian Magnate Wars

THE HEART OF A HUSSAR

A Hussar's Promise ~ Excerpt
(Book 2 of 2)

Betrayed by the lord he has served since boyhood, Jacek Dąbrowski, captain of winged hussars, has just been exiled to a remote fortress along the Polish-Lithuanian Commonwealth's southeastern border—a dangerous no man's land where reviled Tatar raiders constantly hunt for fresh slaves to satisfy the Ottoman Empire's insatiable appetites.

But Jacek's lord, Eryk Krezowski of Biaska, has taken far more—he has also taken Jacek's only love, Oliwia, for himself. Determined to forget Oliwia and Eryk, Jacek grinds out a new life in the war zone that is now his home. When tragedy strikes and he is called back, he cannot refuse and must once again confront those who have betrayed him.

Once a Russian peasant, Lady Oliwia Krezowska has risen to a lofty perch she never sought. The reluctant lady of a vast estate, Oliwia has everything a woman could want—except Jacek, the only man she's ever loved. Even if she weren't bound to Eryk by marriage, she has no hope of recapturing Jacek's heart—his bitter hatred toward her is an impenetrable wall.

Upon Jacek's return to Biaska, secrets are revealed and he realizes much of what he once believed is wrong. He embarks upon yet another mission with newfound purpose, only to be confronted by an enemy he never saw coming. Just as one dream is realized, another is shattered. Jacek's fortitude will be tested again and again as he endures battles no man should in an effort to reclaim his life and his love.

Meanwhile, a different foe, one who was but a shadow of a threat before, continues to grow, becoming more powerful every day. That enemy's sole quest is to destroy Biaska and everyone in it, including Oliwia and everyone she loves.

Though worlds apart, Jacek and Oliwia are in the battles of their lives—*for* their lives—from which neither may survive.

THE HEART OF A HUSSAR

Chapter 1 – Beginnings

The thunder of pounding hooves and billows of dust engulfed Jacek, stinging his eyes as he rode behind his four outriders. The landscape they traveled was an unending expanse of tawny grasses, resembling a great suede cloak tossed over the earth. He squinted into a late-day, azure October sky streaked with filaments of white, but nothing moved along the flat horizon. Today's journey was no different from yesterday's, or the day before, or the day before that, and it jabbed at his raw nerves. But instinct told him the Tatars still roved, searching for human treasure, and he could not let down his guard.

He blew out a breath. Since he'd been assigned command of the border outpost at Silnyród months ago, his life had been one long series of skirmishes with the cunning raiders. Jacek chuckled wryly to himself. *Assigned*. Banished was a more apt description. Banished to a decrepit fort in Podolia for loving the wrong woman.

And now his days were spent hunting. But it wasn't for venison or pheasant among other noblemen as he'd once done. No, he hunted Tatars, small bands splintered from a thousands-strong army pushing into Muscovy for the sole purpose of carrying off Slavic slaves. The devils! They had no trade but slaving. It was these harriers his undersized garrison scouted and fought. In the last few weeks, they had scattered like autumn storm clouds—which prickled him all the more. The Tatars were sly, and they were quick. Would they slither through border patrols, past spies, unnoticed? Where would they come from next? Would they strike at night as villagers slept? Or now, over the next swell of ground?

The enemy had devastated harvests and stores of food to keep its army going. Would they leave when none remained? Or grow so fat with plunder that they would return to the warmer climate of their Crimean homeland? The time wasn't here yet. Maybe never. They might remain and raid throughout the long winter, and if they did, the outpost Jacek commanded needed more shoring up.

Of late, daily patrols and scouting missions turned up nothing. No raiding parties to kill, no captives to save, no enemies to question. Not even signs of the damned Zaporozhian Cossacks, whose unlawful forays into

Ottoman territory sparked vengeful counterattacks against defenseless folk. Folk he was resolved to safeguard.

For now, he and his limited force chased ghosts across the plains.

Waning golden light signaled the end of the day's scouting, and the party turned for home. As they approached in the gloaming, Silnyród's fortress walls loomed like an enormous galley on a deserted sea. The surrounding flat ground was broken up by breastworks bristling with wooden spikes, a ditch, and stone barricades stacked the height of two men. Though not tall enough to prevent a determined enemy scaling the walls, the stone was more solid—and more defensible—than the rotting wooden palisades he'd found when he'd first arrived. To the right, on the fortress's eastern flank, smoke from sprawling cooking fires blanketed the village.

Guards on the battlements hailed Jacek and his troop as they clattered across a bridge spanning the ditch. Behind them, men secured the fortress's giant doors against the night and lit torches braced to the thick walls.

"Has everyone reported?" Jacek dismounted, tossing his reins to a stable lad.

"Yes, and they saw nothing," his second, Lesław, replied.

Jacek nodded and pulled off his plumed helmet, ruffling his short brown hair to cool his sticky scalp. Another lad began unbuckling his gorget, breastplates, and vambraces as something clamped on his heel. He jerked his leg, but the vice held—and growled.

"Jesus, Tymon! What in blazes is wrong with your devil of a dog?" Jacek shook his ankle, but the small beast held.

"Damn it, Statyw! Release the lord!" bellowed a stocky man heading briskly for Jacek.

Jacek lifted his boot, and the dangling mongrel attached to it, and let the stable master at it.

"Keep that blasted thing away from me." Jacek scowled as Tymon unclamped the offending mutt and dropped it to the ground. Jacek sprang back as the fiend lifted one of its three legs to wet his boot.

"My apologies, Captain Dąbrowski." Tymon erupted in a string of oaths and chased after Statyw. The mongrel was Jacek's most spirited adversary of late. How good it would feel to be rid of the damned thing!

Jacek stalked through mud to the log manor house, reminded by its sadly hanging thatch that its roof needed repairing. He flung the front door wide, setting a few serving maids to squealing. When they recognized him, the young ones smiled and the old ones scowled. He ignored them all, save one.

That one, Bogna, the capable commander of his household, accosted him as he navigated the hall. "My lord, your boots?" She pointed behind him at lumps of muck in his wake.

He shrugged. "It's all off by now."

"Tchah!" She threw up her hands, her wizened face scrunched in a scowl.

Men crammed tables, slurping and grunting their way through their servings. Jacek wended his way round them, nearly grinding his hip on a table corner. The men stopped to acknowledge him, and he waved them back to their meals.

"Bogna, why are the tables this way?" he asked as he pulled off his gloves.

With an eye-roll, she said, "Lately, you have brought on so many soldiers, my lord, all of them hungry, that we needed more seats. This was the best arrangement." Leathery hands on her hips, she added, "Your meal is ready, my lord."

He nodded. "I shall wash first." He thought he heard her mutter, "Take off those boots."

The smell of *bigos*—hunter's stew—filled his nostrils, setting his stomach to growling. Stepping through a doorway off the main hall into a low-ceilinged room, Jacek smacked his forehead on the frame—again—and cursed. *Jesus, damned door!* As he rubbed his head, he paused before his makeshift shrine that held a candle, the wooden rosary his mother had given him, a crucifix, and a depiction of the Black Madonna—Our Lady of Częstochowa. Here he crossed himself and mumbled a quick prayer to be forgiven his incessant blasphemies, a habit he'd never broken and likely never would. Then he threw his gloves on one of two trunks and glanced at the painting of his beloved mare, Jarosława, suspended above it. The piece had been given him by Oliwia four years ago at Christmas when he'd been twenty-two and she sixteen, and though he hadn't fallen in love with her until the following year, he had treasured the picture even then. He still did despite everything. It was one of two remembrances he allowed himself of Oliwia.

Just as he sank into the furs covering his rough wood-framed bed, there came a rustle. In the doorway stood a beaming serving maid with a pitcher of water.

"For you to wash up, Pan Jacek," she said sweetly.

"Leave it there," he grumbled and jerked his chin toward a rickety washstand as he rose.

She poured water into a cracked porcelain bowl before setting down the pitcher, then held her hands out to him. "May I take your cloak and *kolpak*, m'lord?"

"No." He dropped the fur cap beside the gloves and whipped off his cloak and pegged it. She stood still, watching him as he began unbuttoning his mud-spattered *żupan*. With an exhale, he said, "What is it?"

She fumbled and reddened. "I merely ... I wondered if there is aught you need, m'lord."

"Yes. To be left alone." He closed the door on her crestfallen countenance, then dipped his hands in the bracing water and scrubbed his bearded face. After pulling on a fresh garment, he trudged out the door and took his seat at the head table among his fellows. Materializing from the shadows, the same maid hurried to fill his tankard with *piwo*, then painstakingly placed a full trencher before him. It was a wearisome routine, and he had scant patience for the fawning tonight. Even if he were to find himself in a moment of weakness, he knew better than to seek pleasure in his own house. *No entanglements.* Entanglements had always proved messy, and he'd avoided them—save the one which had shattered his heart.

Before Oliwia, he'd always found women wanted far more of him than the lone tryst he wanted of them, and he'd rarely fancied lying with whores. After Oliwia, even trysts held little appeal, for she became the measure by which he judged all women, and they could not compare. She'd ruined him. In the end, it was far easier to forgo intimate encounters altogether and focus on his prime objective, which was to build his reputation as a commander and gain the king's notice—and an estate. If he had to do it in this godforsaken place, then so he would.

He shoveled spoonfuls of bigos into his mouth amid the soldiers' good-natured jibing directed at a young, dark-haired garrison soldier.

"Anyone see Florian trip over himself today when Luiza brought out the slop?" a soldier chided. "Never seen a lad so eager to feed swine before."

THE HEART OF A HUSSAR

"No," another replied, "but I saw him trip when he ran to pull up a water bucket for her."

Florian's curls twitched as he shook his head. "You lot are jealous."

"You stole my favorite tavern maid, you cur," the first soldier complained.

"She wasn't yours to steal," Florian retorted, pointing his eating knife at him. "Jaromir promised her to me at the first, soon as he saw I'm the best man for his daughter." Florian turned to Jacek. "Luiza told me to be sure you will come to the wedding, Captain."

"I will not miss it," Jacek replied.

The first soldier hooted. "'Luiza told me.' You're already whipped, Florian."

"Florian, you are *not* invited to come with us to Milda's tonight," said a different soldier.

"Milda has nothing I want." Florian grinned. "Take Benas," he added, jerking his chin toward a young Lithuanian soldier. The lad had just arrived from a nearby village to train with Jacek and Lesław.

"Benas, you may accompany us tonight to Milda's, but don't think you're getting a go at the new girl," the first soldier chortled.

"Why not let the pup have a go?" said an older soldier as he sucked on a pipe. "He'll be done before he starts, and you lads won't have to wait." The men exploded in guffaws and pounded hands round the table. His face red, Benas stared hard at his platter.

Thank the saints for the new girl! Jacek had added men to the garrison, but brawling had become all too common among those vying for the hand of any unmarried maid or the services of the overworked Milda and the few whores in the village. Though he was pleased to add the soldiers, Jacek begrudged the fact that to keep them he needed the whores too—or rather, he needed to help Milda recruit them any way he could. It wasn't that he minded whores, but Jesus, he had better things to do! Nonetheless, the new girl's novelty had so far distracted the men from fighting each other while giving Milda a much needed rest *off* her back.

Florian piped up, interrupting Jacek's inner grumbles. "Captain, with harvest over and the Feast of St. Hedwig upon us, surely Bater Beg's army has turned for home by now."

Jacek grunted and reached for the bread, tearing off a hunk before the maid could do it for him. "We've had no new reports of their movements.

Crown Hetman Żółkiewski's patrols have uncovered little, and his spies cannot predict when the devils will be done ravaging Muscovy and go home. And then there are the damned Cossacks."

"Which ones?" asked Benas.

"The Zaporozhians." Jacek washed down the dry bread. Bogna shooed the maid away and refilled his cup. He thanked the old woman and took a swig.

Benas wore a puzzled expression. "But they are with us, yes?"

"Most times, but if they smell opportunity, then hang alliances," Jacek replied.

"Do you mean they fight against us?" Benas's growing confusion deepened the lines between his brows.

"No, but they cause problems for the Commonwealth when they raid Ottoman territory. They break the truce between our countries, and the Turks strike back," said Florian.

"An eye for an eye?" asked Benas.

"Usually, they send the Tatars to do their dirty work, though," one soldier added.

Finished with his meal, Jacek dropped his napkin on the table. "Żółkiewski's duty-bound to enforce peace with the Ottomans. But the Zaporozhians don't follow rules and raid anyway. So Żółkiewski apologizes to the Turks and pleads with the Cossacks, and when the Turks retaliate, guess who has to defend?" Jacek pointed from his chest to Benas's and back again.

A soldier's son burst into the hall on a gust of wind and hurried toward Jacek.

"Captain, I was told to give you this!" He thrust a bundle in his hands. Jacek scanned the packet, recognizing the seal belonging to his master, Lord Eryk Krezowski. The one who had stranded him here.

"Bogna, see the messenger gets something to eat," Jacek mumbled as he rose. He crossed to his chamber and barred the door. Seated on the edge of the bed, he unfurled the bundle in the glow of the bedside lantern. What he unwrapped was a dagger with a letter penned by Lord Eryk. Puzzled, he inspected the dagger and recognized it as his own. Then he read the note twice before tossing it aside.

The missive delivered only cheer. Or so Eryk asserted. Deputy Witold Bilicki had concluded Jacek was not responsible for the brutal murders of two women. One had been a tavern maid he'd argued with—whose mutilated body had been found beside his stolen dagger—and the other a whore who'd taken him in later that same night when he'd passed out in a drunken stupor. Both had been alive when he'd left them, and neither had deserved her fate. But now someone had been arrested and had confessed, and Bilicki had returned Jacek's knife. The other bit of "good news" stole Jacek's breath like a well-placed fist to his stomach.

Jacek lay back, his arm folded under his head, and stared at the hewn ceiling. Reaching into his żupan, he extracted a bound lock of sable hair and drew it over his mouth, under his nose. The scent was long gone, but he rubbed it against his cheek, the silky strands catching on his beard. His mind unexpectedly jumped to the maids in his kitchen, in the tavern, and the wenches in the village. But thinking of them stirred not even a modicum of desire.

Why is it the ones you don't want make nuisances of themselves, while the one you do want ...

"The one you *do* want belongs to someone else and now carries his child," he muttered aloud. It was one thing to fool himself into believing no intimacy took place between the woman he desired and her husband, but it was quite another to be slapped with the evidence that his self-deception was utter fantasy. He tucked the precious tress back in its place against his heart.

As he looked up at the ceiling, he tried to focus on one point, tried to lock out all the commotion in his head, but he could not expel the disturbing images of Oliwia in Eryk's bed. His mind wandered backward, along a familiar path, to Oliwia before she married Eryk, when Jacek had believed she was his. He grew more agitated, berating himself for losing her.

If only I'd secured her promise before leaving on campaign, or returned when I said I would instead of chasing my dream. She would be mine now.

He imagined never seeing her again; he was destined for battles, and she now for childbirth. Would she survive its perils? Fear chilled him, and in that moment he cared little that his own fate might lie at the point of a Tatar's scimitar. It was a long while later when fatigue finally claimed him, and he drifted off, quite alone.

Yelling startled him awake in the dark hours. He flung off his covers and began pulling on clothes while his door rattled in its frame.

"Captain! Captain!"

Bootless, Jacek shot to the door, unbarring and opening it in one motion. Benas stood in the frame, his eyes wide, his breathing rapid.

"We're under attack! The village and part of the fortress are in flames."

"Tatars?" Jacek grabbed his boots and weapons. His retainer, Marcin, materialized out of the main hall murk.

Benas shook his head. "Uncertain. It's chaos."

"Did any villagers get inside the walls?" Jacek asked as Marcin helped him into his armor. Jacek buckled on his sword belt and slid his *szabla* in its scabbard, then gripped his favored weapon, the *nadziak*—his war hammer.

"I don't know, but the tavern's one of the buildings ablaze."

Jacek grasped Benas's shoulder. "Where's Florian?"

"None have seen him."

"Christ! Marcin, roust Lesław. Benas, get to the stables and tell Tymon to start saddling the horses.

End of Chapter 1 from A Hussar's Promise
Coming November, 2020

Acknowledgments

To Eryk Jadaszewski of Polish Hussar Supply Plus, a fountain of knowledge he shared so freely, and to Joan Karasinski, the gracious queen who welcomed me into her court and allowed me to hang out in her tent during the reenactment of the Siege of Jasna Góra.

To all the living history reenactors who teach us about Poland's storied past and keep its memories vibrant. I'm honored to have been so warmly welcomed by all of you and humbled by your knowledge and your passion. Never stop. Na zdrowie!

To Dr. Radosław Sikora, who so generously shared his narrative on the Battle of Kłuszyn, and whose books grace my bookshelf.

To Sophie Hodorowicz Knab, who so patiently answered my questions about Polish traditions and customs.

To the countless history professors, who replied to my queries and whose knowledge can be found woven into the details.

To Jennie Quinlan, editor extraordinaire, whose expertise, honesty, and belief in the story helped get it to the finish line.

To fellow author, Barbara Tyner, for the generosity of her time, her thoroughness, keen eye, and invaluable feedback.

To fellow author, Elizabeth St. John, for her unfailing patience, support, and guidance.

To my Scribophile critiquers, Janet, Andrea, TZ, Wendy, Kurt, and Paul, for sticking with the story and helping me craft a better one.

To Francisco Cordoba of HippoCampus Publishing, for his input and attention to detail.

And especially to my family. Kyle, Matt, and Ryan, my incomparable cheerleaders, whose enthusiasm encouraged me to keep going. To my husband Tim, who sat and listened to the story as I reeled it out of my head one night over pizza and beer, and whose spark made me believe. Whose support never wavered. Who was the first to slug through my rough early chapters. Who shared his knowledge of period-specific weaponry, and who willingly researched the more elusive details. Who gifted me with a nadjiak and hussar sabre (best presents ever!). Who cheerfully shared our home with all my characters, though it got crowded. Who was my sounding board and plotting partner when I was stumped. I couldn't have done this without you.

Connect

Want to know about character and historical insights, exclusive bonus content, and upcoming releases? Be the first to find out by signing up for my email list.at www.griffin-brady.com.

Other ways to connect:

Facebook: https://www.facebook.com/AuthorGriffinBrady
Twitter: https://twitter.com/griffbrady1588
Website: www.griffin-brady.com
Or email me! griffin@griffin-brady.com

GRIFFIN BRADY

Also by this author

A Hussar's Promise, Book Two
(coming November, 2020)

Writing as G.K. Brady, award-winning contemporary romance author of The Playmakers Series

Book One - Taming Beckett
Book Two - Third Man In
Book Three - Gauging the Player
Book Four – The Winning Score
(Coming September 30, 2020)

About the author

Griffin Brady is a historical fiction author with a keen interest in the Polish Winged Hussars of the 16th and 17th centuries. She is a member of the Historical Novel Society and Rocky Mountain Fiction Writers. *The Heart of a Hussar* took third place in the Rocky Mountain Fiction Writers' 2018 Colorado Gold Contest and was a finalist in the Northern Colorado Writers' 2017 Top of the Mountain Award.

The proud mother three grown sons, she lives in Colorado with her husband. She is also an award-winning romance author who writes under the pen name G.K. Brady.

GRIFFIN BRADY

Made in the USA
Coppell, TX
15 September 2020